TOM BALE

THE CATCH

arrow books

Published by Arrow Books 2014

2 4 6 8 10 9 7 5 3 1

Copyright © Tom Bale 2014

First published in Great Britain in 2013 by Preface Publishing

Arrow Books
Random House, 20 Vauxhall Bridge Road,
London SW1V 2SA

www.randomhouse.co.uk

Addresses for companies within The Random House Group Limited
can be found at: www.randomhouse.co.uk/offices

The Random House Group Limited Reg. No. 954009

A CIP catalogue record for this book is available from the British Library

ISBN 978 0 09955 944 3

The Random House Group Limited supports the Forest Stewardship
Council® (FSC®), the leading international forest-certification organisation.
Our books carrying the FSC label are printed on FSC®-certified paper.
FSC is the only forest-certification scheme supported by the leading
environmental organisations, including Greenpeace. Our paper
procurement policy can be found at: www.randomhouse.co.uk/environment

Typeset in Electra LH Regular by
Palimpsest Book Production Limited, Falkirk, Stirlingshire

Printed and bound in Great Britain by
CPI Group (UK) Ltd, Croydon, CR0 4YY

THE
CATCH

Tom Bale was born in Sussex in 1966. He worked in a variety of jobs while pursuing his lifelong ambition to be a writer. His first novel, *Sins of the Father*, was published in 2006 under his real name, David Harrison. After that he acquired an agent, a pseudonym and a publishing deal with Random House. He now writes full time and lives with his family in Brighton. Find out more at www.tombale.net and follow him on Facebook.

Also available by Tom Bale

Skin and Bones
Terror's Reach
Blood Falls

For my daughter, Emily

THE
CATCH

One

It was sold to Dan as a mercy mission, a favour for a mate. There was never any suggestion of trouble. He just had to be there with Robbie, a supportive presence in the background while the handover took place.

Dan agreed to it for Cate's sake: that was the noble motive. But he also had a favour of his own to ask, and a lot riding on the answer. So he ignored the voice in his head that urged him to let Robbie sort out his own mess for once.

He should have known better. Because Robbie had this ability to drag you in, enticing you to share his burden whether you wanted to or not, and once committed you felt obliged to stay and see it through.

A painful lesson, as Dan later reflected, that the path of least resistance can sometimes be the route to disaster.

The pub was busier than either of them had expected. On the drive over Dan had remarked on a recent news story on the death of country pubs, and they had reminisced about the dives they'd visited over the years: grumpy landlords, terrible decor, flat beer and greasy food; pool tables where the balls wouldn't roll straight. At twenty-nine they were old enough to enjoy an occasional wallow in nostalgia; young enough to giggle and splutter as they competed to find the ideal name for a pub in decline. 'The Sack of Shit' was declared the winner.

In the same vein, The Horse and Hounds had been rechristened The *Hearse* and Hounds, though it turned out to be a handsome Tudor hostelry on a lonely rural track a few miles north of Steyning. 'Middle of bloody nowhere,' as Robbie put it.

The car park was almost full, necessitating a tricky reversing manoeuvre on Dan's part, easing his weary old Fiesta into a gap between a Land Rover and a trade-waste bin. He made it, but only just, and there was the usual teasing from Robbie about his shortcomings as a driver.

The pub was divided into two bars. Most of the action seemed to be in the public bar, and the reason soon became obvious: live music.

Robbie groaned when he heard the first strains of what sounded like a fiddle. 'Not folk,' he said. 'Anything but folk.'

Now came a flutter of acoustic guitar, the sly rattle of brushes on a snare drum.

'Folk rock, maybe,' Dan said. 'Some kind of fusion. That drum sound is almost . . .'

'Jazz,' Robbie finished for him, and they grimaced in unison. 'Shit, no, it's jazz folk. Jolk.'

'It's no jolking matter.'

Laughing, Robbie punched Dan on the arm. 'For that, you're getting the first round.'

First they checked the saloon bar. It was whisper quiet, the room deserted but for a prim middle-aged couple sharing a banoffee pie, and an elegant young woman sitting alone in the corner. Dan would have waited until he could meet her eye, but Robbie dragged him away.

'Don't stare at her.'

'I wasn't. Anyway, this client of yours isn't even—'

'It's a precaution, all right? We have to act like we're nothing to do with her.'

For that reason, Robbie wanted to wait in the public bar, despite the fact that his dislike of the music intensified a hundredfold once he was physically in the presence of the musicians – four of them, all silver-haired but youthful in manner and joyful in mood. It was too noisy to talk properly, which didn't suit Dan's purpose. As he watched Robbie drain his first pint in double quick time, it dawned on him that this was the reason he'd been lumbered with driving: Robbie wanted a night out on the lash.

Then the musicians took a break, and after Robbie had bought more drinks Dan managed to steer the conversation round to his business venture.

'I went to see some brilliant premises in Hurstpierpoint, perfect for a coffee shop. Empty at the moment, but it's got an A3 classification.'

Robbie didn't exactly yawn, but neither did he exhibit much interest. Undeterred, Dan went on: 'I had a meeting with the bank last week. It's not looking good.'

'Course it's not. The economy's fucked.'

'So I reckon we may need to find an alternative source of finance—'

'Honestly, mate, you're insane to think about starting a business. You wanna stay where you are till things improve.'

'But Denham's isn't secure. It's only a matter of time before the online retailers wipe us out.'

'At least there'll be some redundancy in it.'

'That's what Hayley says. But it feels wrong. Like we're wishing it to fail.'

'You mean Hayley and me agree on something? Jesus, I'd better retract that.' Robbie's glass was empty once more. 'Your round.'

'Give me a chance.' On the tiny makeshift stage the musicians were preparing to resume. Dan checked his watch: it was almost ten p.m. 'Do you think he's coming?'

'Of course he is. I'll tell you what, we'll go next door. I can't listen to any more of this shit.'

'All right, but how long are we going to wait?'

3

A harsh note on the fiddle delayed Robbie's reply. 'Plenty of time left yet. I wanna get this sorted tonight.' A fierce glint in his eye as he emphasised *tonight*. It was a look that Dan knew well – and should not have ignored.

Afterwards he thought about that a lot. He could have done something right then, just put down his drink and walked out, and to hell with Robbie and his silly, greedy mistakes.

But he didn't. Mainly because of Cate, of course. He didn't want to let her down.

So he stayed, and they all went to hell.

Two

Cate watched as they trooped in from the other bar, refugees from a maudlin Celtic ballad. She saw from Dan's body language that he didn't want to be here any more than she did – and not just because of the entertainment on offer.

But here they both were, and having waited nearly an hour she was just daring to hope it had been a wasted journey when she received a text: Running late. There in five.

Bugger. Dan and her brother were buying drinks from the sulky barmaid, who had added weight to a theory of Cate's by perking up the instant Robbie walked in.

As the two men chose a table at a discreet distance from hers, Cate took out her phone, still debating whether to pass on the message. Far more tempting to text Robbie and tell him the client had cancelled. Half an hour from now she'd be tucked up in bed with a mug of hot chocolate and a good book. She was three hundred pages into a Stephen King epic, *11.22.63*. Not in the same league as her all-time favourite, *The Stand*, but still an enthralling read.

Tempting . . . and yet she knew she wouldn't. Robbie was like a big soppy dog, a family favourite who could do no wrong, seducing everyone he met even as he slobbered over their clothes and left his mess on their carpets. *And along come Cate and Dan with their buckets and mops and their endless supplies of patience . . .*

5

No, not endless. She gazed at her brother's broad back, at the mop of dark hair that spilled over his collar, and she vowed that this would be the last time. No more bailouts. No more favours.

But then she had made that vow before, and no doubt so had Dan. As he took his seat he offered her a quick, grudging smile: *What the hell are we doing here?*

Cate had always liked Dan. Liked him more, in some ways, than she did Robbie. Her brother had so many layers, what seemed like wholly different personalities ghosting behind the dazzling screen of his surface charm. Dan was a lot more straightforward: what you saw was what you got.

He had an open, friendly face, his features not as chiselled as Robbie's; a smile that was warm and genuine rather than calculated to impress. He was an inch or two shorter than Robbie, though in terms of physique they were fairly evenly matched: both men slim, well toned, still in fine shape on the brink of thirty.

And yet, her theory went that if you presented the two of them to a room full of girls who'd been primed to make an instant choice, around eighty per cent would go for Robbie. In Cate's view, that probably said less about their respective merits than it did about young women and their tastes in men.

Listen to me, she thought. *A dry old maid at thirty-three.* Perhaps she was being too harsh on her brother. Besides, who was she to pass judgement when her own life was hardly a resounding success?

She picked up her handbag, a big heavy Gucci, crammed with all manner of junk that she was definitely going to clear out *any day now*. Even though she could plainly see the envelope, wedged between her purse and a packet of wipes, she felt the need to reach in and hold it for a second, the contents yielding slightly as she squeezed them between her fingers.

This was *so* unethical. And never mind that, if Mum ever found out . . .

Cate became aware of her heartbeat, a dryness in her mouth. This felt like the moment before she had to stand up in court, tense but excited, eager to do it if only to have it done.

The last favour, she reminded herself, and at that second the door of the saloon bar was flung open and in he strode. The client.

His name was Hank O'Brien. The first time she'd heard it, Cate had made a face and said, 'Hank?' and Robbie had said, 'He's not American. He's just a twat.'

She had a horrible feeling that her brother was spot on. Hank O'Brien was in his fifties, short and round and bustling with self-importance. He had wispy brown hair and the complexion of a dedicated drinker. A little rosebud mouth that might have been engineered for disapproval.

He came in, wincing at the music. His gaze took in the couple finishing their dessert, then lingered for half a second on Dan and Robbie, who were hunched over the table, conversing in a grinning, blokey manner designed to exclude everyone else.

It worked a treat. Dismissing them as irrelevant, the gaze moved on, and when it alighted on Cate something changed in O'Brien's face. He looked like he'd sucked on a lemon only to find it infused with sugar.

Cate's heart sank. Her job had just been made easier, but almost certainly at a cost.

She stood to greet him but he waved her down with an imperious flap of his hand. 'Miss Gilroy?'

'Mrs,' she said. A lie, but only a tiny one. 'Call me Cate.'

They shook hands. His grip was firmer than she'd expected, but a little damp. He reached inside his jacket and produced a slim wallet. 'To drink?'

'Nothing for me, thanks.'

'Go on. I'm sure I can tempt you . . .' When Cate shook her head, those rosebud lips tightened a fraction. 'One minute, then.'

He greeted the barmaid with the same bluff, over-familiar air and, oblivious to the girl's indifference, updated her on his progress in a local golf competition. He returned holding a double of something, raising the glass in a toast as he sat down.

'Can't beat a fine single malt at the end of a busy day.'

'Quite,' said Cate, thinking: *Probably more than one, in your case.*

'I was delayed by a conference call with a major supplier. CEO was in Aspen and the finance chap's holed up in bloody South Korea!' The tone was one of mild exasperation, but it was obvious that he intended for her to be impressed.

'What is it that you do, exactly?'

He hesitated, as if suspicious of the question. 'You name it. Number crunching. Problem-solving. Public-private partnerships and what have you.' A chuckle. 'I could spill out acronyms until your ears bleed.'

'Sounds fascinating.'

'No, it doesn't.' He was watching her closely. 'Anyhow, we have more important things to discuss.'

Cate nodded. 'We're glad this can be resolved amicably.'

'I bet you are. Director of Compton's, are you?'

'I'm freelance. I advise them on legal matters.'

'A lawyer? Huh. Got a law degree myself. I suppose that little prick thought I'd be intimidated?'

'Not at all. Mr Scott is keen to see this settled to your satisfaction.'

O'Brien grunted. Cate couldn't tell if his reaction meant: *Glad to hear it,* or: *You're talking bollocks.* Right now she hardly cared which. She wanted to grab the envelope and throw it across the table at him, then leave at once – a feeling that intensified when she caught him ogling her breasts.

'I know why they sent you, my dear. Done it myself often enough, deploying the totty for a charm offensive.' He rubbed his chubby palms together. 'Mother Nature certainly poured you into a tasty little mould, didn't she?'

'Mr O'Brien—'

'My error not to have anticipated it. I'd have arranged to meet at my place.' A gulp of Scotch, then he hefted his belly tight against the table, squeezing in as close as he could get. His voice became low and seductive. 'A ten-minute stroll, or two minutes if we take your car. I'll give you the full tour.'

'No. Thank you.'

'I insist.' He raised his eyebrows. 'I can't imagine you'll object to being plied with the best champagne?'

'I'm afraid your imagination's faulty. I don't drink champagne.'

Mild as it was, the insult made O'Brien flinch. He narrowed his eyes and leaned back until his chair groaned in protest.

'Of course, you hardly need a tour of my house. You and the whole world have seen inside it. And that's why you're going to do as I say, lady, and show me a damn sight more respect into the bargain.'

Three

On the face of it, Robbie's justification was simple enough: it had seemed like too good an opportunity to resist. Up to a point, Dan could see the truth in that. *Never look a gift horse in the mouth*, as his aunt would have put it.

Robbie's mother, Teresa Scott, owned a company called Compton Property Services. Launched in the mid-1980s, the core business involved the purchase and renovation of large old houses to sell on at a profit or convert into student lets. From that came a subsidiary operation that managed rental property on behalf of mainly high-net-worth clients.

Hank O'Brien had placed his sumptuous converted farmhouse on their books three years ago, following an acrimonious divorce. Tenants were found and signed up to a long-term lease, but a death in the family meant they had to terminate after less than a year.

While the house was still vacant, Robbie happened to get chatting to the friend of a friend of a location manager, scouring the south of England for a large rural property needed for several weeks of filming. A quick guided tour later and Robbie had secured himself a nice little bonus: five grand straight into his pocket. The film people were done within a few weeks, and then the house was taken on a new short-term let; O'Brien himself moved back in just under a year ago, with nobody any the wiser about Robbie's deal on the side.

Except that the movie, a mid-budget Brit-flick comedy, proved to be an unexpected hit. Not to Hank O'Brien's taste, particularly, but three weeks ago it happened to be the least worst option on his British Airways flight from Tokyo to Heathrow. Waking from a brandy-induced slumber, Hank had opened his eyes to find two vaguely familiar actors engaged in a passionate clinch on what was unmistakably his living-room carpet.

For Robbie, the only saving grace was that he'd intercepted O'Brien's complaint before it reached his mother's ears. But even the briefest of conversations convinced Robbie that he lacked the diplomacy to massage Hank's wounded ego. Robbie didn't do grovelling apologies.

In desperation he had enlisted his sister's help. Cate had taken over negotiations and swiftly agreed to pay Hank three thousand pounds in cash, with an undertaking that neither party would breathe a word to the taxman.

Robbie had correctly sussed that O'Brien would have an eye for the ladies: another reason for Cate to conduct the handover. But his sister would do it only on the condition that she had backup close at hand.

Hank had never met Robbie face to face, so that was fine. Dan was roped in to make Robbie's presence less conspicuous, and once he'd learned that Cate had been saddled with the most difficult role Dan had felt obliged to go along with it.

A messy business, but at least O'Brien was here now. Soon it would be over and they could all go home.

'Has she given it to him yet?' Unwilling to turn and look, Robbie was relying on a running commentary from Dan, who had pulled a face when he saw the way O'Brien was leering at Cate.

'They're talking.'

'What is there to talk about?'

'I think he's coming on to her.'

'Christ, he must be desperate.'

'Don't be stupid.'

Robbie made a crooning noise. 'Ah, you've still got the hots—'

'Sshh. Just leave it.'

At the other table O'Brien abruptly leaned back, his expression hostile, while Cate drew herself upright and crossed her arms. There was only one explanation for such negative body language. She had rebuffed him.

Dan felt glad, as well as relieved that Robbie had no way of influencing the conversation. To save his own skin he'd want Cate to flirt shamelessly with the man.

'He'd better not try renegotiating,' Robbie muttered.

Cate was talking in a low, steady voice, O'Brien scowling as he listened. She produced the envelope from her bag and handed it over. Hank lifted the flap and peered inside. His eyes widened greedily.

'She's given it to him.'

'Good. He can take it and piss off, and I'll have a drink to commiserate.'

'You're still two grand up.'

'Technically, yeah. But it was spent eighteen months ago. I had a nightmare getting that lot together.'

'Oh well. Put it down to experience.' Dan found it hard to be sympathetic. When Robbie was flush he could cheerfully blow in an evening what Dan took home in a month.

From the other bar, a song ended on a wave of heartfelt applause. It only diverted Dan's attention for a second, but by the time he looked back it was already too late to do anything.

The timing was ironic – just as Cate dared to believe she could wrap this up without any great unpleasantness.

O'Brien seemed happy enough as he examined the contents of the envelope. She'd been worried that he might insist on counting it out, note by note. If he did, they would have to go somewhere more private, and Cate couldn't bear the idea of being alone with him.

But Hank merely slipped the envelope inside his jacket and offered his hand. It was only as she went to shake it that she spotted the malevolent gleam in his eyes. He grabbed Cate's wrist and hauled her towards him.

'The price just increased.'

'What?'

'I want the other two thousand. And a kiss.'

'Let go of me.'

'You're coming back to mine. We'll talk about it there.'

'I'm not going anywhere with you.' Twisting away from him, she tried to wrench her arm free but he was too strong. He swooped in on her, his pink lips puckered, the large pores on his nose glistening with sweat.

Filled with revulsion, Cate acted on pure instinct: she punched him in the face. She had to use her left hand, so it lacked the power of her dominant arm; the noise he made when her fist connected with his cheek was more an exclamation of surprise than a cry of pain.

But his retaliation was brutal. Releasing her arm, he shoved her backwards, putting all his weight behind the move. Cate hit the side of her chair and tumbled over it. As she fell she glimpsed the middle-aged couple bolting for the door. Beyond them, the barmaid's hand was clamped over her mouth. In the other bar, the band had struck up a new song, a jauntily inappropriate soundtrack to the brawl.

Hank growled a threat as he came round the table: he wasn't done hurting her yet. Cate tried to curl into a protective ball but the overturned chair was jabbing into her side, impeding her movement. She was conscious of her brother on his feet, but he kept his back to her, reluctant to get involved.

O'Brien was lining up to kick her when Dan wrestled him away, allowing Cate to wriggle clear of the chair. In the calm that followed

Robbie turned, surveying them with a kind of bemused detachment, as though the whole display had been staged for his entertainment.

'Glad to see you're enjoying it!' she shouted, and Robbie glared at her, no doubt because she'd broken cover.

Sure enough, Hank was turning to inspect him. As he did, Dan gripped his arm. 'You need to leave.'

Another voice broke in. 'That's right, Mr O'Brien.' It was the barmaid, gesturing towards the public bar. 'Lance won't stand for any trouble.'

Dan said, 'It's sorted. He's going.' He regained O'Brien's attention. 'After you apologise to this woman.'

Hank gave Dan the same suspicious appraisal. 'What's your part in this? Do you know her?'

'Just leave it and fuck off,' Robbie said. 'You're outnumbered.'

'Are you threatening me?' O'Brien took a step forward, his face blazing with fury, and Cate saw the moment it dawned on him.

Dan saw it too: the man's eyes narrowing, his brows dipping together.

'You're Robert Scott. You're the scrote that cheated me.'

'No, I'm not.'

'I recognise your voice. You made a major mistake, buddy, thinking you could swindle me. The film-makers paid you five thousand, not three.' Puffing himself up, he jabbed a finger at Robbie. 'I'll see to it you lose your job over this.'

'I dunno what you're on about, mate. You're pissed.'

Affecting disdain, Robbie turned away. Hank lunged at him and once again Dan thrust himself into the gap. He caught a faceful of the man's sour, booze-sodden breath and nearly gagged.

'I want you out,' the barmaid shouted. 'Otherwise you're gonna get barred.'

At this, O'Brien faltered, giving Dan the chance he needed.

'You're mistaking him for someone else. My friend's name is Gary. The only reason we got involved is because I saw you hit this woman.

We don't know her, and we don't know you, but unless you leave right now we'll call the police.'

'Just go,' Cate added as she climbed to her feet. 'Please.'

Hank glowered at them for a few more seconds while he summoned up some dignity. 'I will,' he told Cate. 'But you mark my words, lady. You haven't heard the last of this.'

Four

Nobody spoke as they watched Hank O'Brien depart. A deeply unpleasant man, for sure, and now a deeply unhappy one. Dan had no doubt that O'Brien would make good on his threat.

'Thank you for helping,' Cate said, pointedly ignoring Robbie.

'Are you okay?' Dan asked, seeing that she was fighting back tears.

'Actually, no. I'm in a stinking temper, which is why I'm going to get out of here before I say something I might regret.'

She picked up her bag. Dan said, 'Shall I walk you to your car, in case he's still out there?'

'If he is, I'm going to bloody kill him.' From the look on her face Dan wouldn't have bet against it. She gave her brother a similarly ferocious glare, then marched out.

Robbie waited till she'd gone before he met Dan's eye. '*Gary*? Do I look like a *Gary*?'

'It was the first name that came into my head.'

'Mm. Quick thinking, I'll give you that.'

Dan grunted. 'We may as well get off now.'

'Just a second.'

Leaving Dan to pick up the overturned chair, Robbie sauntered over to the bar, choosing a spot about six or seven feet from where the barmaid was standing. Dan knew it was one of Robbie's golden rules: *Always make them come to you.*

And the girl took the bait. She was around twenty, with jet-black hair, pale doughy skin and piercings in her nose, lips and eyebrows. Far too stocky and unkempt for Robbie's taste, Dan would have said, but it was clear what he intended to do. He was already leaning on the bar, his head tilted at an angle that oozed sincerity.

In little more than a whisper, he said something that elicited a yelp of laughter. Within seconds she was gazing deep into Robbie's eyes, the stud in her lower lip bobbing gently as she recited something to him: probably her phone number.

Robbie nodded, then deftly planted a kiss on her cheek: too quick for the girl to react, but afterwards she looked thrilled.

Turning away, Robbie caught Dan's eye and winked. 'Okay. We're done here.'

The car park was just as crammed as before, save for a space where Cate's Audi TT had been parked. Dan relaxed at the knowledge that she had left without further incident.

They crunched over the gravel, avoiding puddles from a recent shower. The night air was damp and fresh and fragrant, and Dan felt his spirits lift at the thought that they were heading home.

He climbed into the Fiesta, nearly bumping his head as Robbie simultaneously dropped into the passenger seat, causing the car to rock on its suspension like an ancient pram.

'How about we grab a nightcap in Brighton?' Robbie said.

'It's too late.'

'Should take around twenty minutes if you floor it. We'll cruise West Street, see who's available.'

'If you're on the pull, what about that barmaid?'

'Leave it out. I wouldn't do her with yours. I was just making sure she was cool with what happened.'

'And you got her phone number?'

'In one ear, out the other.' Robbie tutted. 'Ah, come on. Dump the car at my place and we'll go somewhere in Hove. Get a few shots inside us.'

'Yeah. You're two minutes from home, but I'll have to get a cab.'

A snort from Robbie, as though he'd hoped Dan wouldn't spot the flaw in his plan. He waited a second or two, then said, 'You were telling me about these cafes. The bank gave you the cold shoulder, yeah?'

'Pretty much. I was thinking . . .' Dan checked the road was clear, pulled out of the car park and accelerated. 'Either we have to raise the money from somewhere else, or maybe find someone who can lease the premises at a really good rate—'

Robbie's laughter was loud and coarse. 'No chance. And believe me, you wouldn't wanna do it. My mum's a slave driver.'

'So you keep saying. But I've always got on well with her.'

'Yeah, in a civilian relationship. Going into business with her is a different ball game.'

'But isn't it worth having the conversation, at least?'

'Not when she's watching every frigging penny like a hawk.' He gave a deep sigh. 'How am I gonna stop her from hearing about Hank the Wank?'

'You're not. You're better off coming clean.'

'Bollocks, am I. Any excuse to cut my wages and she'll do it.'

Now it was Dan's turn to sigh. With the banks so risk-averse, he'd hit on the idea that Robbie's mother could be his potential saviour.

'Surely her core business is sound enough? I mean, with the property portfolio?'

'Oh, she's sitting on a fortune. But nobody's gonna prise her hands off that till she's dead and cold. I bet the old witch'll live to a hundred just to spite me . . .'

His voice dwindled to silence. Dan's parents had been killed in an accident when he was fourteen.

Robbie shifted in his seat. 'Sorry, mate. You know what I mean, though?'

'Mm. Seems we're both out of luck.'

'Yep. Life's a bitch and then you die.' But this was followed by another change of mood; a jubilant cry: 'Hey hey, well, look who it is!'

Five

It all happened so quickly.

Dan knew it was a dreadful cliché, even as the thought passed through his mind.

The road was narrow and dark, hemmed in by overhanging trees on the left and a dense hedgerow on the right. There was no other traffic. No street lighting, no moon or stars.

At first Robbie's shout made no sense. Perhaps his night vision was superior to Dan's, or perhaps he'd caught an earlier glimpse of the pedestrian as the car's headlights swept round a bend in the road.

It was Hank O'Brien. He was on the left-hand side, walking on the uneven grass verge along the edge of the tree line. Stomping home, no doubt plotting his revenge.

He should have been on the other side, Dan thought, dredging up a memory of the Highway Code. At night you're supposed to walk *towards* the traffic.

Dan automatically lifted his foot from the accelerator. By now the lights had picked up O'Brien's unsteady gait. There was room for him to shift another foot or so away from the road, but with typical arrogance he made no concession to their approach. Maybe he was too preoccupied – or too drunk – to react.

Fortunately there was no oncoming traffic, so it was perfectly safe for Dan to encroach on the opposite lane. That was exactly what he set out to do.

He was conscious of glancing at the mirror, noting the darkness of the landscape behind him; he felt the subtle shift of the muscles in his arms as he eased the steering wheel to the right—

Then Robbie said, 'Let's scare the shit out of him,' and he leaned over and yanked on the wheel.

The Fiesta, in the process of drifting right, made an abrupt lurch to the left. Dan felt the loss of traction as the front tyre slithered on to wet grass and mud. Then an impact, grotesquely loud and somehow unexpected, a voice in his head shrieking: *How the hell did that happen?*

There was a startled cry from Robbie as a fist-sized spider web of cracks materialised in the top left-hand corner of the windscreen. A heavy form thumped against the passenger-side window and was gone.

Dan was already correcting the steering, the Fiesta slipping obediently back on to the road, Robbie also straightening up, his arms flopping demurely into his lap as if nothing had happened – and even if it had it was nothing to do with him. Dan hit the brakes, remembering too late that he ought to check his speed. It would be important to know exactly how fast he'd been going.

For the investigation.

For the trial.

By the time he looked, the needle was juddering towards zero. No use to anyone, but it couldn't have been more than forty to begin with, and the limit for the road was, what, sixty? Fifty, at the very least.

Well within, he thought, and the phrase became a nonsensical litany repeating in his head. He might not be very confident, but that didn't make him a bad driver. He was safe, sensible, cautious. He was *well within*.

Then it registered that the car was stationary, and Robbie was staring at him with a look of horror and disbelief that must have mirrored his own expression.

'I just wanted to scare him,' Robbie said. 'He'll be all right, won't he?'

21

'We knocked him down.'

'He'll be okay. Let's just go.'

It took Dan a few seconds to digest the idea, so terrible and so attractive, before he managed to respond.

'No.'

He heard himself say it, and was perplexed that a sound could emerge so calmly from a body where every cell felt weak and flaccid, sloshing around like water in a bag.

Robbie twisted in his seat, looking over his shoulder. 'It's still clear. Come on.'

Ignoring him, Dan checked the mirror, then kangaroo-hopped the car forward like some hapless novice driver, parking with the nearside wheels up on the verge. He activated the hazard lights, turned off the ignition and took the keys with him as he got out of the Fiesta. Deep in his mind the possibility must have lurked that Robbie might commandeer the car and abandon him to his fate.

And it was a fate Dan saw clearly, as he stepped into the vanilla-scented air of a spring evening. It dropped into his vision like an elaborate stage set, gliding down on silent ropes and pulleys.

He saw newspaper reports and TV footage. Grainy photos of a thin, haunted man attempting to shield his identity from the cameras as he was marched into court. He saw the shame etched indelibly on the face of his aunt – Dan's surrogate parent these past fifteen years – as she contemplated the process by which his disgrace would contaminate and quite possibly destroy her life.

He started to move to the rear of the car. In the darkness he could barely see where the road ended and the verge began. The poor visibility offered itself as an excuse to give up, to tell himself he'd imagined it.

Then he heard the passenger door open, Robbie climbing out, and he knew there was no question of driving away. They had to do the right thing.

* * *

22

'Can you see him?' Robbie asked.

Dan didn't respond. He crouched down and examined the verge. Maybe he *had* imagined it. Maybe Hank had slipped through a gap in the trees and continued on his way home across the fields. What they'd hit was merely a rabbit or a badger, something that would lie unnoticed, unmourned, quietly decomposing by the roadside.

Then he saw the shape: twisted, unnatural, far too large to be an animal. It was further away than he'd expected, lying partly in a shallow ditch at the base of a tree.

Dan made it to within six or seven feet and then stopped as emphatically as if a force field had come down around the body. Later he would question whether it was purely fear, or revulsion – or whether a sense of self-preservation had been kicking in, even then.

Don't leave any evidence at the scene.

'Oh, shit,' Robbie whispered. 'We hit him. We really did.'

Dan fumbled for his phone, nearly dropping it. He looked at the display. 'No signal.'

'What?' Robbie saw the phone and gave a tiny shudder. 'We've got to get out of here, mate. Right now.'

'What if he's still alive?'

Robbie said nothing for a moment. Then he swore again, softly. 'Oh, fuck. He could identify us.'

He brushed past Dan, who was about to explain that he didn't mean it like that. If O'Brien was badly injured then they had to help him. Raise the alarm, somehow. Even transport him to hospital themselves, if need be.

But Robbie was right, too. As dreadful as it was, it might actually be better if Hank was dead . . .

The thought produced a tingling in Dan's temples. A cold sweat broke out on his back and suddenly he was fourteen again, coming home from school to find not his mum but his aunt waiting for him, a police car parked outside and two officers in uniform standing in the kitchen. One of them, a young woman, had greeted Dan with the most hideously false smile he'd ever witnessed—

'I'm going to throw up.'

'Not here.' Robbie made an urgent flapping gesture to shoo Dan away from the body. Dumbly comprehending, Dan staggered back to the Fiesta and then beyond it, to the opposite verge. Along with the roiling nausea in his gut came an even more sickening realisation.

He was a coward.

Six

If anyone should have been chucking up, Robbie thought, it was him. All that lager and a couple of lines of coke – and now this.

Instead, somehow, he felt fine. Clear-headed and stone-cold sober.

Robbie had always considered himself good in a crisis. The trick was never to look too far ahead, never *over-worry*, as his dad used to put it, before he buggered off and stopped worrying about anyone.

Now Robbie assessed the situation with a cool, clinical logic. The first stage was acceptance. He had done something really dumb. Despite what Dan might think – despite what *anyone* might think – there hadn't been any malicious intent. But it was done, and it couldn't be reversed, so there was no point dwelling on it. The consequences were all that mattered now. The consequences – and how to avoid them.

He took a few steps towards the body. His foot touched something solid and there was a faint sucking sound as he lifted it away.

It was the envelope. The frigging envelope full of cash. He picked it up, saw it was coated in blood. Part of his footprint was visible on the outer edge. For that reason alone, he couldn't leave it here.

'Mine, I think,' he murmured. He shoved it into his pocket, glancing round to make sure Dan wasn't watching. Then he moved closer to the body.

O'Brien had been thrown about ten or fifteen feet. It might have been further if a tree hadn't got in the way. He lay slumped and twisted, his head half buried in the ditch, his chubby limbs flung out at crazy angles, as though he'd been frozen in the act of an ill-advised star jump.

Reluctantly, because he knew that every second they stayed here could condemn them, Robbie eased into the ditch until he found a position that allowed him a view of O'Brien's face.

At first all he noticed was the blood, dribbling from the nose and mouth. More blood on his head, dark as treacle in his hair. Blobs of it on his bushy salt-and-pepper eyebrows. Blood everywhere, and yet—

Hank's eyes were open.

Robbie thought his heart would stop. He had to straighten up and take a deep breath. He checked on Dan: a distant silhouette, doubled over and coughing.

One second, two, Robbie's mind busy processing, processing . . . and then a decision.

Couldn't let him live. Not if it meant going to prison.

He looked round for something to use: a rock, or a branch. A branch would be best, given that the guy had already hit a tree.

Then some gut impulse had Robbie bending low, looking at the eyes again. Not just at them but *into* them, gazing deep as though there was a seduction to be had.

Nothing. Not a blink. Not a flicker.

Result.

Robbie let out a sigh, the relief now coursing through his veins, a thrumming in his ears like something mechanical. Like a distant engine, almost.

He shut his eyes, willing the sound to be inside his head and nowhere else.

But it wasn't, and when he opened his eyes he saw, off to the north, the probing lights of an approaching car.

'Dan!' he yelled.

＊　　＊　　＊

Robbie leapt out of the ditch, one foot skidding as he landed awkwardly. He turned his ankle and grunted with the pain, but still had the presence of mind to check the verge for footprints. In a few places the grass had been flattened, but it should spring back up. The body might not be discovered for hours yet, whereas if another motorist came past and saw them . . . that would be game over.

He started running. Dan was a few feet from the car, gaping like an idiot.

'Get in.'

'But—?'

'He's dead. Nothing we can do for him.'

'We have to report it.'

'You said there's no signal. Let's get out of here, find somewhere to make the call.'

Looking uncertain, Dan climbed into the car and switched off the hazard lights. As the engine started, some wily instinct made Robbie grab the rear door rather than the front. He saw Dan reaching for his seat belt and shouted, 'Leave that. Just go.'

Robbie threw himself on to the back seat, twisting round to get the door, but the momentum as Dan pulled away was enough to swing it shut. Robbie lay back on the seat and stared at the car's roof, watching the ghostly shadows of trees gliding across the rear screen.

'Not too fast,' he cautioned.

There was a sarcastic snort from Dan: as if he ever drove too fast. The Fiesta wobbled on the road as he briefly let go of the wheel to secure his seat belt. 'See if your phone has a signal,' he said.

'All right. When we reach the main road.'

Silence for a few seconds. Then Dan glanced over his shoulder, noting that Robbie was still lying on his back. 'What's up?'

'Feel sick myself,' Robbie said, putting a groan into his voice.

'I don't see why we're doing this.'

'Just giving ourselves a choice. Some time to think.'

'But that's wrong. We should have—'

'Hank's dead, okay? It makes no difference now.'

A disgruntled noise from Dan, and a wash of light through the rear window. 'The car's gaining on me.'

'Pick it up a bit, for Christ's sake.'

'But we're leaving the scene of an accident!' Dan sounded wretched, like a kid caught cheating by his favourite teacher. 'What if he's lying there, unable to call for help . . .?'

'He's dead, believe me. Half his bloody head's caved in.' Robbie let that image take hold, then said, 'You know, we're better off going back to mine. Report it from there.'

'Why?'

'We'll be calmer. We can get our heads straight.'

Dan fell moodily silent, to Robbie's relief. He wanted Dan to forget he was there, at least for a couple more minutes.

The car stayed on their tail until they reached the junction with the A283, where Dan made a hesitant left turn. The car behind went right.

When he was certain it had gone, Robbie gripped the front passenger headrest and loomed up into the rear-view mirror like something from a horror movie.

Dan let out a yelp of alarm. 'Oh, Jesus Christ—'

Robbie shouldn't have smiled, but he did. There were still problems to solve, of course; various issues that might need to be addressed. The barmaid, for a start, and maybe the pub's other customers.

For now, though, only one possible witness had seen them on the road. That witness probably wouldn't recall much about the Fiesta, but if by chance they did they ought to be clear on the fact that the car had just a single occupant. A driver, but no passengers.

Result.

Seven

Dan decided to leave Robbie in the back seat. He couldn't face pulling over, even for a few seconds. If he stopped now he might never drive the car again.

That was also why he reluctantly accepted Robbie's advice. It shouldn't take long to get back, and then he could explain why they hadn't been able to call any sooner. Hank O'Brien was, after all, tragically beyond help.

Besides, the shock was taking hold, creeping through his body like a slow immersion in ice. It was a fight to keep control of his hands and feet. More than once a corner approached and he felt certain he'd be incapable of anything but driving straight ahead, ploughing into a tree or an oncoming car.

And would that be so bad? Better that his aunt suffer a genuine, unexpected bereavement than the disgrace that he was about to inflict upon her.

So he thought, and yet each time he found the strength, the will to keep the car on the road, and that only seemed to emphasise the depth of his cowardice.

It was nearly eleven when he turned off the A27 and threaded through the quiet streets of suburban Hove. Robbie lived virtually rent-free in one of his mother's properties, a two-bedroom flat in a red-brick Gothic pile in The Drive, a few hundred yards from the seafront.

Dan pulled in at the kerb. Suddenly eleven o'clock didn't seem very late at all. There were plenty of lights on in the buildings all around them; a middle-aged couple strolling past; a dog walker crossing the road just ahead of them. No one paid them any attention.

And why should they? Dan thought. It wasn't as though the nature of their guilt was painted on—

His gaze came to settle on the cracks in the corner of the windscreen. He gasped. Ignoring a bemused question from Robbie, he opened the door and in his haste almost tumbled out of his seat.

Dan stood facing the car. Robbie joined him, and both men confronted the evidence of their crime.

The bumper was barely affected, just a scuff mark on the black plastic, and the lights were undamaged. But there was a long, deep crease on the bonnet, running from front to back, directly beneath the crack in the windscreen. More damage on the roof: several indentations in the corner above the door frame. The bodywork was crumpled but not cracked, so perhaps it could be repaired without too much difficulty . . .

Then Dan spotted the blood. Half a dozen drops on the roof, glistening blackly beneath the glow of the street lights. Another thin smear along the glass where the windscreen bonded to the frame.

'Look at this,' he said.

'Got a cloth?'

Dan opened the passenger door. There were tissues in the glovebox. He used a couple to wipe up the blood, shuddering at the thought of where it had come from, then stuffed the soiled tissues in his pocket.

'Let's go in,' he said. 'Make the call on your landline.'

Robbie didn't move. He stared at Dan, a curious look in his eyes. Amusement, almost.

'What?' Dan said.

'You really wanna do that?'

Dan felt his heart rate go up a notch. A crippling weight pressed on his stomach, like something trying to shove his organs apart.

'Of course. We have to—'

'No, we don't. We don't have to tell anyone.' Robbie moved a step closer, his eyes blazing with intensity. 'It was an accident, pure and simple. O'Brien is dead, and that's terrible for him. But let's be honest, he was a piece of shit.'

'You can't say that for sure.'

'Look how he treated Cate. An arrogant old lech who wouldn't take no for an answer. Imagine what he might have done to her if we hadn't been there . . .'

Dan was shaking his head, not wanting to be persuaded. 'But what about his family? If he's got kids . . .'

Robbie shook his head. 'He hasn't, I'm sure of that. He divorced a few years back. Lived on his own. And even if there were kids, they'd be grown up by now.'

You can't imagine what it's like, Dan thought. The whispered condolences. The sorrowful smiles. The way the whole world suddenly collapses, folding in on itself, and you're trapped in a suffocating darkness that might never end . . .

He cleared his throat. 'He's still going to be missed. What about his job, his colleagues?'

'All I know is he travelled a lot. Maybe he worked for himself?'

'You're trying to tell me the guy lived in a void, but I don't buy it, Robbie. This has made a hole in someone's life, you can be sure of that.'

'All right. But nothing we do now will bring him back. It'll only ruin *our* lives, won't it?'

Dan swallowed. His mouth had become too dry for him to speak. Again he thought of his parents, and the manner in which he had lost them, and now the appalling irony that he could even contemplate running away from a situation like this.

If you do something wrong, put your hand up. That was what had been drilled into him. *Take your punishment, and in the long run you'll be a better person for it.*

* * *

31

Robbie was studying his face, waiting for his argument to hit home. Then he added: 'It's not just us, Dan. Think of our families. Cate. Your brother. And Joan. What will this do to Joan?'

Dan knew he was being manipulated, but he also knew that Robbie had a point. Was Dan so adamant about this that he'd subject his aunt to more tragedy, more heartbreak?

Then he remembered: 'O'Brien texted your sister. The police will track her down.'

'I'll speak to Cate, don't worry.' Robbie's attitude became a little more brisk. He gestured at the car. 'You'll have to get this fixed up. But not through the insurance.'

'I can't, anyway. I don't have comprehensive cover.'

'Okay. Well, it needs to go somewhere that won't ask questions. I could try and find a place if you like?'

'Robbie, this is *wrong*.'

'You wanna go to jail, do you?'

'Of course not. But maybe that's what we deserve.' Dan placed a hand over his mouth for a moment, as if to block the words before they emerged. 'I don't know what to say. Are you really suggesting we should just do nothing?'

Robbie gave a benevolent smile. 'In a way, the hard part's already done.'

'But I can't bear the thought of leaving him there. Perhaps if we reported it anonymously . . .'

'You're kidding? The technology these days, they can trace the phones in a heartbeat. And they record all the calls. Once they play it on TV, somebody's bound to recognise you. They'll have you banged up in no time.'

'So we own up to it, then. We tell the truth.'

'That it was an accident? They won't buy it. Not once they find out what happened in the pub. They'll think you hit him deliberately. And we can't prove that you didn't.'

'Oh, Jesus, Robbie—'

Dan pushed his hand through his hair, while Robbie gazed into the distance, his eyes misty with regret.

'I s'pose we *should* have stayed at the scene. Now it's just gonna look like you ran off.'

'But I *said* that.' It was almost a shout. Dan had to make a real effort to lower his voice, talking through gritted teeth. 'I wanted to stay. *You* were the one who insisted on coming home.'

'Mm. Bad call on my part. I wasn't thinking straight.'

Dan turned away, his body almost writhing with misery. 'This is insane. We should have flagged down that other car to fetch help.'

Nothing from Robbie. When Dan turned back, what he saw made him flinch: an expression so cold that for a second this didn't look like Robbie at all, but a stranger.

'At the end of the day, though, it was your decision.'

'*What?*'

'You were driving, Dan. Not me.'

Dan stared at him, at a friend he had known since primary school. The most important friend he'd ever had.

'You grabbed the wheel.'

'I was just trying to beep the horn, that's all. Make him jump.'

'No. You grabbed the wheel. That's why we hit him.'

Robbie opened his hands: *whatever*. 'Look, I hate to point this out, but all the police will care about is that *you* were driving. It's your car. You were in control of it. I was just a passenger, yeah?'

His eyes widened, and what they told Dan was clear: *I won't go down for this. I won't take any responsibility.*

The betrayal winded him. Dan raised a hand to wipe his eyes, not wanting to bear the scorn that would greet the appearance of tears. But a sudden burst of rage drew the hand into a fist, the movement into a punch.

It struck Robbie on the chin and sent him floundering, completely unprepared for it. Along with surprise, and anger, there was a hint of

33

grudging admiration on his face. Then a cautious look round to see if anyone had noticed.

Dan did the same thing, realising how reckless it was, drawing attention to himself next to a car dented from a recent collision. But his heart was pounding and his fists remained clenched. If Robbie came at him now he thought it would probably end in murder: neither of them would back down.

But Robbie only rubbed his jaw and gave Dan a long, calculating look. 'Don't do something you'll regret, eh? Go home. We'll talk about this tomorrow.'

It was good advice, and despite every primitive instinct to have it out with Robbie there and then, Dan relaxed his hands, turned and got back into his car.

Eight

Cate drove faster than was sensible on the journey home. With nine points on her licence, one more encounter with a speed camera and that would be it: a driving ban. Luckily, there were no fixed cameras on her route back into Brighton, and she barely considered the possibility of a speed trap. Too preoccupied.

She lived in a two-bedroom terraced house in Victoria Street, in the Montpelier district of Brighton. Parking was sometimes a pain, even with a resident's permit, but tonight she was lucky. She slotted the Audi into a tight gap right outside her front door. Funny to think that she'd once dreaded parallel parking: now it didn't faze her at all.

'Skillage,' she muttered, and laughed. She was blatantly trying to pump up her mood, but every train of thought led back to her brother, and what he'd put her through, and then on to contemplation of the ways in which he might be made to suffer.

For starters, he could decorate her back bedroom. Maybe tile the kitchen as well. And if he tried wriggling out of it, she would tell Mum everything. Not just the scam with O'Brien, but all the other stunts he'd pulled over the years. Like sleeping with his clients, and taking back-handers, and the company profits that had disappeared up his nose.

Cate realised she was gritting her teeth. She shoved the front door open with more force than was necessary and made a note that Robbie could give it another coat of paint.

She punched in the alarm code, shut and bolted the door, kicked off her shoes. Took out her phone, dropped her bag on the floor and then stood still for a second, closing her eyes while she took a deep, calming breath. She was home. The nightmare was over.

But it wasn't, of course. Hank O'Brien had made that abundantly clear. And if he should discover Cate's family connection to Compton Property Services – or report Cate's part in the affair to her real employers – the consequences didn't bear thinking about.

She checked her phone, but there were no messages. Nothing from Robbie, begging forgiveness. He was probably still in the pub, stringing the barmaid along and getting merrily rat-arsed . . .

She sighed. She felt so weary, so drained, that the only sensible option now was to go to bed.

Very sensible, she thought, as she took a bottle of Pinot Grigio from the fridge and poured a generous measure into a wine glass the size of a fruit bowl. What finer proof of her self-discipline than that she didn't tip the whole bottle in?

Then into the lounge. It wasn't a large space, but it was her favourite room, her cocoon. There was one long sofa, an extendable dining table in light oak with four leather chairs, a bespoke set of matching oak shelves for her books and DVDs, and her main indulgence, a *fuck-off* forty-two-inch plasma TV, wall-mounted at the optimum height to enjoy movies and sport. Cate's ideal Saturday involved a top Premiership game on Sky, then an evening of action movies: anything with Denzel Washington, Liam Neeson or Matt Damon – but *never* Jason Statham, and the jury was still out on Gerard Butler.

She reached the sofa, tucked her legs beneath her and lifted the glass to her lips. At precisely the moment that the wine made glorious contact with her taste buds, the doorbell rang.

*   *   *

36

Robbie? That was her first thought – she'd misjudged him, and he was here to apologise in person.

A gulp of wine, then she set the glass down on the floor and went to answer. There was a semi-opaque panel in the front door: all she could make out was a head in silhouette, probably male.

'Who is it?' she called, and had a sudden chilling thought that Hank O'Brien had found out where she lived.

'It's me.'

Not O'Brien, or Robbie, but somebody equally cocky.

Making sure to sound confused, Cate said, 'Who?'

'*Me-ee.*' A single drawn-out note that started off grouchy, then softened, as if he'd spotted the danger that she would leave him standing on the path.

Cate sighed. She opened the door a fraction.

'Hello, Martin.'

'Come on,' he said, irritated again.

'Do you know what time it is?'

'I came round earlier and you weren't here. Are you going to let me in?'

'What do you want?'

He sighed, jerking both arms in a helpless spasm. 'I need to talk to you. Please.'

For the second time this evening Cate put the needs of an immature male before her own best interests, and opened the door wide. Martin gave a wince of a smile and stepped inside. He was a tall man, six foot three, with a noticeable stoop and a face that seemed destined not to age well. At thirty-four the angular features that she'd once so adored were beginning to thicken and sag; the flesh on his cheeks was puffy and sallow.

'Have you put on weight?'

He grunted. 'Stopped going to the gym. You look amazing. Better than ever.'

Moving swiftly on, she thought. 'I take it this isn't a social visit?'

'Not really.' He gazed at her for a few seconds, as though he'd lost the thread of some internal monologue. Then he dragged his hands across his face and said, 'Christ, I'm knackered.'

'Janine working you too hard, is she?'

Cate expected the wisecrack to earn a rebuke. Over the past eighteen months Martin had stated repeatedly that he saw no reason why they couldn't all just get along – Martin and Cate and Janine, his ex-wife and his current squeeze, blissfully united in their devotion to one very special man.

As if.

Now, however, Martin did something very uncharacteristic. He blushed. Cate couldn't recall the last time she'd seen him blush – certainly not when he'd told her he was leaving. Not even when she'd guessed it was Janine he had been shagging for months.

'What?' she asked, feeling like she was pulling the pin from a grenade.

Still nervous, Martin dipped his head. His hair was military short and jet black, but Cate thought she spotted one or two silver strands. Distracted by this discovery, she nearly missed his mumbled reply.

'Janine's pregnant.'

Cate blundered into the lounge. A shrill voice had started up in her head. The thoughts it expressed were hers, but the voice seemed to belong to someone else: the kind of harridan she'd sworn never to become.

What are you doing here? Why are you telling me this? Is it to rub salt into the wound, or is there another reason?

Martin trailed after her, stopping abruptly when she turned on him. 'What do you want from me?'

'No one else knows yet. I thought you should be first.'

Cate nodded, but this declaration had her stumped. In silence they stared at one another, a little too close together in the cosy room. Martin tried to sidle past and there was a high-pitched popping sound, followed by the crunch of broken glass.

'Oh, bloody hell, Martin!'

'Sorry. I didn't see it.'

'It was right there in front of you.'

'Yeah. On the floor. Who leaves a glass of wine on the floor?'

'I didn't ask you to come in here. God knows, after the night I've had—'

'I said I'm sorry. I'll get a cloth, shall I?'

'No, I'll do it. You pick up the glass.'

Martin hesitated in the act of kneeling. 'Don't suppose you have any gardening gloves handy?'

'What?'

'So I don't cut myself.' He gestured at the floor. 'Well, come on. I'll never hear the last of it if I get blood on the carpet.'

Sweet Jesus, it's as if we've never broken up . . .

The thought made Cate laugh out loud, which provoked a frown from Martin: he hated being teased. And to think she'd almost believed him capable of appreciating how much anguish his news had caused her.

She fetched some kitchen roll and the dustpan and brush. Martin had located the largest fragment of the wine glass and was methodically collecting the smaller pieces, stacking them in order of size as though they were parts of a puzzle that had to be assembled in a precise sequence.

He moved back to give her space, and as he watched her sponging wine from the carpet Cate experienced the weird telepathy that exists between couples – even those who are no longer a couple – and knew exactly what he would say next:

'At least it wasn't red wine.'

She didn't dignify the comment with a response. Shifting position, a twinge of pain in her leg brought back the memory of Hank O'Brien shoving her to the floor. She tried to counteract the negative image with a better one: the moment she had punched him in the face.

*   *   *

Cate leaned forward, her head bent over, and dabbed at the carpet. Perhaps not the most effective way to clean up, but at least having her back to Martin made the conversation easier.

'Congratulations, by the way.'

He snorted. 'Thanks.'

'I wasn't being sarcastic.'

'Oh.'

'I take it you're pleased?'

'Delighted.'

'Now who sounds sarcastic?'

'No, I am. Honest.' She heard a creak as he sat on the sofa. When he spoke again his tone was no longer defensive, but softly apologetic. 'The thing is, I've done a lot of growing up lately. I think I'm ready to start a family now.'

Cate shut her eyes tightly, perhaps testing to see if there was a tear or two to be squeezed out, but nothing emerged.

'That's all good, then, isn't it?' she said.

No reply. Cate plucked an overlooked sliver of glass from beneath a dining chair and dropped it into the dustpan. Then she turned, shuffling round on her knees. Martin was gazing at her, his face slightly flushed, his mouth moving in silence as if he'd been robbed of the power of speech.

'What's wrong, Martin?'

'I'm glad about becoming a father, really I am. I'm just . . . I'm not sure if I'm having a kid with the right woman.'

He sat back with a sigh, as though grateful to have relieved himself of a mighty burden. For Cate, the only saving grace was that he didn't seem to expect a response. She felt a torrent of emotions, welling up behind the dam of her poker face, and knew that, no matter what happened, that dam must not burst until Martin had gone.

Nine

Dan was on autopilot for the drive home. It was a route he'd driven countless times, on the nights when Robbie wanted company and Dan either didn't feel like drinking or couldn't afford an expensive taxi ride.

Home was a three-bedroom semi in Hollingbury, a quiet district on the northern edge of Brighton, high up on the Downs. Following the death of his parents, their small house in the centre of town had been sold and the proceeds pooled with the resources of his aunt, Joan, who had purchased this house as a compromise: close enough for her to stay in touch with her friends in Woodingdean, where she had lived before, while allowing Dan to remain at his school in Surrenden Road.

The property came with a garage, but it tended not to be used because of the narrow shared driveway. Joan had sold her own car as soon as she became eligible for free bus travel.

Dan didn't relish putting the Fiesta on the drive. The angle of the dropped kerb was too steep. Unless he got it just right the bumper would scrape noisily over the concrete and wake the whole neighbourhood.

He took his time, praying that his aunt wouldn't come to the door. Inching over the kerb, he drew level with the house, then stopped. He had to turn the engine off because he needed his keys to unlock the garage. For good measure he switched the car's lights off as well.

As the retractable garage door creaked on its elderly runners, he was vaguely aware of a car pulling up in the road behind him. A door opened and shut. Then a voice called out: 'Hey!'

He turned, saw Louis walking unsteadily up the drive. Dan hurried from the garage, intercepting his brother as he drew level with the back of the Fiesta.

'You putting the car away?'

'Electrics are playing up.' Dan indicated the night air, the hint of a candyfloss mist for which he was, at that moment, absurdly grateful. 'Where have you been?'

Louis shrugged, turning to avoid interrogation. 'Out.'

'You have college tomorrow.'

'Not till ten, on a Wednesday.'

'Even so, Louis. You shouldn't be getting drunk at your age.'

'I'm seventeen. I can do what I want.' He pouted, but there was little malice in his voice. Dan knew they were both uneasy about the father-son dynamic that seemed to encroach all too often nowadays – it was too stark a reminder of what they had lost.

Louis moved away, then wheeled back round, nearly tripping over his own feet. He grabbed the roof of the car for support. Now he was on the passenger side, leaning against the rear window.

'Where you been tonight, anyway?'

Dan tried to look nonchalant while hurrying around the front of the car to block Louis's path. Another couple of steps and he would see the damage.

'Nowhere special. I was with Robbie.'

'Pussy hunting, were you?' Smirking, Louis slid drunkenly along the side of the car. 'Legs won't hold me up!'

'You need to get indoors.' Dan placed his hands on his brother's shoulders and tried to ease him backwards. 'Go to bed.'

'You nag me too— Hey! Wassup? You look like shit.'

'So do you.' Dan could feel a bead of sweat running down his spine. 'Now come on, before Joan sees you in this state.'

'Get off me! I'm not a little kid.'

'So you keep saying. Maybe it's time you stopped acting like one.'

'Piss off. Always bossing me around, like you're so bloody superior.'

'That's bollocks, Louis, but I'm not going to argue with you.' Dan had him backed up to the corner of the house. 'Got your keys?'

'Yeah, but—'

'Then in you go. And keep the noise down.' He propelled his brother away with enough force to cause Louis to stumble. Dan hated laying down the law, but any amount of bad feeling was preferable to having Louis dragged into this . . .

Conspiracy, said a voice inside his head.

With his brother fumbling to unlock the front door, Dan got into the car. Starting it up, he over-revved and had a vision of hurtling into the garage, slamming the Fiesta against the rear wall.

That might not be such a bad thing. Writing the car off would obscure the earlier damage. But the thought shocked him.

He was thinking like Robbie.

Hiding the car brought only temporary respite. Dan regarded it as a breathing space, an opportunity to think through his options before making a calm, careful decision.

Tomorrow. If it was already too late to expect a decent hearing from the authorities, then sleeping on it couldn't make the situation any worse.

He locked the garage and remembered there was a spare key in the house. He'd have to put it somewhere Louis or Joan couldn't find it.

The front door had been left open. There was no sign of Louis, but his aunt was descending the stairs, wrapped in a thick pink dressing gown.

'Your brother's in a dreadful state. Did you bring him home?'

'Someone dropped him off. I don't know where he's been.'

'He's in the bathroom, being ill. I'm just fetching the ibuprofen.'

'Perhaps a bad head is what he needs.'

She gave a wistful sigh. 'He just seems so young . . .'

'He always has,' Dan said. *And he always will.*

Joan kissed him lightly on the cheek. 'Did I hear you putting the car in the garage?'

'Yeah. The engine was cutting out.'

'Oh, goodness. It's one thing after another, isn't it?'

He nodded, stepping back to let her go into the kitchen. He had hung his jacket on the peg when he remembered the bloodstained tissues. He retrieved them from his pocket, revolted by the crumpled, sticky feel of them in his hand.

With the bathroom upstairs occupied – he could hear Louis retching noisily – Dan went into the downstairs toilet and dropped them into the bowl. A pink tinge began to spread through the water and it came to him, the stark knowledge: *This is the blood of a dead man.*

He shut his eyes, fighting back nausea of his own. Then he scrubbed his hands clean while staring at the haunted soul in the mirror above the sink. Louis was right: he *did* look like shit. Bags under his eyes, just like his dad's.

Joan had gone back to bed by the time he eme͟ ͟ ͟e climbed the stairs and knocked gently on the bathroom door.

'All right?' he whispered.

Louis replied, in a subdued tone: 'Yeah. Are you?'

For a second Dan was gripped by an almost delirious need to confess. Call Joan and his brother on to the landing and tell them ev ͟thing.

Then the moment passed, and he said, 'Uh-huh. Night, Louis.'

On into his bedroom, where a sudden crushing weariness bore down on him. Without bothering to switch on the light, he wriggled free of his shirt and stamped out of his jeans, mashing them into the carpet as he collapsed on to the bed.

He didn't expect sleep to come easily, but it was virtually instant-aneous: more like passing out than dozing off. His very last fear, the one he carried into oblivion, was that the evening's tragedy would feed into the nightmares that had stalked him since childhood: his parents' fatal accident re-imagined in endless gory detail.

But it wasn't the accident he dreamed of, or Hank O'Brien, or Mum and Dad. It was Cate. He dreamed that she had loved him all along, and it broke his heart to know he wasn't worthy of her.

Ten

The call came at just after three a.m. The dead hour.

The landline extension was on Gordon's side of the bed. He jerked awake, registered the time on the clock radio and knew immediately that it was bad news. Nobody phoned with good news at three in the morning.

Even as his hand reached out to pick up the phone, he was praying: *Please don't let it be about Lisa.* He thought it unlikely. His daughter was a plain, undramatic woman in her late twenties, in good health, not given to risk-taking. Even so, he felt a frisson of alarm which didn't entirely fade until the phone was at his ear and he heard and recognised the caller's voice.

It was Jerry Conlon. And Jerry was nothing to do with Lisa; had never set eyes on her.

But Gordon was still right about one thing.

He listened to thirty seconds of explanation. Jerry Conlon was pushing sixty, a lifelong drinker and smoker, and on the phone some of his words got lost in the phlegmy South London growl. Fortunately Gordon knew the man's speech patterns well enough to fill in the gaps.

Afterwards, Gordon couldn't think of much to say. Part of his mind was still rejoicing that Lisa was safe. So he said, in a cautious whisper:

'Yes, yes, absolutely,' and after Jerry had spoken some more: 'No, you were right. Yes. Do that.'

And then, because it seemed there was nothing else to be discussed, he terminated the call. But as he leaned out to replace the handset there was an ominous stirring on the other side of the bed, and Gordon knew with a familiar sinking feeling that he hadn't got away with it.

The bedside light snapped on: Patricia, wide awake and springing into action, pushing back the old-fashioned silk eiderdown and reaching for her glasses, as though there might be documents to read, orders to give.

'A problem?'

'Could be. That was Jerry.'

Patricia sat bolt upright, her expression fierce enough to boil water. Gordon flexed the muscles in his arms and legs, trying to stay relaxed, but he could feel the sleep oozing from his veins.

'He's concerned about O'Brien,' he told her. 'He hasn't been able to reach him this evening.'

'You mean he's not answering his phone, or he's gone missing? What, exactly?'

'Both. Jerry wonders if he's out on a bender, but Hank hadn't said he was planning on anything the last time they spoke.'

'And when was that?'

Gordon flinched. He had enough self-respect not to wriggle out of sight beneath the covers. He could try it, in a light-hearted fashion, but Patricia wouldn't see the funny side.

She thrust out her hand. 'Phone.'

While Patricia dialled the number, Gordon found himself wondering if her first concern, like his, had been for Lisa, or whether it had even crossed her mind that her daughter might have been in distress.

'Jerry, it's me. The full story, please.'

Closing his eyes for a moment, Gordon imagined he could feel the body of his wife thrumming with a furious energy; almost enough to make the bed vibrate. Then he realised it was actually his own body trembling, probably because he was tired, and anxious – and fearing his wife's overreaction.

Sighing, Patricia said, 'And what time was this?' Gordon strained to hear the other side of the conversation, but all he could make out was a distant low-pitched rasp, like someone sweeping concrete with a stiff broom.

'No,' she said. 'Go at seven. Make sure you're not seen. You have keys, don't you?'

'Hasn't he looked inside?' Gordon hissed.

Patricia held up a hand to command silence. 'Seven o'clock. If he's there, you should be able to rouse him. If not, you call me.'

She passed the phone back to Gordon, who went to say goodnight to Jerry, only to find that the line was dead.

'Well?' he said, because some degree of analysis was now unavoidable.

'This could be bad.' Patricia had crossed her arms and was staring intently at the far wall. 'This could be very bad.'

Patricia Blake was a large woman, although Gordon preferred to think of her as 'solid'. She had always been that way: solid, well-built, wide at the hips and shoulders. Thirty years ago there had been a softness in evidence as well, in her eyes and her skin; even in her manner when the occasion called for it. But time and bitter experience, rather than wearing her smooth, had instead created furrows and ridges in her character, had made her coarse and abrasive.

She remained a handsome woman, however, and Gordon knew he wasn't the only one who thought so. She took great care of herself. Her hair and nails were regularly and discreetly maintained, so that from one month to the next her appearance barely changed at all. Her hair was longer than many would consider appropriate for a woman in her mid-fifties, but in public she wore it piled up in a chignon, which lent her a somewhat sexy, girlish quality. In a certain light – admittedly a rather low light – Gordon fancied that she bore a resemblance to Leslie Caron in her middle years.

To many people, Gordon was aware, his wife was regarded as a sour old battleaxe. He could understand that. What successful middle-aged woman didn't attract such epithets? And Patricia was never one to hold back her opinions: she had pricked a fair few egos over the years, and made enemies as a result—

'Gordon! I hope you're not dozing off?'

'No. Sorry.'

'I was saying, Jerry last spoke to him yesterday afternoon. O'Brien didn't mention any plans for the evening beyond a drink at his local pub.'

'Perhaps he met a friend and went on somewhere?'

'Mm. Jerry said there are lights on at the house, but no sign of Hank.'

'Do you think he might have been taken ill? A heart attack, or a stroke?'

'I hope not.' Patricia shuddered. 'Not after everything we've invested in him.'

'But if he could be in the house, unable to call for help . . .'

'Jerry suspects the alarm code has been changed. Hank mentioned upgrading his security a few weeks ago.'

'Then why didn't—?'

'Why didn't Jerry action it there and then? That is a question we'll address when this present crisis is resolved. He didn't say anything to you about it?'

'About the security? No, of course not.'

Patricia nodded, but her eyes were narrowed, as though some doubt lingered. 'If necessary he'll have to disable the alarm. But if O'Brien's in there, sleeping off a night on the tiles, he's going to wonder how and why Jerry obtained a set of keys.'

Silence for a minute or two, mulling it over. It was three-fifteen, and Patricia had told Jerry to call again at seven. Gordon tried to calculate how many hours were left for sleep, but his brain refused to do the arithmetic. Three or four – and then only if Patricia agreed that nothing could be achieved by staying awake. Sometimes she enjoyed batting a problem back and forth, the way a cat will toy with an injured bird, not to find a solution but for the sheer pleasure of it.

'There's no sign of a disturbance at the house?' he asked. When Patricia shook her head, he said gently: 'Then let's not get too despondent. Perhaps Hank has acquired a lady friend.'

'I sincerely hope not. If he's seeing somebody and we don't know about her, it raises the question: what else don't we know?' She exhaled loudly, nostrils flaring. 'This comes back to Jerry. If O'Brien's hiding something, it means Jerry isn't doing his job properly. And he's going to suffer for that.'

Wisely, Gordon said nothing. For Patricia, issuing threats was a form of therapy. It helped to purge the anger from her system.

He shifted across the bed, snaked out one hand beneath the covers and located her thigh, which he began to stroke. 'Lie down.'

She cast him a glance. 'You're not seriously expecting . . .?'

'No. No, I'm not.' Gordon was hurt. She didn't have to sound quite so appalled. 'Let's go back to sleep. If there is a problem, we need to be fresh and alert in the morning.'

She made another huffing noise, but he could sense that he'd won her over. She turned off the light and shuffled down, coming to rest with her head lying sideways on the pillow. He could just make out her eyes, shining with a malevolent glow.

'All these years,' she said. 'Everything we've put into this, and just when it's coming to fruition—'

'Ssh, I know. I know, my darling.'

'I won't stand by and watch it fall apart. I mean it, Gordon. I won't let anything stop us from getting what's rightfully ours. Anything,' she said again, much too vehemently for a quiet bedroom in the bleakest hour of the night. 'Or anyone.'

Eleven

Dan couldn't remember much about his dreams the next morning; only that they had involved an intense desire for Cate which, upon waking, provoked a nanosecond of guilt – before such trivial concerns were obliterated by his first clear memory of the previous evening.

I ran down a pedestrian and left him dead at the roadside.

He buried his face in the pillow and held out until his heart was pounding, his body awash with an almost delirious need for oxygen. Then he flipped on to his back and drank the air in hungry gasps, watching black spots dance across his vision. It was a vain attempt to solve his problem. There was only one decent thing he could do now.

Confess. Call the police, or better still hand himself in. There was a station in Hollingbury, just across the road from the Asda supermarket where they did the weekly shop. Probably less than a mile away.

Dan had only a vague idea of the procedures, but guessed it would be far from pleasant. Would he be released upon completion of his statement, or held in custody? The thought of confinement – and more than that, confinement in the company of violent, dangerous men – tempered his enthusiasm for the idea.

He sighed. From downstairs came the sound of the toilet flushing, then Joan's heavy footsteps on the kitchen floor. A burst of music from the radio, before she lowered the volume. Any second now the alarm on his mobile phone would be trilling—

His mind jumped back to *radio*.

TV.

News.

He sat up too quickly, making his head spin again. Thought about skipping a shower, then decided he shouldn't depart from his normal routine. Trudging into the bathroom, he automatically locked the door, then with a shudder he flipped the bolt back, barely able to comprehend how it would feel to have that mundane power taken away from him.

There was a sour smell in the room, a couple of nasty stains on the floor where Louis had been less than diligent in cleaning up. Dan found a bottle of detergent and used a wad of toilet paper to remove the mess. Another foretaste of prison life: mopping up other people's bodily wastes.

By the time he had shaved, showered and dressed, it was almost seven o'clock. Descending the stairs, holding fast to the nonchalant expression he had perfected in the bathroom mirror, Dan felt he was beginning the first day of a new life, in an unwelcome new skin.

The skin of a liar, a coward, a killer.

As their surrogate mother, Joan prided herself on preparing breakfast for 'her lads'. Somehow Louis was able to get away with declining, grabbing an apple or a cereal bar because he was invariably running late. Thus it fell to Dan to submit to a proper breakfast, knowing it gave shape and purpose to the start of his aunt's day, even though he would have been happier with toast or a pot of yoghurt.

Joan didn't seem to notice anything untoward as they exchanged greetings. She indicated the mug of coffee already waiting for him, then went back to monitoring the bacon under the grill.

'Ready in a jiffy.'

'Lovely. Thanks.'

'Louis said not to wake him till nine.'

She sounded doubtful, but Dan shrugged. 'It's up to him to know his own timetable.'

'Yes,' she agreed. 'Yes, it is.'

The radio was on at a low volume, tuned to the BBC. Dan couldn't change it to a local station without arousing suspicion. He took his coffee into the lounge, put the TV on and went searching for local bulletins. Joan came in as he caught the tail-end of a weather forecast.

'More rain, likely as not,' she remarked. With some good-natured tutting about poor table manners, she had brought his plate in on an ancient wooden tea tray.

Dan had dreaded this moment, having to fake his eagerness to consume a plate piled high with scrambled egg, bacon, mushrooms and toast. In fact, his stomach gave an urgent grumbling at the sight of it, and he realised he was starving.

While he ate, he switched back and forth between the two main channels and eventually saw both segments of local news. There was no mention of any hit-and-run in West Sussex; mostly it was the same old bureaucratic shenanigans and travel chaos.

Once or twice Joan popped in and stood, dishcloth in hand, watching the screen with her head tilted to one side. Clicking her tongue, she would issue one of her customary pronouncements: usually 'Shocking, the way people treat each other,' or 'I don't know what the world's coming to, I really don't.'

When Dan carried his plate out, having devoured every last scrap, she said, 'I do hope your car starts all right.'

It threw him for a second. Somehow he'd managed to forget all about the Fiesta. There was no way he could use it in daylight. As he pictured them now, the dents were practically an imprint of Hank O'Brien's body.

'Oh, er, no.' He smothered his confusion in an air of weariness. 'I don't want to risk it cutting out on me. I'll walk.'

Joan nodded, but went on gazing at him. She was his dad's older sister, short, grey-haired and comfortably plump. But there were times, especially when she frowned, that he could see enough of a family resemblance to imagine how it might be to have his father standing here now, regarding him with the same tender concern.

'Daniel, dear . . . is everything all right?'

'Fine. Just had a bad night.' He took a glass from the cupboard and ran the cold tap. 'You haven't seen my blue fleece, have you?'

'I think I put it in your room. Unless it's still in the ironing pile . . .' Mumbling to herself, she made for the dining room, where newly washed clothes were stacked on a chair ready to be ironed or put away.

As soon as she was gone, Dan rooted around in the odds-and-sods drawer and found the spare key for the garage. He slipped it into his pocket and took a sip of water. Joan returned, looking mystified.

'Are you sure it's not upstairs?'

'Maybe. I probably just didn't notice it.'

With a chuckle, she said, 'You men are all the same. Can't see what's right under your nose.'

Dan struggled to maintain his smile, imagining how the same feeble defence might be offered up in court.

Twelve

Cate spent a restless night trying to sleep, one minute too hot, then too cold. Even with an entire king-size bed at her disposal, there never seemed to be enough space to stretch out and relax. It already worried her how often she ended up sleeping diagonally. If the opportunity for another serious relationship came along, she wasn't sure how she'd feel about relinquishing half the space she had at present.

She feared that this was how it began, the conversion to permanent spinsterhood – with an unwillingness to compromise on the little day-to-day preferences.

Bloody Martin. She had turfed him out with a promise, made under duress, that she would call him in a day or so, once she'd had a chance to let the news sink in. It was his plaintive declaration that had done her in. *I'm not sure if I'm having a kid with the right woman.*

But what did he mean by that, exactly? That he wasn't committed to the relationship with Janine? That he regretted running out on Cate, and wished he was having a child with her?

If so, he certainly won top marks for irony, not to say bare-faced cheek. This was the same Martin who'd told her, time and time again, that he wasn't ready for the demands of parenthood: 'I don't want the little brats interfering with my lifestyle.'

And when she had caught him shagging Janine, he'd had the temerity to blame the affair on Cate. In his view, their marriage had soured because of her unrelenting desire to have children, which had compelled him to seek relief elsewhere. As he had put it: 'We want different things, that's all.'

'Yeah,' she had agreed. 'I want a child, and you want to act like one.'

And now this. Cate told herself it was the hypocrisy that upset her most, but the doubts had come creeping up on her during the night. The truth was, she didn't just feel angry; she felt jealous. Her longing to be a mother was as powerful as ever, but there was precious little sign of a prospective father on the horizon.

And that prompted a truly ghastly thought: perhaps she didn't just envy Janine because of the baby growing inside her – but because Janine had Martin and Cate didn't. Was it possible that she still had feelings for her ex-husband?

'No chance.' Cate said it aloud, as she lay defiantly sideways in bed. Sod the next occupant, whoever he might be. They'd get separate beds.

The brooding meant she was awake earlier than normal. Enough time for a run, if she wanted. It was only half an hour down to the Hove lawns and back. Burn off that eleven o'clock pastry in advance.

Yeah, right. Better to go into work early and steal a march on the day. There was a huge backlog of non-urgent emails in her Inbox, all the routine stuff she ignored until it reached critical levels.

But that plan was thwarted, too. Her phone rang as she was brushing her teeth. Much as she'd like it to be Robbie, finally apologising for last night's fiasco, there was little chance of him calling at this hour.

She had a good memory for numbers, and this one wasn't at all familiar. She answered with a cautious: 'Hello?'

'Good morning,' said a cheery, well-spoken male voice. It sounded quite rich and appealing, Cate thought.

'Who is this?' *A wrong number, but maybe I should ask what you look like.*

'Detective Sergeant Thomsett of Sussex Police. May I ask who I'm talking to?'

'Uh, Caitlin Scott,' she said, her voice wobbling on a note of alarm. 'How did you get my number?'

Silence for a second or two. Then he said, 'I'd rather explain that face to face.'

Dan left the house at a quarter to eight. It was a still morning, warmer than of late, with only a few wisps of cloud in a sky criss-crossed with slowly dissolving vapour trails. A fresh-washed day, full of promise and opportunity. He ought to have been strolling down Ditchling Road with nothing on his mind but his plans to open a coffee shop and be his own boss.

Instead he kept reminding himself to savour every precious moment of freedom, but it was impossible while he was fretting about how and when that freedom would be taken away.

The spectre of incarceration had him pondering Robbie's advice. Forget it happened. Hank was a nasty bit of work. Nobody would miss him.

But was that true? Robbie had seemed sure of it, but then Robbie would say whatever it took to convince you to see things his way. Hank might have a partner, although the way he'd come on to Cate suggested not. And children, maybe, though it was a fair point that they'd probably be grown up. Older, at least, than Dan was when—

When the same thing happened to me.

Eager for a diversion, he pulled out his phone and dialled Robbie's number. Tough luck if it woke him.

Robbie answered with a bleary, 'What?'

'Day off, is it?'

'Gotta go in later.'

'We need to discuss what happened last night.'

'Nothing happened last night. Nothing worth talking about *on the phone*, if you get my drift?'

Dan frowned. Surely it was paranoia to believe their call would be monitored by the security services – MI5 or GCHQ or whoever it was?

Then it occurred to him that Robbie had a far shrewder concern: a fear that Dan was recording the call, trying to entrap him.

'So let's meet up.'

'Yeah. I'll ring you later.'

Dan sighed, put the phone away and continued down the hill. He pictured the country road they'd driven along, now bathed in a soft morning light, farmers and postmen and early commuters making their regular journeys. How soon before a driver, perhaps in the cab of a truck or high on a tractor, spotted something that didn't look quite right?

Once found, the body would tell its own tale. Hit and run. A pedestrian knocked down by a vehicle and left to die in a ditch.

You were driving, Dan. Not me.

That was undeniable. Even though Robbie had grabbed the wheel, Dan couldn't prove that, and no one would believe it for a second. So if he was going to hand himself in, it had to be with the certain knowledge that he, and he alone, would be taking responsibility for what had happened.

As if emerging from a daze, Dan found he had reached the busy Fiveways intersection. He paused, gazing absently at the small parade of shops across the road. An ideal location for his dream cafe, this: an affluent part of Brighton, with plenty of small commercial properties to rent or buy . . .

Except that it was never going to happen. The banks wouldn't lend to him and neither would Robbie's mum. Dan's future had been precarious enough before last night. Now it lay in tatters. Even the most lenient of sentences would put his ambitions beyond reach for ever.

And without the business there was little prospect of owning property, of getting married. Everything had rested on Dan and Hayley striking out on their own.

But it didn't have to be this way. Did it?

He stared at the shops, a row of recycling bins lined up outside the Co-op; at the cars queuing impatiently at the lights, the drone of their engines like white noise. There was a definite moment when he felt the tension ease, and he understood that in the depths of his primitive subconscious mind, programmed over millennia for survival against the harshest of odds, a crucial decision had been made and would not be reversed.

He wasn't going to take the punishment on Robbie's behalf.

He wasn't going to own up to the crime.

Thirteen

Robbie would have gone back to sleep but for the text he received while he was playing stress counsellor to Dan. It said: Jimmys in cab 2 gatwck 4 day at haydock & overnite. Cum c me pleeese! Xx

Bree.

Robbie sighed. His head said no, he had better things to do. Another hour's sleep, a decent breakfast to soak up last night's booze, and then some actual work. He had calls to make, clients to sweet-talk, a new property to view somewhere near Lewes.

He was still lying there, debating it, when she texted again: Like NOW hun. Im wet 4 u xxxx

At which point another part of his anatomy made the decision for him. He tried to argue against it, because it wouldn't just be sex. There was a power play at work here. He'd been guilty of indulging her, especially while he was trying to rustle up the three grand to pay O'Brien. But now that cash was back where it belonged, stashed in his floor safe, so he had no reason to waste time with Bree and her stupid bloody schemes.

But it was no good. On matters like this, rational thought was no match for his libido. He shot back a text: 20 mins. Stay wet. Then dragged himself out of bed to answer the call from his bladder, his mood lifted by a glimpse of sunshine through the blinds: the first morning in ages which hadn't begun with mist or rain. Maybe it was an omen.

In the bathroom Robbie made a snap decision not to shave. Two days' growth: it made him look a little more wild and dangerous. And if it scratched Bree's baby-soft skin and left incriminating burns on her inner thighs, well, so be it.

He knew she was crazy for him, which he thought was entirely appropriate. His wariness stemmed from the fact that she was probably also a bit crazy, full stop.

Still, there was no denying that nature had been kind to Robbie. He was a shade below six feet, weighed twelve stone, could wear his dark hair either swept back or artistically mussed up – each to fairly devastating effect. He had clear blue eyes and good cheekbones and teeth that were small and neat and brilliantly white. Add to that a quick wit and an easy line in charm and you had a package that had undoubtedly smoothed his path through life.

He didn't feel gratitude, particularly, or guilt. If he was lucky, so be it. Some people were lucky. Some weren't.

And we're back to Dan, he thought. *Poor sod, losing his parents, lumbered with a kid brother and an ageing aunt. Not to mention that mouthy bitch of a girlfriend . . .*

Breakfast was coffee and a fistful of Frosties: without milk, because the last carton was sitting empty on the counter. Jed had finished it and neglected to buy more. The absence festered while Robbie crunched the dry, sugary cereal and brushed the crumbs from his hands.

He waited till he was ready to leave – suited and booted because he'd have to go to work after he'd seen Bree – and knocked sharply on the door to the flat's second bedroom.

'Wha'?' came a voice from within.

Robbie gripped the handle, hesitated a moment, then thrust the door open. He never quite knew what he would find when he ventured into Jed's room – it made him feel like he was the parent of a wayward teenage boy.

The sight that greeted him today was about average: lots of empty cans and bottles, discarded fast-food cartons, several screwed-up balls of aluminium foil and the bottom section of a plastic lemonade bottle that still held what appeared to be a little dirty liquid.

Jed Armstrong was submerged in a pile of clothes and tatty old blankets which he'd brought with him when he moved in, and which for no obvious reason he favoured over Robbie's Siberian Goosedown duvets. Jed was a Geordie of indeterminate age and background. Robbie put him in his thirties, or maybe forties, but he could just as easily have been a twenty-something who'd lived a very hard life.

He was a friend of a friend of a guy Robbie sometimes drank with: another of those haphazard social collisions that, as with the location manager, had led to an unexpected and not entirely positive outcome. In this càse Jed had been in need of a place to crash, Robbie had plenty of space, and it transpired that Jed could pay his keep in cash or in kind: herbs or pills or powders, in a seemingly inexhaustible supply.

At first it had seemed like the perfect arrangement, but four months in and Robbie was having his doubts. For one thing, Jed wasn't supposed to keep his stash on the premises – or at least no more than could be deemed for personal use. Robbie was far from confident that Jed had adhered to this rule. Adhering to rules wasn't Jed's thing.

'Time is it?' he growled.

'Uh, ten to eight.'

'Is there a fucking fire, Robert?'

Robbie chuckled, but it didn't come out right. 'Nah, it's just we're out of milk, and you were gonna—'

'You woke us up for that? Jeezus Christ, man, you want me to bang on your fucking door at four in the morning to tell you I've wiped my arse on the last sheet of bog roll?'

Jed twisted round, squinting out from the covers like some kind of nocturnal creature leery of surveillance. 'I see you're all tarted up for a day at the office, so you'll be on the way out now, will you?'

Robbie could hardly deny it. 'Yeah.'

'Well, tell you what then, Rob. Grab some milk while you're gone, will ya? 'Cause some twat just woke us to say we're clean out.'

Cackling, he vanished beneath the blankets.

Robbie stomped out, distracting himself with the question of where to get Dan's car fixed. Perhaps he could enlist Jed's help to find a suitable place. At the same time there was an alternative plan brewing – a plan that Dan wasn't going to like one bit.

The flat came with a parking space at the rear of the building. Robbie's motor was a BMW 335i Coupe, bought new four years ago when his profit-share from Compton's was still healthy enough to sustain such extravagance. Last year he'd counted on trading up to something hotter still, but Mommie Dearest had quashed that idea. It meant he'd had to take it for an MOT, which in his eyes was a humiliation.

He got in the car, started her up and checked his look in the mirror: eyes clear and bright and clever. He smiled: *Life is good.* The two and a half grand he owed to various people was sitting in the safe, but now his wallet contained five hundred quid that he hadn't expected to see again. A bonus, right?

And Hank the Wank was probably still lying in the ditch. Fox food.

Driving into the sunshine, Robbie felt the first proper stirring in his groin and knew that he'd done the right thing in answering Bree's call. Sometimes you had to put everything else to one side and just listen to what the big feller in your pants was telling you.

Fourteen

The detective wanted to see her as soon as was convenient. Cate was about to suggest meeting him at work, until she thought of the questions that his presence might prompt from her colleagues. Instead she gave him her home address, then called the office to say she'd forgotten to mention a doctor's appointment.

Thomsett hadn't supplied any further information on the phone, and Cate made her brain hurt trying to figure out what he wanted. Something related to the business with Hank O'Brien seemed the likeliest answer. Hadn't he warned them that this wasn't the end of the matter?

She knew that Robbie's actions had been underhand, and he'd certainly breached the terms of the property-management agreement with O'Brien, but Cate couldn't see why a detective would be particularly interested. Unless Hank had dressed up his grievance in more serious terms – alleging fraud, perhaps?

Or assault. After all, she *had* punched him in the face.

She considered calling her mother, but decided that it made no sense to spill the beans – and provoke her mum's wrath – until she knew precisely how much trouble she was in.

Instead she began to assess her case for self-defence. The problem was that she'd need to involve Dan and Robbie as witnesses, but doing so would expose the lie that they were merely strangers who had come to her aid. Suddenly Hank would appear to be the victim of a full-blown conspiracy. And any half-decent barrister would take her apart.

One stupid favour for her brother and now she was looking at a criminal conviction; maybe a prison term. At the very least, her career would be finished.

Cate found herself picturing her own disgrace and ruin, while Martin and Janine frolicked gaily over sunlit meadows with their beautiful bundle of joy . . .

The doorbell cut through her misery. She opened the front door and took an involuntary step back. The detective was tall and dark-haired, with strong features, rich brown eyes and the sort of winning smile that conveyed an intelligent, easygoing manner. What with that gorgeous voice, she could imagine him presenting an upmarket property show on daytime TV: *Today's couple are from Swindon, and they have a budget of six hundred thousand pounds* . . .

'Miss Scott?'

'Uh, yes. Caitlin. Well, Cate, actually.'

'Right. And is this Hove, Actually?'

Her brain was so scrambled that by the time she got the reference it was too late to laugh. Feeling like a halfwit, she heard herself say, 'No, we're still in Brighton here.'

He nodded, holding his warrant card at chest height. 'Lame joke. I'm DS Guy Thomsett. This is my colleague, DC Bill Avery.'

He indicated a heavyset man with a mop of russet-coloured hair, trudging up the hill from a badly parked Renault Saloon. Avery had a pink, blotchy complexion, a misshapen nose and a decidedly unfriendly scowl.

'Bugger to park round here,' he muttered in a soft Yorkshire accent.

'You get used to it,' Cate said, wishing there was some way she could invite Thomsett into the house while leaving his subordinate on the pavement.

As she led them into the living room, she couldn't help glancing at the spot where Martin had kicked over her wine. Thank God it had been white and not red: they might have thought it was blood.

Thomsett, she noticed, was nearly as tall as Martin, but not lanky or awkward with it. He took a seat at one end of the sofa, and as Cate sat at the other end she spotted flecks of grey in his hair. Same as Martin, but it suited him better. She put him in his mid-to-late thirties.

Avery, who was perhaps five years older and a good deal shorter, chose to stand almost directly in front of her, his arms crossed, the muscles bulging beneath his crumpled suit. A rugby player in his spare time, or a boxer.

'We're here in connection with a man named Hank O'Brien.' Thomsett was watching her intently enough to see her flinch. 'May I ask how well you know him?'

'Hardly at all.' The detectives gave her a second or two to elaborate, but Cate knew how that game was played and did nothing to fill the silence.

Avery's scowl intensified. 'When did you last see him?'

'Yesterday evening.'

'And where was this?'

'At a pub. The Horse and Hounds, near Partridge Green. I had a meeting with him.'

He exchanged a glance with Thomsett. 'Concerning?'

'A property rental,' Cate said. 'My mother owns Compton Property Services.'

'I know it.' Now Thomsett looked sombre. 'We found your number on his phone. He texted you at ten-oh-four.'

'Yes, to say he was running late. He was supposed to meet at—' She frowned. 'What do you mean, you found my number?'

'I have some bad news, I'm afraid. I have to inform you that Hank O'Brien is dead.'

Cate stared at Thomsett in astonishment. This time it barely registered how closely both men were studying her reaction.

'How? Did he have a heart attack or something?'

'No. He was knocked down and killed on the B2135, approximately two-thirds of a mile from the pub.'

Bree Tyler was the epitome of a trophy wife. Aged twenty-seven, a former swimwear and lingerie model, she was tall and lithe and perfectly honed. Hailing from Whitehawk, one of the city's most notorious estates, she was so proud of having outgrown her humble origins that, far from concealing the fact, she broadcast it to practically everyone she met.

Her husband, Jimmy, was more than twice her age. Short and thin with a big pot-belly, his hair slicked back like a 1950s greaser, he was an old-fashioned East Ender who talked like he'd just stepped out of a low-budget British crime movie, one of those films where everyone says: 'It's all gorn fahking pear-shaped.'

Robbie had no idea what Jimmy did for a living: Bree was worryingly vague about it. All she could say was that he spent his days at the horses or the dogs, mostly but not always in southern England. Whether gambling was his main source of income, or whether he used the gambling to launder money from elsewhere, Robbie frankly preferred not to know. But on the days when Jimmy travelled further afield, Bree liked nothing more than to summon Robbie for a horizontal workout.

The Tylers lived in a Tudor-style home in Woodland Drive that put Robbie's apartment to shame in terms of both luxury and vulgarity. The living room had dark oak panelling on the walls and teak parquet flooring. It also had the largest TV he'd ever seen, and a dartboard right next to the French doors that overlooked the patio and swimming pool. One corner of the door frame was studded with tiny holes from stray darts, looking like it had been attacked by woodworm.

Bree greeted him at the door wearing a towelling robe. Robbie had barely stepped inside before she shrugged it off to reveal hold-up stockings and a lacy bra-and-knicker set.

'I was gonna get properly dressed but then I thought: why waste time?' She giggled wildly, and Robbie felt a twinge of concern. If she'd been at the Buck's Fizz for breakfast he'd never get away.

'Like what you see?' she asked, preening for him. 'We can spend the whole day in bed if you want.'

'I've got to work later.'

'Really? That's not like you.' Another giggle: it set his teeth on edge. Bree tilted her head and drew her perfectly threaded eyebrows together. 'What's up, hun?'

'Nothing.'

'Jimmy texted from the airport. Him and the boys were having a full English and a few pints before the flight.' She wrinkled her nose. 'Thank God he's not back till tomorrow. Fried food makes him fart like a camel.'

'I'm not worried about Jimmy,' Robbie said, then realised it was virtually an admission that he *was* worried about something.

'Is it your mum? Honestly, what a cow she is.'

Robbie shrugged, then looked at his watch. Bree slapped him on the arm.

'All right, you're in a rush.' She tutted theatrically. 'You know you can't be this grumpy when you're doing it for a living.'

'I'm not gonna be doing it for a living.'

Ignoring the denial, she poked him in the tummy. 'Better get to work on that six-pack, Mr Sex God.'

Sulking, he grabbed her arm, and was rougher than he intended. Her yelp of surprise turned into a moan as he slipped the bra strap off her shoulder and eased one perfect breast free from its cup.

'I told you,' he murmured, his lips moving from her cheek, towards her neck. 'I don't need to do that.'

'You liked the idea last week.'

'That was last week. Things are looking up.'

'Wouldn't have guessed it from your face.' She shivered, and made to undo his belt. 'You gonna tell me about it?'

'No. The thing is, Bree, I'm really pushed for time—' A gasp as her fingertips caressed his groin. 'How about just oral, yeah?'

She snorted. For a second Robbie thought she was going to back off completely.

'All right, babes, but on one condition.'

'What?'

'It's my turn first.'

Fifteen

Denham Electricals was a modest, family-owned retailer situated in an unfashionable part of Lewes Road, just north of Elm Grove. It was both an anachronism and a minor miracle. Unable to compete on price or range with the Internet retailers or the big chain stores, it concentrated instead on the quality of its service, and somehow it was still breaking even.

Dan Wade had been an integral part of that service for a little over eight years, having risen from a lowly retail assistant to his present role of sales manager. That sounded more impressive than it was, given that the store employed only eleven sales staff, of whom seven were part-time. There was a service department as well, dealing with repairs and installations. The recent TV switch-over to digital broadcasting had caused a welcome spike in business.

Add a pair of delivery drivers and a handful of office staff dealing with stock orders, accounts, personnel and payroll, and the building employed a total of twenty-six people under the benevolent, slightly erratic gaze of the managing director and third-generation owner, Willie Denham.

Only one member of the sales team had served a longer term than Dan, and that was Hayley Beaumont. Two years his junior, she had begun as a Saturday girl, aged fifteen, and then went full-time after leaving school a year later. She was a small, curvy, intense woman with dark wavy hair and warm brown eyes. She had doll-like features and a quiet, sensual manner which had disarmed Dan from the beginning, and which neatly camouflaged a will of iron.

Their relationship had begun seven years ago, and for more than half of that period they'd rented a flat near Queens Park. Then, just under two years ago, they'd split up by mutual agreement, Dan returning to his aunt's while Hayley first shared with a female friend before going back to her parents' home in Newhaven.

After six or seven months apart, during which time both of them had had a few casual dates, they had drifted back together. This time, however, they saw no point in renting: instead the seven or eight hundred pounds a month could be saved towards a deposit on a place of their own.

Or on a coffee shop. Dan felt that should be the priority. In the long term they stood a better chance of buying a home if they could rely on the income from a flourishing business. Hayley hadn't opposed the idea, but he was aware that she wanted to fit the acquisition of a business in and around buying a house, getting married and having babies.

Today, because he had walked, Dan arrived later than usual. Hayley was waiting for him in the staff car park at the rear of the shop, sitting behind the wheel of her cherry-red Vauxhall Corsa.

She looked startled when he came around the corner on foot, and it struck Dan just how much effort would be required to maintain the illusion of normality: not only with Hayley and his family, but with colleagues and customers, with everyone he encountered. Having to behave as though nothing in his world had changed fundamentally since the day before.

He felt a surge of revulsion at the thought of kissing Hayley. He was unclean, contaminated by guilt and shame.

Perhaps the fear showed in his face, because Hayley wore a deep frown as she emerged from the car. 'What's happened to you?'

'Nothing. Why?'

'You look terrible. Where's your car?'

In a flash of inspiration he tapped his temple: 'Bad head.'

'I thought you were driving last night?'

'I was. We ended up in Hove. I got a cab back.'

She clicked her tongue. 'Cabs cost money, Dan.'

'I know. Sorry.' He forced a smile. When she took a step towards him he braced himself for a kiss, but instead she lifted her nose to his face and sniffed.

'What?'

'Checking your breath. Can't have you breathing alcohol over the customers.'

'Bloody hell, Hayley, I'm the manager.'

'Exactly. It would look really unprofessional.'

After Robbie had done wonderful things with his mouth and Bree had reciprocated with her usual enthusiasm, they both lay shoulder to shoulder on the bed, resting.

'Jesus,' he said. 'You could win awards for the way you do that.'

'You were a bit selfish today. I'd have liked it slower.'

'Didn't hear you complaining.'

'Oh, you're still good, babes. Could earn a fortune if you put your mind to it.' A pause. 'Except you don't seem to need it any more.'

'Not really.'

'So what's changed, then? Last week you were desperate to lay your hands on some cash.'

'Had a bit of a windfall,' he said. 'A lucky bet.'

'Oh yeah?' He could tell Bree didn't believe him, but she didn't push it. 'Anyway, it's worth thinking about.'

'What's your obsession with this? Do you wanna be my pimp or something?'

'Yeah, your business manager. Love it.' She sniggered. 'It's just such an opportunity, you can't let it go to waste. Jimmy's got all these mates,

73

and if you saw their wives . . . Most of 'em are twenty, thirty years older than me, but all they talk about is *sex*. Lusting after their tennis coaches and fitness trainers, their plumbers, electricians, gardeners – even their bloody *hairdressers*. They are just *gagging* for it.'

'Yeah, and I bet they're a right bunch of trogs.'

He copped a playful punch for that. 'A bit past their best, maybe.'

'Saggy as Bagpuss and twice as ugly.'

She laughed again, shuddering. 'Ooh, stop it. I can't imagine getting all old and wrinkly, can you?'

'No. And you want me to have sex with 'em.'

'But for good money, babes. I'm sure they'll pay a *fortune* for a bit of fun with you.'

Sounded like a fate worse than death, but as his phone bleeped Robbie said, 'I'll think about it. Right now I've got other stuff going on.'

He scooped up the phone. Bree nuzzled against him, trying to see the display.

'I bet it's your mum, getting on your case again.'

'No.' It was his sister, but he wasn't going to tell Bree that. He wasn't going to answer it, either. 'Gotta go.'

He rose from the bed, moving out of range before she could deploy her one foolproof method for dissolving his willpower: clamping her mouth around his cock. But as he got dressed he sensed that the atmosphere had cooled. She was sulking about this gigolo thing.

It was his own fault. He'd suggested it, as a joke, when he was frantically trying to raise the cash for O'Brien. Stupid of him, especially as Bree didn't have enough going on in her life. Something like this promised her easy thrills: once it was set up she could sit back and enjoy it while he took all the risks.

She accompanied him to the front door in only her bra and knickers, then waved him off in full view of any neighbours who might have been watching. *Crazy bitch*.

'He's away all night, remember,' she called. 'Come back later if you've got time.'

'I'll see how I go.'

No chance of that, even if Robbie did get in the mood for another helping. According to his phone he had four missed calls from Cate. That had to mean grief of some kind.

It turned out to be an agonisingly slow morning, Dan nursing his fictitious hangover under Hayley's watchful gaze, pretending to be grateful that there were so few customers to serve.

A large part of the showroom was devoted to a display of televisions, most of which, for demonstration purposes, were kept on during opening hours. On some they played carefully selected DVDs, but others were tuned to BBC1 and ITV1, and that meant regular news bulletins.

The distinctive drum-heavy theme that heralded the BBC news soon inspired a Pavlovian response in Dan. He found himself irresistibly drawn towards the nearest screen, even though a simple hit-and-run was unlikely to feature on the national news. It might not even make the local news.

But he had to be sure. Even when Hayley noticed he was behaving oddly, he found it hard to resist the lure. It was like scratching at a scab, and he wondered if this was how his guilt would undo him.

There was a strict ban on the use of mobile phones in the sales area, which meant that he didn't see Cate's text until he popped to the rest room for a coffee at about eleven-fifteen. Sent almost two hours before, it said simply: Call me!

There was also a voicemail message. Dan had just noticed it when Hayley walked into the room. Ignoring his phone for a second, he put the kettle on.

'Still quiet out there,' Hayley said.

'Mmm.' There was no way he could sneak off now, but he was desperate to hear the message. He dialled, fighting the urge to turn away from Hayley. She was pretending to study the staff noticeboard, watching him from the corner of her eye.

The voicemail was from Cate, too: 'Dan, I'm off to work now, but the police have just turned up.' He heard her pause, breathing rapidly from shock. 'This sounds mad, but Hank O'Brien was killed last night, on his way home from the pub. I think we need to talk. You, me and Robbie. Phone me, please.'

He deleted the message. Looked up to find Hayley staring at him. 'Who was that?'

'Just Robbie.' The lie was automatic. 'Suggesting a hair of the dog.'

'Are you going to?'

'Doubt it.' Thankfully the kettle boiled, and he could give it his attention. 'Want a tea?'

'No. I just came in to make sure you're all right.'

Trying not to sound irritable, he said, 'It's only a hangover.'

'Why don't we walk along to the Level at lunchtime?'

Dan had no good reason to refuse, so he nodded. 'Yeah, okay.' All he could hear was that one word repeating inside his head, pulsing like an abscessed tooth.

Police.

If the cops had already found Cate, then it was as good as over.

Sixteen

Gordon loved nothing more than the mornings he spent pottering around the house. As far as his wife permitted, he strove for a lifestyle that could be described as at least semi-retired.

The Blakes lived in a five-bedroom Victorian rectory in a charming village on the North Downs, within a brisk hike of Box Hill. The kitchen had been extensively remodelled and now incorporated what had once been the scullery and a small additional sitting room. The result was a magnificent space with vast windows facing south and east to catch the morning sun. The sight of its golden warmth streaming through the glass rarely failed to lift Gordon's spirits – although today it was a close-run thing.

Unless work or some kind of marital duty intervened, his favourite routine was to lose a couple of hours with a pile of newspapers and Google News on his laptop, Radio Four playing in the background, a couple of fresh croissants from his favourite bakery in Dorking, and the Krups coffee machine filling the room with an aroma so intoxicating that he barely needed to drink the coffee. Sheer bliss.

But not today.

Today the kitchen had the tense atmosphere of a war room: Patricia pacing restlessly, her heels click-clicking on the limestone floor. Gordon almost expected her to requisition the breakfast island as a plotting table; in full Churchillian mode she could spread out a large map of Sussex, adding little weighted flags or models to denote Hank O'Brien, and Jerry Conlon, and the driver of the mystery vehicle that had smashed all their dreams to kingdom come.

The bad news accumulated in dribs and drabs, starting with Jerry's first call at seven a.m. As instructed, he'd already been out to O'Brien's but had to abort his mission after spotting a police car on the driveway.

After that, a nail-biting wait for more information – and Patricia didn't take kindly to waiting. The next update wasn't until nine, after Jerry had thought to investigate in the village nearby. He'd discovered a hive of activity along the road north-west of O'Brien's home: police, and forensics people, and what might have been a mortuary van.

Shortly after that, another report. The talk in the village was of a road accident, a hit-and-run, the body discovered by a farmer around five-thirty a.m.

'Best guess is it happened last night.' Jerry's voice had taken on a rueful tone, but there was an undercurrent of excitement. Jerry enjoyed a drama, especially if he was close to the centre of it.

'We need an identity,' Patricia told him. 'Find out if it's Hank.'

'Everyone's saying "he", so I'm pretty certain it's a bloke.'

The most productive conversation occurred after he'd visited the local pub. The police had already talked to the barmaid, who'd confirmed Hank's presence in there the night before. Patricia, her face grave, had put the phone on to speaker in time for Gordon to hear Jerry say: 'It's only her word for it, we gotta remember.'

'This barmaid, is she reliable?' Patricia asked.

'Seems to be. I was listening to her holding court with a load of regulars. From what she said, it sounded like Hank all right. And it fits, dunnit, with him vanishing off the radar?'

Gordon leaned in, closer to the speaker. 'Was Hank on his own in the pub?'

'Dunno. She got called away before I could have a word.'

'Try again,' Patricia said. 'We need to know if he was with anyone. As much detail as you can get.'

'But you don't think it could be connected . . .?'

'At this stage, we don't know,' Patricia said.

'Best to be careful what we discuss by phone,' Gordon chipped in.

'Eh? Oh. Yeah, I get you.'

'In fact,' said Patricia, 'I suggest you pay us a visit, as soon as you have everything you can find. And try the house again. If you can get in safely, bring his laptop with you.'

After the call, Gordon poured fresh coffee for them both. While reaching for the sugar he caught his reflection in a glass-fronted cabinet and had to pause. Much of the time he fought against his natural vanity, but every so often he didn't see the harm . . .

At fifty-two he was still slim, youthful, a full head of grey hair trimmed every three weeks at a salon in Richmond. He wasn't tall, about five seven, but he kept a surprisingly muscular physique, thanks to regular gym sessions which had, if anything, grown more addictive in recent years.

And he was good-looking, he felt, albeit in a slightly old-fashioned way. The faithful sergeant to the maverick cop in a 1980s TV show. He had pale green eyes and a sensuous mouth. The lines of age on his forehead had been welcomed: they made him look serious, wise, pragmatic. He was a *man*, not a boy. Whatever the situation, whatever the challenge, he was there to meet it.

With this in mind, he placed the cups on the counter and addressed his wife in his best stern-but-caring voice. 'No more pacing, darling. Come and sit down.'

Patricia saw that he meant it and did as she was told. She picked up her spoon and absently stirred the coffee, even though it was still swirling from when Gordon had seen to it.

'So where are we?'

This was her invitation for Gordon to do what he did best: deconstruct a problem, identifying the separate components in a way that enabled Patricia to see the whole picture, analyse it and come up with a solution.

'O'Brien's dead. If we take that as our starting point?'

'I agree. Even Jerry couldn't have got that much wrong.'

'So we act on the basis that, barring a miracle, Hank is no more, and the work he was doing may have perished—'

'No.' Patricia raised an imperious forefinger. 'Focus on what happened to Hank.'

'A hit-and-run accident. Late at night, a lonely country road—'

That finger was up again: a false nail, painted scarlet, shaped like the head of a spear. 'No, Gordon, no. A hit-and-run doesn't necessarily equate to an *accident*.' Seeing him look baffled, she smiled a tiny schoolmarmish smile. 'Think about it, darling. If you knock somebody down and drive away, isn't there every chance that you did it on purpose?'

Gordon took a sip of his coffee: scalding hot, just as he preferred, but Patricia winced when it made him slurp.

'You think Hank was murdered?' he said.

'We'd be foolish to rule it out.'

'But why? What motive?'

'In the best-case scenario, it's something completely unrelated. Some murky secret we know nothing about.'

'And the worst case . . .?'

'I hardly need say, do I? Worst case, it's *us*.'

Gordon had just taken another sip of coffee. Unable to speak for a moment, he raised one eyebrow in a question: his little Roger Moore parlour trick.

'It's not entirely logical,' Patricia added. 'If I were Templeton, I wouldn't deal out retribution until I knew if Hank was working alone. And, if not, who were his co-conspirators?'

'In which case, they'd be kicking down our door . . .' Gordon gave an uneasy glance at the hall.

'Exactly. On balance, it's more likely Hank was the author of his own misfortune. Perhaps he sought out a new partner and it backfired. We always considered the possibility of a double-cross. And Jerry's clearly been asleep at the wheel.'

'A horribly apposite phrase in the circumstances.'

She shrugged. 'Did Hank decide his efforts could be better rewarded elsewhere, I wonder? Or did he simply go it alone and try to extract a settlement from Templeton without reference to us?'

Lulled by the solemn tone of her musing, Gordon sighed. 'I dare say we'll never know for sure.'

Patricia snapped him out of his trance. 'Of course we will. It's imperative that we find out who we're up against.'

Gordon nodded briskly, as if he'd never held a contrary view. 'But if the police are at the house, we may already have lost the chance to retrieve —'

'Hank would have known to hide the important material. And there's no reason to believe they'll carry out a forensic examination.'

'If only we could get to the laptop first.'

'Well, so far Jerry has been as useful as a chocolate coffee pot, or whatever the saying is. I suspect we need to bring in somebody of a higher calibre. Somebody who won't blanch at the first sign of difficulty.'

He already knew who his wife was describing. He saw it in her eyes; he could hear the little thrill in her voice that appeared whenever she talked about him. Gordon wouldn't dare let on, but it was a name that always filled him with dread.

'Stemper.'

Seventeen

Dan made himself a coffee, then checked that Hayley was back in the showroom before he hurried out to the car park and rang Cate's mobile.

She answered immediately. 'Dan, thanks. I've been trying to reach my brother, but he won't pick up.'

'What's this about the police?'

'Hank O'Brien's dead. Knocked down by a car.'

'Oh God, that's terrible.' Dan hoped he sounded genuinely shocked.

'The police found my number on his phone. I've just had a visit from two detectives from Major Crimes. They're working with the Road Policing Unit to try and trace the driver.'

'I see.' After a respectful pause, Dan said, 'I take it the police asked about your meeting with Hank?'

'Yes. I didn't own up to knowing you two, but I had to mention the rest of it. The fight and everything.' In a low voice, she added, 'I've got somebody waiting. Can we get together after work?'

'Okay.' Dan felt a watery ache in his stomach at the prospect of having to look Cate in the eye and lie to her.

'I should be free for about six-thirty. How about The William IV?'

'Fine.'

'I'll keep trying Robbie. Can you call him, too?'

'I'll do my best, but you know Robbie.' He tried to chuckle and mangled it badly.

'Yeah.' Cate seemed too preoccupied to notice. 'A walking disaster area, and we pick up the pieces.'

Dan put his phone away, wondering if it might be an advantage if Robbie was absent tonight. Maybe he should confide in Cate, tell her everything.

'What are you doing out here?'

He spun round and found Hayley in the doorway, leaning out as though she'd merely paused in the act of passing by.

'Getting some air.'

'I thought I heard you talking.'

'What? No.' He blushed, wondering if he should confront her: *How long have you been there?*

He settled for shoving his hands in his pockets and striding towards her with a studious *back-to-work* look on his face, but Hayley didn't budge.

'You seem really on edge.'

'Is that why you keep following me?'

'I'm not.'

'Every time I look round, you're homing in on me.'

'And you practically jump out of your skin when I see you.' She gave him an enigmatic smile. 'You haven't made an offer for a business or something?'

'No, of course not.'

She thrust out a hand. 'Let me see your phone.'

'Jesus, Hayley . . .'

'You were talking to someone. Why are you denying it?'

'Okay, it was Cate. We bumped into her last night.'

'You didn't tell me she was there.'

'She called me because she's worried about Robbie. He's got money trouble.'

'Self-inflicted, I bet. Like all of Robbie's problems.' She gave a disparaging sniff. 'What I can't understand is why you stay friends with him.'

'I don't want to get into that now . . .'

'No, all right.' Appearing to be pacified, she turned and headed back into the shop, Dan a pace or two behind. In a light tone, she said, 'Cate's divorced, isn't she, from that Malcolm?'

'Martin.' He'd corrected her before realising that it might have been a deliberate error.

'Whatever.' She stopped abruptly, reached out and caressed his cheek, as if to signal that he was forgiven. 'Are we doing lunch at twelve?'

He looked at her, puzzled, then remembered her suggestion of a walk to the Level. He knew he couldn't cope with a whole hour of cross-examination. 'Sorry, I'd better not. Got a stack of warranty applications to sort out.'

Hayley saw the lie but didn't challenge it. Dan felt a pang of self-disgust. He wished he could say something conciliatory, but healing the rift now would only lead to more interrogation.

It was another hour before he had a chance to call Robbie. He waited till Hayley had gone to lunch, then retreated to the sales office. He rang from the landline so that Robbie wouldn't recognise the number.

'Hello?'

'Robbie. It's me.'

'Oh. Clever.'

'Have you spoken to your sister yet?'

'Been too busy.'

Dan sighed. He could hear a lot of background noise: a hubbub of voices, some of them juvenile, and lots of little electrical bleeps and pings.

'Are you at work?'

'Course I am. Always working, me.'

'You know Cate's heard about the accident?'

'Yeah. No reason to panic.'

'The police have been to see her. She wants to meet us tonight. The William IV at half-six. Okay?'

'I guess I don't have any choice.' For once, Robbie sounded appropriately sombre.

'Too right you don't—'

'What I mean is, I can't risk letting you meet her alone. Not when you're this flaky.'

Dan had that winded sensation again, the shock of betrayal. 'Bullshit,' he said. 'Anyway, we might have to tell her. It's not fair to leave her in the dark when she's already compromised herself.'

'What do you mean?'

'I'll tell you later. Get there for six and we'll discuss it before Cate arrives.'

Dan put the phone down on Robbie's protest, then stared at the desk, glumly convinced that nothing positive would come of the meeting. All that Robbie truly cared about was Robbie. Deep down, he'd always known that, but had chosen to overlook it. Now he was paying the price.

'Silly twat.'

Robbie had instinctively ignored his sister's attempts to contact him. He couldn't see why Dan lacked the sense to do the same. Now they would have to meet up and maintain the lie that they'd played no part in Hank O'Brien's death. And what were the chances of Dan holding it together?

Fucking nil, probably. Still, it was a useful test. If Dan couldn't keep his mouth shut with Cate, he'd be a goner if the police ever tracked them down.

So what can I do about that . . .?

The options were pretty unpalatable. He remembered the moment when it had seemed that O'Brien was still alive and needed finishing off. But it was one thing to snuff out an arrogant bastard like that; another thing entirely to do it to his oldest friend . . .

He shook off the thought and admired the gadgetry laid out before him. A lot of it was being pawed by grubby little brats with no intention of purchasing anything. Robbie loved the Apple store, but he'd love it even more if they put bouncers on the door. The place needed an age limit and a strict 'no timewasters' policy to keep the chavs out.

Coming here had meant postponing a viewing in Plumpton, which could lose them the business, but Robbie didn't give a toss. It wasn't like he was getting any profit-share. Besides, after all the grief last night he had a burning desire to make himself feel better.

Digging a wodge of cash from his pocket, he snared the attention of a tasty sales assistant. The initial eye contact was promising, so he followed up with his full-on, ten-megawatt smile.

'Hello, darling, I fancy an iPad.' He took his voice down a notch: 'What will you do for cash?'

Eighteen

He was sizing up a space marine when the call came in. After three hours of continuous close work, it was a welcome interruption.

Most of that time had been consumed by the finishing stages, using a fine-detail brush to paint a beguiling character called the Changeling: a trickster who devoted himself to sowing confusion and havoc. Stemper approved of that.

The Changeling was a character from a game called *Warhammer 40,000*. Stemper had only the vaguest notion of how the game itself was played, although for the sake of appearances he pretended to be absorbed by Jacob's lengthy and garbled explanations.

What attracted Stemper was the challenge. He had always been fascinated by tasks that involved extraordinary levels of self-control. The concentration and dexterity required of a model painter were, he thought, comparable to those of a watchmaker, a neurosurgeon, a bomb-disposal expert.

Or, indeed, a bomb-maker.

When the phone buzzed he sat upright in the chair, savouring the burn as the muscles in his back unfurled. He flexed the fingers of his right hand, made a tight fist, flexed them again, and picked up his mobile.

The caller began to introduce herself, but there was no need. 'Patricia,' he said. 'Wonderful to hear from you.'

'Thank you. I take it you're free to talk?'

'Of course. How may I help?'

'I think we have a problem. Something rather, uh, delicate.'

Stemper smiled. He could do delicate, as the beautifully decorated Changeling would attest. He could also do confusion and havoc.

It took her less than two minutes to set out the reason for her call. He regarded brevity as an essentially masculine trait, but Patricia was adept at getting to the crux of the matter. He might have complimented her, but for the fact that he had been placed on speakerphone.

Gordon Blake hadn't yet said a word, but Stemper could hear him breathing: a faint nasal purr that would irritate if Stemper gave it too much thought.

'Intriguing,' he said, when Patricia's account was complete. 'As you've suggested, a lot rests on whether it was deliberate or accidental.'

'What's your gut feeling there?'

Stemper picked up the box of space marines and idly turned it in his hand as he considered his reply.

'I think there's every chance that last night's event is entirely unrelated to your own arrangement.'

Patricia made a noise in her throat. 'I don't know if that's better or worse.'

'Better, surely? And remember, this is nothing more than first instincts. A cold reading.'

'Of course.'

'I'd also say that your chap is probably adequate to the task, as it stands.'

'You think so?' A note of disappointment: she didn't rate Jerry Conlon. She wanted Stemper.

'My services are available if required. For now, there's one thing you should consider.'

'Go on.'

Stemper tipped up the box of space marines: the next project on his list. Jacob liked to participate where he was able, so Stemper would cut the plastic parts from the sprue, using an extremely sharp craft knife, and glue the models together. Jacob, if supervised, could be trusted to spray the undercoat.

'Put yourself in the mind of the culprit. After such an event there's inevitably a period of denial, of doubt, particularly if it was unintentional. He or she will have woken this morning and thought: *Did it really happen?*'

'Yes,' Patricia murmured. 'I can see that.'

'Through the course of the day, that sense of unreality will intensify. There will be an irresistible urge to know for sure.'

'A return to the scene of the crime?'

'It's a cliché precisely because of its strong basis in reality.'

'But it was last night. We're probably too late.'

'Not necessarily. You said the authorities are present?'

'Yes.'

'Certainly when Je— when our friend was there,' Gordon added, in a tone of breathless excitement. Stemper pictured him, sitting with both hands pressed between his legs, his knees swinging open and shut like saloon doors in a gale.

'I imagine they'll be there for some hours. But once the body's removed, and a thorough search completed, they'll leave the scene unguarded.'

'What do you suggest we do?' This time Gordon was subdued, as though reeling from Patricia's disapproval.

'Tell your friend to find a suitably discreet location with a clear view of the road. Somewhere he can hide for several hours. If they come back, it'll be before three a.m. He should note the registration of every vehicle that passes twice or more, or anyone who slows down to look.'

Gordon said, 'But don't crime scenes always attract, what do they call it, "rubberneckers"?'

'Yes. And among the rubberneckers, you'll often find the perpetrator.' He added, 'Regarding the numbers, I do have a database chap if you need one, though for DVLA records it does tend to be quite pricey.'

'Thank you, but we have our own contacts,' Patricia said.

'Of course. Well, do let me know if I can be of any more help. A pleasure to talk to you again.'

Stemper put the phone down, thinking: *They will need my help.* Especially if their only assistance was coming from a phlegmy old reprobate like Jerry Conlon . . .

He pushed the chair back on its castors, crossed his arms on the desk and lowered his head until his chin rested on his forearm. Now he was at eye level with the Changeling. It glared at him with a righteous fury, daring him to do what he did best: fight fire with fire.

Footsteps clattered on the stairs. Stemper checked his surroundings – the desk, the floor, the laptop screen – then relaxed. A quick double knock and the door burst open. Against the rules, but Stemper had a smile prepared.

Jacob bowled into the room. His face lit up. 'Ah, you painted it! Amazing!'

Stemper gave a modest nod. The boy ran towards him, arms up as if seeking a hug, then dropped them at the last second. He stood over the model, close enough for Stemper to taste the heat and sweat pumping from him. His blond hair was wet and spiky. There were grass stains on his school polo shirt.

'Can I touch it?'

'Not just yet.' Stemper noticed a small twig matted in the boy's hair. 'You look hot and bothered.'

'Went to the park on the way home. Nathan was there, and Mattie Clark. We were fighting and stuff. Doing karate.'

'Sounds like fun.' Stemper thought about reaching over and plucking the twig out, but while he was deliberating he heard movement on the landing.

'Jacob! I've told you not to disturb Mr Hopper.'

'But he's finished the Changeling for me!'

Stemper swivelled the chair towards the doorway. Debbie Winwood was the epitome of a gently disapproving mum, arms folded across her breasts, love and tolerance in her eyes. She flashed Stemper a knowing look.

'You're very lucky, Jacob. Have you thanked him?'

'Thank you,' Jacob said dutifully, then went back up a gear: 'Can we do the marines now?'

'You've got homework tonight.'

The boy groaned. His fingers were fluttering above the Changeling, desperate to hold it. Debbie lingered in the doorway, needing to establish control over her son but respectful of Stemper's territory.

He picked up the box of space marines. 'I tell you what, Jacob. I'll prep them tonight, and then maybe you can do the base coat tomorrow.'

'Yeah! Will you help me with them?'

'If I can. I might have to go away for a few days.'

Debbie's ears pricked up. 'On business?'

Stemper nodded. 'There's the possibility of a new contract.'

'Oh. Long-term, do you think?'

He saw the worry in her face. Over the past two months the rent he'd paid and the help he'd offered around the house had made him virtually indispensable. Everything had gone beautifully to plan.

He said, 'Not necessarily. I should know more later this week.'

She nodded, then winced as an elbow bumped her arm: her daughter, Brooke, cradling an open laptop and trying to slither past with her back to the room.

'Be more careful.'

'Sor-ry.'

'Come and see the Changeling!' Jacob cried. 'It's all painted.'

Brooke turned just long enough to pull a face, her tongue bulging against her lower lip: as if Jacob was insane to think a thirteen-year-old girl would be interested in anything that excited a nine-year-old boy. Like, *why?*

The dynamics of family life enthralled Stemper. His expression conveyed that, whilst he wasn't taking sides, he understood her attitude entirely. Brooke saw it but maintained the sneer. She spent a lot of time monitoring Stemper in her peripheral vision; rarely if ever did she look him directly in the eye.

'Right, Jacob,' Debbie said. 'You need to get out of that filthy uniform. And Mr Hopper needs peace and quiet.'

Reluctantly, the boy traipsed out, and Debbie offered another apologetic smile.

'I've put the kettle on. Do you want . . .?'

'Not right now. Thank you.'

Stemper waited until the door had closed, then turned the chair back towards the desk. *Peace and quiet*, he thought. *Or confusion and havoc.*

He knew which he preferred.

Nineteen

When they told him the plan it was clear that Jerry wasn't impressed, though he wouldn't actually come out and say it.

He arrived half an hour after the conversation with Stemper, while the Blakes were still hyper – or rather, Patricia was hyper and Gordon was surging in and out of her slipstream. Gordon didn't appreciate how much it had affected them until he caught the look that Jerry gave Patricia. Ravenous but wary, as though a voice in his head was telling him to be careful what he wished for.

Gordon couldn't help smacking his lips together, relishing the surprise they had in store for him.

Patricia, who favoured directness, had said, 'I don't care how tedious it is for him. If he'd kept a closer watch on O'Brien, we wouldn't be in this position.'

That wasn't necessarily true, although Gordon didn't say so. 'Can we trust him to get this right?' he asked.

'Frankly, who knows? Are you volunteering in his place?'

And he'd laughed. 'No, not me, darling. I get far too fidgety, don't I?'

Conlon arrived in his rented VW Golf. His own car was some kind of absurd vintage Cadillac, restored at great expense over a period of many years. As to why Jerry had bothered, Gordon had no idea. A big flash car was about as foolish a choice of vehicle as you could imagine for a man in Jerry's current role of low-key, unobtrusive gofer. The Blakes had duly insisted on more anonymous transport.

Nudging sixty but looking a decade older, Jerry Conlon seemed to believe he was entitled to a perpetual mid-life crisis, as if an early brush with the rock-and-roll business had endowed him with the gift of immortality.

He was painfully thin, except for a roll of flab around his middle that resembled a bicycle inner tube. He wore tight jeans, leather coats and bootlace ties. Permanently unshaven, his uneven white stubble was more Steptoe than Bruce Willis, and his curly grey hair was stained an unappealing nicotine yellow. With his sunken cheeks and wheezy south London voice, he could have been an escapee from a 1950s sanatorium.

In the living room, over a pot of Earl Grey, he updated them on his progress. 'I managed to blag a chat with this barmaid. Traci, with an "i". She's about twenty. A fat, rough-looking bird. Supposed to be a goth, but take it from me, she ain't the real deal.'

Gordon snorted. Another of Jerry's delusions was that he had his finger on the pulse of youth culture. For a man who looked like his own pulse was thready at best, Gordon thought he'd be wiser to concentrate on a lifestyle more befitting his age.

'What did she tell you, Jerry?' Patricia said.

Conlon gave his nose a savage rub with the side of his hand. 'It is O'Brien. Dead as a doornail when the farmer found him this morning.'

A moment of glum silence. They had known all day, but the news sank deeper now.

'And we're in the clear as regards your contact with Hank?' Patricia asked.

'Totally. I only ever used the mobile you gave me. I assume it's untraceable?'

Patricia nodded. 'What about the house? The laptop?'

'No chance. The fuzz were still there.' Anticipating their displeasure, he raised a hand. 'But I got another snippet in the pub. Turns out Hank met up with some bird.'

'A woman?' Patricia said. She and Gordon exchanged a glance: just as they had speculated.

'Yeah. Dunno if it was a date or what, but it didn't go well. Traci said they had a row. O'Brien pushed the girl over, then these blokes went wading in.'

'Who?' Patricia barked.

'Just two blokes that were in there drinking. They broke up the fight, and O'Brien scarpered.'

Patricia seemed poised to speak, but in fact she was just drawing in a long, slow breath. Gordon knew it as an *uh-oh* breath.

'Did you get any information about them?' she demanded, splaying her hand and ticking off each point on a different finger. 'Their ages. Their descriptions. What they said. What they did. What sort of *car* they drove.'

Jerry shrivelled under the onslaught. 'Hey, it was hard enough getting that. The pub was heaving, and the fuzz were in and out all the time. This was a hit-and-run, remember? If they clock me taking too much interest, what do you think they're gonna do?'

'Hmm.' The look Patricia gave him made it apparent that she took a dim view of his excuses.

'I suppose we have a bit more to go on,' Gordon said.

Patricia, still studying Jerry, said: 'Which brings us to your next task . . .'

Once they had explained it, Jerry took a noisy gulp of tea and sighed. 'So I'm camping out for the night, basically?'

'Till three a.m.,' Patricia said. 'Just make sure you're not seen. I trust there are suitable places to hide?'

'Only in a field, or up a fu— up a tree.'

Savouring the misery on Jerry's face, Gordon said, 'A touch of good fortune tonight and the mystery will be solved.'

'And what if nobody shows up?'

Patricia said, 'We'll reassess tomorrow. Gordon and I have already discussed how we can enhance the team.'

Jerry looked indignant. 'You mean get outside help? Like who?'

'Stemper.'

'Shit.' Jerry swore with such comic timing that it should have provoked a smile, but Gordon didn't feel like smiling. His own reaction, safely internalised, had been much the same.

Patricia was affronted. 'What do you mean by that?'

'Nothing. It's your decision, I suppose.' Unconsciously, Jerry was shaking his head, but Patricia didn't seem to notice.

'You're quite correct, Jerry. It *is* my decision.'

Twenty

Dan was in the pub by ten to six, having fled the shop and jumped on the first bus that came along.

In the final hour of trading Hayley had begun chatting brightly about a wedding fair taking place this Sunday, at a hotel near Crawley. It was the sort of thing he'd struggle to be enthusiastic about at the best of times; right now even a lukewarm interest was beyond him.

'I know it's not likely to be relevant for years yet.' Here she'd left a pause, during which he was probably expected to contradict her. 'Mum's keen to come, but she won't if you'd prefer it to be just the two of us.'

Dan had shrugged. 'No, let her go with you if she wants.' Then one of the other assistants had interrupted with a question about wireless routers, and Dan gave a silent blessing for his lucky escape.

Later, as they were leaving, Hayley pounced again. 'So? Are we all going?'

'What?'

'God, Daniel, it was less than twenty minutes ago. The wedding fair.'

'Oh. Didn't you say you're taking your mum?'

For a second he thought she might slap him. Instead she shook her head, a small vicious movement.

'Forget it. All you care about is this . . . this *dream* of owning a cafe.'

97

'What's wrong with that?'

'It's starting to feel like an excuse.'

She said it quietly, but there was no mistaking the challenge in her voice. A couple of colleagues were easing past; they offered bland farewells, but once outside there would be smirks, whispers, gossip.

'I can't talk about it now.' He pushed through the exit. 'I'll see you tomorrow.'

'Aren't I giving you a lift home?'

'Er . . .' He recalled his lie from this morning. 'No, I have to pick up my car from Robbie's.'

Hayley gave a long-suffering sigh. 'I suppose I could take you over there.'

'It's the opposite direction for you.'

'I don't mind. It would give us a chance to talk.'

'No, the bus is much easier. We may go for a quick drink. Non-alcoholic in my case,' he added. Gave her a peck on the cheek and said, 'Sorry. Got to run.'

The William IV was only moderately busy, with a small group of after-work drinkers at the bar. There was a TV mounted on the wall, but it wasn't switched on. Probably for the best, Dan thought. He needed to forget about the news for the time being.

While he waited to be served, his stomach roiled with a kind of pre-performance nerves. On the bus he'd rehearsed various expressions, settling on one that he hoped would make him look appropriately concerned, but essentially innocent. He must have been unconsciously practising again, for one of the bar staff appeared from the back and gave him a curious glance.

He ordered a pint of lager, carried it to a vacant table at the back of the pub and nursed it for a good ten minutes till Robbie walked in, a stern look on his face. He got a pint for himself and joined Dan. No greeting as he pulled out a chair, just: 'Bloody Cate.'

'You dragged her into this mess.'

Robbie scowled. 'How did she sound? Suspicious?'

'No. She just wants to discuss this visit from the police.'

'Can't be too terrible. Nobody's arrested us.' He registered the look on Dan's face. 'You wanna tell her, don't you?'

'I'm not sure.' Dan had been wrestling with that question for most of the day, and still wasn't able to articulate how he felt. 'She has a right to know, doesn't she?'

'Not really. And you won't be doing her any favours. At the moment she's innocent. She hasn't had to lie to that cop, because she was genuinely unaware of the accident.'

'But she *has* lied. That's what I was getting at on the phone. She told him she didn't know who we were.'

Robbie looked relieved to hear it. 'Cool. That's a minor detail. As long as they don't suspect her for the accident, they're not gonna push her on the two guys who came to her rescue . . .'

You didn't come to her rescue, Dan thought. Robbie seemed to read his mind, flashed a grin and ploughed on.

'Whereas, if we own up to it, and then the Old Bill come sniffing round again, she's bound to give something away.'

Dan shrugged. But he could see Robbie's point.

'Like today,' Robbie said. 'She'll have reacted with surprise, which is almost impossible to fake. The cops are trained to spot it. Do you wanna make things harder for her?'

'No. Of course I don't.'

Robbie leaned forwards, fixing him with a steady gaze. 'The worst thing you can do now is blab. Do you see that?'

'Yes. I suppose so.'

'And you'll keep your mouth shut? No cracking, even if she starts accusing us?'

Dan nodded, under duress, then caught sight of movement over Robbie's shoulder. It was Cate, marching towards them.

Twenty-one

Cate stepped over the threshold and looked round for Dan, hardly expecting Robbie to be present. She was surprised to see the pair of them sitting at the rear of the pub.

Something about their postures gave her the sense that they were conniving. Robbie had his back to her, but Dan glanced in her direction and quickly looked away.

As she reached the table, she exclaimed: 'My God, you made it!'

Her brother turned, a lazy smile at the ready. 'Anything for you, my darling sister.'

Dan, already blushing for some reason, was rising to his feet. 'Drink?'

'I'm okay, thanks.'

'A short meeting, is it?' Robbie said. 'Good.'

'Don't get lippy. I want to know if the film company paid five thousand for using the house.'

'I had expenses. I had to get it ready for them. Some of the furniture had to go into storage—'

'Robbie, I agreed three thousand with Hank in good faith. It's no wonder he got so upset.' In frustration, she swatted him on the head. 'It'll be a long time before I forgive you.'

He winced, rubbing his scalp. 'Yeah, yeah. So what's the story now, then?'

Cate sat down next to Dan. There was plenty of room for them both, but he shifted an inch or two away from her nonetheless. He looked embarrassed by Robbie's flippant tone.

'Hank O'Brien was a horrible man,' Cate said. 'And when he left the pub last night, I dare say I'd have relished the idea of him being knocked down by a car.'

Robbie spluttered: 'I hope you didn't say that?'

'No. But I didn't hide how I felt, either.' She rounded on her brother. 'It's obvious they'll interview everyone who saw O'Brien in the pub. You don't think it would look strange if I'd pretended Hank and I were best buddies?'

'She's right,' Dan said, and Robbie, though he avoided her eye, seemed to agree.

'This isn't a joke, Robbie. And it didn't feel very pleasant to come under suspicion.'

Now both men were staring at her. Dan said, 'What do you mean?'

'DS Thomsett wanted to look at my car. His colleague, DC Avery, made it clear that they'd be asking at the pub to see if anyone can corroborate that I was driving the Audi.'

'They don't seriously suspect you?'

'Thomsett, not so much. Somebody in the other bar saw Hank taking a pee in the bushes before he set off for home, which would have been when I left. But, even so, Avery kept looking at me like I was a . . . a worm on a hook.' She shivered. 'He reminded me that he could easily check the ownership records with the DVLA, as if I might have swapped cars overnight.'

'That's ridiculous,' Dan said.

'But imagine how it looks to them. Hank and I have a fight, and within ten or fifteen minutes he's dead at the roadside.'

There was a glum silence; even Robbie seemed affected by it. Then he said, 'You didn't tell them the whole truth, though?'

'About you two? No, I didn't.' Her tone was intended to leave him in no doubt as to the debt he owed her. 'I said there were a couple of lads drinking nearby. They broke up the fight and sent Hank on his way.'

Robbie groaned. 'So we'll be the chief suspects?'

'Well, how else was I supposed to describe it?'

'It's only what the other witnesses will say,' Dan pointed out to him. 'Did the cops want descriptions of us?'

Nodding, Cate said, 'I was as vague as I could be. Whether anyone else remembers you more clearly . . .' She opened her hands, and in the pause that followed the voice that had been nagging at her all day finally asserted itself: *Ask them. You have to ask them.*

Cate swallowed. She looked from Dan to Robbie and said, 'Please tell me the truth. Were you involved in what happened to O'Brien?'

It felt disloyal. She told herself that was why she'd been reluctant to ask the question. But the reality, Cate suspected, was somewhat darker. She was scared of the answer she might receive.

'Involved?' Robbie echoed, as though baffled by the concept.

'Yes. I'm asking whether you knocked him down.'

Robbie's gaze shifted to Dan, who opened his mouth, but no sound emerged. There was a brief, wallowing silence. Cate experienced a twinge of shame.

'I wouldn't normally go flinging accusations, but it's not unreasonable, is it? We were all pretty worked up after the fight, and you'd been drinking, Robbie.' She hesitated. 'In fact, I wondered if you'd persuaded Dan to let you drive . . .'

'So you thought I did it? Well, thanks a lot, sis. The answer is no, I didn't. All right?'

Dan was nodding in confirmation. 'I'd never have let him get behind the wheel. It was me who drove home last night. And I didn't kill O'Brien.'

Chastened by the emotion in his voice, she said, 'And neither of you saw anything? You didn't pass him on the road?'

Robbie drained his pint and gave her a gloating smile. 'We may have done. But if he was lying in the ditch, we wouldn't have known, would we?'

'You're a heartless bastard.'

'Hank was a twat. I'm not gonna mourn him.' He looked at his watch. 'We done now? Interrogation over?'

Before she could reply, Dan said, 'These detectives, did they say how likely it is that they'll find whoever did it?'

Cate shrugged, recalling how her initial reaction to DS Thomsett had been soured by the presence of his colleague. 'There's no CCTV in the area. They mentioned something about looking for traces of paint on Hank's body. From the car.'

'Half of that CSI stuff is bollocks,' Robbie said cheerfully. 'You can't identify a car from a few flakes of paint.'

'If you say so. But both of them struck me as bright, and dedicated, and Avery is one of those cops who can make you feel guilty even if you're pure as the driven snow.' She eyed Robbie. 'So we'd better hope the other witnesses can't describe you too clearly.'

'No reason why they're gonna trace me – as long as you stick to your story.'

'Actually, no. If they decide to gather some background info on the deal with Hank, they'll be off to Compton's to speak to you.'

'You really think they'd be that thorough?'

'I do. And there was something else. An odd reaction when I told them about the money.'

Dan leaned forward. 'Odd in what way?'

'Just . . . they really pounced on it. Wanted to know exactly how much was there, in what denominations. What size and colour was the envelope? Did I recall which pocket Hank put it into?' She gave another shiver. 'It was as if they didn't know anything about it.'

Twenty-two

The shock was so great that Dan couldn't stop himself from reacting, but he managed to turn his exclamation into a cough. While Cate give him a quizzical look, Robbie filled the silence with a single word: 'Weird.'

A quick warning glance at Dan, then he added, 'Maybe it fell out of his pocket when he was hit.'

Cate nodded. 'That's what I wondered.'

'But they'd have searched the whole area, wouldn't they?' Dan knew he shouldn't be inviting speculation, but there was a spark of fury burning inside him and he wasn't about to extinguish it yet.

'Not necessarily. If the car hit him at high speed, the envelope might have gone flying. It could be lying in the middle of a field right now.'

Robbie even gave a wistful little sigh. Perhaps Cate was fooled by it, but Dan wasn't.

He said, 'Either that, or he was robbed.'

'You mean, after he was dead?' Cate was aghast. 'I suppose, if the driver got out to see what he'd hit, and then spotted the money . . .'

Dan nodded. 'Not only killed him, but stole from a corpse.'

'Disgusting. To think there are people who'd stoop so low—'

'Isn't this getting a bit morbid?' Robbie cut in. 'Like I say, the cash is probably still there. I've a good mind to go and look for it.'

Cate gasped. 'Don't be so silly. Anyway, I expect DS Thomsett has organised a thorough search.'

Another pensive silence. Dan glared at Robbie, who avoided his eye. Cate picked up her bag and slipped it over her shoulder. 'Well, I've said my piece. I'll leave you two to enjoy the rest of your evening.'

'Thanks for letting us know about this.' Dan rose alongside her. Because of their proximity it seemed possible that they would kiss goodbye, but after leaning forward he hesitated, unsure if it was appropriate. Cate sensed the movement and turned, so Dan had no choice but to plant a clumsy kiss on her cheek. He sat down, red-faced, Robbie sniggering as Cate stepped past him.

'Don't kiss me!' he cried.

She gave him a slap. 'Your first task is to tile my bathroom.'

His muttered response was unclear, but sounded like: 'Fuck that for a laugh.'

'Oh, you're doing it – or I'll fill Mum in on last night's escapade, and perhaps a few more things besides. Understood?'

Robbie glowered. 'Yeah, well, give me a shout when you've bought the tiles.'

The pub was busier now. Dan watched Cate weaving her way through a group of men in suits clustered around the side door. She attracted several admiring glances but appeared not to notice.

For ten seconds he said nothing. This was Robbie's chance to come clean, but he went on staring at the table, not a trace of shame or guilt on his face.

'You took it, didn't you?'

'Come on, Dan. What was I supposed to do?'

'Leave it there!' Dan didn't intend to shout. A couple of people looked round. He continued in a harsh whisper: 'Leave it for the police to find, so that Cate's story held up.'

'It was the heat of the moment. I couldn't just leave it there for some lucky bastard to take. You don't think one of the cops wouldn't help themselves?'

'No, I don't. Most people are honest.'

A growl from Robbie, as though he couldn't be bothered to debate the point. 'That fucking Hank. If he hadn't texted Cate, the cops would never have found her. I still don't see why she had to tell them about the deal.'

'It was her innocence that made her so convincing, remember? She had no reason to lie, because she didn't realise her brother was a dirty, unscrupulous . . . grave robber.'

'Hey, it was my bloody money in the first place!'

Dan took a deep breath. 'You should be thankful Cate lied about not knowing us. Otherwise we'd be sitting in a cell right now.'

'Except, like she said, they may come sniffing round at work, and then I could be in the shit.' Robbie sighed, still looking to Dan for sympathy.

'You've got no idea what you've done to your sister, have you?'

'It was one little white lie . . .'

'They won't let it go now. Cate told these detectives that she handed over three thousand quid. If they can't find it, they'll conclude that this wasn't just a hit-and-run. So they'll keep up the pressure on Cate, and they'll also start looking at you. The missing money gives them a mystery. Your best hope of staying out of this is to remove that mystery.'

Robbie looked blank. Either he didn't understand, or more likely he was pretending he didn't.

'How?'

'You take it back,' Dan said.

Robbie seemed genuinely astonished. 'You've gotta be kidding me?'

'As if I'm in the mood for that.'

'But you heard what Cate said. They'll have searched the road by now.'

'Yeah, and I heard what *you* said. It could have gone anywhere. They'll think the search team missed it first time round.'

Robbie snatched up his glass, only to find it was empty. He glanced at the bar.

'Uh-uh. You're driving.'

'You really are serious?'

'Absolutely.' Dan checked his watch. 'You can't go yet. Better to wait till about half-nine, ten.'

'What if the cops are still there?'

'You drive on past. Nothing suspicious about that.'

'Look, Dan, it's not that simple. There are people expecting that money back—'

'You've spent it, haven't you? One bloody day later and you've blown it already.'

'Only a bit. About four hundred.' Robbie's voice was high-pitched with indignation. 'One minute I was skint, the next minute I had three grand back in my pocket.'

'So now you're skint again?'

'Yeah. I haven't even got the four hundred.'

Dan could barely contain his fury. He knew exactly what Robbie was angling at. 'How much *have* you got?'

'I can scrape together a couple of hundred.' He frowned. 'And I threw the envelope away.'

'Okay. So you get the two thousand eight hundred and an envelope. And I'll loan you the other two hundred.'

Robbie nodded, still more aggrieved than grateful, until he caught Dan's glare. 'I'll pay it back next week.'

'Yeah. You will.'

'I promise.' Robbie slapped his chest, an oath of sorts. 'Can you come with me? Be my point man . . .'

Dan pulled a face, but he'd been half expecting the request. 'I suppose so.'

'Cheers.' Robbie sat forward, his hand drifting towards the empty glass. 'I was impressed by how well you held it together. Smooth as silk when she put us on the spot. A born liar, eh?'

'I didn't lie to her. I told her that I hadn't let you drive, which is true. And I didn't kill O'Brien.'

'But you hit—'

'You grabbed the wheel, Robbie. You'll deny it till you're blue in the face because that's your style. But the fact is, I know you did it and so do you.'

'I was mucking around,' Robbie protested. 'You don't honestly think I meant to kill him, do you?'

'I don't know,' Dan said. 'I really don't know.'

Twenty-three

Jerry was in the shit, both literally and metaphorically, and it was all because of Stemper. Stemper – and the damn retainer.

The retainer was Jerry's lifeline, and he couldn't turn his back on it. He had sod all in the way of a pension: didn't even want to think about how he'd fund a retirement that was conceivably only a few years away. He almost hoped he would die first, rather than end up alone and decrepit, mouldering in some filthy flat with ice on the inside of the windows, spooning cold baked beans out of the tin . . .

The Blakes had brought him on board at a time when he was slipping into the final act of his patchy, eclectic career: still making a living, but only by jumping through hoops, and tiring fast.

He'd assisted a former Cabinet minister in writing his memoirs. Did book research for various politicians and through them landed PR duties for a quango or two. Some investigative work for a TV documentary, and then his journalism – rock and roll and classic cars, both of the vintage variety – but less and less of that once news went online and everyone expected to read it for free.

For a pittance, he still wrote book reviews: favourable ones for his mates or media people who might be useful to him; negative for everyone else, to demonstrate that he wasn't a soft touch.

The Blakes turned all that into a sideline. Thirty grand a year, and all he had to do was be available when they needed him, for whatever it was they wanted him to do. Within reason, of course.

Within reason. They had all used that phrase, in perfect agreement, but no one had ever spelled out what constituted 'reason'.

You never do, in the salad days.

Bitching aside, Jerry accepted that tonight's second task probably fell within those parameters. Tramping through mud in the cold and dark was far from pleasant, but it wasn't like going hand-to-hand against the Taliban, either. And yet . . .

There was a nagging sense of disquiet; almost fear at times, insubstantial but *there*. All he kept thinking, in his natty journalistic style, was that the retainer had provided a lifeline, but could yet end up as a noose.

He wasn't normally this morbid, but then he didn't normally have to contend with Stemper. That the Blakes would bring him in seemed grimly inevitable. And Stemper had something missing. Jerry could see that clearly, though it amazed him how many people failed to notice.

Jerry had first met him at a function organised by the Blakes. Stemper had been charming, even gregarious, and Jerry had watched him closely and known that it was an act: a brilliant performance that even managed to encompass flashes of humour. Jerry had met plenty of psychopaths in his time – at record companies, fashion houses, and of course Parliament – but he'd never encountered one who could fake a sense of humour.

Everyone said Stemper was excellent at his job, but nobody ever went into detail about precisely *what* he did, or *how* he did it. Instead there were euphemisms like 'mission accomplished', 'a job well done', 'top-flight performance'. In the absence of solid information, Jerry could only let his imagination fill in the gaps.

He'd swear blind that tonight's escapade was Stemper's idea. And because the Blakes were so in thrall to him, they couldn't see it was a complete waste of time. If he valued his dignity, Jerry knew, he ought to walk away now. Tell them where to stuff their retainer.

But thirty grand a year. If that vanished, so would Jen-Ling – and she was all that stood between him and those cold baked beans . . .

Couldn't risk that. He just couldn't.

The accident site was on a long country road with narrow verges, trees one side, a hedgerow on the other; nowhere to stop and pull in. It was a dry, clear evening with a few wispy streaks of cirrus, glowing white against the darkening sky.

Jerry reached the spot where Hank O'Brien had met his end. It was marked by a couple of signs, a semicircle of plastic bollards and some crime-scene tape fluttering between the trees. Jerry saw how easy it would have been to knock down a pedestrian on this stretch of road. Especially a tosser like Hank, probably marching along with his back to the traffic.

About two hundred yards further on Jerry found the entrance to a field, barred by a gate. A dirt track led across the field, roughly in the direction of O'Brien's home. Perhaps this was the route he'd intended to take.

It was too conspicuous to park here. Knowing his luck, the bloody farmer would turn up on a tractor.

Swearing softly, Jerry did a clumsy five-point turn and drove back to the pub. His third time there today. For that reason he wouldn't go inside, though he'd have liked to grab some peanuts or crisps. Maybe a quick Scotch to warm himself through.

The car park was nearly full, and he could sense the buzz of activity coming from within the pub. A lot to talk about, after last night.

He set off slowly, partly out of reluctance, partly because he needed the cover of darkness. He had a small rucksack containing water, a bag of Glacier mints, a notepad and pen, and the camera. There were also latex gloves and a hunting knife, just in case.

Once he was on the open road a mean wind seemed to spring up from nowhere. Jerry shivered. He'd put on a shirt, a fleece and a leather jacket. Thought that would be plenty, but it didn't feel like it now.

'Fucking Stemper,' he muttered.

The idea of climbing a tree had a certain juvenile appeal: took him back to the halcyon days, playing Robin Hood and Davy Crockett with his pals in Battersea Park. And the branches might offer shelter from the wind.

But the trees, which from the car had appeared so dense and solid, were in reality thin and fragile and knotted together like wicker. They weren't strong enough to bear his weight, and at ground level the foliage was too thin for concealment.

Jerry was forced to cross the road and squeeze through the hedge, almost directly opposite the accident site. In the fading light he failed to notice a stray bramble, which tore the skin from his forehead.

'Shit!' He burst into the field, only to tread heavily in a cowpat. Blood trickled down his face as he peered at the mess on his boot.

He dug around in the rucksack and found a crumpled napkin to stem the bleeding. Then he stumbled along the edge of the field, the earth soft and squishy, like walking on butter.

He stopped at a point where he could observe the road, perhaps thirty or forty feet from the accident site. He could hear the police tape vibrating in the wind with a *thoc thoc thoc* sound that made him think vaguely about boats, sailing, summertime.

He popped a mint into his mouth, telling himself to suck it slowly. Within a few seconds he forgot, crunching it down and praying his teeth would cope, given the cost of dentistry.

A few minutes passed before he thought to try the camera. It was a Canon, a simple point-and-shoot. He leaned through the hedge and snapped off a shot of the road. The flash bloomed like a tiny supernova and the shock made him reel back, nearly falling into the mud.

Shit. He fumbled with the buttons, trying to switch the flash off, but none of the icons on the screen made any sense. Snarling and cursing, he came close to pitching the damn thing across the road.

A couple of cars passed before he'd worked out how to do it. His next practice shot was of a van, heading south. Jerry had to kneel in the weeds to get the right angle. He pressed the shutter, the camera at arm's length and tilted diagonally. But the picture was useless, the van no more than a white blur in the darkness.

Without a flash, the exposure time was far too long. He'd never get the registration plates that way, and he was buggered if he was going to jump back and forth through the hedge to scribble down the numbers like some lunatic bloody trainspotter.

Jerry's resentment was building with every minute. The Blakes shouldn't have placed him in this position. It was downright demeaning.

That wimp Gordon. If he got his woman in line, instead of constantly deferring to her. Anyone could see that Patricia had the hots for Stemper, but Gordon seemed oblivious to it. And God only knew what Patricia saw in Stemper – the guy looking at them all like they were specimens on his laboratory bench.

Jerry shuddered. *What a waste of fucking time. No one's gonna turn up.*

That thought went round and round in his head for the next hour, the way a song lyric would get lodged in his brain when he couldn't sleep. *No one's gonna turn up. It's a waste of time. No one's gonna turn up.*

And he went on believing it, with bitter conviction, until they turned up.

Twenty-four

They held off and held off, but finally they had to go. It was Dan's idea to keep waiting. He told himself he was doing the sensible thing, rather than delaying because he was scared. But the ever-present sense of foreboding gave the lie to that.

Before they left the pub, Dan had a second pint of lager. Robbie wanted another drink, but had to settle for a J20. He didn't take kindly to that, nor to the reminder that Dan's car still had to be sorted out.

'If what Cate said is true, and they find paint from the Fiesta on his . . .'

'Yeah, all right. I'm dealing with it.'

'Soon, Robbie. It has to be soon.'

'I hear you, okay?'

Tired and irritable, they wandered through The Lanes in search of food. Ended up at a chain Italian. Dan ordered a pizza and ate it mechanically, each mouthful dropping into his gut like a stone. Another hour crawled past.

Robbie received a couple of texts during the meal. After reading the first one he snorted and put his phone down without a word. But the second one drew a sigh.

'Who is it?'

'Bree.'

It took Dan a second to place her. 'You're still fooling around with her?'

Robbie nodded. 'Amazing in bed, but she's getting clingy.'

'If her husband catches you . . .' Dan realised what he was saying, and let it drop. After last night, he should know better than to caution Robbie about his behaviour.

Their next destination was an ATM in North Street. Dan said a silent prayer as the machine spat out a thin sheaf of notes. *Please forgive me, Hayley, for lending him our money when I know he won't pay it back. And forgive me for not telling you in the first place . . .*

Then on to Compton's. The office was located in a narrow three-storey building in a part-residential terrace in the North Laine area, just down the hill from the railway station. The area beyond it, east of the station, had undergone extensive redevelopment, with a new supermarket and gleaming apartment blocks. The Compton property portfolio included several flats in the new complex, and Dan, at Robbie's behest, had been one of the first people to tour the finished apartments – all of them way out of his price range.

Standing in the tiny lobby, watching the teasing blink of the light on the alarm box, Dan felt like an inept cat burglar, braced for the shock of a police floodlight. It was a grim rerun of last night, the same sick jumble of obligation, guilt and resentment – except that now those feelings were magnified through a lens of sheer terror.

One mistake tonight and he could be spending the rest of his life in prison.

Armed with a replacement envelope, they walked to Robbie's car, which he'd put in the NCP in Church Street. There were parking bays in front of the office, but Robbie had avoided using them. 'Keeping out of Mum's way at the moment,' he explained.

'That's probably wise.'

At Robbie's flat, Dan made no move to get out of the car, and

Robbie didn't invite him in. Dan knew that the lodger, Jed, had outstayed his welcome.

'Was he there?' he asked, when Robbie stalked back to the car.

'Gone out. And he hadn't locked the door properly.' Robbie was gripping the envelope in one hand, and only reluctantly passed it to Dan, who tutted.

'If the police come round and find his drugs, it won't just be Jed in trouble.'

'He doesn't keep them there.'

'You don't sound very sure.'

'All right, but who says the police are gonna . . .?'

He tailed off, noticing that Dan had opened the envelope and was peering inside.

'It's all here? Exactly three thousand?'

'*Yes*, it fucking is,' Robbie said, irritably enough to put an end to conversation for another ten minutes.

They retraced their route from the night before, but in Robbie's fast, whisper-quiet BMW. There was a surreal quality to the journey, as though they were going back in time.

Perhaps they were, Dan thought. Perhaps they'd return to that country lane and there would be nothing to see because nothing had happened. They'd reach the pub and Hank would arrive soon after, safe and sound, and once the transaction was concluded Robbie and Dan could happily depart, and all would be well . . .

It was a quarter to ten when they turned right on to the B road, heading north through a serene rural landscape. The fields and hedgerows were a shade or two darker than the sky, thin trees looming over them in bony silhouette.

Robbie's hands fluttered restlessly on the steering wheel. He cast a covetous glance at the envelope.

'Oh, man, do we really have to do this?'

'If it keeps us out of prison, Robbie . . .'

'It wouldn't necessarily come to that. With the right legal team, we could work something out. Cate would help. She'd make a great witness.'

'So now you're expecting your sister to commit perjury for the sake of a few quid?'

'It's not a few quid.'

'There's no point having this conversation,' Dan said. 'We're doing it.'

Getting close now. Dan's heart was beating faster, his breath coming in short gasps. He leaned forward, one hand on the dashboard as he willed the car onwards; now just wanting it over, wanting to know for sure that this was real and not a nightmare.

'There,' Robbie said, jiggling the steering wheel to the right. The car jerked sideways and Dan had to stifle a shout: he heard the thud, the body tumbling over the Fiesta's roof.

Then he saw that the shifting headlights had picked up a couple of little red dots. Plastic bollards, grouped around the site where Hank's body had been discovered. And there was a reflective yellow sign in the road, an appeal for witnesses to contact the police.

'Nobody here,' Robbie said. 'Where shall I stop?'

'Go past,' Dan said. 'Maybe fifty feet away.' Thinking: *If anyone sees us here . . .*

But the alternative was worse. There was nowhere else to leave the car, other than at the pub, and that was out of the question.

Robbie braked as they rolled past the site. Didn't even give it a glance. Dan tried to look but couldn't see much.

Steering the BMW on to the opposite side of the road, Robbie stopped tight against the verge. As he put the handbrake on he glanced in the mirror and swore.

There was a car coming up behind them. Still quite a way back, but if they drove off now it would look even more suspicious. Robbie activated the hazard lights while Dan had another idea. He offered Robbie his mobile. 'Pretend to be talking.'

Robbie put the phone to his ear. Moments later the car flashed past, the driver only a vague blur to them, as they were to him.

'I'd say turn the hazards off,' Dan said. 'It's calling attention to us.'

Robbie handed the phone back, exchanging it for the envelope. 'You're getting good at this, mate,' he said. Half-teasing, half-admiring.

'Yeah, well, I've had to be, haven't I?'

Twenty-five

Jerry heard a car slowing down. As he moved to get a better look he heard another one approaching behind it. This was the first traffic for a good five minutes or so, and the way he'd been crouching had cut off the circulation in his lower legs. The pain as he stretched out made his eyes water.

Fucking Stemper.

The second car was moving fast. He ducked away from the wash of its headlights, waiting for it to pass, and as he looked up he heard the clunk of a door opening.

A couple of seconds, then another clunk. Jerry eased his upper body round, careful to avoid a clump of nettles, and squinted into the darkness.

The car had pulled up on the wrong side of the road, close to the accident site. Two men were getting out. The passenger shut his door after him, but the driver's door was left open, almost touching the trees beyond the verge. Both men looking around, scanning the road in both directions. Nervy, furtive movements.

Jerry knew he had to get the plate number, but he was too far away. He couldn't risk approaching along the road. Instead he withdrew into the field. For a better vantage point he'd have to creep along until he was almost level with the rear of the car.

He had to be careful, though. Two against one – not the sort of odds he fancied. And these were young men: he could tell that much. Young and fit.

And killers, maybe.

Dan had intended to stay in the car, until he realised that he didn't trust Robbie not to slip a few hundred pounds into his pocket.

He got out, shut his door and looked around. It was dark, and quiet, and yet his nerves were screaming danger at him. This felt like an act of gross stupidity; a suicide mission, almost. Returning to the scene of the crime . . .

And then a dreadful thought: what if the police had anticipated that? What if they'd set up a hidden camera, filming everyone who went past?

'Robbie . . .' he whispered, and then heard in his mind the derisive laughter, and when Robbie gave him a questioning look he shook his head. 'Never mind.'

'So where we gonna leave it?'

'Far enough out that they might have missed it during a search.'

Dan examined the trees, trying to work out the distance from the lonely semicircle of bollards. At close range he could see yellow paint sprayed on the road: this must be where the police investigator had marked the point of impact. Dan shuddered, picturing O'Brien's body being hurled through the air.

'No flowers,' he murmured.

'What?'

'These days you normally see flowers laid at the scene of an accident.'

'Yeah, but who's gonna miss Hank the Wank?'

'I thought someone would.' Dan sighed. He spotted a break in the trees, pointed it out to Robbie. 'Through there?'

Robbie stepped towards the gap. Dan turned, checking the road again, and something moved in the hedge behind him.

*   *   *

'What was that?'

Robbie gave a start. The envelope leapt in his hand and he had a horrifying vision of a cop car gliding up just as the money spilled out into the ditch.

'Frigging hell!' He saw Dan was stock-still, half-crouched, facing the opposite side of the road.

'There's something in the hedge.'

'Probably a fox.'

The passing seconds were ticking in Robbie's head like a bomb waiting to go off. He gave Dan's concern a moment's thought, then dismissed it. He pressed through the trees, trying to bend the branches rather than snap them. The field beyond looked recently ploughed, the soil gleaming in the early starlight. It had a rich, honest aroma that made him think of childhood, but he had no idea why.

There was no way he could go into the field without leaving incriminating footprints. It would have to be option two: the frisbee method.

He knelt down, got ready to do it, then hesitated. He was *literally* going to throw away three thousand pounds. It almost brought tears to his eyes.

Come back and get it tomorrow, a wicked voice spoke up.

He answered it with: *Maybe*.

Partially consoled, he was able to toss the envelope gently into the field. It vanished into the darkness, landing with a soft thud. Job done.

Easy to find in the morning.

Robbie turned back. Dan was still facing the other way. He'd moved closer to the hedge.

'There!' he said. 'Did you hear that?'

Jerry had the rucksack at his side. He could barely see the guy beyond the hedge, but he could hear him coming closer. Moving nothing but his right arm, Jerry reached into the rucksack, probing for the knife.

'There!' said the man. 'Did you hear that?'

Jerry froze again, comforted just to have a weapon in his hand. If the guy suddenly came at him there should be time to shove the knife through his heart. And if it happened, Jerry would have no qualms about doing it. He was cold as stone inside.

It's him or me now: simple as that.

Dan was dimly aware of Robbie throwing the envelope; he registered the scudding noise as it hit the earth. But his focus remained on the hedgerow. He was certain that he'd sensed a quiet rustling, a subtle rearrangement in the tangle of shadows.

Someone was in there, watching them.

He took another step, was sure he could see the faintest glimmer of reflected light: a pair of eyes, staring straight back at him. It could be a fox, like Robbie said.

Or maybe there was nothing: just his overcharged imagination.

'Well?' said Robbie, and Dan gasped.

'I don't know.'

'Come on, then. Let's get the hell out of here.'

Dan wrenched himself away, hurried to the car and found Robbie gazing forlornly into space.

'What really hurts is that they've probably finished the search.'

'What?' Dan was still lost in thought. *Didn't look like a fox's eyes . . .*

'After Cate told 'em about the money, I bet they came back here and looked for it this afternoon. All that's gonna happen now is some bloody farmer will stumble on a windfall.'

'If that happens, we have to hope he does the decent thing.'

'Yeah, right.' Robbie started the engine and pulled away. 'What the fu—?'

The BMW lurched as he reacted to something in his rear-view mirror. There was a crunching noise from the gearbox, the car losing speed, dying on them.

*   *   *

Dan turned, saw a figure running in the road, only yards behind. 'Go!' he yelled, and Robbie got himself together, rammed the gearstick into second and hit the accelerator. Dan's head bounced off the headrest but he barely felt the pain. The figure was still lumbering towards them, his arms moving together, not flailing but with purpose, as though he had—

A blinding flash of light through the back window. Dan's immediate reaction was that they'd been shot at, and he yelled again and ducked sideways. The BMW swerved and corrected, and then Robbie floored it and they sped away.

'What the hell was that?' Robbie shrieked.

Dan looked back, his eyes still smarting from the flash. Not a gunshot: he knew that now.

'A camera. He took a photo.'

'Oh, Christ! The number plate . . .?' Robbie had lifted his foot off the pedal, enough for the car to lose momentum.

'What are you doing?'

'Should we go back? It was only one man, right?'

'No. In case he's a cop.'

'Ah, fuck, no.' Robbie increased speed again. Neither said a word, both frantically thinking it over. Then they spoke at once.

Robbie: 'He can't be a cop—'

Dan: 'The picture might not come out—'

'What?'

'It depends on the range of the flash. Most photos taken at night are rubbish.'

Robbie nodded, eager to believe it. 'If he was a cop, he wouldn't be there on his own. And there'd be a roadblock.'

That brought fresh fears, but a minute later they were at the pub. The car park was heaving. A knot of smokers stood outside the door, but no police, no cars or barriers in their way.

Keeping to a sensible speed, Robbie drove on, continuing north until he reached Partridge Green, where he took a right towards Shermanbury and could head south again.

'Oh shit, Dan. If he's not a cop, who the hell is he?'

'I don't know.' Paralysed by confusion, Dan could only recall what he had said to Robbie the night before.

This has made a hole in someone's life, you can be sure of that.

Twenty-six

It had been a long and miserably tense day, and by the time Jerry finally got in touch they were both past their best.

Patricia had declined Gordon's offer to wait up alone. 'I'll only have to get up when Jerry arrives.'

'But it could be hours yet, and even then there might be nothing to report.'

'Gordon, I am perfectly capable of enduring a late night.'

And she was. She sat with Gordon in the living room, sneering at *Newsnight* and its attempts to portray a world they knew far more intimately than any BBC apparatchik could describe.

'State-funded television, it's an obscenity,' Patricia said. 'Should be wiped out, and one day it will be.'

Gordon agreed wholeheartedly, of course; although occasionally he would succumb to the lure of nostalgia: David Attenborough, the Morecambe and Wise Christmas specials; the coverage of great state occasions. Wimbledon fortnight.

The phone rang at about ten to midnight. Gordon hit the button for the speakerphone and Jerry's voice drawled out in a low-pitched gurgle of excitement: *'Only fucking got 'em!'*

'I beg your pardon?'

'Am I on the speaker? It's safe to talk, yeah?'

'Yes, Jerry,' Patricia said. 'Explain, please.'

'There were two of 'em. Turned up in a BMW around ten o'clock.'

Gordon glanced at his wife: it was just as Stemper had predicted.

'Did you get a clear look at them?' Patricia asked.

'I couldn't. I was hiding the other side of the hedge. One of 'em nearly spotted me.'

'All right. What can you tell us about them?'

'Young blokes. Twenties, early thirties. Both quite tall, slim builds. Reasonably well-spoken, but not posh like—'

Like you two, he'd been about to say.

Gordon smiled. 'You mean educated?'

'Yeah. One sounded worried, like he knew they were taking a big risk.'

'What did they do?'

'That's the weird part. I had one staring right at me, and the other one was in the trees across the road. I reckon he was looking for something.'

Gordon frowned at Patricia, who said, 'If they left anything at the scene, surely the police would have found it?'

'Yeah, you'd think so.'

'What about the car? You took the number down, I hope?'

'Better than that,' Jerry crowed. 'I got a picture.'

Patricia gave him no time to savour his achievement. 'Has it come out clearly?'

'Well, it looks pretty good on the screen. I had to use the flash, which meant waiting till they were back in the car. Then I jumped out, took the photo and legged it back into the field.'

'Good work,' Gordon said, while pulling a sarcastic face. Jerry was childlike in his craving for plaudits: for this he'd want a gold star.

'So it's gotta be the two lads in the pub, hasn't it? The ones who broke up the fight with Hank and his lady friend.'

'It's possible. When can you bring us the picture?'

'I've got something else, as well,' Jerry said. 'I took another look at Hank's place. Cops had gone, and it turns out he hadn't changed the alarm.'

'Has anything been taken?'

'Not as far as I could see. That big filing cabinet in his study looked the same as normal.'

'Good,' said Patricia, though there was little danger that Hank would have kept anything significant in his study. 'And his computers?'

'Both still there. I brought the laptop with me.'

'Well done. What time will you be here?'

Now there was a pause. 'In the morning.'

'Oh,' Patricia said, very distinctly.

'Where are you?' Gordon asked.

'Back home. Look, I'm cream crackered. I'll be round first thing, all right?'

Patricia went to speak; Gordon placed a hand in the crook of her arm: *Don't fight this skirmish.*

'Tomorrow, then.' After ending the call, she growled: 'His instructions were to come straight here.'

'But he's not getting any younger. And, sad to say, my darling, neither are we.'

'But the photo, the car registration—'

'Nothing we can do with that until the morning. In any case, I wouldn't get my hopes raised.'

'No, but I won't take insubordination from that man. Something will have to be done about him.'

'In due course. For now, let's accept that we've taken a major step forward. We know there's some kind of conspiracy.'

'Mmm. In that case, we can't entrust the work to an amateur like Jerry.'

She looked to him for agreement, and here Gordon had to fake some enthusiasm. His wife's eyes had lost focus, her expression almost savage as she gazed at some imagined future vengeance.

'Stemper will hunt them down. And when he does, they'll wish they'd never been born.'

Twenty-seven

Dan barely slept. Wide awake from around three until past dawn, the bleeping of his alarm was the first indication that he'd finally managed to doze off.

He tried to get up, then slumped back as if locked in place by the sheer weight of defeat. Haunted by the figure who'd crept from the hedgerow and fired his camera in their direction. Plagued by the only explanation that made sense.

Someone was trying to find them.

On the drive home Robbie had latched on to the idea that the flash wouldn't have been capable of illuminating the BMW's number plate.

'But if it does,' Dan had said, 'I assume it's registered to you?'

'No, the company.'

'They'll still trace you easily enough, if this bloke reports it.'

Robbie, busy grieving for the lost money, had merely grunted. There was silence for a while as the BMW sped through the countryside, headlights picking out small creatures scurrying away from danger.

Dan said, 'I suppose he could have been a reporter.'

'Like paparazzi? You don't reckon they've got better things to do than sit in a field on the off chance that . . .'

That the killers will reappear. But Dan couldn't say it aloud either.

'A sicko, more like,' Robbie said. 'Jed knew somebody who used to rob stuff from roadside memorials. Collected all the little cards and messages and put 'em on a corkboard in his kitchen.'

'Hm.' Dan didn't think that explained it.

Robbie gave a sudden cry, slapping a hand against his forehead. 'Fucker's gonna get my cash.'

'He'll never find it.'

'What if he's got a torch? Or he waits till the sun comes up?'

Dan sighed. If the money disappeared it would mean their mission tonight had been for nothing. Worse than that, because now they were in danger of being identified.

'There was no way we could anticipate this,' he said. 'At least, if he takes the money, I suppose he's less likely to report us.'

'Always look on the bright side, eh?'

'Well, yeah. We can't change what's happened.'

'We could turn around—'

'We are not going back,' Dan said vehemently. 'That would be crazy.'

One more crazy thing, he thought, added to the great pile of crazy things they'd already done.

But, for now, life went on. Dan dragged himself up, remembering that he'd have to walk or take the bus to work.

He'd just stepped out of the shower when he caught the faint chime of the doorbell. Even through the steam on the bathroom mirror he could see how stricken he looked. The door was unlocked, and it actually crossed his mind to leap over and slide the bolt home – as if that might make a scrap of difference.

'*In other news, the suspect in a fatal hit-and-run managed to evade arrest this morning when he locked himself in his bathroom and refused to come out . . .*'

He grabbed a towel and dried off with frantic haste, desperate not to be naked when they came for him. The photo must have captured the number plate. From that the police had found Compton's and then identified Robbie, who'd sold him out within seconds—

There was a tap on the door. A sardonic female voice said: 'Taxi for Mr Wade.'

Dan had to take a breath before he could reply. 'Hayley?'

'Er, correct. Who did you think it was?'

He laughed away his embarrassment. 'Just a sec.'

'I'll be waiting downstairs.' Then, presumably in answer to a question from Joan, she called out: 'Love one. Thanks.'

Dan's relief was short-lived. This latest scare only emphasised that he was caught in an ever worsening tangle of lies.

He got dressed, descended the stairs and found Hayley sipping tea and chatting with Joan, who was leaning against the door frame, regulation dishcloth in hand. On TV a politician blustered in unpleasant close-up: there was a badly concealed shaving cut on his neck.

Dan kissed his aunt on the cheek. 'I'll skip breakfast, thanks.'

'But the bacon's on . . .' She gestured towards the kitchen. 'You've plenty of time, haven't you?'

Hayley nodded for him, sitting with her back straight, stomach pulled in and knees together. She had both hands cupped around her tea, as though it was cold in the room.

'All right,' he said. 'Can I just have a sandwich?'

'Bacon buttie coming up. What about you, Hayley?'

'No, thanks. Too many calories.'

'Tsk. Listen to you. Lovely figure, you have.'

As Joan turned away, Hayley's expression hardened and Dan realised that they hadn't kissed; hadn't greeted one another at all.

She asked, 'Where were you last night?'

'Robbie's. Like I said.'

'Collecting your car?'

Dan shrugged. 'I ended up staying for a couple of drinks.'

A look of pain crossed Hayley's face. She held his gaze for a moment, then stared at the TV. The politician's interrogation was over, but Dan remained on the hook.

'Didn't you get my text?'

'Yeah. Sorry. By the time I noticed it was a bit too late.'

She snorted, easily detecting the lie. 'When you didn't reply, I phoned here,' she said quietly. 'I spoke to Joan.'

'Uh-huh,' Dan said, as if he couldn't see any problem with that. But his heart had begun to beat wildly

'I mentioned you having to collect your car. Joan had no idea what I was on about.' Hayley speared him with a look. 'She said the Fiesta's in the garage. It's been there since Tuesday night.'

Dan nodded: *Yes, it has.* He wondered if it showed in his eyes: the fear, the frantic calculations.

He swallowed hard and said: 'I'm sorry, Hayley. I lied to you.'

Twenty-eight

'Oh my God! What have you done to your hair?'

'Thought I'd try something different. Don't you like it?'

Bree pressed a finger against her plump painted lips. 'I'm not sure, babe. That fringe . . .' She giggled. 'It's a bit Justin Bieber, but like a year out of date.'

Robbie had only a hazy idea who she was talking about, so he said nothing. She reached out and stroked his forehead, flicking his hair to one side.

'A nice parting there would suit you. The older ladies really go for that look.'

'Christ, Bree. Don't you ever give up?'

'No way, babe. If I did, I'd still be in a shitty flat in Whitehawk.' She allowed him to step inside and nudge the door shut. 'You're bright and early.'

'Woke up horny.' His arms circled her waist and his hands slid greedily over her bum and down between her legs. He gasped as he pressed against her. 'When's Jimmy back?'

'Not for hours yet.' She grasped his hands in hers, gently but firmly bringing his exploration to a halt. 'So we can take our time . . .'

Hayley waited for an explanation. Dan sat in one of the armchairs, snatching another second or two in which to assemble his story.

'I did drive home on Tuesday night. But I shouldn't have.'

'You were over the limit?'

'Only a couple of pints, but . . .'

'You said your head felt terrible.'

'Yeah, well.' He shrugged, content for her to believe he was lying about how much he'd drunk.

'What if you'd been stopped? You'd have lost your licence.' She looked appalled. Dan wondered if she was thinking about his parents' accident.

'I know. Sorry. Do you mind not . . .?' He nodded his head towards the kitchen. A moment later Joan came in with his sandwich and a mug of coffee, just as Dan glanced at the TV and saw a man standing in front of the Sussex Police logo. The volume was low, but Dan made out the presenter's voice-over: '. . . appeal for witnesses.'

Joan handed him the plate. She looked subdued, as though she'd picked up on the tension in the room. Dan took his coffee, straining to catch every word of the news report while appearing not to give it any undue attention.

A caption identified the man as Detective Sergeant Thomsett. Dan's heart stuttered. Joan was asking if Hayley was sure she didn't want something to eat, and Hayley replied that she'd had cereal and a banana, all she was permitted on her current diet, and Dan, pretending that this conversation was infinitely more compelling than anything on TV, took a bite of his sandwich and heard the detective say: '. . . in particular we'd like to speak to two men who were in the saloon bar of the Horse and Hounds public house at around ten p.m. on Tuesday.'

Dan jumped up, terrified that if Hayley or Joan heard the news report they couldn't fail to make the connection.

'Shall we get going? I'll eat this on the way.'

Joan gazed at him, troubled. 'Well, if you like. I'll fetch some kitchen roll.'

'So is there something wrong with your car?' Hayley asked – and

Louis chose that moment to stroll in, bleary-eyed, hair poking out at wild angles. He was wearing only pyjama bottoms, and he brought a pungent teenage smell into the room.

'Hiya, Hales.'

'Morning,' she said, trying not to recoil as he pecked her on the cheek.

'You not got it fixed yet?' Louis asked his brother. 'Hey, you haven't pranged it, have you?'

'No,' said Dan, a lot more indignant than was necessary. 'It's the electrics, I think.'

'Do you want me to have a look at it?' Hayley had recently taken a car-maintenance class at night school, a fact of which she was inordinately proud.

'No, I'll sort it out. Let's just go, shall we?'

Before she could object Dan strode out of the room, hoping they hadn't registered the fact that his face was burning with shame. The only consolation was that the news bulletin had ended.

Another ordeal had been endured, but there would be many, many more to come.

In having sex with Bree, Robbie had to find a delicate balance – work hard enough to make it special for her, but not so special that she might question his motives.

And time was a factor. Bree liked it slow and sensual, and why not? She had sod all else to do with her day, frankly. It was different for Robbie. He had duties, responsibilities, problems to solve . . . and securing Bree's cooperation was only one factor in that quest for solutions.

So while he tried not to fret over every passing moment, he wasn't entirely successful. Fortunately Bree seemed not to notice that when he came up for air he was checking the bedside clock.

She was, as ever, full-blooded in her appreciation of his skills, climaxing with a long squeal of pleasure. She lay still, panting hard,

135

one finger idly stroking the sheen of sweat that coated her taut brown belly.

'Oh baby, that was . . .' She shuddered, bumping her knee against his thigh as he moved alongside her. 'Just give me a second, yeah? That was *so* good.'

'Fine.' He couldn't help but grimace: he'd probably overdone it.

A minute or so passed, the silence easy enough. But it was another minute when Robbie should have been somewhere else.

He took a deep breath, almost a gasp, as he found himself reliving the scene last night: the menacing figure in the rear-view mirror, Dan's panicked cry and the flash of a camera. Neither of them could say what it meant, who the guy was or what he wanted. But even Robbie, the eternal optimist, couldn't deny that it spelled trouble.

'I may need to ask a favour,' he said.

'Oh yeah?'

'Nothing much. Just want you to say I was with you on a couple of dates.'

'Okayyy.' A long, weighted pause. 'Who is it I'm gonna be telling? Your mum?'

'Well, yeah. For starters.'

'Who else?'

'I don't know yet. Might not be anyone.'

The bed rocked as she turned sideways. She put her face close to his, all the better to scrutinise him.

'What have you been up to, Robert Scott?'

He grinned at the playful tone, but knew he'd have to give her something; a morsel of truth, at least.

'A little bit of naughtiness – nothing to do with women,' he added hastily. 'Business deals. Better if you don't know the details.'

'You sound like Jimmy.' She looked fretful. 'So you want an alibi, if the cops come sniffing round?'

Robbie smiled. *Bree, my darling, you're brighter than you look.*

'They probably won't. But just in case . . .'

'And what if Jimmy's home when they turn up?'

'No. All right. I'll ask somebody else.'

He turned his head away from her, but she stayed put. He felt a cool hand grazing his thigh.

'What dates?'

'Last night, and Tuesday evening. That's all.'

'I'm not promising,' she warned him, but her fingers were moving with silky affection, prompting a fresh pulse of interest. 'All these favours, and yet the fuss you make when I come up with a brilliant idea for you . . .'

He shut his eyes, trying to contain his weariness. He'd known there would be a price to pay.

'I'll give it a try.'

Bree let out a screech of delight that almost burst his eardrums. 'Yes! You won't regret it, babe. You'll be a *star*. You'll be *rolling* in cash—'

'Yeah, yeah.' Robbie held up his hands. 'Find me one that's half decent, as a trial run.'

She was nodding enthusiastically, plans already forming. Then she frowned, directing attention to his groin.

'It's still all floppy.'

'Uh, yeah, I'm not really in the mood right now.'

She wagged a finger at him. 'A professional is *always* in the mood, Robbie. He doesn't have a choice.'

Twenty-nine

The Blakes had woken to a soft drizzle and a veil of misty cloud that obscured the Downs and made the view from the picture windows seem commonplace and uninspiring. There were a few breaks appearing by the time Gordon had cleared up the breakfast crockery. He refilled the coffee maker and tried yet again to appease Patricia, but he could do little to lift the gloom that had settled over their kitchen.

Finally the doorbell rang, an interruption both expected and startling, like the end of a demanding exam. It was Gordon's role to greet visitors but today he found Patricia snapping at his heels. Such eagerness didn't bode well: he felt it could only lead to disappointment.

His misgivings were confirmed when he opened the door. Jerry Conlon looked tense rather than jubilant: this wasn't the demeanour of a man bearing gifts. He was dressed in absurdly low-slung jeans, a graffiti-splattered T-shirt and a bikers' jacket, and he sported the kind of shoulder bag you might see on a hip young advertising executive in the West End.

His gravel voice had barely managed a greeting when Patricia barked: 'It is now nine twenty-six. Evidently your definition of "first thing" differs markedly from ours.'

They filed through to the kitchen. Gordon's beloved Sony Vaio laptop was up and running on the table. Setting his bag down beside it, Jerry glanced at the coffee maker and muttered – with reckless courage, Gordon thought – 'I'm parched.'

Ignoring the hint, Patricia dragged the bag away from him and opened it up. 'This is Hank's laptop?'

'Yeah. I ain't had a chance to look at it yet—'

She peered into the bag. 'Where's the camera? You're two hours late and you've forgotten to bring the damn camera!'

'Hang on a minute—'

'No, Jerry, I won't "hang on". This is intolerable. It makes me wonder why we ever believed we could entrust you with . . .'

Gordon took a step towards his wife, fearing he might have to physically restrain her, but Jerry had stepped out of her range and was dredging the pocket of his too-tight jeans, performing what looked like a squirming dance before his hand emerged and he slapped a tiny square of plastic on to the table.

'Memory card.'

Patricia regarded it for a long second. 'I see.'

'You don't need the camera. Pictures are on there.'

'Yes.' She took a deep breath. 'Well, let's examine it, shall we? Gordon will make you a coffee.'

At first Jerry didn't move, and Gordon wondered if he would demand an apology: the mouse that roared.

Then he nodded brusquely, pulled out a chair and said, 'Two sugars, ta.'

It was ironic, as Gordon was to reflect later, that Patricia's initial outburst ending up saving Jerry's skin. The misunderstanding over the camera served to dilute her anger, so that when the moment came she lacked the appetite for another tirade.

Because the results of last night's expedition were a disappointment. The memory card yielded a single photograph, a poor-quality shot of a car that was undeniably a BMW. Gordon enlarged the photo to 150%, then to 200%, but the number plate remained unclear, a maddening blur of shapes that might have included a B, a 2, possibly a W.

They were staring at the screen in dismay when Jerry, perhaps emboldened by his earlier moral victory, said, 'I know you can't read it too well, but I was thinking you could get it enhanced somewhere. They reckon NASA have software that—'

'We're not minded to involve NASA, now, are we?' Patricia said.

Jerry gave a half-hearted shrug. 'I dunno.'

'What about utilising *this* little gizmo?' Patricia tapped her skull. 'Why didn't you memorise the number?'

'It was too quick. Anyway, I thought the picture was gonna come out fine.'

'You should always have a backup plan. *Always.*'

Gordon decided it fell to him to stay positive. 'We have something here, at least.'

Patricia snorted. 'Only in as much as Stemper got this exactly right. Which demonstrates the wisdom of having him on board.'

Jerry wore a grim look. 'So I'm off the case, am I?' To Gordon's ear, he didn't sound entirely unhappy at the prospect.

'Not unless you wish to sever your relationship with us?' Patricia asked.

'No, of course I don't—'

'Good. Because I'm sure you'll have an opportunity to redeem yourself. Beginning with this.'

She nodded towards O'Brien's laptop. Gordon opened it up and pressed the power button. Jerry, still uneasy, scratched his head fiercely enough to make Patricia wince.

'But I'm gonna be working alongside Stemper?'

'That's correct.'

As Patricia focused her attention on the laptop, Jerry glanced in Gordon's direction, as if hoping to share a moment of fellow feeling. Gordon pretended not to notice.

'Great,' said Jerry weakly.

Thirty

Cate bought a cappuccino and retreated to the furthest recesses of the cafe, ignoring vacant tables at the front. She was meeting DS Thomsett for the second day running and her instinct was to find somewhere discreet.

Despite her best efforts to shrug it off, last night's conversation with Dan and Robbie kept playing on her mind. It was hard to define exactly what made her feel uncomfortable. She had asked them, quite bluntly, if they were involved in O'Brien's death, and they had denied it outright.

She tried to remind herself that, whatever reservations she might have about her brother's honesty, she had none where Dan was concerned. He had been at the wheel, not Robbie; therefore his denial ought to be good enough for her. It was time to stop torturing herself with pointless speculation.

The detective had requested an urgent meeting. He'd sounded slightly irritable on the phone. To avoid office gossip she'd suggested they meet at Giardino's, one of the cafes in the food hall on the top floor of the Churchill Square shopping centre.

It was almost eleven o'clock. The cafe was only moderately busy, though there was a constant stream of teenagers and young mums passing to and from the McDonald's across the way. Cate added a single sugar to her coffee, wishing she could have more, then noticed she'd received a text.

It was from Martin: one of the puerile jokes he liked to dispatch to his entire address book. Cate knew he'd deleted her number during their acrimonious separation, so he must have restored it – perhaps after his visit on Tuesday night. Evidently she was back in favour, but whether that fact pleased her or not she couldn't actually say.

She looked up and saw DS Thomsett walking into view past the cafe's stand of complimentary balloons. He gave her a taut smile and indicated the shelves of pastries at the counter: *Did she want anything?* She shook her head.

He was wearing a charcoal suit with a crisp white shirt and a spotted purple tie. Boots rather than shoes, and they were dark brown, not black. His hair was a little more tousled than before, as though he'd been running his hands through it. Even while buying coffee, his posture exuded authority. You would not underestimate this man, Cate thought. You would not lie to him.

Except that she *was* lying to him. *She was lying to a police officer in a fatal-accident investigation . . .*

He picked up his tray. As he approached, Cate took a deep breath, willing herself to be calm. Thankfully there was no sign of his sidekick, Avery.

'Hi, there,' he said.

'Morning – oh, you've got tea!'

'Yes.' He gave her a curious look. 'Is that permitted?'

'Of course. It's just . . . don't most people drink coffee these days?'

He frowned, as if correctly deducing he was in the presence of a madwoman. 'Coffee's trendier, I suppose. But I've always preferred tea.'

'I like the aroma, but not the taste.' Cate laughed, far too heartily for such an innocuous comment. She wasn't just making an idiot of herself; she was betraying her nerves, giving Thomsett reason to wonder why she was so jittery.

He sat down opposite her, deftly transferring the contents of his tray to the table. He'd bought a couple of croissants, and invited her to share them.

'Have to eat when you get the chance in this job,' he said with a rueful smile.

'Mm. I know the feeling.'

'Well, you've probably gathered that I didn't ask you here to debate the relative merits of hot beverages.' The smile had vanished, and there was a wary look in his eyes. 'This money you gave to Mr O'Brien, three thousand pounds in a brown envelope?'

Cate nodded, struggling to make out his voice over a sudden ringing in her ears.

'It was found this morning, in the field beyond the accident site.'

He said nothing more. Cate waited, perplexed, and then said, 'That's good, isn't it?'

'It should be. Except that yesterday the field in question – the whole area, in fact – underwent an extremely thorough search.'

'Oh.'

'Normally in this situation the SOCOs would get hauled over the coals. But they're trained to find the smallest traces of evidence, like glass fragments, flecks of paint. I don't see them missing an A5 envelope, do you?'

'I suppose not.'

'The other notable fact is that the money was found by a farmer.' He tore off a piece of croissant and popped it into his mouth. 'The same man who discovered the body yesterday morning.'

'Do you think he'd pocketed the money . . .?'

'Then got cold feet and put it back.' Thomsett nodded. 'It's plausible. DC Avery is interviewing him as we speak. He has rather a knack for frightening people.'

It was said with a chuckle, but did he also send her a warning look? Cate could feel a cold dread crawling over her skin.

She said, 'This farmer, you don't believe he had anything to do with O'Brien's death?'

'I doubt it. But if he's hiding something, we'll know soon enough.' Another chunk of croissant was consumed, quickly but with a certain delicacy. Thomsett dabbed a napkin to his lips. 'That drizzle overnight hasn't done us any favours. The envelope was wet and muddy, so it might not yield any prints.'

'That's a shame.'

'Well, we'll see. They can work miracles these days. Correct me if I'm wrong, but what we should find on there is the farmer's, Hank O'Brien's, and yours. And your brother's, presumably, if you were meeting Mr O'Brien on his behalf?'

Cate nodded. 'And other people from his office, potentially.'

'So four lots of prints, minimum. Compton's is just along Foundry Street, isn't it?'

'Frederick Street. That's the one above Foundry.' Cate felt sick. Would it look suspicious to ask where he was going with this, or was it more suspicious *not* to ask?

'Perhaps I'm being dim, but I don't see how testing the envelope will help in the search for the driver who hit O'Brien.'

There was a moment of heavy silence, in part because Thomsett had the cup of tea at his mouth, and his eyes seemed to shine with regret. Cate felt sure that somehow, inadvertently, she had incriminated herself.

The detective swallowed. 'You're not dim. The truth is, it probably won't help at all. But the fact we only found it this morning is an anomaly, and therefore it has to be investigated. Same with the traces of paint on Mr O'Brien's clothing. It's gone off for analysis, but without more debris at the scene there's little chance of pinpointing the vehicle.' He sighed. 'So now it's down to the TV appeal.'

'TV appeal?' Cate echoed.

'I featured on the local news this morning. Didn't you see it?'

'No. I don't usually watch . . .'

'Doesn't matter. Alexander Armstrong can sleep easy.' He grinned, but she saw a hint of disappointment that she'd missed it. 'There was one spot of good news, though. The couple who were dining in the pub have come forward and confirmed your account of the altercation. They also remember seeing your Audi in the car park.'

Somehow Cate managed a wry smile. 'I bet that came as a blow to DC Avery.'

Thomsett chose that moment to take another drink, and didn't respond. 'Unfortunately they couldn't tell us much about the men who broke up the fight. We've got the barmaid helping us put together e-fits this afternoon —'

'I have a meeting with some insurers, I'm afraid.' Seeing his face, Cate paused. Felt herself blush. 'I mean, if you wanted me to . . .'

'It's fine. What I will do is ask you to take a look at the images and tell us if you think they're accurate.'

'Oh, right. Okay.'

Thomsett finished off the first croissant and pushed the plate in her direction. 'Sure you won't have some? Feels rude to be eating alone.'

'Thanks.' She took a small piece: if nothing else it was a distraction.

Thomsett looked pleased. 'You probably know yourself, witness evidence is notoriously unreliable. You end up with a suspect who's tall and short, fat and thin, blond and dark, bearded and clean-shaven . . .'

'It doesn't arise as much in my line of work. Civil law, it's mostly accidents, compensation claims. We rarely have to do identity parades.'

'You've got it cushy,' he said, teasing her. 'You never fancied getting down and dirty on the criminal side?'

'I considered it, but the idea of being called to a police station at three in the morning didn't appeal.'

'I don't blame you. Plays havoc with your personal life, too.' A micro-pause, but both of them took note of it. 'Are you married? Living with someone?'

She narrowed her eyes, not maliciously but to show her surprise. 'Is that an official question?'

'Nope. Just general nosiness on my part.'

'I was married,' she said. 'We divorced last year.'

'Oh, I'm sorry. Same here, two years ago. Weekend dad.'

She liked the fact that he didn't try to sound jocular; instead the pain was there to see and hear.

'For us, one of the saving graces was that we didn't have children.' Cate heard her voice wobble: *dangerous territory, girl*. She picked up her phone to check the time, remembering the silly text from Martin. 'If there's nothing else, I'd better be going . . .'

'Yes, of course.' Thomsett stood up and they shook hands. 'I'll be in touch with those e-fits, then. And watch out for me on the box. I'm hoping they'll repeat it on tonight's news.'

'Yes. I will.'

'Let's hope we get a lucky break, eh?' He smiled, perhaps quite innocuously, but to Cate it seemed to say: *I know what you're hiding, and you're not going to get away with it . . .*

Thirty-one

Willie Denham was a small, rotund man, with thick white hair and a neatly trimmed white beard. He had kind eyes and ruddy cheeks and he reminded Dan of Richard Attenborough, circa *Jurassic Park*.

He was quietly spoken, too, but his gentle, twinkly manner concealed a savage desire to protect the family business. Over the years Dan had seen a number of staff make the assumption that the boss was a soft touch, and none of them had survived for long.

Normally Denham's fondness for floor-walking and deceptively innocuous chat didn't worry Dan at all. He was proud of his sales team and knew they wouldn't let him down. Today, though, he couldn't shake off the conviction that Denham had rumbled him.

It was bad enough that every TV in the store exerted a terrible grip. The 24-hour news sites were the worst, although none so far had featured the hit-and-run. Dan was now dreading the lunchtime news, when both BBC and ITV would broadcast local bulletins.

If there was one tiny consolation, it was that Hayley wouldn't be there to see them. She'd pointedly informed him that she was meeting her best friend, Miranda, who worked in a bank in North Street. Dan had no doubt that his erratic behaviour would be high on the agenda. While outwardly pleasant, Miranda was an emotional vampire, and this current crisis would give her plenty to feast on.

'Slow day.'

Dan jumped. Denham had materialised at his side. Because of the height difference, Dan found himself looking down at a small bald patch on the older man's crown. There was a sprinkling of dandruff on the shoulder of his suit jacket.

'Afraid so,' he said.

'Thursdays are always unpredictable, of course. Weather's neither one thing nor the other . . .' Denham peered in the direction of the windows, the shop momentarily darkening as a bus rumbled past. 'But I dare say things will pick up, given time.'

Dan half turned, as if scanning the shop for a cluster of hitherto unseen customers. It was about as rude a dismissal as he dared, but Denham merely stood in silence, nodding to himself. Several excruciating seconds passed before he spoke again.

'You know, I do feel you're—'

'Dan! Phone for you!' It was one of the assistants, Maisie, who hadn't noticed Denham's presence. 'Somebody called Cate?'

Apologising to his boss, Dan hurried away. When he reached the office he glanced back and saw a troubled-looking Denham gazing in his direction.

'Dan?' The tone of Cate's voice made his stomach lurch. 'They've found the money.'

'Have they?' Dan thought he sounded fairly normal, under the circumstances. He felt confident enough to add: 'Good to hear it.'

'That's what I said. But DS Thomsett doesn't think it adds up.'

'It was the wrong amount?' he blurted. *Robbie must have palmed a few notes . . .*

'No, I don't mean that. He says the whole area was searched the day before.'

'That's a bit strange.' Now he was beginning to doubt his delivery. Gauging the right level of concern was almost impossible.

The office door opened and Tim Masters, the service manager, came in. Nodding at Dan, he sat down at the adjacent desk and began riffling through a stack of invoices. Dan turned away from him and said quietly, 'In that case, I guess someone slipped up.'

'Maybe. Although Thomsett has other theories.'

'I see. Look, I'd like to hear more but it's a bit tricky right now.'

'I know what you mean. Are you free to meet after work? Same place as yesterday, six o'clock?'

'Fine.' He put the phone down, and told himself that this wasn't too bad. He'd wanted the police to find the money, and they had.

'Interview, is it?'

Dan gave a start. Tim wore a sly smile as he gestured at the phone. 'You can tell me, chum. Who's poached you?'

'No one.' Dan knew his denials would fall on deaf ears. Tim was not only notoriously indiscreet, but he also behaved as though he and Dan were in competition, even though Denham was scrupulously fair in his treatment of the two departments. It didn't help that, during Dan and Hayley's brief separation, she had dated Tim for a while, claiming afterwards that it had been more a friendship than a romance.

'Good luck!' Tim called as Dan left the office. 'Just don't let the old man get wind of it till you're ready to walk out the door.'

Jerry ordered a lemonade, lime and Angostura bitters, handed the barmaid a twenty and said, 'Get yourself a drink, love.'

She nodded, with less gratitude than Jerry had expected, and said she'd take the cost of half a lager.

He planted his elbows on the bar, making it clear he was going to talk to her whether she liked it or not. 'Bit quieter compared to yesterday.'

'Yeah, it was mad.' She frowned. 'I thought I'd seen you before.'

'We were talking about that poor geezer who got knocked down.' He smiled, but had a feeling it didn't help his case much. 'Traci, isn't it?'

She nodded. 'Just moved here, have you?'

'No – well, yeah. Kind of . . .'

A customer approached the bar and Traci gravitated towards her as if Jerry had ceased to exist. He took a big mouthful of his drink and told himself to be patient.

He was still smarting at the way Patricia had treated him. How was it his fault that the bloody registration number couldn't be read? He'd done his best – and he'd suggested getting it enhanced. The Blakes knew all sorts of people: cops and spies and politicians. But no, they'd scorned the idea, and now he was lumbered with playing second fiddle to Stemper.

After serving the customer, Traci didn't return to Jerry's end of the bar. He was forced to drain his glass, draw out a tenner and wave it in the air, silently praying that the Blakes would reimburse him.

The girl dragged her feet coming over. 'Same again?'

'A Coke,' said Jerry. 'And get yourself another.'

This elicited surprise, then a foxy look as she reached for a clean glass: she'd worked out what the deal was.

'So you were saying this bloke, the one that died, he had a fight with his girlfriend?'

'Dunno if she was his girlfriend.' She set his drink down, but Jerry kept the money in his hand. He'd seen the movies: he knew how this was done.

'I mean the woman he was with. And a couple of other blokes got involved as well?'

''S right.' She was staring at the tenner. Jerry waited, but that was all he got.

Bitch, he thought. 'They locals, were they?'

'You what?'

'The two men. Knights in shining armour. I wondered if you knew—'

'Are you from the papers? The cops said they might come sniffing round, asking questions like this.'

Jerry glanced left and right, then gave her a conspiratorial wink. He snapped the tenner in the air as he handed it over. 'That's right, love.'

Eyes on the till, she said, 'They told us to be careful what we said, but I don't think it's any of their fucking business whether I talk about it. Do you?'

Jerry grinned, trying to disguise the fact that he hated it when young women used the F-word. 'Fucking right,' he said. 'Free country, innit?'

'Which one you from?'

'*Sunday Times.*' It was the first title that came into his head. Aim high, he thought.

Traci gave a nod, trickling coins into his palm. 'So you've got ID? One of those . . . what is it, a press card?'

Taken aback, Jerry reached into his jacket, then started patting his pockets with all the subtlety of a pantomime dame. 'Uh, must have left it at home.'

'Ohh. Pity, that.' Traci turned her back on him. He was sure he heard a snort of laughter.

Jerry gave it a few minutes, sipping his Coke, but it was clear she wasn't going to come near him. Cursing her, he ambled out of the pub, upping his pace when it struck him that if the bitch was really suspicious she might take a note of his car, and then he *would* be in the shit.

What made it worse was that he did have an old press card at home, but hadn't thought to bring it.

Another foul-up. That was how the Blakes would see this. And they'd compare him with fucking Stemper.

Stemper would have got her to talk.

Thirty-two

Robbie reached the office around eleven, having made a couple of visits first: routine checks on some existing Compton rentals.

As it turned out, his mother was off in the badlands of Hastings, and of the three other full-time staff only one was present today: Indira, an attractive married woman in her mid-thirties with whom Robbie had once enjoyed a brief fling. Now the rumour was that she and her husband were trying for another baby. Robbie might have offered to help her practice, but frankly he had enough on his hands at the moment.

Still, Bree had come good, agreeing to provide an alibi. After the weirdness of the guy jumping out on them with a camera, Robbie accepted that he had to take this seriously. He had to have a plan.

Driving home last night, he'd nearly raised the subject of precautions: lining up an alibi, changing their appearance. But then he had thought better of it. If Dan had any sense he'd work it out himself.

Besides, it wasn't Dan who was at risk. The BMW was registered to Compton's, so if the mysterious photographer somehow traced the number it would lead him to Robbie.

Unless he claimed that somebody else had been using the car . . .

He looked up, caught Indira's eye and grinned. She responded with a more guarded smile; nothing that could be misconstrued. Now that he thought about it, she was rarely alone in the office with him. She hadn't even remarked on his new hairstyle.

Not Indira, he decided. But maybe he could put one of his other colleagues in the frame.

As he pondered, his gaze was drawn to the window. The BMW was sitting in a parking bay out front, where a tall man in a decent suit was examining the vehicle with a more than casual interest.

Was this it? Robbie wondered. *Had they found him already?*

He did nothing for a while, just watched the man slowly circle the car, peering down to study the offside wing, the bonnet and bumper, then the nearside wing. Rising to his feet, and ignoring a quizzical look from Indira, Robbie approached the door.

The man was now at the rear of the car, hands in his pockets, an intrigued expression on his face. He was smart, well-groomed, but not slick. From a distance you might have concluded that he was soft, even slightly feminine, but close up, when you saw the look in his eyes, that image was quickly dispelled.

'Gonna make me an offer?' Robbie drawled.

'Is it for sale?'

'No, but seeing as you're so interested . . .'

The man shook his head. A warrant card was produced, just as Robbie had feared.

'Detective Sergeant Thomsett. Would you happen to be Robert Scott?'

'That's me.'

'I was speaking to your sister earlier. She didn't tell you?'

'No. Why?'

Thomsett seemed gratified by Robbie's answer. Cate had dumped him in it, then.

'I'm investigating the death of a client of yours, Hank O'Brien.'

Robbie nodded slowly. 'I heard about that. Nasty business.'

'It is. I understand your sister met Mr O'Brien on your behalf, just prior to his death.'

'That's right. Cate probably told you the details.'

Thomsett smiled, but without much humour. 'Why don't you give me your version of events?'

Robbie began by explaining that O'Brien had accepted a fee of three thousand pounds for some 'additional services' arising out of the property rental, but Thomsett pegged him back, asking about the role of the film company and how the opportunity had arisen in the first place.

'Your failure to inform Mr O'Brien of these "additional services" was an oversight?'

'Something like that. Anyway, we got it sorted, and my sister went to the pub to give him the money.'

'Why was that?'

Robbie pretended not to understand, but Thomsett pushed him on it. 'Why her, and not you?'

'Hank could be a bit . . . prickly. Not easy to deal with.'

'Hence the altercation in the pub. Is it true to say he felt you'd cheated him?'

Robbie shrugged. 'He seemed happy enough with the three grand that Cate agreed over the phone. What I heard was that he made a move on her, then got nasty when she blew him out.'

Thomsett nodded thoughtfully, as if some of this might have been news to him. Robbie realised he should have gone through it with Cate, point by point.

'The fight was broken up by two young men at an adjacent table. Obviously we're very keen to talk to them.'

'You think they killed Hank?'

'Not necessarily. But the longer we go without them coming forward, the more it suggests they have something to hide . . .' A heavy pause, then he added: 'Can you tell me where you were on Tuesday night?'

'Sure. With a girlfriend.'

'Her name?'

Robbie scowled. 'Bree Tyler.'

'Address?'

'It's complicated. She's, uh, what you might call . . .' Robbie grinned, hoping they could share a 'men of the world' moment.

'Married?'

'That's the word.'

Thomsett looked disgusted. 'I'll be as discreet as I can, sir.' From his tone, that meant not very discreet at all.

Trying to inject some levity into his voice, Robbie said, 'Come on, you don't really think I was waiting outside the pub, ready to knock him down?'

Thomsett held his gaze. 'It doesn't sound particularly ludicrous to me.'

The detective took out a notebook. 'So, your girlfriend's address? A phone number would be useful, too.'

Robbie gave him the details, reading Bree's number from his own phone. He watched the cop writing it down, telling himself it was a bluff.

Adding insult to injury, Thomsett was resting the notebook on the roof of the BMW. Sensing Robbie's unease, he said, 'I take it you own this vehicle?'

'Yeah. Well, no.'

Thomsett slowly looked up. For a second Robbie couldn't decide which answer was best. Did the detective somehow know they'd returned to the scene in the BMW?

'It's registered to the company, but I use it most of the time.'

Thomsett made another note. Robbie was determined not to be unsettled by him.

'So what happens now?' he asked. 'To the three grand.'

'Currently it forms part of the evidence in our investigation. In due course it'll be added to Mr O'Brien's estate.'

'I don't think he had much family. The ex-wife is probably rubbing her hands together. Have you asked where she was on Tuesday night?'

Thomsett declined to answer. 'His next-of-kin is a sister, I believe. But you can be assured that we're pursuing all relevant enquiries.' He put the notebook away. 'We plan to conduct some tests on the envelope that contained the money. Can you tell us who handled it prior to your sister and Mr O'Brien?'

'Just me, as far as I recall.' Then, for a moment, he faltered. *Dan.* Hadn't he given it to Dan in the car?

Doesn't matter, he thought. Dan's prints weren't on file anywhere. No harm done.

He relaxed again, nodding to confirm that he stood by his answer. But he knew that Thomsett had spotted the hesitation.

'We may need to take a sample of your fingerprints. I'll be in touch.' The detective thanked Robbie for his cooperation and sauntered away.

Robbie didn't want to be caught watching him go, so he went back inside. His immediate desire was to get hold of Cate and give her hell, but there was a more important priority: Bree.

Thank Christ he had prepared the ground this morning.

Thirty-three

Stemper experienced a quiet satisfaction when Patricia Blake called to engage his services. He was gratified to hear they had followed his advice and delighted that his hunch had proved correct. He shared her disappointment, bordering on disgust, that Jerry Conlon had failed to obtain the registration number of the car.

His landlady was close to tears when she heard he was going away, perhaps fearing he would demand a refund of the extra money he paid for food and laundry. She brightened up at the news that he had no long-term plans to leave, and he insisted on paying his rent in full even if he was absent for a week or two.

As a lodger, Stemper seemed almost too good to be true – with the emphasis on 'almost'. He took care not to cross that line and arouse suspicion about his place in her life.

Debbie Winwood had worked in the accounts department of a major defence contractor until a dispute with her supervisor led to her resignation, amid allegations that she'd been the victim of bullying and sexual harassment. As well as launching a case for constructive dismissal, Debbie had let it be known that if she lost her case she would blow the whistle on certain financial irregularities and breaches of EU procurement rules.

The company's owner, Robert Felton, had hired Stemper to gain her confidence and assess what degree of threat she posed. As a single parent, newly unemployed, Debbie had been forced to rent out her spare room to help with her finances. Stemper, a quiet, well-mannered professional, happy to help around the house, happier still to indulge her son and his obsession with this *Warhammer* nonsense, had been a godsend.

With a little more effort, and perhaps a few modifications to his personal appearance, Stemper knew he could make her fall in love with him. It wasn't a prospect he relished, but if it proved necessary he would do it.

The same pragmatic approach was required for the second stage of the assignment. If Stemper concluded that she posed a credible threat to Robert Felton's business, he would have to neutralise that threat.

He had already decided that a house fire was the ideal scenario: clean, efficient and relatively easy to stage.

For the sake of completeness the children would have to perish along with their mother. It wasn't just that it was more tenable; a family tragedy made for a much better story.

That lay in the future. In the meantime, there was this pleasant diversion for the Blakes.

Stemper knew Brighton quite well, though it had been years since his last visit. This was a place where he felt comfortable, a city of many faces: busy, cosmopolitan and tourist-friendly, but also dark, seedy, dangerous.

Snarled up in traffic on the one-way system, he gazed at the familiar landmarks: St Peter's Church, the Royal Pavilion, the blocks of magnificent Regency architecture, now interspersed with newer and, for the most part, sympathetically designed apartment buildings.

The open spaces that divided the main road were crowded with language students and feckless daytime drinkers, men and women in shabby clothes sprawled on the grass, mangy dogs lying at their feet. Stemper was visited by a memory of his father.

Gas the lot of them.

* * *

A succession of traffic lights changed in sequence, a benevolent hand waving him forward, and at last the sea came into view, lying calm and quiet beyond the gaudy enticements of the pier.

Stemper had booked a room at a guest house in Kemptown, east of the city centre. He avoided larger hotels because of the preponderance of CCTV, though on this occasion he would also concede to an element of nostalgia in his decision.

He found the address and managed to park his rented Ford Focus a short distance away. He collected a briefcase and a holdall from the boot, then paused to take in his surroundings. The tight, narrow street was just as he remembered it: hemmed in by the high terraces and tilting towards the coast; the sea a distant beguiling dazzle, like a torch shone into a tunnel.

The air had a distinctive briny smell, and the squawk of a seagull could be heard clearly above all human sounds. It sat on the roof of a splendid building painted in cream and terracotta. Imperiously it tracked his progress along the street, as if Stemper had no right to be there. A brutal creature, big and ugly, with a harsh unpleasant voice.

His father had liked Brighton for reasons that had never been apparent to Stemper. As a child he'd probably attributed it to the seaside, or some appreciative quality of the audiences here, but now he guessed it was more likely there was a woman involved.

He entered the guest house and was swiftly intercepted by the proprietor, a small, neat man wearing a pink shirt with a bold Paisley bow tie and a sleeveless pullover in dark grey. His head was slightly too large and too round, putting Stemper in mind of a clock face. There was a smear of black hair plastered to his skull. His features were small and delicate, each one marooned in an ocean of pallid skin.

'Mr Hooper? I'm Bernard Quills. Let me take this for you.'

He was reaching for the briefcase but Stemper swung it gently beyond his grasp. 'I can manage.'

'Of course.' Quills stepped back, one hand flat on his stomach, a matador's pose. 'Your room is on the second floor. Rather a steep climb, so do take care.'

The guest house was gloomy and overheated and smelled of wet laundry and radiator dust. From deep in the building, Stemper could hear music playing, something tinny and frivolous. The stair carpet was dark green at the edges, paler in the centre where years of tread had almost worn it away. The walls were hung with Anaglypta, painted with a brownish cream gloss. At regular intervals there were framed prints of old Brighton: the chain pier, the Volks railway, the beach at Black Rock.

A museum-piece Hoover stood sentry on the top-floor landing. Pausing, Quills gave Stemper a careful appraisal and made a clicking sound with the roof of his mouth.

'In general I don't offer more than b&b, but I've a stew in the oven, if you're peckish at all?'

Stemper smiled. 'Very kind of you, but I have a prior engagement.'

'I see. Well, the offer's there.'

Quills opened the third of four doors along the landing and showed Stemper into his room. The decor was just as tired, but the room seemed clean enough. There were fresh flowers in a vase by the bed, and bowls of potpourri on the window ledge. More historic prints on the walls. Stemper set his bags down while Quills lingered in the doorway, anxious for a verdict.

'All to your liking, I trust?'

'Yes.' Stemper approached the window, which was obscured by a net curtain. There was no view, other than that of the building in the street behind.

'So what brings you to these sunny shores?'

'Business meetings.' Stemper noticed two flies caught in the net: one dead, one still struggling.

'You're not an actor, then?'

'An actor? No. Why?'

Stemper turned in time to see the proprietor shrug. His hands were clasped wistfully against his chest.

'You might laugh, but I pride myself on guessing a profession, and I had you down as something theatrical. Definitely a touch of the Alec Guinness about you.'

Stemper shook his head. 'Nothing as glamorous, I'm afraid.' A teasing pause, then: 'Yourself?'

Quills beamed with gratitude. 'Oh, I only dabble these days. Amateur stuff, though I was a background artist on the remake of *Brighton Rock*. Have you seen it?'

'No.'

'A wonderful experience. I worked alongside John Hurt and Dame Helen Mirren. Such a gracious lady, Dame Helen—'

Stemper nodded. 'Marvellous. Well, I had better get unpacked.'

'Of course. Please do call if you need anything.'

The door closed, but Stemper could sense the other man standing outside, listening. He didn't move until he heard the creak of floorboards along the landing. While he waited he reached out and crushed the desperate fly with his thumb.

After locking the door, Stemper opened the briefcase, removed his netbook and sat down on the bed. On the opposite wall a framed poster from a 1960s variety show spirited him back to his childhood.

His father, nearly sixty when Stemper was born, and coming to the end of a long and patchy career as an entertainer, one of the last of the spirited all-rounders who had been, in his time, an actor, singer, comedian, clown and illusionist. Stemper's mother, more than a generation younger than his father, had been a dancer, a chorus girl and finally her husband's foil and assistant.

By the time Stemper came along she'd had her fill of the showbiz life, and her lack of enthusiasm must have shown in her performances. What Stemper remembered most clearly were the muffled screams, late at night, as his father had remonstrated with her, pinpointing each error, each failure on her part to provide the support that he demanded. First the lecture, then the beating, the cries that she tried to suppress – for Stemper's benefit, perhaps, or so as not to scandalise their fellow guests in the small down-at-heel establishments so much like this one.

Even at five or six years old, Stemper had grasped exactly what was going on. He had listened carefully to every word, every blow, and he had seen how important this was to his father; how much he cared; his merciless, unrelenting insistence on *perfection*. Perfection at all costs.

Stemper had listened, understood, and approved.

Thirty-four

Robbie tried Bree's mobile but got her voicemail. That could mean hubby was back, in which case leaving a message would be risky.

He gave it a few minutes, picturing Bree with a gaggle of her female friends, idling over a boozy lunch in Terre à Terre or Due South. It made him resentful. Why didn't she keep an eye on her phone, for Christ's sake?

He rang again. Somebody answered but immediately cut the connection. Shit.

He stood up, aware that Indira was surreptitiously watching him. 'Just gotta pop out.'

'Problem?'

'No such thing, Indira. You know that.'

'Sorry. "Opportunity in disguise"?'

'Exactly.' He treated her to the same smile that had gifted him a blow job in the ladies' toilets at the Metropole during the firm's summer party.

He'd already passed off Thomsett's presence with the explanation that he was just some guy interested in buying the same model BMW as Robbie's. He didn't think Indira believed a word of it, but at least he had put something on record; just in case she should decide to pass it on to his mo—

* * *

Indira gave a mocking laugh as the Jaguar XK pulled up next to his BMW. 'A few more seconds and you'd have made it.'

Robbie quickly strode outside. If there was going to be a confrontation, he didn't want Indira listening in.

Teresa Scott was a tall woman, with broad shoulders and a once-athletic frame that had thickened somewhat with age. In her teens she had played both hockey and netball at a county level, and nowadays she ran in charity events like Race for Life, as well as regular half-marathons. She boasted that she was fitter than either of her children: Cate might have disputed that, but Robbie didn't.

It went without saying that she was far more driven to succeed than either of them. In her Jaeger suit and Valentino heels, she was an imposing figure. After retrieving her briefcase – Prada, of course – from the passenger footwell, she turned to face her son. 'What the chuff have you done to your hair?'

'Looks good, doesn't it?'

'Huh. No wonder you've been keeping such a low profile. To what do we owe the pleasure today?'

'I'm on top of things, don't stress. How was St Leonard's?'

'A whole morning I'll never get back. KM and bloody A are already deep in the developer's pockets.' She looked him up and down. 'Where are you off to?'

'Got a quick meeting,' he said airily.

'And is this "meeting" actually related to the business that pays you such a handsome salary?'

He thought about lying, then grinned. 'Not directly, no.'

Teresa sighed, extending a long manicured forefinger and pinning it against his chest. 'I can't keep making allowances for you, Robert. It's a constant battle just to keep my head above water.'

'I know. We should have a proper catch-up. Dinner, maybe? My treat.'

Robbie grasped his mother gently by the shoulders but her finger was still in place, as if poised to skewer him. He leaned in, pressing his lips against her cheek, and for that he earned a reluctant smile.

'I have no idea what you're up to, Robbie, and I probably don't want to know. But wherever it is you're going, will you *please* try to drum up some bloody business while you're there?'

His phone rang as he was cutting up a delivery van on the roundabout at Seven Dials. The driver blew his horn and gave Robbie the finger. Robbie stuck his arm out of the window and made a 'wanker' gesture, then accelerated across the junction into Dyke Road and took the call.

'What is it?' Bree hissed.

'I need to see you. I'm on my way over.'

'You can't. Jimmy's home.'

'It's urgent, Bree. Really urgent.'

She sighed. 'Okay. Hove Park, in ten minutes. By the Goldstone.'

Robbie made sure the van wasn't pursuing him, then eased up on his speed. At least it looked like he would reach Bree before DS Thomsett did.

He started thinking about how to play it, but his mother's parting shot lingered on his conscience. There was no doubt that he needed to accrue some brownie points. One solution might be to throw himself into this proposal of Bree's, then find a way to launder some of the proceeds into Compton's to improve the balance sheet . . .

No. Bad idea. If he was going to have sex with dodgy older women, he wanted to make sure that every penny went into his own pocket.

He left the BMW in the retail park, thought about a quick scoot around Comet to look at gadgets, then remembered that he was down three grand, last seen disappearing into a muddy field. DS Thomsett had his mitts on it now.

Crossing the road, he saw Bree jogging towards him through the park. The sight of her in skintight black Lycra made him forget all his troubles for a moment. He wanted to drag her into the bushes and shag her senseless.

She slowed her pace, checking over her shoulder before accepting a kiss. He went for her lips but she presented her cheek instead. Robbie frowned.

'He hasn't followed you, has he?'

'Not the speed I run. Even so, you never know who's watching.'

'That didn't seem to bother you yesterday, posing in the doorway in your knickers.'

'Yeah, well, I was excited about seeing you.' Another look behind her. 'But we ought to be more careful. Jimmy's come back in a really funny mood. Like, normally, even when he's dead on his feet he wouldn't say no to a hand job.'

Robbie grimaced. 'Too much information.'

'So it's making me wonder if he's getting it elsewhere.'

'One less chore for you.'

'He's my *husband*. And I'm not a fool. I know he married me for my body. So if he's found someone else he prefers . . .' She shook her head, as if despairing that Robbie could understand. 'Anyway, what's the big emergency?'

'Turns out I will need that favour.'

'Oh.' Bree looked doubtful. 'And you still can't tell me what it's about?'

'Best if you don't know. You've just got to say you were with me the last two evenings, from about eight till midnight. Keep it simple, say we took my car and parked up by the King Alfred while we talked, and maybe fooled around a bit.'

'And who is it I'll be telling?'

'A DS Thomsett, or one of his colleagues.'

'DS Thomsett?' she echoed. 'So it is a cop?'

'Sshh.' Robbie winced, looking round. 'It's fine, honestly.'

There was a buzzing noise: Bree's phone, stored in a Velcro pouch on her belt.

'Can you imagine how Jimmy's gonna react if the cops turn up on his doorstep?'

'Thomsett promised me he'll be discreet.'

'Yeah, right. And the next thing the whole of Sussex police will know every detail of my sex life.' For all the scorn in her voice, Robbie sensed she was just blowing off steam.

She took out her phone and checked the display. He watched as her features were transformed by a triumphant smile.

'I've got your first client.'

'What?'

'Maureen Heath. Her hubby's playing golf in Portugal this weekend. She's dying to meet you!'

Thirty-five

Brighton was tawdry and brash, full of what Patricia still liked to call 'the lower classes', their numbers greatly swelled by unchecked breeding, courtesy of the welfare state and, latterly, by a massive influx of foreigners.

'Everywhere you look, Gordon. Immigrants. Parasites.'

Gordon gave a murmur of assent, but he saw things slightly differently. Yes, the place was brash, but it was also vibrant and thrilling. It was a city for the young, he thought, and he couldn't avoid a wistful tug of longing. To be young, attractive, wealthy: that was the holy trinity.

Their destination was one of Brighton's finest seafront hotels. After parking beneath the building, they walked around the exterior to the bar where the meeting was due to take place.

Reaching the corner, their attention was drawn to a cluster of people on the promenade across the road, pointing and staring out to sea. It was Gordon who spotted it first: movement in the sky beyond them, a mysterious shifting cloud of . . . insects?

Never before had there been such a plague of locusts—

'Starlings,' he exclaimed, with genuine relief. 'They fly in formation at dusk. I saw it on a nature programme.'

Patricia harrumphed. 'It never ceases to amaze me what tiny minds find entertaining.'

But she paused, all the same, watching the flock as it danced and writhed, now fat and billowing like a sail, now elongated and sinuous as a serpent. A minute or two passed, and then she said, 'Actually, it is a rather compelling sight.'

Gordon agreed. 'There's something almost supernatural about the way they change shape, keeping perfect time with each other.'

'The herd instinct at work.' Patricia snorted. Her hand grazed Gordon's in a gesture that seemed intentional. 'It's served us well enough, I suppose.'

It was their first visit to the hotel for some years. Patricia was aghast to hear Eastern European accents in the lobby – from guests as well as staff. Gordon's practised eye had noted that the girls on reception had the kind of peachy complexion and fine bone structure that you rarely saw on English women.

In the bar they found Jerry Conlon nursing a pint of bitter. Patricia suggested a more remote table, requiring him to move. A waiter took their order: mineral water and a bottle of Sauvignon Blanc. As soon as he was out of earshot, Patricia wanted to know how Jerry had got on.

'I spoke to that barmaid again, but there was nothing new.' Anticipating Patricia's scorn, he added, 'I pushed it all I could, but she was getting suspicious. She asked if I was a journo, so I said I was.'

'Well, you are,' Gordon said. 'After a fashion.'

'Yeah, but I didn't want to give her my press card. Too risky, innit?' Jerry shrugged, then made a none-too-subtle attempt to deflect attention from himself. 'How did you get on with the laptop?'

'It's clean,' Gordon said. 'No hidden files. No encrypted documents.'

'What we need,' Patricia added, 'is a *genuinely* thorough search of the house.'

Jerry's protest was cut short by the return of the waiter. They shared a glassy smiling silence while the wine was poured. When it was safe to resume, Gordon said, 'There was one oddity. What do you know about a movie called *Entwined*?'

'Never heard of it.'

'Apparently it's a British romantic comedy. Hank had emailed an acquaintance at Channel 1, asking if he knew anyone at the production companies who made the film. He specifically asked about the location manager, but didn't say why he was interested.'

Jerry looked perplexed. 'He never mentioned it to me.'

'The acquaintance was away. He replied a week later, unable to help, but Hank said he'd already made contact through other means.'

'And nothing about why?'

Gordon shook his head. 'We were hoping you could shed some light on it.'

'This might be important,' Patricia said. 'Think very carefully.'

'I dunno. I remember him in a stinking mood, around the time he came back from Tokyo. I turned up one day and he was on the phone, shouting and bawling about being taken for a ride.'

There was a moment of ominous silence. Then Patricia said, 'And you didn't ask him what it concerned?'

Jerry gulped his beer and kept the glass raised, like a shield. 'I think I did, but he just sort of fobbed me off. I assumed it was a utility company or something. You know the grief you get with those bloody call centres.' He scratched his head with his customary ferocity. 'I can't for the life of me see how there'd be a connection between a British movie and what happened to Hank.'

'Perhaps there isn't,' Gordon said. 'But in a situation like this we must leave no stone unturned.'

Patricia nodded: not just agreeing with Gordon, but indicating the figure that was bearing down on them.

'Here's the man for turning stones,' she said.

* * *

Before any of them could react, Stemper had slipped into the armchair beside Jerry. There were no elaborate greetings, no handshakes or kisses: nothing that would draw attention to the group.

'Glad you could join us,' Patricia said, beaming. Gordon nodded in agreement, but Jerry only sniffed and shifted in his seat.

'My pleasure,' Stemper said. He didn't appear to have aged in the couple of years since Gordon had last seen him. His face a little puffy but unlined, the features nondescript. There was a smattering of grey in his light brown hair, but Gordon had a feeling that it had always been there. Hadn't it?

'Can we get you a drink?' Patricia asked.

'I'll have some of this water, if I may.'

'Of course.' A nod to Gordon, who duly poured mineral water into one of the spare glasses. Rather than hand it to Stemper, he slid the glass across the table in his direction.

'Since none of us want to be here all night,' Patricia said, 'we'll confine ourselves to the broad outline for now.'

She paused, looked round the room and cleared her throat.

'For many years Hank O'Brien was a Whitehall civil servant. A high-flyer, tipped as a future Permanent Secretary. I first encountered him when I was a special adviser at the Home Office during the Major administration. This was around the time that the government started using PFI.'

'Private Finance Initiative,' Gordon chipped in.

'He's quite aware of that,' Patricia snapped. 'Anyway, Hank grew increasingly frustrated with the public sector, quite understandably. In the late nineties he jumped ship to a company who'd been awarded a major construction contract – a contract that Hank himself had negotiated on the government's behalf some months earlier.'

Jerry muttered, 'Jobs for the boys.' He probably hadn't intended Patricia to hear it, but she lasered him with a glare.

'Quite. And where would you be without it, Jerry?'

As Conlon's face reddened, Stemper gave a thin smile. 'If that's the system, only a fool would decline to take advantage of it.'

'Precisely. Gordon describes it as "gamekeeper turning poacher". It's an inevitable consequence of greater private-sector involvement, and of course the late nineties was like a gold rush in that respect. Consequently, O'Brien was headhunted by another firm, keen to benefit from his inside knowledge.' She paused. 'The firm was Templeton Wynne.'

'Ah.' Stemper gave Patricia a look which, to Gordon's eye, seemed rather too knowing. It made him wonder what else had been said over the years: conversations between them to which Gordon had not been privy. 'So there's a personal element to this?'

'Intensely personal,' Patricia agreed. 'We made Mark Templeton who he is, and in return he cut us dead.'

Thirty-six

Tonight it was Cate who arrived at the pub first. When Dan walked in she gave him an uncertain smile. He joined her at the bar, and because they had kissed upon her departure yesterday it seemed natural to greet her with a kiss now.

As he did, he placed a hand on her arm to steady himself and was seized by a sudden urge to pull her into an embrace. He quickly withdrew, scared that his self-control might desert him.

Cate insisted on buying the drinks. Dan chose orange juice. He wanted to keep a clear head.

'Robbie's supposed to be joining us,' Cate said.

'Really? Did you twist his arm?'

'I didn't have to. DS Thomsett paid him a visit this afternoon.'

'Oh.' Dan's response was casual, until he remembered that he was entitled to feel concerned about this. 'How did it go?'

'Robbie didn't tell me. He was in a foul mood because he thinks I dropped him in it. But I wasn't sure . . .' She hesitated. 'I can't decide what's natural or normal any more. I'm second-guessing everything I say and do.'

Dan nodded. He knew exactly what she meant.

Cate went on: 'The trouble is, nobody can keep up a deception for ever. And listening to Thomsett, I don't think he'll stop chipping away at this. He's certain the money would have been found during

173

the initial search, which can only mean that somebody took it, then panicked or had an attack of conscience and brought it back.'

'That sounds like a crazy risk, doesn't it?'

'You'd think so. But Thomsett told me that the farmer who found the money is the same man who discovered the body the day before.'

'So he's the likely suspect?' Dan realised he sounded far too eager.

Cate nodded. 'DC Avery was questioning him today. But if he flatly denies it, I don't see what they can do. The fingerprints aren't going to prove anything either way.'

'Fingerprints?' A wave of nausea swept over him. Cate started to speak, then glanced to her right and flinched: reacting to her brother's hostile gaze.

'Hold on,' she said. 'I may as well explain it to you both.'

Robbie marched straight up to the table. He looked different: a new hairstyle that didn't suit him. Dan went to make a sarcastic comment and then understood why Robbie would want to change his appearance.

'Thanks very much!' Robbie glowered at his sister as he sat down next to Dan.

'I didn't warn you in case it was a test. Thomsett might have told me on purpose to see if I tipped you off.'

Dan nodded. 'Cate's right. It would have seemed even more like you had something to hide.'

A couple of slow blinks signalled that Robbie was thinking it through; then he seemed to relax slightly.

'Luckily for us, DS Thomsett has other things on his mind.' Cate told him about the farmer, and that the detective intended to test the envelope. It wasn't news to Robbie.

'He said he may want to take my prints.'

Cate seemed relieved that Robbie already knew about it. In some respects, Dan thought, this was the perfect outcome: the farmer under suspicion, Robbie questioned without incident and Cate satisfied that her brother had played no part in O'Brien's death.

But the fingerprints . . . the fingerprints could be their undoing.

'Anyway,' Robbie said, 'what does the money have to do with whoever killed Hank?'

'I asked the same thing. It's an inconsistency, pure and simple. But I don't know how far they'll pursue it. The damp weather might have destroyed the prints—'

'It rained!' Dan exclaimed. Cate gave him a troubled glance, while Robbie nudged him with his foot.

'You guys are getting too worked up,' Robbie declared. 'Of course these cops will put us under some pressure. We just have to soak it up till they get bored and go away.'

'Blasé as ever,' Cate said. 'I only hope you're right.'

'Me too,' Dan said. 'Are you sure Thomsett doesn't suspect it was you in the pub on Tuesday?'

Robbie shook his head, but he looked shifty. 'I told him I was out with a "friend" that night.'

'That was quick thinking.' Cate's response gave Dan a second to process his shock. 'A female friend, I assume?'

'Is there any other kind?'

Robbie laughed, a deep lascivious *heh-heh-heh*. Cate narrowed her eyes and said, in disgust, 'You are a piece of work, you really are.'

'What?' Robbie seemed genuinely mystified; then he caught Dan's eye and growled in frustration. 'Oh, come on, I didn't mean that *we*'re not friends – me and Danny boy. Of course we are. Best buddies, eh?'

Dan shrugged, while Cate shook her head. Leaving her drink half-finished, she stood up.

'You don't deserve him, Robbie, I'll tell you that for nothing. You don't deserve either of us.'

Thirty-seven

Still bitter that his wife might have been confiding in Stemper, Gordon decided he should take a greater part in the conversation. First he poured more wine. He regarded it as safe to drive on up to half a bottle.

'It was called Templeton Wynne from the start, but there was only ever Templeton in charge. The name was a silly pun to bolster his ego. "Wynne" as in "winner".'

Patricia took over. 'It was my address book and Gordon's PR skills that launched his business. Practically every contract, every connection that made him successful, he owes in some form or another to the assistance we gave him.'

'Billions of pounds in PFI contracts,' Gordon said. 'Not to mention all the direct government funding for his management services and assorted claptrap.'

'Right from the start he failed to give us credit. And this was when we'd just begun our own political consultancy. Gordon and I were slaving night and day to make it work. It wasn't unreasonable to expect some mutual support. Instead, he simply cast us aside the moment we'd served our purpose.'

'Did he ever explain his reasoning?' Stemper asked.

'Not a word,' Patricia said. 'Not a damn word.'

Gingerly, Gordon added, 'There had been one or two minor disagreements. Spats. But nothing to justify his treatment of us.'

'He saw to it that we lost out on some very significant contracts. There's no other reason to account for why we were passed over . . .'

'And in the meantime he was raking in a fortune.'

Stemper gave a sombre nod. 'I imagine the recent knighthood must have rubbed salt into the wound . . .?'

Gordon cringed. Of course, Stemper wasn't to know the subject was strictly off-limits.

Patricia said, with frosty disdain: 'I shan't comment on whether "Sir Mark" deserves his title. But it's a given that he'll be in the Lords within a year or two. His Party donations are already into seven figures, much of it funnelled through proxies.' A bitter look at Gordon. 'And to think that I was the one who introduced him to David.'

'Of course,' Gordon said drily, 'we hadn't the vaguest notion how important that smooth young man would later become. No one did.'

More sympathetic noises from Stemper. He was sitting very straight, his hands folded neatly in his lap. His only movements were regular glances to his left or right, apparently casual, but Gordon sensed he was absorbing every detail of the room and its occupants.

He said, 'And how does O'Brien's death link in?'

Patricia nodded. 'I'm sorry, we've gone off-track. It's a badly kept secret that Templeton is cashing his chips. Even with the spending cuts, the government is intent on outsourcing to an extent that will make the last gold rush seem like small change. In health, in education, social security, policing, you name it. There are hundreds of billions up for grabs, and of course the American conglomerates are determined to get their noses in the trough. One of them decided that a merger with Templeton Wynne offered the perfect route to the front.'

'"Merger" being something of a euphemism,' Gordon said.

'Exactly. Not that Mark Templeton will care much either way. Even on conservative estimates, he's looking at an instant personal gain of around a hundred million pounds.'

*   *   *

Stemper didn't do anything as coarse as whistle, or even shake his head. He simply digested the news with a sip of water and nodded at Patricia to continue.

'The one saving grace was that Templeton wasn't aware of my past association with Hank O'Brien—'

Jerry chose that moment to cough loudly, and not entirely convincingly. Gordon glared at him, wondering what he knew – or what he thought he knew. Someone as boastful as O'Brien might well have spoken out of turn, and Gordon squirmed at the idea of his dirty linen being aired in public.

'As I say,' Patricia quickly went on, 'this gave us a marvellous opportunity. We worked on O'Brien for years, until he came round to our way of thinking.'

'Which is?'

'Put simply, that Templeton owes us. From our own experience, we were certain that there would be excessive profits, much of it derived from fraud. When a private company lands a lucrative government contract, it's like being handed a blank cheque. How many of us can say we wouldn't add an extra nought?'

'Or three extra noughts?' Gordon said.

They all chuckled, politely, and Stemper said, 'Did Hank confirm this?'

Gordon nodded. 'For nearly five years he's been collecting evidence, not just in the UK but from Templeton subsidiaries across the globe. Canada, Australia, Hong Kong.'

'Part of the deal was that Hank insisted on keeping the incriminating material until we were ready to proceed,' Patricia said. 'It's a decision that with hindsight I bitterly regret.'

'Fair enough, really, though.' This was another unexpected contribution from Jerry, who looked taken aback when everyone stared at him. 'I mean, that was his insurance policy, if anything went wrong.'

'He didn't need an insurance policy,' Patricia said, which Gordon knew was slightly disingenuous. In the event of disaster, their clean-up strategy would have entailed recruiting Stemper to neutralise any threat to the Blakes – and that had included O'Brien, and, indeed, Jerry himself.

Stemper said, 'If O'Brien held on to the documentation, might he have felt he could go it alone?'

'It was always a possibility,' Patricia said. 'But a solo venture posed various dangers for him.'

Gordon said, 'We had guaranteed protection for Hank, particularly if the whole affair went public.'

'I still have many high-level connections, both politically and in the media,' Patricia reminded them. 'Hank was aware that we could shield him from a firestorm.'

'Even if that meant revealing your own part in the affair?'

She shrugged. 'This was in the context of a total meltdown. We had no reason to believe it would come to that. But you're right to highlight the importance of secrecy. It was – no, it *is* imperative to the success of our plan that Templeton has no inkling that we're behind it.'

'Understandable,' Stemper said. 'But it made you vulnerable. I wonder if Hank merely exchanged your protection for that of another party . . .'

'And something went badly wrong.' Patricia nodded grimly. 'You're completely in tune with our thinking.'

'So what now?' Stemper asked. 'Granted, you need to know why Hank died. But on the larger issue of Templeton – and the money – can you walk away from it?'

This was the central question of the meeting, and they all knew it.

'The honest answer?' Patricia said. 'I'm not sure that we can.'

'How much is it worth to you?'

She glanced at Gordon. 'Templeton is in the United States at the moment. We have private detectives monitoring the negotiations in Delaware and New York. Once we received notification that the agreement was ready to sign, Hank was going to confront his boss with a weight of accumulated evidence. If Templeton didn't pay up, that material would go to the authorities in half a dozen countries. It would obliterate the value of his company and put Templeton behind bars for a very long time.'

She hesitated, expertly building the tension. Jerry was gaping at her like some docile beast, his mouth lolling open.

'In return for silence, our price was fifty million pounds.'

Once again Stemper didn't flinch. But there was a noticeable gleam in his eyes, as if everything had become much clearer. Jerry closed his mouth with an audible snap. He'd never been told exactly how much was involved, and Gordon regretted that he was present to hear it now.

He said, 'The crucial thing is to locate the paperwork. If Hank partnered with someone else, his accomplice may be preparing to use it to extort money from Templeton.'

'Or from us,' Patricia said. 'It's not inconceivable that Hank kept incriminating documents relating to our part in this.'

Stemper said, 'Is his death likely to jeopardise the merger?'

'We've had no indication of any problems.' The thought provoked a weary sigh. 'I dearly hope not.'

'Hank was senior, but nowhere near business-critical,' Gordon said. 'And the due diligence is already complete. I suspect the Americans will never even hear of it.'

Patricia said, 'The key point is that on Tuesday night we lost control of our own destiny, and we don't know if that control was wrested from us deliberately or quite inadvertently.'

Stemper nodded. 'You shouldn't rule out a coincidence. But with fifty million at stake, that becomes rather more difficult to believe.'

'If there's a conspiracy, it must revolve around this woman in the pub with Hank, as well as the two men who returned to the accident site.'

Jerry stirred into life again. 'A couple of young guys? I don't see them cooking up something on this scale.'

'Foot soldiers, Jerry,' Patricia declared crisply. 'They come in all shapes and sizes.'

Stemper agreed. 'It's prudent to assume the existence of an unknown adversary. Are there any obvious candidates?'

'None we can think of. It really did seem watertight. And we're so close – only a week or two away.' She made a fist. Gordon saw the liver spots on her hand stretching tight over her knuckles 'If we can find an answer quickly, we should be able to retrieve the situation and lay our hands on what's rightfully ours.'

Stemper, pragmatic as ever, said: 'Is the house still unoccupied?'

The Blakes looked at Jerry, who said, 'Far as I know.'

'Good. I suggest we search it tonight.'

Gordon sensed an inward groan from Jerry. Chiding himself for enjoying it, Gordon thought he should mention what they had found on the laptop. He described the email that referred to the British film.

Intrigued, Stemper said, 'I'd recommend getting hold of a copy on DVD, if you can.'

'I suppose we have nothing to lose by checking it,' Patricia said. 'And your last hunch was certainly spot on.'

Stemper inclined his head, modestly, and returned the compliment: 'That was an excellent briefing. Thank you.'

Gordon could feel the glow of pleasure emanating from his wife. Stemper picked up his glass and gently swirled the water round. 'Let's reconvene tomorrow for a progress report.'

A handkerchief had materialised in his free hand, which he used to wipe the glass. Gordon was astonished – even more so by the fact that neither Patricia nor Jerry appeared to notice what he was doing: removing his fingerprints.

Patricia leaned forward, eager to capture Stemper's full attention. There was an unmistakeable sheen of tears in her eyes.

'Those funds weren't intended to squander on the comforts of retirement. The bulk of it was earmarked for a specific project. We were going to do a lot of good with that money, and now someone—' the sadness turned to rage as she snarled '– some *animal* has taken that from us.'

As she stood up, Stemper rose with her and nodded solemnly 'I understand.'

She took a step away from the table, moving out of Jerry's earshot. Gordon also stood, determined to remain privy to their conversation.

In barely more than a whisper, Patricia said, 'There are three things we have to find out. Who are they? Why did they kill Hank? What do they want now?' A glance at Jerry, and another, less hostile, one at Gordon, and then she added: 'And when we know that, we make them pay for what they've done.'

Thirty-eight

After Cate's departure, an uneasy silence. Dan barely trusted himself to speak, so it was Robbie who gave way first.

'I dunno why she had to get so worked up. We're still mates, aren't we?'

'You changed your hairstyle and set up an alibi, but didn't think to mention it to me. Is that what a "mate" does?'

'Dan, you're in the clear, remember? It's not your workplace this cop's gonna come sniffing round.'

'Not yet. But if they lift the fingerprints it'll make no sense. O'Brien's won't be on there. Neither will Cate's. That'll send DS Thomsett back to you for an explanation, and the more he looks at you the more he'll start to wonder if you were at the pub . . .'

Robbie nodded glumly. 'I know. It's not good.'

'*My* fingerprints are on that envelope.'

'Yeah, but it's not as though they've got them on record, have they? Unless you've got a criminal record you never told me about.'

A lopsided grin. Dan made a face. 'Funny.'

'Look, it was a damp night. They probably won't get anything.'

'We've got to pray they don't.'

Robbie gave him a thoughtful look. 'You might wanna do something with your hair, though. How about a flat-top? Or a number two all over?'

He rubbed his scalp, mimicking the actions of a razor. Dan was incredulous.

'I can't believe you're treating this as a joke.'

'Ah, Dan. You need to try and relax a bit. Otherwise you're gonna keel over from the stress.'

It was advice that Dan neither wanted nor needed from Robbie. He picked up his phone, hoping for an excuse to leave. But he didn't need an excuse, did he?

'You getting them in?' Robbie asked as Dan stood up. Then he groaned. 'Aw, come on. The night is young.'

Dan ignored him. He marched out, and was halfway along New Road before Robbie caught up. The street was busy with after-work drinkers and early theatregoers. The noise of the traffic from North Street was like a brass band tuning up.

Robbie grabbed his sleeve, a gesture of clumsy affection. 'Sorry, man. I know this is really hard on you.'

'You don't give a toss about me. Or anyone else.'

A hollow laugh from Robbie: Dan's temper had always amused him.

'I'm still gonna sort out your car, I promise.'

Dan was only half listening. He reached North Street and turned left, towards the bus stop. It wasn't until a procession of vehicles had rumbled past that he noticed the altercation taking place across the road.

A taxi had pulled up at the kerb, its front passenger door open. A group of young men were clustered around it, haranguing the driver. The pedestrians flowing past were studiously ignoring the swearing.

'Unhappy customers,' Robbie muttered. Then he said: 'Hey—' as Dan sprinted across the path of a bus.

He only just made it. Adrenalin pumping, Dan burst into the group, grappling with the man who had launched an angry kick at the car's tyre.

There were shouts of alarm as the others realised what was going on; one or two lashing out at Dan with clumsy punches. He moved away, turning so they could see him clearly, but his attention remained locked on the man – the boy – he was holding.

'Louis! What the hell do you think you're doing?'

His brother's mouth opened but he was too stunned to speak. His eyes wouldn't focus properly. He reeked of booze.

There were angry cries of 'Get off him' and 'Leave him alone, wanker'; and then someone muttered 'It's his brother'; and at that the group fell silent and abruptly resembled nothing more than schoolboys in the presence of a teacher they respected.

'Fucking hooligans,' the taxi driver yelled. 'Few years in the army, that's what they need.'

He drove away, a couple of the boys flipping him the finger. Louis shook off his brother's grasp. He was red-faced now, his voice an octave too high when he tried to explain. 'He wouldn't take us to Hove. We offered him good money, but he treated us like shit—'

'I don't want to hear it,' Dan said. 'This isn't how you behave, and you know it.'

'Our money's good as anyone's.'

'You can't afford taxis. Where were you going, anyway?'

'Strip club!' one of the others shouted, to guffaws. Dan gave the boy a contemptuous glance, then he realised it was Miles, who'd been friends with Louis since infant school. The Miles that Dan knew was shy and polite: a wallflower. What had got into them?

'Louis, you need to go home.'

'Piss off. I don't have to obey you.' Louis stepped away from him, swaying slightly. His eyes were dilated and his gaze wouldn't settle on anything for more than a second or two. *This isn't my brother*, Dan thought. *It's an impostor.*

He turned to address the group. 'Have you been drinking all afternoon?'

There were a few grunts of assent, with a defiant edge.

'What else have you had, besides the alcohol?'

No one answered, but Miles betrayed them with a goofy smile. Dan became aware that Robbie was loitering nearby, staring at Louis. When he sensed Dan's attention he looked away.

The distraction was Louis's cue to move. 'Come on, we're out of here.'

'You're going home.' Dan reached out but his brother chopped viciously at his arm.

'Make me.'

There were snorts of laughter as the boys jostled past him and set off up North Street. For all their youth and bluster, Dan knew he couldn't physically stop them; nor did he want to. He'd never in his life struck out at his brother. The thought of doing so made him feel sick.

Sidling up, Robbie said, 'Best to let 'em go.'

'Did you see the state they were in?'

'You were seventeen once, remember?'

'I didn't go round behaving like that. They could have got arrested.'

Robbie shrugged. 'They weren't doing any real harm. You've got to realise, your brother's a free spirit. A bit like me,' he added.

'I hope not,' Dan said, making sure Robbie understood that he wasn't joking in the slightest. 'Anything but that.'

Thirty-nine

Stemper had pictured O'Brien's farmhouse as an imposing period building, Grade II-listed, tile-hung in the Sussex fashion, boasting oak beams and tile floors and great open fireplaces. In fact it was a modern four-bedroom house that wouldn't have looked out of place on a 1970s estate of executive homes. The main benefit, as far as Stemper could tell, was the seclusion offered by the extensive grounds.

A night visit was far from ideal for a thorough search, but Stemper was eager to create some momentum. This evening's meeting had left him in no doubt as to the importance of making a swift breakthrough.

What shocked him most was that the Blakes had entrusted Jerry Conlon with the task of watching over an asset worth fifty million. Stemper wouldn't have relied on Jerry to take his suits to the dry-cleaner's.

He'd insisted that they wear latex gloves, overalls and woollen hats to minimise the trace evidence. He could tell Jerry thought this an absurd overreaction. Conlon looked like a refugee from some hideous alternative-theatre group: without the greasy mop of hair on his brow, his face resembled that of an elderly lizard.

Stemper said, 'I understand there was talk of the alarm code being changed?'

'Yeah, but it wasn't.'

'I know that. Didn't you find out why he'd considered changing it?'

Jerry sneered. 'You never met him, did you? Hank was always bitching about something or other.'

'He was of vital importance to the Blakes, and your job was to protect their interests. You should have made it your business to know.'

A moment of icy silence, then Jerry sniffed and said, 'Yeah, well, water under the bridge. Let's get on with it, eh?'

Inside, the decor was an uneasy mix of traditional and modern. Nowhere was this more evident than in the main living room, which had a 1970s-style split-level layout and bare-brick fireplace, as well as white leather couches and smoked-glass tables.

The farmhouse was visible, at some distance, from a couple of neighbouring properties. Since flickering torchlight was more likely to arouse suspicion, Stemper decided it was better to close all the curtains and blinds, and then use the normal lights, one room at a time.

It took only a few minutes to complete the initial reconnaissance, Jerry scurrying behind him like an overexcited but cautious puppy; one that knew what it was like to feel his master's boot.

The results were disappointing. There was a safe hidden within a wardrobe in the master bedroom, but it wasn't much larger than a shoebox: designed to take passports, jewellery, cash.

'We might have to get inside.' Stemper was troubled by the possibility of a flash drive: a USB stick could hold a room's worth of documents.

Jerry didn't feel it was likely. 'What we're after will be on paper. I can guarantee it.'

'Really.' Stemper wasn't as sceptical as he sounded. The Blakes had said as much themselves. But the house's construction seemed to preclude the possibility of a hidden strongroom or a walk-in safe.

They began the methodical search in the office, situated in the larger of the two back bedrooms. The Blakes had already trawled through the work laptop, and Stemper had recommended that he bring it back here tonight. In addition, there was a desktop PC and also an ancient laptop – kept for backups, perhaps.

Stemper's briefcase contained, among other things, a portable hard drive with a two-terabyte storage capacity. While Jerry powered up the computers, Stemper focused on a large four-drawer filing cabinet.

'I've looked in there,' Jerry said. 'It's all kosher.'

Stemper had his doubts, but he saw that Jerry was correct. All he found were conventional company documents, most bearing the glossy emblem of the Templeton Wynne group and distribution lists that went far wider than any illicit paperwork would go.

The old laptop interested him more. There were signs that the hard drive had been wiped. Setting his data-recovery software to work, Stemper examined the desktop PC. It had a single user account, no password protection, and the files and folders consumed only eighty-one gigabytes of the 250-gig hard drive.

Stemper wondered if there was an element of double bluff: hide the evidence in plain sight. It seemed unlikely, but the Blakes could check it for themselves when he delivered a copy of the hard drive.

'You say he would have favoured paper over digital. Could he have stored it offsite somewhere?'

Jerry screwed up his face while he thought about it. 'Nah. That wouldn't be Hank's style. He'd want it close.'

'The outbuildings?'

'There's a garage, an old barn. Couple of sheds. Have a look when we're done here.'

'I intend to.'

Jerry gulped audibly and focused his attention on the laptop. 'Aye aye,' he said, blatantly relieved. 'Looks like you've got something here.'

The software was busy plucking out files that had been buried deep but not beyond reach. Even Stemper couldn't suppress a smile at the titles: *Girls 'n' Dogs, Dirty Virgins, Little Darlings, Deflowered.*

'Filthy bastard,' Jerry muttered. 'Underage stuff, you reckon?'

'Could be.'

'I'm glad he's dead, then.'

'They'll have to be checked, in case he's hidden anything amongst them.'

'Yeah, well, the Blakes can handle that. I'm going nowhere near any paedo shit—'

A sharp noise made him jump. It was the sound of glass giving way.

Stemper, perfectly calm, exchanged a glance with Jerry, who looked like he might be about to soil himself.

'I think we have company.'

Stemper removed a couple of items from his briefcase and slipped them into the deep pockets of his overalls.

'Police?' Jerry said, his dry lips smacking noisily.

'No.' Stemper indicated the desk. 'Sit there. Don't move. Don't make a sound.'

Jerry nodded, immensely grateful to be assigned such a straight-forward task.

Stemper descended the stairs and crept into the hall. He heard a thud from the living room. From the doorway he saw a torch beam roaming the room like a distressed insect. The light settled on the entertainment consoles beneath a plasma TV. A soft exhalation as the intruder assessed what he could take.

He would kneel down to disconnect the cables.

Stemper made no sound as he entered the room. He was holding his breath, though he nearly let it go when he saw the white stripe glowing along the leg of the man's trousers. A burglar clad in tracksuit bottoms with white piping, and big white trainers that also shone in the half-light.

No professional, then. But Stemper didn't see that as grounds for leniency.

He took out the stun gun. Acquired in America, it delivered a charge of five million volts that would render a grown man insensible for several minutes.

The intruder was sifting through a pile of Xbox games when Stemper reached him. He had possibly half a second's awareness that he wasn't alone before the stun gun did its work.

Stemper had ample time to put the light on and drag the intruder into the centre of the room, where he sat him up against a coffee table. He removed the man's cheap plastic jacket, tied his hands with the sleeves and used the rest as a hood. Pulled tight over his face, it would leave him struggling to breathe, disorientated and afraid.

The man was groaning, his breathing ragged. Stemper considered the possibility of a congenital heart defect. A corpse on his hands tonight would be an unwelcome complication.

He gave his prisoner a slap. 'Wake up.'

The man writhed for a moment. 'Who the fuck . . .? What d'you do to me?'

'I'll show you.' Stemper pressed the stun gun into the man's side.

'No! Leave it out—'

'Who sent you here?'

'No one.'

'You're lying. Tell me who you're working for.'

'I came here 'cause I thought the house was empty.'

'How did you know that?'

He shrugged. 'Just did.'

'Wrong.' Stemper moved as if to strike again.

'Don't! I heard a whisper . . . The owner wound up dead the other night.' He was growing more confident. 'Me and a mate thought we'd take a look. He's keeping watch. You'd better let me go. He's tooled up, 'n all.'

It sounded blatantly untrue, and Stemper said so. 'Who told you about the owner?'

'Just picked it up.'

'Someone gave you the address. Tell me.'

His body sagged in defeat. 'Just some girl, all right? Works in a pub round here.'

'And she tipped you off?'

The man only grunted in response.

'Where does she live?'

'What? Ah no, you got no right—'

Stemper gave him another shock, for a shorter duration this time. The man screamed but did not lose consciousness.

'Yeah, yeah. It's Worthing, okay? Broadwater Street. There's a block of flats just past the churchyard. Traci's the ground floor. Number six.'

Stemper heard movement behind him and turned, braced to take on the man's accomplice. But it was Jerry Conlon, open-mouthed with shock. Stemper shook his head fiercely, gesturing back towards the office.

The burglar sensed something had changed, lifting his head and casting blindly around.

'He's out there. You better let me go.'

Stemper didn't think the man had brought an accomplice, but he couldn't discount it completely. He hauled the man to his feet. 'How did you get in?'

'Broke a panel in the conservatory door.'

Stemper wanted him leaving the same way. Boldly opening the front door would emphasise that Stemper was an insider.

He walked the man through the dining room, where an arched opening led to the conservatory. Sure enough, a single pane had been punched out; foolishly, Hank had left a key in the lock.

Stemper took a look outside. The night was still and very dark, low cloud blotting out the moon and stars. There was no sign of anyone else.

'Remember this,' he said quietly. 'I saw your face when you blacked out. You haven't seen mine. If any word of this leaks, you won't see me coming.'

'I get the message. I'm hardly gonna blab, am I?'

'Nothing to Traci, either, or I guarantee she'll suffer.'

He propelled the burglar across the patio, the man stumbling, pulling at the coat that still covered his face. Stemper locked the door, removed the key and retreated from sight.

Jerry was in the office, biting so intensely on a nail that he could have chewed half his finger off.

'Small-time burglar,' Stemper told him. 'I don't think he poses a risk, but we'd better get out of here.'

'Was that Traci he mentioned?' Jerry gave a bitter laugh. 'Did she put him up to it?'

'I'll be finding out.' Stemper pointed to the computers. 'Let's shut these down.'

'This is a nightmare. It's like there's a frigging curse on O'Brien.'

Or on you, Stemper thought. But he didn't say that. It made no sense to give Jerry any warning.

Forty

On Friday morning Cate woke in an unexpectedly positive mood and went for a run. The air was cool but fragrant, stirred by the lightest of sea breezes. A thin veil of cloud glowed with the promise that eventually the sun would break through. Cate managed two miles along the promenade, exchanging rueful smiles with the other masochists out early to run, cycle, rollerblade or walk their dogs.

She tried not to dwell on Robbie or Hank O'Brien. Instead she thought about work. There were medical reports to read and schedules of loss to prepare, and she was determined to get up to date before the weekend.

She was back home by twenty to eight, feeling virtuous enough to contemplate cookies for elevenses. She showered, dressed and was seconds away from leaving when the doorbell rang.

It was DS Thomsett, clutching a document wallet. Avery, the unruly henchman, lurked behind him.

'The e-fits. Do you have time to take a look?'

A disarming smile overcame Cate's defences. 'I can spare a few minutes. Come in.'

She led them into the lounge, then remembered there was a bra on the radiator – not a decent bra, either, but an everyday one from M&S that had gone grey with age. Casually, she managed to unhook it and let it drop out of sight beneath her dining table. Thomsett gave no indication that he'd noticed, but Avery made a sarcastic noise in his throat.

She was given two sheets of paper. Concerned that her hands would shake, she clutched the papers tightly until she had sat down and could rest them on her knees.

Each image was a full-face portrait, rendered in a slightly unreal, cartoon-like style. Cate squinted, trying not to overdo the austere concentration; at the same time anxious that she didn't betray any flicker of recognition.

She saw a definite likeness to Robbie and Dan, but realised it was largely because she'd been expecting to see them. The closer she looked, the more she noticed details that didn't match. It struck her then that Robbie had changed his hairstyle because of the e-fit – which was, she had to admit, a wise move on his part.

'Anything you'd alter?' Thomsett asked.

After a respectable pause, she placed a finger on the one that represented her brother. 'His face was longer, with a narrower chin.'

Avery snorted, as though he knew precisely what she was doing. She forced herself to meet his gaze, until he shrugged and said, 'What about the other one?'

Dan's likeness wasn't as accurate. Cate wondered if that was because the barmaid had been smitten with Robbie.

'Darker hair, perhaps. And the nose was fatter, sort of bulbous.'

'Here . . .' Thomsett gently took the paper, brought out a pencil and sketched the changes, while Avery went on staring at Cate with a peculiar half-smile on his lips. Thomsett showed her the results. 'Any good?'

'I think so.'

'Okay. I'll get these updated.' And then, in an offhand tone, he added, 'I paid your brother a visit yesterday.'

* * *

Cate's mind went blank. She hadn't warned Robbie in advance, but surely it would seem odd if he hadn't said something to her?

'He mentioned it last night.'

'I got the impression he's quite sore about the loss of that three thousand pounds.'

'Is he? I suppose it must seem ironic, handing over the money to somebody who dies so soon afterwards . . .' She tailed off, aware that she was straying on to dangerous ground.

'That's probably it.' Thomsett leaned towards her and tapped one of the images. 'You don't think that looks a bit like your brother?'

'Him?' She made a show of examining it again. 'Vaguely, I suppose. The man I saw wasn't as tall as Robbie. He was better-looking, too.'

'Took a shine to him, eh?' Avery piped up. 'You didn't get his number, by any chance?'

'No, I didn't.'

Thomsett frowned, possibly unhappy with his colleague's intervention. 'We're told that Mr Scott was with his girlfriend on Tuesday night. A "Bree Tyler".'

Cate shrugged. 'Okay.'

'Have you met Mrs Tyler?'

Thomsett's emphasis on *Mrs* was subtle, but not so subtle that she wasn't intended to notice. Cate raised a hand, palm out.

'That's an area of his life I steer well clear of.'

'Something of a playboy, is he?' Avery said.

'Well, women seem to go for him. I can't say I see his appeal myself, but there you are. He's in no hurry to settle down.'

Thomsett smiled. 'Do I sense that you disapprove?'

'Oh, I don't know. Maybe I'm just envious.'

It was slightly too intimate a disclosure for the circumstances, and an awkward silence followed. Cate checked her watch. 'I'd better be going.'

Thomsett got up. 'Thanks for your help. I'll run these amendments past the other witnesses.'

Cate nodded, wondering what would happen if the barmaid disagreed. Would the detectives attribute it to witness unreliability, or would they suspect a more sinister motive?

Thomsett led the way out, with Cate behind him. As they passed through the hall, Avery murmured in her ear: 'A bit of friendly advice, love. Lie to us, or hold something back, and we'll destroy you.'

Cate flinched, but was in control of her expression by the time she turned. She faced him down, and said quietly, 'I'm not.'

'Fair enough. Just don't say you weren't warned.'

Thomsett was opening the front door, apparently unaware of the exchange. Cate wondered if he deliberately let his subordinate do the dirty work.

He stepped outside, then turned back. 'Are you aware there's a man in a grey Toyota Avensis watching your house?'

'What?' A flare of panic, which subsided when Cate leaned out and saw the Avensis. The car must have been new, but the occupant was sadly familiar.

'That's my ex-husband.'

'Is it?' Thomsett sounded grave. 'Would you like me to have a word with him?'

'I don't think that'll be necessary, but I appreciate the offer.'

'All right.' He stepped back to let Avery past. 'You have my number. Please don't hesitate to call me.'

Cate watched them drive away. Only then did Martin extract himself from the Avensis, his limbs as cumbersome as ever. Looking shamefaced but also slightly peeved, he advanced on Cate, who remained in the doorway, her expression hard and unfriendly.

'I'm already late for work, so this had better be good.'

Martin gestured in the direction the detectives had taken. 'Who the hell were they?'

'Jehovah's Witnesses.'

'No, they weren't.'

'Insurance salesmen?'

'You don't want to tell me, I get it. But I saw how you were looking at the tall one. You didn't mention *him* on Tuesday.'

Cate laughed with disbelief. 'What do you want, Martin?'

'You said you were going to call me.'

'I've been busy this week.'

'So I can see. So what does he do? Another solicitor?'

'No. He's a detective sergeant.'

That had the required effect. Martin blinked a few times, nodding stiffly. 'A police officer?'

'That's right. And he noticed you sitting there.'

'Wh-what did he say?'

'Not much. I told him I can deal with you myself.'

'Oh.' Martin had never been particularly good at thinking on his feet, and now he looked completely lost. Cate almost – *almost* – felt sorry for him.

'How's Janine?'

Martin looked morose. 'She keeps throwing up, but that's normal, isn't it?'

'She must be touched by your concern.'

'The bathroom stinks,' he said, as though that were reason enough to resent his wife's condition. 'Look, I'm sorry we've got off on the wrong foot again—'

'Yeah. Anyone would think we weren't supposed to be together.'

'You can joke about it, but maybe we shouldn't have given up so easily.'

'Nobody "gave up". You ran off and slept with another woman.'

'And I've apologised, haven't I?' He didn't wait for a reply, possibly because he knew it wasn't true. 'Are you free tomorrow afternoon?'

'No.'

'Tomorrow evening, then? I'll tell Janine I'm out with my brother . . .'

Cate's sigh was loud enough to cut him off. 'I can't deal with this right now. Just leave me alone, Martin. Otherwise I'll take up my friend's offer to have an official word with you.'

Forty-one

Robbie made it to the office before nine, feeling smugly pleased that he'd roused Jed and pressured him to find somewhere to offload an unwanted car. Too sleepy to ask questions, Jed had muttered something about a place in Hampshire.

When his mother came in, Robbie mocked her for being late and endured her amazement that he was in at all. She claimed to have been working from home since seven. This was just a quick visit to collect a contract before heading off to East Grinstead.

'Got my eye on a block of flats coming up for auction.'

'It's out of our ideal area again, though.'

'Yes, Robbie. But you remember that phrase about beggars and choosers?'

She was pulling a face at him, so he pulled one back. He could have told her he knew that phrase only too well.

He'd already had a text from Bree: `Have you called her yet?`

He ignored it for a while, and actually got some work done. Sorted a couple of maintenance headaches. Then another text: `Call her, Robbie. £200. EASY monee ;-)`

Bree was right. With a heavy heart he found the number. Maureen Heath, husband in Portugal. He was some kind of builder. Maureen was in her early fifties, a mother of four grown-up children. Robbie wondered idly if any of the four were female.

He'd always been choosy about his sexual partners, even the one-night stands. Of course he'd made exceptions, usually when the evening was wearing on and the choice was limited. It never bothered him much because he was invariably off his head on the good old party powder: the phrase beloved of those in the know was *Never mind the 'beer goggles', try the 'coke glasses'.*

But this would be different. He'd have to be sober, clear-headed. Professional. What Bree had in mind for him was whole new territory: sex as a chore.

Christ, if he wanted that he'd get married.

He tapped out the number. When it went to voicemail he held his nerve and left a brief, grudging message. Maybe his tone would put her off . . .

She called back a few minutes later. She had a throaty voice, not unattractive, though something about it gave him an impression of heft. And Robbie definitely liked his women slim: that was non-negotiable.

'Mr Scott? I wonder if I could make use of your services?'

Seemed a funny way to put it, but he supposed he should be glad she wasn't playing coy.

'Absolutely. When's a good time for you?'

'Pardon?'

'For me to come round. I assume we'll meet at your place, or did you want to book a hotel?'

There was a pause. Then she said, 'I suspect we're at cross purposes here. Do you handle property rentals?'

'Yeah. Isn't this Maureen?'

'No. My name is Cheryl Wilson. I'd like to engage your services to rent out my brother's house. Well, technically it's mine now,' she added grimly. 'My brother died.'

'Oh, I'm very sorry to hear that.' Relaxing back in his chair, Robbie went into full-on smarm mode. 'Delighted to help. May I ask how you found us?'

'Certainly. You rented it out once before. I have the paperwork here. A farmhouse near Ashurst. Hank O'Brien?'

Robbie nearly tipped the chair over. He grabbed the desk and righted himself, scrabbling to keep hold of the phone.

'Mr Scott?'

'Yes. Sorry.'

'I wondered if I'd lost you there.'

He gave a bark of insincere laughter. He was fighting an impulse to ask whether this was a joke. Nothing in her manner suggested she was anything but serious.

Unless it was the police, hoping to trick him into an indiscretion.

He said, 'I'm very sorry to hear about your brother.'

'Horrible business. Knocked down by a car, and the evil buggers didn't stop.'

Buggers, plural. A figure of speech, or was this deliberate, to see if he contradicted her?

'Horrible. So, er, how do you want to proceed?'

'There's still probate to be granted, but I might as well get the ball rolling. The market's not right for a sale at present, and I have no desire to live here. Renting seems the best option.'

'Of course. I'd better have a look round, in case anything's changed since last time.'

'Splendid. Tomorrow morning any good?'

'Uh, where are we . . .?' He pretended to check a diary. 'Saturday, ah, yes. Is eleven o'clock convenient?' Robbie wondered if she could hear him smiling. He felt increasingly sure that this was the real deal.

'Eleven's fine,' Hank's sister told him.

'Great. See you tomorrow.'

The door opened and Indira came in. 'You look pleased with your-self,' she said.

'Indeed I do.' He hammered out a drum roll on the desk. 'What's that old saying? *May you live in interesting times.*'

Forty-two

Dan would have called in sick on Friday, but for the poor example he'd be setting to his brother. It was a good job he didn't, because when he got to the shop he learned that Hayley had a stomach bug and wasn't coming in.

He tried phoning her but there was no reply. This felt like fate at work. Disaster would pile upon disaster – unless or until he did the right thing.

It was never far from his mind, the idea that he should give himself up. Then he had two options. The first was to tell them the actual truth: perhaps it wasn't so unlikely that Robbie had grabbed the wheel . . .

Except that Robbie would deny every word. So Dan's other option was to say he had done it. Forget trying to implicate Robbie: just take full responsibility and get it over with. In a strange way this seemed like the more honest course of action. More honourable, certainly.

But what about his aunt? Did he have the right to inflict so much pain with what would be essentially a lie?

Dan couldn't decide. His brother's behaviour was now an aggravating factor, with Joan having confided that she was worried sick about Louis. Blaming herself, even, that she had failed as a surrogate parent.

Although Dan had done his best to reassure her, he shared her

204

concern. He hadn't mentioned the incident with the taxi driver, but there was no disguising the state of Louis's inebriation when he finally stumbled in at eleven o'clock last night, having ignored various texts and calls.

After making sure he was all right, Joan had swiftly retreated to her bed. Louis had done the same, but in the early hours Dan had woken to the sound of his brother being violently sick.

He'd knocked on the bathroom door, but the only response was a sombre: 'Go away.' Louis sounded like he'd been crying, and Dan decided it was better to leave him.

In the morning Joan checked his college timetable and found that Louis wasn't due in until ten-thirty.

'I'll give him till nine. Do him a nice egg-and-bacon sandwich.'

'You know, we really don't deserve you,' Dan said.

'Oh, nonsense.' She smiled, but he could see the anguish in her eyes. And now he had to add to the burden of anxiety.

'You haven't noticed any money going missing, have you?'

'Money? No, why?'

Dan saw the shock as it dawned on her. With hindsight it was what troubled him most about last night: not the loutish behaviour but the fact that Louis could afford to stay out drinking and doing God knows what else. He'd had a Saturday job at HMV, but had walked out a couple of months ago. Since then his only disposable income had been fifteen pounds a week in pocket money that came from his trust fund, set up with part of the proceeds of their parents' estate.

Joan looked heartbroken. 'You both know where I leave my purse. I'm not in the habit of counting every penny, but I think I could tell if someone was helping themselves.'

'Okay. Sorry I asked.' Dan kissed her cheek on his way out, making sure he held her a little more firmly than usual.

The next instalment of grief came mid-morning: a text from Cate, wanting him to call her. Willie Denham was on the prowl, so Dan had an anxious wait until the old man made himself scarce and he could slip away to the office.

'Those detectives were round this morning to get my opinion on the e-fit pictures.'

'How did they look?'

'It's hard to say. Because I know you, I could see the resemblance. But I suggested a couple of changes that made them less like the two of you.'

'Thank you,' Dan said. 'I hope that's not putting you at risk.'

'So do I. Every time I open my mouth it feels like I'm digging a deeper and deeper hole.'

'I appreciate it. I'm sure Robbie does, too.'

'Really?' Her sigh was almost savage in its intensity. 'It feels like he expects us to ease his path through life, without ever accepting responsibility for what he does. The Teflon man.'

'I agree. But I don't think you could ever disown him, any more than I could with Louis.' When he explained what he'd witnessed last night, Cate was astonished.

'Louis was always such a sweetheart. And he worships you.'

'Didn't sound like it when he was telling me to piss off.'

'That's in the heat of the moment.' She sighed again. 'The thing about a family member is that you have to see the best in them when nobody else does. So if you can keep faith with Louis, I'll try and do the same with Robbie. Deal?'

Dan managed a laugh. 'If you say so.'

Forty-three

A visit to the barmaid was exactly what Stemper needed to restore his equilibrium. When it came down to it, extracting information was the essence of his job. It meant he could lead, not follow. Influence events from the beginning, rather than simply react to them.

The break-in last night had been a shambles, and he had admitted as much to the Blakes. Patricia was astounded by the news of the burglary. Predictably, she viewed it in the context of a larger conspiracy.

'I'm almost certain it's unrelated,' Stemper had told her. 'I'll know very soon.'

'And what about Jerry?'

'I've told him to keep watching the farmhouse.'

Her voice dripping with scorn, Patricia had said, 'If you think he can be trusted to do that properly.'

Bernard Quills had been happy to give Stemper a key, saying he understood perfectly that some of his guests liked to stay out late. Stemper had returned at four a.m., only to encounter Quills on the first-floor landing, wrapped in a bright red silk kimono. There was no way the man could have heard Stemper come in, but they both went through the motions of pretending that Quills had been disturbed in his sleep.

'Takes a lot to sneak up on me in the small hours!' he'd joked.

Ignoring the implicit invitation to try, Stemper had made his way to bed, aware that through no fault of his own another complication had arisen.

The next morning Quills had been thrilled when Stemper agreed to take tea and toast in the spacious but fussy dining room.

'It's all included, you know. Have the Full English if you like. I've kippers, too. Not much call for them these days . . .'

And so he had wittered on, Stemper indulging him, even while the plans quietly formed: both short- and long-term. He ate a single slice of toast, with a rather nice thick-cut marmalade. Quills reappeared the moment he had finished, a photo album under one arm.

'May I? Just quickly.' The proprietor nudged his way into a chair next to Stemper and handed him the album. 'Photography was expressly forbidden on set. Terribly naughty, but how could I resist? Look.'

The pictures showed Quills in a vintage brown suit and a fedora, standing amongst a group in similar garb, on a stretch of promenade that Stemper guessed was Hove. There was a line of brightly coloured beach huts in the background. In one, a man that Stemper recognised as John Hurt was talking to a woman in a dowdy costume who might or might not have been Dame Helen Mirren.

'The third AD said I was wonderful.' Quills gave a little sigh, and corrected himself. '*Looked* wonderful.'

'What lovely memories,' Stemper said, returning the album.

'Thank you. I wish I'd been more involved on that one. Fortunately you get a lot of films made down this way. Brighton's a magnet for artistic types, as you probably know.'

'So I've heard. Does a movie called *Entwined* ring any bells?'

Quills arched one eyebrow. 'Yes. A rom-com, wasn't it? Haven't seen it myself, but I believe there was some location filming in Sussex.'

'When was that, do you recall?'

Another probing glance from Quills, then he gazed skyward and stroked his chin.

'Summertime, it would have been. Late summer.'

'Last year?'

'Oh, no. Year before, I think.' His eyes flashed. 'I'm dying to know why you're interested.'

'Just enquiring for a friend.' Stemper decided he had nothing to lose by being enigmatic. No matter what else he said or did, they were set on a path now, he and Quills.

'Hmm.' The proprietor wagged a finger at him. 'There's a quality to you . . . Are you sure you're not in the business?'

'Let's just say I'm of it, not in it.'

Quills waited for him to elaborate, saw it wasn't going to happen and spluttered with laughter.

'Oh, you're a tease . . . You know, I'd very much like to get drunk with you one night.'

Stemper smiled, stretching the silence almost to breaking point before he responded.

'I'd like that, too.'

Stemper had only the dimmest memory of Worthing. He thought his parents had played here at some time in the early 1970s, but he couldn't recall having visited it since. Just another South Coast seaside town, a little down at heel but somehow charming with it, not as attractive or prosperous as Brighton, but not so evidently in decline as Hastings, which Stemper knew quite well.

He had a sneaking affection for such places, clinging on for survival in the face of an economic storm that could strip a town of its vitality as savagely as any Atlantic hurricane. A storm that no one could understand, much less contain.

He parked at the far end of Broadwater Street and set off on foot, an anonymous figure in a dark grey suit. He carried a briefcase and wore glasses with a strong black frame and clear lenses.

It was a warm day for late March, spring-like but not fragrant: too far inland to smell the sea. There was something man-made in the air; a vaguely unpleasant chemical aroma.

Stemper found the building. Having been prepared to bluff his way inside, he was gratified to find the outer door gliding slowly towards the latch as one of the residents entered ahead of him. He caught the door and paused until the resident was out of sight. The communal area was in a poor state of repair, with peeling paintwork and a large stain on the carpet – animal urine, possibly – that should have been cleaned with stronger detergent.

He made his way to number six: treading lightly, because footsteps reverberate. Reaching the door, he was unfazed by the existence of a peephole. The glasses were the crucial detail. People instinctively discounted the threat of violence from a man wearing glasses.

He listened for evidence of movement. She might not be alone, but he could deal with that. If she was out, he'd have to consider a visit to her workplace, which would require a more delicate approach.

He knocked and waited, not looking directly at the peephole. He heard a bolt being drawn back and the door was opened by a woman who matched Jerry's description: young, pale, heavyset and miserable. She wore a big shapeless sweater that hung to her knees, and black tights with a couple of holes at the feet.

She had the sort of face that looked unformed without make-up, like a mask that had been taken too early from its mould. There were fashionable chunks of metal embedded in her skin, and a raw hole in her lip from which a piercing had been removed.

She held an unlit cigarette in one hand, a lighter in the other. Her expression was devoid of fear or curiosity.

'I'm from the managing agents,' Stemper said, angling his body so that she automatically matched him, turning sideways and opening a gap for him to exploit. 'Safety assessment. Won't take more than two minutes.'

'But haven't they—?'

He was already striding past, the briefcase held up as a barrier between them. It would put her at ease, this unwillingness to risk physical contact.

'I shouldn't be telling you this,' he called as she shut the door behind him. 'We've had problems with the picture windows.'

He'd reached the living room, which was tidier than he had expected, and set the briefcase down.

'I didn't hear about that.'

'Hinges failed. One of your neighbours had a very lucky escape.' He nodded at the doorway behind her. 'Is that your boyfriend or partner?'

She turned to see what had caught his attention. 'There's nobody—'

He moved extraordinarily fast. Partly it was adrenalin, partly practice, but it was also, he liked to think, a natural gift. Stemper had been born a predator.

He took hold of her dominant right arm and grabbed a fistful of hair, pulling her head backwards while he pressed his foot against her knee, urging her body to the floor. A tiny clatter as the lighter slipped from her grasp.

'I won't hurt you, Traci. But you have to cooperate.'

'Who are you?' She didn't quite shriek, but she was too loud. He adjusted his grip on her arm, found the pressure point just above her elbow and gave her a taste of pain.

'Do as I say, Traci. Settle down. Be quiet. Listen.'

This time, there was a squeal of capitulation. He knelt behind her and used one hand to remove his tie, looped it over her head and around her neck: a good makeshift noose.

'Hank O'Brien, you remember him?'

Her body tensed, and she struggled: a sudden fit of panic. He quelled the movement by throttling her for ten seconds, then released the pressure.

'A friend of yours tried to burgle the house. You're an accessory to that crime.'

'I . . . I dunno what you mean.'

'Traci,' he said quietly, and began to tighten the noose. She gasped, begging him to stop.

'I just mentioned what had happened. I didn't realise he was gonna—'

'I'm not interested. Tuesday night, O'Brien was in the pub with a young woman. How did the fight start?'

'Uh . . . He got lairy with her, I reckon. She hit him, then a couple of guys waded in.'

'Did you know any of them?'

'Apart from Hank, no. That's who the police are searching for. The men, I mean. I think they know who the woman is.'

'Describe her.'

Another quiver of panic. 'Uh, oh God . . . uh, taller than me. Slim. Dark brown hair, shoulder-length. Quite pretty. Good complexion.'

'Age?'

'Thirty-something. She looked . . . serious. She had a suit on. Oh, and this green bracelet. Hermes, I think. I noticed it when I was serving her.'

'Well done. Now tell me about the two men.'

She gave the sort of big heaving sigh that he associated with teenage torpor: *Do I have to?* His response was ten long seconds with the tie pulled savagely tight.

'Both late twenties, maybe. One of them was really hot. He had dark hair, not curly exactly but like wavy. His mate had light brown hair.' Another sigh. 'Look, I did all this with the fucking police. They've done these e-fit things. They'll be on TV.'

'But you saw them in the flesh. You heard their voices. What accents did they have? Common or well-spoken?'

'No accents. They weren't posh or nothing, but not rough. Just normal. Same as you.'

'After they'd broken up the fight, what happened then?'

'The woman left first. She—' Traci stopped abruptly. 'I can't swear to this, but I sort of had the feeling she knew them. The way she spoke to them, especially the fit one. She looked well pissed-off with him.'

'What did the police say about this?'

'I didn't tell 'em. I mean, it's only a guess. And I don't wanna get involved.'

'Did the police mention the woman's name?'

'No. Just said they were gonna ask her to look at the e-fits. I've got no idea who she is, honest.'

Stemper said nothing. His hand twitched, eager to go back to work.

Flinching, she said, 'There's something else. The money.'

'Yes?'

'The farmer that discovered the body, he reckons the next day he was walking his dog and he saw this envelope in the field, right? With *three grand* in cash.' True amazement in her voice, as though this represented unimaginable wealth.

'He found it the following day? Wednesday morning?'

'No. That's what's so weird. He found it on Thursday, after the cops had searched. In the pub last night he was really freaking out. The cops were saying he must have took it when he found the body, but chickened out and put it back. Only he swears he didn't.'

'What do you think?'

'He wouldn't have the balls to lie to them. He's so straight, he goes to church and everything.'

Stemper smiled. He couldn't claim to know what this meant, but it felt like a major step forward.

Forty-four

At lunchtime Dan knew he had to escape the stifling atmosphere of the shop. He walked along to the Sainsbury's on the Lewes Road gyratory, reflecting on the fact that the air around him was probably richer with exhaust fumes than it was with oxygen.

But it was a pleasant enough day, and the walk and the solitude were beneficial to his mood. He bought a sandwich and strolled back, crossing the road to avoid directly passing the shop, then made for the Level, a large communal space with a children's playground and a skatepark. There were avenues lined with elm trees, and a patch of open ground which often played host to travelling funfairs.

He found an unoccupied bench and sat down. While he ate his sandwich he tried to let his mind go blank, as if his worries might float away like untethered balloons. Little hope of that, but perhaps it brought his blood pressure down by a point or two.

He'd rung Hayley a couple more times and had no response. He was reluctant to leave a message, since almost every communication between them seemed to go wrong. Now he tried again, and when it tripped over to voicemail he said, 'Hayley, I hear you're not well. I hope it isn't too serious. Call me, please, because we need to talk.'

She must have been screening her calls, for she rang back immediately.

'How are you?' he asked.

'Not great. Hardly surprising, really.'

Dan decided not to comment. 'Take it easy today, then.'

'I am. That's why I wasn't answering the phone. But I'm glad to hear what you said.'

'Well, this week's been weird. We keep falling out for no reason . . .'

'No reason? Come on. Your message said we need to talk, so let's talk. What did you do last night?'

'Hayley—'

'It's a simple enough question. Did you stay in? Go out? What?'

'I had a drink with Robbie.'

'Oh, *Robbie*.' Her voice was loaded with sarcasm. 'You two are inseparable at the moment, aren't you?'

'Look, I rang to see if you were okay. What is it, a bug? Something you ate?'

'Maybe. Or maybe it's how my body's reacting to emotional stress.'

'Hayley, I don't understand—'

'I just want the truth. Stop lying to me, Daniel. I'm not a fool, and I won't be treated like this.' She cut the call on a sob of despair.

But Dan was nothing if not a masochist, so on the walk back to work he called Robbie.

'With a client. Ring you back in two secs.' Piling shock upon shock, Robbie was true to his word. 'You done anything about that makeover yet? Before the e-fits come out.'

'No,' Dan said. 'But Cate's tried to have them changed to look less like us.'

'Yeah, she told me. Smart cookie, my big sis.'

'She is, and she's really gone out on a limb for us. You can't afford to keep upsetting her.'

'Ah, it's just sibling stuff.' A sly smile in his voice. 'How was little Louis this morning?'

'Suffering. And it serves him right.'

'A man after my own heart,' Robbie declared. 'Anyway, I was gonna call you. Guess who's after my services? Only the delightful Mrs Cheryl Wilson . . .'

'Who on Earth is she?'

'Cheryl Wilson, *née* O'Brien. Sister to the late unlucky Hank.'

Dan was crossing a road; he stumbled on the kerb and nearly fell back into the traffic. 'What are you on about?'

'She wants me to rent out the farmhouse.'

'Tell me you turned her down.'

Robbie's laughter sounded distant, as though he'd moved the phone away from his ear in anticipation of Dan's outrage. But Dan was too shocked, too weary to shout.

'Oh, Robbie . . .'

'What reason did I have to refuse? Chances are, she knows nothing about the film company or the deal I did with Hank. She found the paperwork from last time and thought we'd be the obvious choice.'

'But what if she *does* hear about the deal? Surely the police will mention it when they explain where he was the night he died?'

From the way Robbie sniffed, Dan had the impression that this hadn't occurred to him.

'I'll deal with that if it arises.'

'You're playing with fire, Robbie.'

'Maybe, but I'd still argue it would look more suspicious if I'd said no. The cops could well make something of that.'

Dan sighed. 'It isn't just the police. There's the man who jumped out on us the other night.'

'What about him?'

'If he's trying to find out who killed Hank, don't you think he might be watching the farmhouse?'

Robbie was in Preston Park Avenue, having visited a tenant whose boiler was playing up. He'd expected Dan to go apeshit about taking on the farmhouse, and felt almost let down by this subdued reaction.

A good point about the mystery photographer, though. Robbie should have thought of that himself.

'I can't really see it,' he said. 'Does make you wonder what sort of things Hank was up to, though.'

'I don't want to speculate.'

'No? Well, I think there's something to be said for knowing your enemy.' Before Dan could give him grief, he said, 'Your car. I should be able to sort it this weekend.'

'You've found a repairer?'

'Ah, well, I've come up with a contingency plan.'

He was saved from further interrogation by the news that Dan was back at work, with Willie Denham in the vicinity.

'That senile old git?' Robbie joked. 'I'd swap my boss for yours any day of the week.'

Ending the call, he pondered for a while. It seemed to him that there were all kinds of opportunities opening up here. Sure, he'd have to be careful, but he had no shortage of confidence in his own abilities.

Keeping those plates spinning; it was what Robbie excelled at. Cate, Bree, Hank's sister . . .

And Mr X, the mystery photographer.

Everyone had something to hide: experience had taught Robbie that. So what were *Hank's* little secrets?

Forty-five

Their day began badly, as Gordon had feared it would; and then grew steadily worse.

It promised to be a long and gruelling job, reviewing the contents of the hard drive that had extracted the guts from Hank O'Brien's computer. Gordon insisted they take a proper break for lunch: to hell with time constraints.

First there was a call from Stemper, checking that Jerry had delivered the hard drive. He also added some detail to Jerry's barely credible account of the break-in.

'Thank God they were there to stop it,' Gordon said afterwards. But Patricia was in no mood to be reassured.

Jerry Conlon delivered the next blow. 'Don't blame the messenger, but access to the house just got tricky. This woman's turned up in a Lexus. I reckon it's Hank's sister.'

To Gordon's relief, Patricia greeted this news with equanimity.

'That had to be expected. I'm sure Stemper will have another chance to go in soon.'

'But if she hangs around . . . do we approach her?'

'As a last resort. Not if we can avoid it.'

The Blakes had encountered the sister only once, at a party thrown by O'Brien to celebrate his divorce. Gordon remembered a handsome, forthright woman, a little too similar to Patricia in both manner and appearance to be of much interest to him.

Patricia, needless to say, had loathed her on sight.

Back to the computers. Gordon was reviewing the files recovered from Hank's spare laptop. It was mostly porn.

Jerry's warning about the nature of the material had made him sound laughably prim. *Don't tell me you've never watched the sick stuff*, Gordon had thought – but hadn't quite dared to say.

Watching it cold wasn't much fun, although inevitably there were one or two moments that produced an involuntary response. Nothing he could do to ease the pressure when he had Patricia sitting opposite him. There was no hope of persuading her to take a break and retire to the bedroom: not in the midst of a crisis. Not in daylight.

Instead, Gordon had to file away a few beguiling moves for re-enactment on his next visit to Alexia, a high-class escort based in Kingston-upon-Thames. Over the years he'd auditioned a wide selection of female talent, gradually reducing them in number in the manner of those Simon Cowell TV shows, and Alexia had emerged the winner.

The X factor, indeed.

He finished with the porn, deleted it with a military-grade destruction program, and was making a fresh pot of coffee when Stemper phoned with a positive report.

'There's no wider conspiracy. The barmaid has confirmed the burglar's story. He's strictly small-time, an opportunist.'

'Any danger to us, going forward?' Gordon asked.

'I don't believe so. Neither of them wants anything else to do with this. Or with me,' he added.

Patricia took her coffee from Gordon and cupped it in both hands, smiling into the steam as it warmed her face. 'That's a marvellous relief.'

'In fact, Patricia, last night's intervention proved a godsend. The barmaid had some very interesting news.'

'She was willing to cooperate, then?'

Stemper chuckled. 'Let us say she was quickly convinced. As you'd expect from the company she keeps, she's no ally of the police. She held back from them a very significant point.'

'Go on.' Patricia flashed a look at Gordon: *This is more like it.*

'She thinks the woman with your chap may have known the men who broke up the fight.'

'Accomplices,' Patricia murmured. 'But *why* terminate him in the way they did?'

'I'll find out. I have basic descriptions of all three, and I'd venture that the men in the pub were the same pair in the BMW.'

'If only that photo had been clearer,' Gordon said.

'It was a setback, but I do have some clues as to what the men were doing there.'

'Oh, really?' Patricia was so thrilled that she overlooked the sound of Gordon slurping his coffee.

'It's no more than a theory at present. One question, though. Do you know where your man was based during the summer and autumn of 2010?'

Patricia flapped her hand at Gordon, who called up the Microsoft Project document that detailed – in code – Hank's movements, object-ives and results.

'Travelling far and wide. In fact, the whole year he was barely in the UK for more than a week at a time, and he stayed in a London hotel.'

'Not at the farmhouse?'

'No. He'd put it on the rental market following his divorce.'

A brief silence. Somehow they both understood that it boded well, for once.

'Does that help?' Patricia asked.

'Absolutely,' Stemper said. 'Remember to watch the film. Before tonight, if you can.'

'We've not forgotten,' Gordon told him. And when the call had ended, he said crossly: 'I do resent the way he doles out orders. As if we have nothing better to do than lounge in front of the TV.'

Patricia was unmoved. 'As far as I'm concerned, he's earned the right. He gets results.' Then an excited smile. 'Something's put a spring in his step.'

Gordon shuddered. He doubted that Patricia had given much thought to the methods that Stemper might have employed to extract information from the barmaid. The girl, as pictured in Gordon's imagination, was a sweet vulnerable little bird, terrified by Stemper's raptor-like demeanour.

'Whatever the reason,' he said, 'in my book it fully justifies a proper lunch.'

Patricia pursed her lips, but he added sternly, 'No arguments. Love, honour and *obey*, remember?'

He drove them into Dorking, to a charming Italian restaurant where the management knew them well. The food was simple, unpretentious; perfect for a not-too-heavy lunch.

As they sat down, Gordon surveyed the diners at surrounding tables and was struck by how similar everyone looked: nearly all couples, nearly all in late middle age and sleekly prosperous. *We're the golden generation*, he thought. *The last of the lucky baby boomers*.

It prompted a plaintive question: when will it be *my* time to relax? With Patricia so driven to succeed, he found it hard to imagine being granted a life of unlimited leisure. As became clear during the meal, her ambitions were undiminished by the dreadful setbacks this week.

'It's the children I feel for. If somebody else has appropriated our scheme, you can bet they won't have our good intentions at heart.'

Gordon, who'd taken to researching yachts in the three-to-six-million price bracket, swallowed a mouthful of fettuccine and said, 'I know. It was a fabulous idea.'

'And so it remains. We made a pledge, Gordon. A promise to

ourselves. And if we don't find a way to see this through . . .' He was greeted by the remarkable sight of a tear rolling down her cheek. 'We can't fail them. We simply can't.'

'I know. But if Stemper's right, and these three were working together in the pub, it occurs to me that they were planning something else. What the Americans call a shakedown.'

Patricia frowned. There was a dab of cheese sauce on her lip. Fifteen – perhaps even ten – years ago, Gordon could have kissed it away without fear of censure.

'Explain,' she said.

'We know he was a randy bugger. Maybe they'd set him up to allege sexual assault, then blackmail him.'

'So why kill him?'

Gordon threw up his hands. 'That's what makes no sense. Unless that was never their intention. Perhaps something went wrong.'

'Then we're back to square one. The fact is, we still have no clear idea what's going on.'

'I'm sorry. Just thinking aloud.' Gordon took another mouthful of his delicious pasta. Looking around at all the silver hair, the pearls, the golfing attire, he doubted that any of the other patrons were having a conversation quite like this one.

Patricia was studying her phone: a text had come in.

'Templeton's on his way to New York. All still on track, according to our man in Delaware.' She stared at Gordon, suddenly animated. 'Maybe this isn't about us, or Templeton Wynne. What if it's the American angle? A disgruntled shareholder, or even a rival bidder . . .?'

Gordon shook his head. 'There are easier ways of sabotaging the deal than this.' He went to take a final sip of wine and found the glass was empty. 'Now, I know we said only a single drink . . .'

'No. We need to return to work. Any more wine and we'll be dozing off mid-afternoon.'

Reluctantly Gordon agreed. The job of reviewing the hard drives was soporific enough on its own.

The next stop was W.H. Smith to purchase the DVD of *Entwined*. Patricia studied the case and said, 'Looks like utter pap.'

'That will get us dozing, I bet.' They walked on, and Gordon was struck by a fanciful thought. 'Could Hank have been caught in a background shot, perhaps when he was with someone he shouldn't be—?'

'Oh, Gordon,' Patricia said. 'That sounds like the plot of a movie itself. A bad one.'

Back home, they spent an hour reviewing the hard drive, scanning through dozens of dreary emails, before accepting that they were beginning to wilt. Gordon made non-alcoholic fruit cocktails as a pick-me-up, and then they retired to the living room and slipped the DVD into the player.

Jerry called when they were about twenty minutes in. Hank's sister was still at the farmhouse, and there were other visitors.

'Two geezers turned up in a van. They're loading up all the stuff from Hank's filing cabinet. They took his laptop and the PC as well.'

'Templeton's people,' Patricia decided. 'Are you sure you found nothing incriminating?'

'No. Everything they've got is clean.'

'Then it's no cause for alarm.'

When she'd put the phone down, Gordon said: 'Quick off the mark, isn't it?'

'Understandable. Hank did have access to sensitive data.'

'Funny that the sister was so eager to oblige them.'

'Why should she care?' Patricia sighed. 'We *have* to find those documents.'

Gordon said nothing. He leaned forward, almost toppling off the sofa. As Patricia spoke his name he raised his arm, jerkily, like a marionette, indicating the screen.

'Gordon, what's wrong?'

'There!' He fumbled for the remote control, found the pause button, took it back a few frames. 'Look at that.'

Patricia said nothing. Then gasped. Then gestured at him to pause and rewind again.

In a rather ungainly manoeuvre for a woman of her age and build, she moved on to her hands and knees and crawled up to the TV. Gordon tried to ignore the stirring he felt at the sight of her generous backside.

'Is that where I think it is?' he said.

'Yes, it is,' Patricia growled. 'Get that bloody man Conlon on the phone.'

Forty-six

On Friday night Joan had a get-together with her library book group. She'd been going for a couple of years, and through it she had befriended a more recent member, Ron, a widowed retiree in his mid-sixties.

Joan, who had lost her own husband to a heart attack nearly two decades ago, insisted that a romance was out of the question. That didn't stop Louis and Dan from indulging in some good-natured teasing, if only to encourage her that the possibility still existed.

'I'm too old,' Joan had protested, and when Dan had demolished that argument, she had an admission: 'If you want the truth, it frightens me. I've been on my own so long.'

'I understand that, but you'd adjust to it.'

She pulled a face. 'Then there's you two to think of, don't forget.'

'We're fine. Anyway, we'll be off your hands before—'

He realised his mistake when he saw the panic dart across her face. They both smiled and pretended it hadn't been there.

'Ron was dropping hints about a new film coming out,' she confided. 'He told me he's signed up to that Orange Wednesday thing.'

'If he asks you, I want you to say yes.'

'I don't know.' Joan sighed, her gaze growing distant. 'Though it is one I'd quite like to see . . .'

* * *

Dan had texted Hayley, offering to visit her after work. He did so knowing he'd have to take a bus to Newhaven and find a good excuse not to have driven. But Hayley said there was no point. She was still feeling lousy and intended to sleep through the evening.

For once it appeared that Louis wasn't going out. He was ensconced in his bedroom, his music thudding through the ceiling – music that, in most cases, Dan had introduced and recommended to his kid brother: Kings of Leon, Tribes, Arcade Fire.

At around eight o'clock Dan trooped upstairs and knocked on the door. The music abruptly paused.

'What?'

'I'm going to do myself a pizza. Do you want one?'

'No.'

'Sure?'

'Yes.'

Dan sighed. He hated these situations, condemning him to the role of disapproving father figure.

'Come on, Louis. You must be hungry—'

'I don't want anything. Leave me alone, okay?'

The music snapped back on, making further conversation impossible.

Dan heated up a pepperoni pizza. An evening of inane TV beckoned, with beer to blunt the tedium. Earlier he'd caught news bulletins on all the main channels and he'd checked the *Argus* website several times, but there was nothing more on the hit-and-run. No sign of the e-fits, either. Dan wondered if that was because of the amendments suggested by Cate.

He thought about calling her, not to invite her out but just to see how she was. Or maybe he could raise the idea of meeting up for a drink. As far as he knew, she was still single following her split from Martin Gilroy.

Dan had always regarded her ex-husband as a bit of a dickhead, though he'd put that down, in part, to his own jealousy. He had never quite recovered from his adolescent crush on Cate. It mystified him now that she hadn't met someone else. She must be able to take her pick of men.

For a while he sat holding his phone with Cate's number up on the display. One touch away from making contact. It was a pleasant daydream for as long as he could sustain the illusion that he might actually do it; then a longer period of low-level torment once he'd decided that he would not.

There were plenty of sound reasons why he shouldn't. She might assume he was willing to cheat on Hayley – and she was bound to take a dim view of that, given Martin's infidelity.

Then there were the lies, the deceit he would have to maintain no matter how much she challenged him. Because Robbie had been right about one thing: for her own sake, it was essential to keep Cate in the dark about Hank O'Brien's death.

Louis's music was still thumping away. Dan had another beer and watched some of the comedy shows that he normally enjoyed, but the jokes went right over his head. Had anything really made him laugh since Tuesday night? He didn't think so.

Growing maudlin, and reluctant for once to fight it, he fetched a photo album from the dining room. Handling it as he would high explosives, he rested it gently on the coffee table and sat back at a safe distance before flipping the cover open.

It had been many months since he'd looked at these pictures. Most were of his parents in the early days of their marriage: pre-children, or with Dan as an infant. He was shocked to discover how little emotion they stirred. He did not recognise this smiling couple, younger here than Dan was now. The baby they held in their arms could have been any baby.

Over time the photos were losing their power to hurt. Dan couldn't connect to these images – or, rather, to the memories that the images were supposed to nourish. When he tried to recreate important moments he found that his imagination was filling the gaps. His past was becoming fictionalised, to the point where, ten or fifteen years from now, he wondered if he would look back on the events of Tuesday night and find it impossible to believe he had ever been complicit in a fatal road accident.

He closed the album. There were other reliable aids to his memory, of course. For years after his parents' deaths Dan had insisted that Joan use the same washing powder and fabric conditioner. The scent of a freshly laundered shirt or duvet cover could enable him to create, if only for an instant, the illusion that he was still a child, with a mother and father who would always keep him safe, protect him from the world and the monsters that lurked in the dark.

For the same reason he sometimes drank his dad's favourite soft drink, Dandelion & Burdock, even though he'd never liked the taste. He sought out reruns of *Blind Date* and *Only Fools and Horses* on obscure TV channels, because those were shows he'd watched with Mum and Dad.

He remembered the troubling cocktail of jealousy and pride when his brother was born. Showing Louis off to his mates, and even, on one occasion, changing his nappy in front of them, to sniggers and noisy derision that masked a grudging respect. This was so far removed from the experience of most twelve-year-old boys that none of them could decide whether it was 'cool' or not.

Then he recalled an evening when his exhausted mother had spotted the symptoms of an irrational but very real sense of abandonment. Leaving Louis to cry for a few seconds, she had taken Dan in her arms, nuzzled her face against his and told him, confidentially: 'You'll always be my big grown-up boy, Daniel. My hero.'

And now that hero was wondering how long it would take for time to erase the knowledge that he had killed a man.

Forty-seven

Jerry arrived at the Blakes in a sour mood. Once again he'd been up at the crack of dawn to get to Sussex. His miserly employees wouldn't stump up for a hotel, which meant he was spending half his life on the choked-up roads of the South-East. He was going through a small fortune in petrol, and they had the cheek to be funny about it. Wanting to see receipts, as though the price of fuel had passed them by.

Then there was the logistical headache posed by keeping the farmhouse under surveillance when it was on its own at the end of a private lane. Jerry had no choice but to leave the car nearly a mile away, then walk along a succession of muddy, dogshit-splattered footpaths until he found a spot that allowed him a glimpse of O'Brien's property.

In the afternoon he'd just informed the Blakes about Templeton's people clearing the house when Gordon called and demanded an urgent meeting. Jerry was buggered if he was going to drive up there, only to be sent back to Sussex afterwards, so he insisted that he needed to stay and monitor developments for another couple of hours.

Jerry couldn't fathom the Blakes: one minute harassing him to keep a closer eye on the place; the next trying to drag him away. They were pushing their luck, that was for sure.

It was the issue of money that rankled the most. His thirty grand a year didn't seem so generous now he knew they'd been angling for fifty frigging million. He wondered how much of that would have come his way, had they managed to pull it off.

'Sod all,' he kept muttering. 'Not a bloody nickel.'

In the end he rolled up at the Blakes' place around seven, having stopped off at a Harvester pub and treated himself to a steak. Determined not to be hurried, he'd ignored their texts and calls.

The atmosphere was every bit as unwelcoming as he'd expected. As he stepped into the house Patricia remained in the hall, barring his way.

'Where have you been?' she said.

'Bad traffic.'

Patricia gave a dismissive snort: clearly he was supposed to find a way to float above the gridlock. 'And is there anything more to report?'

Jerry didn't care for her tone. It sounded like she knew full well that there was.

'The sister had a glazier round this afternoon.'

'Making good after the burglary,' Gordon commented. If that was intended to mollify his wife, it failed badly.

'So what's up?' Jerry asked, thinking: *I've had just about as much as I can take from you, lady . . .*

Patricia waved towards an open door. 'This.'

He walked into a living room that he hadn't been privileged to enter before now. It was cluttered with antique furniture and made gloomy by heavy maroon wallpaper. There was a TV stuck on freeze frame, the image shivering in the corners as if impatient to move on. A DVD box lay on the floor: *Entwined*.

Gordon, who for some reason was chewing on the arm of Patricia's reading glasses, indicated the screen. 'Recognise this?'

Jerry crouched down. The man in the shot was familiar: not a bad actor. And the woman was a looker, but she—

'Bloody hell.' Jerry stared in disbelief at the room in which the actors were cavorting.

Gordon said, 'We've only been there once, a few years ago. But it looks familiar.'

'It's the farmhouse, definitely.' Jerry's voice was calm enough, but inside he was thinking: *Ohhh shit . . .*

Patricia regarded him severely. 'It's a forlorn hope, I suppose, to ask whether you can make any sense of this?'

'Nope. I'm as much in the dark as you are.'

'But you were paid, Jerry – handsomely paid – to keep tabs on him. As well as your role of intermediary, you were supposed to befriend him, become his trusted confidant.'

'And I did. But I also took your advice that I mustn't make him suspicious. "Don't live in his pocket. Don't make him uneasy." Remember?'

Gordon nodded, shamefaced. 'That's true.'

'And while we're on the subject of money, I wouldn't call it all that "handsome", given some of the crap coming my way.'

Patricia made a spluttering noise, as though her outrage couldn't be funnelled into mere words. Gordon stepped between them, appealing for peace.

'Rather than fall out, let's focus on the issues here.'

'I wish we could.' Patricia snatched the glasses from Gordon's hand. 'But with each development we seem to understand less, not more.'

'Darling, to be fair, this is such a bizarre sequence of events . . .'

Jerry found himself tempted to slip away. As he took a step back Patricia brought her fearsome gaze to bear, jabbing the arm of her glasses in his direction.

'Three days, and all we've had is more questions. More uncertainty. We need *answers*.'

'I can't magic up a solution out of thin air.'

'Then I seriously have to wonder what use you are to us.'

'Fair enough. I'll walk,' Jerry said, hating the petulant tone that always crept into his voice during confrontations. 'But you'll have to make it worth my while to keep my mouth shut.'

A stunned silence. From outside, they heard the rumble of a car engine.

'Are you threatening us, Jerry?' Patricia asked quietly.

He shrugged. He'd been rehearsing an exchange of this nature for most of the afternoon, but now all the clever retorts had deserted him.

Ever the smarmy diplomat, Gordon said, 'Stemper's here. Can I suggest we park this issue for the time being?'

Forty-eight

Nobody had to spell it out: Cate knew what a dismal picture it painted of her life, pushing a trolley round Sainsbury's at seven o'clock on a Friday evening. And not one of the big trolleys, either – which made it all the more obvious that she was shopping for one.

Might just as well write 'saddo' on my forehead . . .

She couldn't remember when she'd last done anything remotely exciting on a Friday, let alone had a hot date. And after this she was going to drive home, put the shopping away, eat a low-fat curry and probably drink the best part of a bottle of Pinot, while telling herself there was really nowhere else she'd rather be than here, on her sofa, watching a DVD.

At least, as it turned out, that was what she *should* have done.

It was an act of lunacy, but at the time it seemed harmless enough. Leaving the supermarket, she let the Audi drift towards the right-hand lane rather than the left.

The house was in Mile Oak, on one of the many new estates that had sprouted up in recent years. The road layout was confusing. A couple of times she was flashed by the car behind when she slowed to read the road signs.

'What am I doing?' Cate said aloud. But the answer was only too clear. She was picking at a scab. The pain Martin had caused her on Tuesday wasn't quite sharp enough to satisfy, or intense enough for her immune system to kick in and heal her. Deep down she understood that she had to feel worse before she could feel better.

She found the address at last, within a cul-de-sac that had only a fraction of the space it needed for parking. It meant that after turning she had nowhere to pull in, but that was fine. She didn't intend to be here for long.

The house that Martin and Janine shared looked impossibly small to contain the three bedrooms which Martin claimed it had. The garden, if they had one at all, must be about the size of a tablecloth. No space for a child to run and play; no room to frolic or gambol or whatever it was you did when you had gorgeous little sprogs and life was perfect.

Although it wasn't fully dark, there were lights on in almost every room. Martin wouldn't like that at all, even if they were energy-saving bulbs. Or maybe Janine was such an enthusiastic provider of oral gratification that Martin had learned to overlook the occasional bad habit?

'God, I'm being a bitch,' she muttered. And she was talking to herself again. 'You're a spiteful cow, Caitlin Scott. And probably going loopy as well.'

No, this was just displacement activity. For the energy-squandering inhabitants of the house had neglected to close their curtains, and as a result Cate was able to see that the bedroom in the top left corner had already been decorated and equipped for its new purpose. It was a nursery, with bright mauve walls and a multicoloured lampshade, and some kind of mobile dangling below the light, a draught causing its shadows to dance and sway.

Cate's imagination did the rest, adding the crib and the cushions and the cuddly toys. A beautifully crafted bookcase filled with all the stories that had enchanted her as a child. The room would have its own special smell, too, of warmth and milk and a mother's love—

'Go!' she cried, and thumped herself on the thigh. 'You pathetic woman.'

Home was still home, but now it felt cold, spare, brittle. Too silent. Before she put the shopping away – before she unpacked, even – Cate drew the last of the wine from the fridge and poured it brimful into a glass. Found a new bottle and placed it in the freezer to cool quickly. This was an emergency, after all.

She was tempted not to eat, but some degree of good sense prevailed. While the meal heated up, she put the shopping away and recounted all the reasons she had to be grateful that she was single, and free – if not exactly young any more.

The curry, it turned out, was indifferent. As a result, when the doorbell rang she wasn't quite as inclined to ignore it and go on eating. Setting the plate down, Cate had a flashback to Tuesday night, the broken wine glass. Perhaps it was female intuition.

Martin was calling her name. He sounded in good spirits; it was more like a serenade than his usual whinge.

But she kept the security chain on. Opened the door and the first thing she saw were flowers. From Sainsbury's: she recognised the wrapping. He was clutching them to his chest, but there was also a bottle of wine in his hand.

That voice in her head said: *See? Be careful what you wish for.*

He greeted her, but didn't ask to be let in, which was as close as Martin came to reverse psychology. Cate slipped off the chain and opened the door. He was grinning like an imbecile. Dressed in newly pressed jeans and a grey shirt with a button-down collar. And he'd overdone the aftershave somewhat. Diesel, she thought it was.

She gestured at the flowers. 'What's this?'

'For you.' He thrust them forward. 'I hope you have a spare vase.'

'Pardon?' Now that he was inside, she had little option but to let him through to the kitchen. She shut the front door and heard a clunk as he put the bottle on the unit.

'Do you have a drink on the go?'

'Yes.'

He was opening cupboards. 'Of course, you're one glass short. Sorry about that. Bloody clumsy of me.'

Next the kitchen drawers, searching for a bottle opener. Cate stood in the doorway and crossed her arms.

'Sorry, Martin. Have I missed something?'

He turned, smiling easily. 'What do you mean?'

'Well, this feels like one of those TV shows where the character falls into a coma for a couple of years, then waltzes in one day as though nothing has happened.'

A tiny frown restored his features to those of an ageing, harassed father-to-be. He indicated the bottle.

'Want a top-up? I need to get one in me quick.' He snorted. 'Dutch courage, I suppose. Isn't that ridiculous, with my own wife?'

'Martin, I'm not your wife any more. We're divorced, remember?'

'How could I forget? But it was a mistake. We both know that now.'

Cate shook her head. 'What are you doing here?'

'Oh, don't give me that.' Martin opened his hands, appealing for reason to prevail. 'I saw you earlier.'

'What?' Cate wanted to sound mystified, but she could feel herself blushing.

'I'm so glad I happened to look out. It's just like when you caught me this morning. We're being drawn to each other.'

'No, I wasn't . . .' She laid the flowers on the worktop. 'I wasn't there because of that.'

'Cate, it's a cul-de-sac. Why else would you be there?'

She bent her head and rested it against the door frame. Then heard him coming towards her, eager to exploit the vulnerability she was displaying. She quickly straightened up.

'Martin, please. Don't push me to explain.'

'I have to, because otherwise you won't admit it to yourself.'

'No. You're imagining things. Look, I'm sorry to be blunt, but I don't love you any more. Coming here with flowers and wine . . . Two, three years ago, I'd have been thrilled by that kind of attention from you.'

'You were parked up outside my house, for Pete's sake.'

He took a step towards her. She retreated a step, into the hall.

'Listen to me, please. I have no desire to get back with you. Your future is with Janine, and your baby.'

His lip curled into a sneer. 'So that's what it is? You're jealous.' Then he saw his error, made an effort to be conciliatory again. 'Don't you see what I was getting at the other night? I *would* have a kid with you now. I'll prove it.' He nodded at the ceiling. 'Let's go and get started, right this minute. No protection.'

She was stunned. 'Martin . . .'

'Come on, we can take the wine with us.' He pursed his lips. 'You can't still be on the pill, surely?'

Cate stepped back again, winded; the words tumbled out: 'Oh, you bastard . . .'

'Well, come on. It's not like you're getting any action.' He advanced and now she was against the wall. She saw his hand creeping towards her and batted it away.

'Don't touch me! Don't you lay a finger on me.'

'How dare you! Are you saying I'm gonna . . .?'

'I'm warning you, that's all. And I'm asking you to leave. Please, Martin.'

'Or what?' he snarled. 'You're practically accusing me of rape. Are you gonna go sobbing to your little detective friend and make up a load of allegations against me?'

✳   ✳   ✳

He was looming over her, so close that there were flecks of his spittle landing on her cheeks. Cate felt paralysed, as if the mere mention of the word 'rape' had been enough to scramble her nervous system.

'All that bullshit this morning,' Martin said. 'You are screwing him, aren't you? Does he know you're desperate to have a kid?' He thumped the wall above her head, and it seemed to shudder against her. She let out a yelp.

'If you don't go now, I'm calling 999.'

'I make you a bloody good offer and you turn me down flat. And yet you'll go and use that cop as a sperm donor. To think you had the cheek to call Janine a slag—'

She slapped his face. Martin recoiled, but at the same time he drew back his fist. Visions of the fight with Hank O'Brien ran through Cate's mind as she ducked low and squeezed through the gap between him and the door frame. Into the kitchen, she dashed for the far counter, grabbed his bottle of wine and turned, gripping it by the neck.

'Get out of here!' she screamed. 'You take one step towards me and I'll kill you.'

He didn't move. Dropping his hands, he regarded her with contempt.

'You're a lunatic. A prick-teasing little whore who belongs in the nuthouse, and one day that's where you're gonna end up.'

He stormed out, slamming the door hard enough to shake the house. Cate managed to put the bottle down safely, then sank to the floor, drew her knees up to her chin and wept.

Forty-nine

Gordon could see how close to meltdown Patricia had come. Stemper's arrival meant the explosion had been delayed, not avoided altogether.

She went to greet Stemper herself, leaving Jerry and Gordon to share an awkward silence. When Patricia returned, Gordon had the impression that she'd been discussing the outburst. The manner in which Stemper's gaze settled on Jerry Conlon brought to mind an undertaker sizing up a body.

They replayed the relevant scene from the movie, and Gordon felt a sense of anticlimax when Stemper failed to exhibit any real surprise. Instead he looked smugly content.

Patricia summarised the day's events: the hard drives had yielded nothing of interest, and O'Brien's sister had taken up what was hoped to be only temporary residence at the farmhouse, where she had overseen repairs to the broken window, as well as the removal of Hank's paperwork.

Then, eyes twinkling, she said, 'I have to confess, I was mystified when you asked about Hank's living arrangements. I take it you already had your suspicions about the film?'

'I merely thought it should be followed up, given the enquiries that Hank had made a few weeks ago.'

Stemper hesitated, as if from what he'd said only a moron could fail to comprehend the situation. In that respect, Gordon knew he would have to fall on his sword.

'Well, I'm still baffled. We keep glimpsing this enormous canvas, but with each sight the picture looks bigger and more confusing than before.'

There was a disparaging snort from Jerry. But Stemper inclined his head and said, 'Eloquently put. In my view, what explains it best is that there isn't one canvas out there in the dark, but two.'

Patricia was the first to grasp his meaning. 'So Hank's death is nothing to do with our scheme?'

'Exactly. That's the good news. The bad news is that I do believe there's another conspiracy, and the movie lies at the heart of it. The farmhouse was used for filming at a time when O'Brien was living elsewhere. Now, his attempt to trace the location manager was made shortly after his return from Japan.'

'Is that relevant?' Patricia said. 'The trip was to a Templeton subsidiary.'

'It *is* relevant, but not in that way. I made some enquiries this afternoon. *Entwined* was part of the in-flight entertainment – if we can assume that Hank flew British Airways?'

'Probably. We can check.'

'So you think that's when he saw the film?' Gordon said.

As Stemper nodded, Jerry clicked his fingers together. 'He was in a steaming mood, you remember?'

'And threatening to change the alarm code,' Stemper said. 'A natural reaction to what he no doubt saw as a violation of his property.'

'Because the house had been used without his permission?' Patricia looked stunned. 'Is this what it's all about?'

'I can't say for sure. But I intend to find out.'

They moved on to the events of Tuesday night. Stemper described the barmaid's claim of a connection between the woman and the men who'd assisted her. He wanted Jerry to verify whether her descriptions matched that of the men in the BMW.

'I had no way of seeing their faces, but sounds like it could be.' Jerry sniffed, rubbing his nose back and forth. 'So how'd you link 'em to the film?'

'Something else I learned from Traci. There was a sum of money found at the accident site, by the same man who discovered the body. A local farmer.'

That had everyone sitting up. Gordon saw how much Stemper enjoyed having them spellbound. A deep vanity lurked inside the man along with God only knew what else.

It was Jerry who dared to break the mood. 'That Traci seemed pretty flaky to me. You sure she's not spinning you a line?'

His gaze pitiless, Stemper said, 'She wouldn't lie to me, Jerry.'

The temperature in the room dropped several degrees. Jerry looked away, and Stemper said, 'The farmer didn't find the money until Thursday morning. And yet the police were at the site all day Wednesday.'

'So this was Hank's money?' Patricia queried. 'How much?'

'Three thousand pounds. One theory is that the farmer stole it when he found the body, then had an attack of conscience. However, Traci doesn't feel he's the sort.'

'And is that what the two blokes were doing there when I saw 'em?' Jerry broke in. 'Searching for the cash?'

Slowly, as if addressing an imbecile, Stemper said, 'No. I think they *returned* the money.'

Patricia shook her head. 'Hold on. Where do we think this money originated? If Hank was passing out envelopes full of cash . . .'

Gordon met her eye, nodding at the implications. But he thought he'd seen what Stemper was getting at.

'Maybe they took the money from Hank, confident that it wouldn't be missed, and then for some reason changed their mind.'

'Yes, Gordon. But where did the money come from in the first place?'

Stemper spoke up. 'One possibility is that it was a pay-off to Hank, perhaps related to the movie.'

'Yes.' Gordon realised his right leg was juddering with nervous excitement, and made an effort to control it. 'They paid him in the pub. Then killed him and took the money.'

'It's feasible,' Patricia said. 'But I don't think we should disregard this farmer.'

Stemper urged caution. 'I can approach him, but I suspect he'll be the type whose silence can't be guaranteed. I feel our priority should be the woman. According to Traci, the police know her identity, and yet they've had to issue an appeal for the two men to come forward. Think about that . . .'

Ignoring the patronising tone, Gordon followed the logic. 'Either Traci got it wrong and the woman *didn't* know them . . .'

Patricia leapt in: 'Or she hasn't admitted the connection to the police. She's covering for them.' There was a new fervour in her voice. 'I see it now. This feels . . . right.'

'I agree. So how do we locate her?' Gordon asked.

Stemper said, 'I want to know how the farmhouse came to be used in the movie. You say O'Brien had put the property out to rent?'

'Through a letting agent,' Patricia said. 'In fact, there could be emails about it on his hard drive.'

'Excellent. That would be the place to start.'

To Gordon's dismay, his wife's enthusiasm departed as rapidly as it had appeared.

'Let's remember, this *film* conspiracy is only one half of the equation. Finding the paperwork remains as vital as ever.'

Stemper said, 'And Hank owned no other property at all? That seems unusual for a man of his income.'

'He was cleaned out during the divorce,' Gordon said. 'She got the London apartment, as well as a holiday home in Greece.'

'All he had left was the house in Sussex.' Patricia displayed a flicker of uncertainty. 'At least, that's all we knew about.'

Jerry was suddenly restless: scratching his head, pulling at the crotch of his ghastly skintight jeans. He stood up.

'Time I was going.'

Patricia looked furious. 'Somewhere you have to be?'

'There is, actually. Friday night, I'm taking my wife out for dinner. Hell to pay if I don't.' He chuckled, but he was the only one who did. 'Where do you want me tomorrow? Or don't you?'

Patricia looked at Stemper, then said, 'We'll call you.'

Jerry shrugged. 'I'll see myself out.'

Patricia motioned at Gordon to follow him. It didn't seem necessary, but Gordon did it anyway, hurrying to the hall in time for Jerry to fix him with a morose look.

'Wish I'd never taken this frigging job,' he said, and slammed the front door behind him.

Back in the living room, Patricia was telling Stemper: 'He's moved beyond insolence and into something far more dangerous.'

'The worm is beginning to turn,' Gordon added, trying not to laugh at his own witticism. 'And what we need is an early bird.'

Fifty

Stemper smiled, for the sake of politeness, but he sensed that Gordon was merely playing with words. If there was an instruction to proceed, it had to come from Patricia.

And she knew it. 'Jerry is now a liability. The fact that he would question his remuneration after such a catalogue of failure . . .'

'He was hinting at blackmail,' Gordon added darkly.

'What do you know about his wife?' Stemper asked.

Patricia snorted. 'South-east Asian, a mail-order bride. Some slip of a girl, I expect.'

'No, she's in her late thirties,' Gordon said. 'They've been together a few years. And she's no slip of a girl, believe me.'

'You seem to be very well-informed.'

'Jerry showed me some photos after their holiday in Cyprus. I seem to recall you made an excuse and vanished.'

'I'm sure I did.' She returned her attention to Stemper. 'Will that be a problem?'

'It's an added complication, but by no means insurmountable.' He went quiet for a minute, keen to see if Patricia interpreted his silence correctly. She did.

'With what we're adding to your workload, we'd better take a fresh look at your own remuneration.'

Stemper beamed. 'Very kind. I'm happy to maintain the current rate, but may I suggest a performance bonus? Another fifty thousand when each objective is fulfilled?'

'Sounds most reasonable.' A glance at her husband. 'You're aware of how much is at stake. If you can find a way to salvage our plan, it goes without saying that the reward will be *extremely* generous.'

'I'll give it my utmost. It's unfortunate that last night's search was interrupted. I need an opportunity to explore in daylight.'

'Except now we have Hank's sister to contend with.'

Gordon gave Patricia a sharp look. 'Are you suggesting . . .?'

'No,' she snapped, though Stemper felt sure that she had, for a second, contemplated drastic measures. 'Let's give her a day or two. If she's gone by Monday, that should leave enough time to get back on track.'

'Providing we locate the papers,' Gordon said.

'We will. And we must also find a replacement for Hank.'

'You mean as the front man?' Stemper said. 'I'm afraid I have to rule myself out there.'

'Of course. We wouldn't ask you to expose yourself like that.'

Gordon spotted the double entendre and choked off a snigger, but Patricia was oblivious.

Stemper said, 'Do I take it that, in the original plan, Hank was expendable?'

After a brief hesitation, Gordon nodded furtively, and Patricia said, 'Yes. I suppose he was.'

'Then his replacement needs to be the same. Someone you can burn without too many qualms.'

'I'd dearly love to nominate Jerry, but he doesn't possess the wit.'

'You might as well send a pet monkey to make the demand,' Gordon joked.

The smile was wiped off his face when Patricia said, 'If we recover the paperwork and there are simply no other options, we shall have to do it ourselves.'

*   *   *

The prospect made Gordon feel physically sick. He didn't like Patricia discussing it while Stemper was present, and he didn't like the way Stemper was, as usual, taking note of every word, every reaction, methodically compiling his vast database of malice.

'I'll see if we can find the name of that letting agent,' Gordon said. When he returned with his laptop, Stemper was declining the offer of refreshments. Gordon didn't get the impression that he'd missed anything of importance.

Stemper said, 'This weekend I'll concentrate on finding the woman and her accomplices. I've been wondering how the police knew who she was. Either she came forward after seeing a news report, or more likely they found her through Hank.'

'So we're back to Jerry and his failings,' Patricia grumbled.

It was in Gordon's nature to offer a defence, pointing out that Hank had no doubt put some effort into keeping his activities secret. But it was late, he felt jaded and weary, and he knew that ultimately it wouldn't make a jot of difference. Jerry's fate was already decided.

Stemper said, 'Presumably the prior contact was made by phone. A pity that Hank's mobile will be beyond our reach for a while.'

'Of course, we do have various acquaintances in law enforcement,' Gordon said, his fingers busily chattering over the keyboard. 'There might be a favour we can call on.'

Stemper vetoed the suggestion. 'If you obtain the information from an official source, it essentially guarantees that nothing untoward can happen to her.'

Gordon hadn't considered that point. He went to say so, but spotted a familiar name on screen.

'Here they are. Compton Property Services. Only the one office, and it's in Brighton.'

'Perfect,' Stemper said. 'I'll get straight on to it.'

'Thank you.' Patricia's voice was husky with emotion. When Gordon glanced up he saw that her gratitude was directed at Stemper, and Stemper alone.

'We're on their trail now,' she said, 'and we're going to make them suffer.'

Fifty-one

Afterwards Dan wasn't sure what mad impulse sent him into the garage. He knew he'd drunk several more beers, had slid past maudlin into the realm of genuine grief, and emerged the other side so numb that he was practically catatonic.

Opening the garage door was impossible without a stomach-churning screech. Dan didn't think about it consciously, but he must have counted on Louis's music to obscure the noise. As he grasped the leading edge and lifted the door, the painful grinding of metal prompted a grisly association with the accident fifteen years ago.

It had happened on the A27, a couple of miles east of Chichester. Mum and Dad had sneaked a rare day out together, leaving Louis with Joan. On the way home they were crossing a roundabout when a Mitsubishi pickup truck came flying out of the road to their left and ploughed into their Vauxhall Cavalier.

They didn't stand a chance. In the weeks and months that followed, Dan eavesdropped this phrase so often, heard it quoted by so many people – friends, relatives, police, social workers – that he grew to detest every word. It wasn't intended to be cruel, he knew that now, but at the time it seemed to have a bitter subtext: *They were hopeless. They were losers. They couldn't find a way to survive . . .*

The driver had stopped, but only because his truck was embedded in the Cavalier. As other motorists rushed to offer help to the victims, the man who had killed them managed to slip away. Apparently a member of the public had given chase over the fields, but lost him in woodland south of the A27. Later it was found that the truck was unregistered, uninsured, had no MOT; its brakes and tyres were illegal and lethal. A small quantity of drugs was found beneath the passenger seat.

The driver was never traced. At first that was irrelevant to Dan: it wouldn't bring his parents back, and that was all he cared about. It was only when he reached adulthood that the injustice began to burn, the way friction rubs away skin, but by then it seemed too late to discuss it with anyone. Instead he'd tried to forget it, and to his eternal shame he had been mostly successful.

Until Tuesday night, when he had become what he loathed.

In the darkness it was virtually impossible to see the damage to the car. Just a series of irregular shadows, the indentations of a glancing blow that had thrown Hank O'Brien into a ditch.

I did it, Dan thought. *Robbie's right. I was at the wheel. I have to take responsibility.*

He sniffed, and realised his vision had blurred. Maybe he was drunk. But it would be so easy, even though it was – *Jesus, eleven-thirty* – to pick up a phone and make the call. Hand himself in.

'What's up?' said a bleary voice.

Dan jumped. Louis was by the door, silhouetted against the pale concrete of the driveway.

'Nothing.'

'Funny time of night to be in the garage.' Louis sounded subdued, but there was a note of his familiar dry humour, perhaps signalling a desire to make amends.

'How are you feeling?'

Louis shrugged. Gazed at his feet and kicked his toes against the dusty garage floor. 'Shitty.'

'That scene last night—'

'You don't have to say it. I was an arsehole.'

Dan nodded. 'I hate lecturing you, Louis. I wish I didn't have to do it.'

'But if you don't, who will, eh? Poor Joanie puts up with enough stress.'

'If either of us lays down the law, it's only because we love you.'

'Do you think I don't know that? Makes it even worse.' Louis shoved his hands in his pockets. He was in jogging pants and a T-shirt, and Dan had to fight an automatic impulse to scold him for not putting a coat on.

'I'm worried about you, Louis. You're at the age where you want to go out with your friends, getting drunk and . . . and whatever.' He decided this wasn't the right moment to delve into the *whatever*. 'But it's also dangerous. Unless someone sets boundaries – unless you know where the boundaries are, at least – there's a danger that you'll end up getting . . . well, *consumed* by it.'

A moment of silence followed his little speech. Dan imagined it was because he'd sounded so inept, so weak and woolly and predictable. But Louis had tears running down his cheeks.

'I feel really inferior to you.' He raised his head and made eye contact at last. 'You're a brother, an uncle and a father all in one. Doesn't leave much room for us to be mates, does it?'

Dan was stunned. 'I've never seen it like that.'

'Yeah, well . . . I look back now and I'm awestruck. I was a two-year-old when they died, I didn't have a clue what was going on. And you were only fourteen, but you had this . . . this *huge* responsibility heaped on you without any warning.'

His voice was so thick that the words were hard to make out. He cleared his throat, acknowledging the struggle with a bemused smile.

'And yet you dealt with it. You lost your mum and dad and became like a parent to me overnight, and I've never once heard you complain. Compared to you, I'm just a silly little brat.'

'No, Louis. No one sees you like that.' Dan opened his arms and embraced his brother, and while they held each other he felt that his heart might break to measure the distance between the image Louis had of him and the grim reality.

Then Louis stepped away, gesticulating as he searched for the words to describe his torment.

'We lost our parents, Dan. It's so unfair, it makes me want to scream. It's *always* there. I can feel it inside me, and it's like . . . it's like the breath of a madman in my lungs. And the brilliant thing about drinking is that when I'm pissed I don't feel that. I don't need to scream for a while.'

Dan nodded. 'I can understand.'

'Can you? How do you cope so well?'

'I'm not sure that I do, particularly.'

'That's not how it looks to me.'

'Appearances can be deceptive. Honestly, Louis. I don't deserve the praise . . .' Now Dan was struggling not to cry. He felt a savage pain in his gut, and from it came a sudden resolve.

Admit it. Be a real man. Tell him.

'I'm a lousy role model, if you want to know the truth.'

Louis took a step back, as if he couldn't believe what he was hearing. 'Why do you say that?'

'Because . . .' Dan swallowed. This was even more difficult than he'd imagined. 'Because I'm a grade one fuck-up. The other night—'

It was the clip-clop of heels on concrete that drew his attention to a noise he'd only dimly registered: the purr of an engine idling in the street. The neighbour's security light snapped on and suddenly Joan was bustling up the drive.

'Well, this is a fine place to hang out, isn't it? Something wrong with the lounge?'

Her face was flushed, and there was an air of suppressed glee about her. Although Louis turned to respond, Dan could sense that his brother was still anxious to hear his revelation.

'Yeah, mad,' Louis said. 'You go in, we're just coming.'

He turned back, but Joan didn't move. Dan quickly murmured: 'Me and Hayley are in a bad way.'

'What are you boys plotting?'

'Nothing,' Louis said, and his gaze fluttered uncertainly between the two of them.

He doesn't believe me, Dan thought. But he knew that the moment to confess had passed. Knew it beyond doubt when Joan grabbed his arm and squeezed it, giddy with excitement as she told him: 'Ron asked me out, and I said yes!'

Fifty-two

Stemper left the Blakes at eleven p.m. He'd spent some time researching the letting agency. He'd also gathered the information he required to deal with Jerry Conlon, mindful that there could be no mistakes.

As he'd pointed out, Jerry was a direct link to the Blakes and therefore posed a tangible threat to them: dead as well as alive.

Before returning to Brighton, he made a detour into London. It was part reconnaissance, part thinking time; and tremendously valuable on both counts.

The late nights were beginning to wear on him. Over the years Stemper had conditioned himself to get by on very little sleep – often just three or four hours a night for the duration of an assignment. But once this was done he would return to the small town near Ipswich and recharge his batteries under the watchful but blissfully ignorant eye of Debbie Winwood.

And when *that* assignment was complete, he would take a proper holiday. By that stage a spell abroad might be advisable in any case.

It was past two a.m. when he reached Kemptown, the narrow street on the hill deserted save for an urban fox, which paused by a discarded fast-food carton, waiting patiently until Stemper had made himself scarce.

Before entering the guest house he glanced down the street, saw the dull black gleam of the sea and felt for a moment the pull of its secret world. This was the hour when his father would have stalked the streets, having slipped away after the show to one of the many private drinking clubs that had flourished in those days. Hours later he would come in drunk, and his vigorous review of the night's performance would commence.

There was no sign of Quills, but Stemper expected him to be awake. The door on the first floor marked 'Private' opened at his touch. On the other side of the door the key was sitting in the lock.

Stemper smiled. This was an invitation that, in all probability, he should decline. But there was no denying that Quills, as a result of his inquisitive nature and his susceptibility to male charm, could one day pose a problem. And that problem wasn't going to resolve itself.

Some of the skills he'd acquired from his father had little practical application. Juggling, for instance. Or tap dancing.

Others were of far greater benefit, and none more so than hypnosis. Stemper had shown a natural aptitude from the beginning. He found it almost absurdly easy to put someone under. Along with his rather bland appearance, he had exactly the right manner – calmly authoritative – and the ideal tone of voice with which to lull and soothe.

He made his way along the hall without resorting to lights. The first door he opened revealed a small, neat living room. The bedroom was next to it, lit by a single lamp draped in muslin.

There was a body beneath the covers, its respiration slow and deep. Stemper crouched beside the bed and placed his hand on the sleeping man's shoulder.

Quills grunted, his body twitching at Stemper's touch.

'Ssshhh. Don't wake up,' Stemper urged him. 'We're going to talk, and you'll stay asleep because you're lovely and relaxed now, and you want to remain that way. In the morning you'll wake and recall how *wonderful* it was, that we shared this experience.'

Quills wriggled. He was lying on his side, and Stemper saw his eyes flicker, trying to open. He laid the back of his hand against the man's cheek, the skin both soft and slightly rough with stubble.

'Sshh. Don't wake up, or I'll have to leave, and that's no way to end such a *wonderful* dream.' He began stroking, slowly, from temple to jaw, and heard a moan of appreciation.

'You're easily besotted, Bernard. You're a lonely man, and you think I'm the answer to your prayers. Well, I've got some good news. I do have the answer. I know the cure for loneliness, and I can help you to find it. But you have to play your part. You have to let me help you, and by relaxing now and remembering how this feels, that warm *wonderful* sense of security that comes from knowing you'll follow me to the very ends of the Earth . . . that's how you'll find the answer, Bernard.'

Quills mumbled a response. Stemper had no idea what he said, but the tone was agreeable, compliant, and that was enough.

'From now on, Bernard, leave the door unlocked and I'll be here again soon. Tomorrow night, perhaps. I'll visit you in your sleep and we'll talk, and at the end you'll come to feel what you already know in your heart – that I understand you better than anyone has ever done or tried to do.'

Another sleepy murmur, another twitch of pleasure.

'I can see into your soul. I see the sweet, lonely man who resides there, so often misunderstood, so often rejected or overlooked. That doesn't matter any more, because now you have someone who truly wants your soul. Sleep now, sleep deeply and remember this: ultimately I want what's best for you, Bernard. I'll be here for you again, very soon. Very soon.'

Quills smiled, but his eyes remained closed. He didn't stir as Stemper got to his feet and left the room.

Fifty-three

Having to be up at eight on a Saturday felt like an imposition to Robbie: practically an abuse of his human rights. Even though it was Compton's busiest day, he invariably managed to wangle a late start or a reason to avoid going in altogether.

Today he was happy to make an exception. Anything for the sister of the late, unlamented Hank O'Brien.

He was gulping down a coffee when Jed wandered in, naked except for a pair of filthy grey shorts. Robbie made a mental note to turn the heating down.

'All right?' he said. Jed rarely surfaced before eleven, especially if he'd been out the night before. Robbie had heard him come in around four.

'That car you wanna ditch? Feller I know works at a scrapyard near Winchester. Says he'll disappear it for you, but best if it's got some serious damage on it.'

'Okay.'

'*Has* it got some serious damage?'

'It will have. How do we get it there?'

'He can collect, if you want.'

'Great.'

'Three hundred,' Jed added. 'Cash, mind.'

Robbie nodded. Dan was going to blow his nut.

'Bit steep, isn't it?'

'He only works there, so he's taking a risk with his job. And since I was getting the impression this was important to you . . .' Jed said it playfully, as if to demonstrate that he already knew the answer.

'It's for a mate.'

'Aye. And you're fretting that he won't wanna stump up the cash?'

'No, no. It's cool.'

'Good. So you'll give us a hundred up front?'

'Now?'

'I'm seeing him later. That's why I'm up at the crack. Doing this for you, Robert.'

Trying to hide his reluctance, Robbie went into his bedroom. Jed followed, and Robbie couldn't think of a way to stop him. He knew a direct request was likely to be ignored, and then what would happen?

Jed leaned against the door frame, absently scratching his groin. Robbie stopped by his bed, not wanting to reach under the mat where his floor safe was concealed.

'Planning to get dressed?' he asked.

'Nah, thought I'd head out naked. Give the womenfolk of Brighton the thrill of their lives.' Jed grinned and crossed his arms. He was going nowhere.

Robbie told himself that it didn't really matter. Jed wouldn't see the combination from where he was standing. But it was the principle that irked him, the feeling that he was being denied privacy in his own home. He'd have to tell Jed it was time he moved on.

He couldn't say it now, of course. But soon.

Keeping his back to Jed, he opened the safe and took out a wad of notes. When he'd told Dan on Wednesday that he was absolutely skint, he had meant it sincerely. This was money he didn't even consider when he was totting up his assets: his ultra, ultra emergency funds. The *do-or-die* money.

He counted out five twenties and returned the rest to the safe. Jed stuck his hand out, a broad smirk on his face.

'Just give us a shout when you want the motor collecting.'

'Soon, probably. A day or two.'

'That'll be swell!' he said in a bad American accent, and he clapped Robbie on the shoulder. 'Always a privilege to help my favourite landlord.'

The weather was dull but dry, so Dan walked to work. Louis hadn't yet surfaced, which wasn't surprising, but even Joan had only got up for a cup of tea and then returned to bed. From the brief chat she'd had with him, it was clear she was still euphoric about accepting a date. Dan knew he would have to ensure she didn't get cold feet between now and Wednesday.

At Fiveways he bought a tube of Polo mints and an *Argus*. He felt sure there would be a shock waiting for him in the paper, and he wasn't wrong. The e-fits occupied almost half a page: Dan and Robbie in grim digitised glory.

Except that it wasn't the two of them; not really. As Cate had said, knowing who the images were supposed to represent made it impossible to evaluate their accuracy.

He binned the paper before he reached the shop. Hayley didn't normally read the *Argus*, so there was no point making it easier for her to see it. She'd texted him to say she was coming in to work today. She'd also asked if his car was fixed yet. He'd replied: `Soon. Looking forward to seeing u xx`

The car park was almost empty, Hayley's Corsa conspicuous by its presence. The shop always had a different feel on a Saturday. The staff cut it fine when they turned up, and the mood tended to be more laid-back. There were jokes about hangovers, the prospects for different football teams, the plans for Saturday-night celebrations.

Hayley was alone in the restroom, eating a low-fat yoghurt and reading a glossy celebrity magazine. Dan glanced at it as he leaned over to kiss her cheek and saw pictures of some C-lister's extravagant wedding. *Uh-oh.*

She seemed to squirm slightly at his touch, and he changed his mind about a second kiss.

'So you're feeling better?'

'Not really. But Maisie's off, isn't she? I didn't want to let the store down.'

He tutted in a way that conveyed both admiration and disapproval. 'I'm glad you're back.'

She shifted round in the seat. 'Are you?'

'Of course. Why wouldn't I be?'

'You tell me.' She dabbed her thumb against her tongue and turned the page: more satin and bows and bottle-brown cleavage.

'I was hoping we'd move on from yesterday's conversation. Frankly it didn't make a lot of sense.'

Hayley said nothing. Dan poured stale water from the kettle and refilled it. He found a clean mug for his coffee, took one out for her, then put it back. If Hayley wanted a drink she would ask for one.

'Well?' he said.

'Well what?'

'I don't know what you meant about "emotional stress". Is that really why you were off sick?'

He heard the snap of another page. 'This isn't the time or the place, Daniel.'

For some reason he thought about Louis, and the quite unwarranted adoration that his brother had expressed last night. It acted to toughen Dan's resolve, so that instead of trying to reason with Hayley he gave a shrug and said, in a voice too low to hear over the burbling kettle: 'Suit yourself.'

Fifty-four

Stemper was almost put out to find other guests in the dining room: two retired couples, by the look of them, dressed in the bright vulgar clothing that he associated with affluent leisure time. Golf, perhaps, or sailing.

He adapted swiftly, exchanging the necessary greetings, then sat at the far side of the room. He didn't much care for breakfast but he needed to see Quills to assess the efficacy of last night's session.

Within a couple of minutes the proprietor emerged from the kitchen, carrying two plates of bacon and eggs. He was wearing a chef's apron over a check shirt, and there were bright spots of colour on his wide cheeks. His first sight of Stemper caused him to break his stride.

Good. Stemper studied the folded card which listed the breakfast menu. He didn't look up until he sensed Quills approaching.

'Good morning! What can I get you?'

'Well, I was going to say just coffee, but those breakfasts look delicious. May I have scrambled egg on toast?'

Quills beamed. 'My pleasure. Anything else?'

'That's all. Thank you.'

They maintained eye contact. Then Quills glanced at the retired couples, before leaning forward and confiding: 'I woke up this morning, convinced that I'd had the most *wonderful* dream.'

'Really?'

'I can't get it out of my mind. Truth be told, I can't get *you* out of my mind.'

A burst of laughter from the other table diverted their attention. Quills quickly reached out and brushed his hand against Stemper's arm.

'It sounds so . . . clichéd, but it's true. And I don't make a habit, I really don't . . . I mean, I'd be mortified if you thought I was . . . well, a predator or something.'

Stemper chuckled. 'Rest easy, Bernard. You're no predator.'

The holidaymakers kept him busy, but once or twice Quills stole a moment to sidle over and engage Stemper in conversation.

'A day to yourself, is it? A chance to see the sights?'

'I'm afraid not. More meetings.'

'Oh, dear. All work and no play . . .'

Stemper nodded. 'I am a dull boy, indeed.'

'And what is it you do, exactly?'

'*Exactly?*' Stemper echoed, with a glint in his eye. 'Well, you probably know that silly phrase: "I could tell you, Bernard, but then I'd have to kill you."'

And for half a second there was silence, before Stemper laughed and Quills, looking slightly uneasy, joined in, slapping his guest affectionately on the shoulder.

'You're a scream, Mr Hooper. So deadpan. You really should be on the stage.'

Stemper left the guest house at eight o'clock. He wore a grey suit and a reversible raincoat, beige side out. He was whistling to himself, cheerful about the tasks that lay ahead. He would earn the first of his bonuses today.

Last night he'd set out his proposal in detail. The Blakes had marvelled at his ingenuity, although his favoured approach was one he'd used on several occasions, and it was far from original. But it was undeniably effective, and it sent the authorities down all kinds of blind alleys.

The Blakes had readily agreed to help with the preparation, freeing up Stemper's time for the immediate priority: Compton Property Services.

Its offices were located in a narrow street a short distance from Queens Road. Stemper was able to pull in at the kerb within sight of the property's frontage, but he was already debating his next move. It wouldn't be long before the city's parking wardens came prowling.

He took out his phone and pretended to be engrossed in a series of texts. In twenty minutes only half a dozen vehicles passed him, including a Royal Mail van making deliveries. He saw the first warden, too, crossing the end of the street and giving him a professional once-over.

A pity. Before he moved on, Stemper wanted something: a development, a sign, a little bit of luck.

He got it. *In spades*, as the saying went.

A car roared past and braked sharply, darting into a marked-out bay in front of the office. Stemper sat forward in his seat, and used the camera on his phone to take a series of shots.

The car's only occupant was a woman in a trouser suit: thirtyish, tall and statuesque. She might have been a candidate for the woman with Hank, except that she was too tall, too heavy, and she was Asian. Stemper guessed that even Traci was sharp enough not to have omitted such a detail.

He waited until the woman had unlocked the door and gone inside, then he called Jerry.

'The BMW on Wednesday night. Could it have been a 335i Coupe?'

Jerry hummed as he thought about it. 'Maybe. I'll check one out on the net later and let you know. Can't do it now. The Blakes have got me back at the farmhouse.'

'Really?' Stemper said, although he knew precisely what Jerry was doing today.

'Yeah, and it's gonna chuck it down later.' Jerry's next complaint was inaudible, and then he said, 'Oh, you need to get the local paper, for the e-fits.'

'I'll take a look. I'm scoping out the property company at the moment.'

'Is that where you saw the Beemer? It's gotta be them, hasn't it?'

'Possibly. I hope to confirm it soon.'

'You will, I'm sure.' He sniffed. 'Well, I've gotta say it, you know your stuff.'

'Thank you, Jerry. I appreciate that.'

Fifty-five

When it came to spinning those plates, manipulating people and situations with consummate skill, Robbie didn't think there was much you could teach him. But he had to admit that Dan had done him a favour with the warning about the mystery photographer.

Before leaving the office last night he'd enquired after Indira's plans for the weekend. Hearing that she was working tomorrow morning, then visiting family in Hertfordshire on Sunday, he had a proposal for her.

'Why don't you have the BMW and I'll use your car?'

Sheer disbelief on her face. 'What do you want in return?'

'Nothing. I only have local calls, so anything's all right with me. Better that you and the family travel in comfort, eh?'

He could see the doubt in her eyes, but it didn't stop her snatching the keys from his hand. Indira was a speed freak, and she'd coveted his BMW for years.

It meant Robbie was saddled with a five-year-old Citroën C4 Picasso. Bree would be less than impressed if she knew, he thought, as he located the address for his next chore of the day.

Maureen Heath lived in a detached house in Shirley Drive, to the east of Hove Park. It spoke of money, if not quite on the scale of Jimmy and Bree, whose home was only a couple of minutes away.

Maureen had returned his call yesterday, suggesting they meet up first.

'You look great from the pictures Bree's shown me, but before I make up my mind I wanna see you in the flesh.'

Like he was a piece of meat. Afterwards Robbie had wondered if he should be charging her for this: she was paying for his time, after all.

He put it to Bree when she called for an update, and she said, 'Oh, don't be a meanie. Just pop round and say hello. I bet she'll be all over you like a rash.'

Nice image. It came back to him now, after a brief journey spent brooding about Jed. No way was that hundred quid going to this mate of his – more likely heading straight for Jed's nearest off-licence or bookie.

If he screws me over, I'll throw him out on his ear.

But the Geordie was unpredictable. To get rid of him safely Robbie would need assistance, ideally in the form of a couple of granite-faced bouncer types. Buy a one-way ticket back to Newcastle or Sunderland or wherever it was, then tell the hard men to haul Jed out of the flat and dump him on the train.

Such an enticing plan, but it felt tantalising somehow, as though it could never go anything like as smoothly in practice. Robbie tutted, and was jolted back to the here and now because he was at the front door and she must have seen him on the path because the door was opening and—

Holy Jesus and Mary . . .

For a second Robbie thought he had said it out loud. He blinked furiously, but the sight before his eyes refused to transform into something more appealing.

At worst he'd anticipated someone on the heavy side, maybe a bit tired-looking, but essentially well-maintained. Bree's friends were, after all, moneyed women with a lot of time on their hands.

He'd been told Maureen was in her early fifties, around the same age as his mother. That couldn't be right, could it?

He said a silent prayer: *Let this be* Maureen*'s mother.*

'Hiya, Robbie. I'm Maureen.' She smiled, revealing uneven yellow teeth that appeared to be edged in boot polish. She was wearing way too much make-up, and the pink dress that encased her frame was obviously something designer but was never going to flatter a shape like hers. She wasn't much over five feet tall, and nearly as wide.

Bree, I'm going to kill you for this.

Even worse was the poor personal hygiene, masked, but not entirely, by a sweet suffocating perfume. Beneath it lurked the odour of a dried-out harbour on a summer afternoon.

There was a meanness in her eyes that didn't match her smile. When she registered the way he was looking at her, the smile vanished but the meanness stayed put. Her gaze dropped and she appraised him from the shoes up, taking her time at groin level, focusing on the bulge that, in the car, he had tweaked and encouraged, because at that point he'd still intended to make the best possible impression.

'Hmm.' She reached out and squeezed one of his biceps. 'Yeah, good. Come on in.'

'I thought this was only—'

'Oh no, just nerves, that was.' Her voice was fast and fluttery, like that Essex girl from *The X Factor* whose name escaped him.

'Well, let's see if we can sort out a date that's convenient, if you're sure you want to go ahead.'

'Nah, I'm sure. Why doncha come in here and get your kit off?'

'I can't. I have to see a client.'

'Bree said I was gonna be your first.'

'No, my day job. I'm due out near Steyning in half an hour.'

'Come back after, then.' She stared him out, pouting. Her lips looked solid and grotesque: collagen?

Robbie swallowed, knowing that it would seem like a gulp. 'This afternoon?'

'Yeah. Bree tells me you're shit-hot. I wanna see for myself.'

Robbie was trapped. He needed the money. More than that, he needed Bree's alibi.

'All right. Should be around two o'clock.'

He started to turn away but she called out: 'Oy, not so fast,' and before he could react she delivered a quick slobbery kiss with all the seductive skills of a clumsy dog. A dog that didn't wash itself adequately.

Whatever his other failings, Dan considered himself a professional when it came to his conduct at work. The idea that he was capable of arguing with Hayley on the shop floor would have appalled him.

She sought his help after being ensnared by a classic time-waster: a young man wearing slacks and a bright green cagoule. He required a detailed comparison of plasma, LCD and LED televisions, and he wanted a demonstration that high-performance HDMI cables provided a better picture than 'bog-standard' cables.

Dan launched his well-practised spiel. Aware that any sign of impatience would invite more questions, his tactic was to display an almost manic enthusiasm for his subject, to the point where, having been out-anoraked, the time-waster became disgruntled and left.

Hayley stayed to enjoy the spectacle. It was showing signs of success when Dan happened to look at an array of televisions just as the e-fits flashed up on every screen. Dan froze mid-word, then forced a grin and tapped his temple.

'Sorry, lost my train of thought there. What was I . . .?'

'Advances in 3D.' The young man greeted the interruption with delight: he'd take this as a points victory. 'I think I have what I need for now.'

He strode off without a word of thanks. When Dan turned back, the news had moved on but Hayley was studying him carefully.

'Are you all right?'

'Apart from wanting to strangle him with a bog-standard cable, yeah.'

'I don't mean that,' she said. 'Those pictures.'

'What pictures?'

She moved directly in front of him. 'Those photofit things. You looked really freaked out.'

'Did I?'

'Yes. What are you keeping from me, Daniel?'

'Leave it, please.' He tried to retreat but there was a display unit in the way.

'You're hiding something. Tell me what it is.'

'Hayley, you're wrong.' He indicated the shop. Other customers were milling around, some of them waiting for assistance. 'And like you said, this isn't the time or place—'

'I don't care any more. Can't you see how hurtful this is?'

And in that instant, terrified by the thought that on the next bulletin she would examine the e-fits and spot the likeness to Robbie or himself, he lost his temper.

'Christ, Hayley, will you leave it alone? Do you think this makes me look forward to married life with you, knowing I'll have to account for every bloody moment of my day?'

A discreet cough, and Denham was alongside, nodding Hayley in the direction of a couple who were gaping at the outburst. To Dan: 'A word in my office, Mr Wade.'

Fifty-six

Stemper remained in position until just before nine, when a Jaguar XK parked next to the BMW. The quality of the cars had him thinking that business must be booming, never mind the financial crisis.

Judging by her Jag and her suit, he guessed this was the company's owner: Teresa Scott. Staff information on the website was sadly lacking, with only a couple of poorly taken group photographs. Perhaps estate agents, even on the letting side, took care not to be recognised in public.

After locking her car, the woman produced cigarettes and a lighter from her handbag and lit up as she approached the door to the building. She took a deep hungry drag, nudged the door open with her foot and began a conversation with someone inside – the Asian woman, presumably, as Stemper had seen no one else go in.

Tapping ash on to the pavement, she glanced along the street and gazed for a second or two at his car. Stemper ignored her, continuing his fictitious phone call until a full minute had passed, then started the car and drove away.

He parked at the railway station, took his briefcase and walked down Queens Road, purchasing an *Argus* en route. In Western Road he found a cafe, drank a cappuccino and checked the paper.

The e-fits were a letdown. He could see the vagueness, the strangeness that wouldn't correspond to any living being. The barmaid's verbal descriptions were more useful than these.

The coffee finished, he went into the Gents and locked himself in a cubicle. Sitting with the briefcase on his lap, he used spirit gum to fix a neat moustache, made from real human hair. He added the glasses, and considered false teeth, before deciding that might be too much.

He ambled down North Street and reached the office for ten o'clock. Both cars were still present, along with a more modest Peugeot saloon. As he drew level with the front window, Stemper saw a man perched on one of the desks inside. But he was in his mid-forties, with thinning blond hair and a hefty beer belly. Not one of the two men in the pub.

After studying the letting notices in the window, Stemper went inside. The man was talking on a mobile, his posture suggesting that he wouldn't be staying long. Teresa Scott was also on the phone, massaging her cheek as if to distract herself from the conversation.

That left the Asian woman. She stood up as he approached and gave him a bright, professional smile.

'Good morning. How may I be of assistance?'

'I'm applying for a promotion that would see me moving to Sussex for at least six months. I'd like to see what sort of home I can rent for my money – that is, my employer's money.' He laughed, and so did she, and he thought: *I'm in.*

And he stayed in for nearly half an hour, by virtue of the fact that he took a slow, methodical look at every current property that met his potential requirements: minimum three bedrooms, maximum rent of four thousand a month. The Asian woman, who'd introduced herself as Indira, expressed only polite admiration for the sum involved, but from then on her eye contact was a lot more frequent, her smile far wider than before.

He gave her a false name and address, but the email and mobile details were valid. She promised to keep him informed of each new property as soon as it came on their books.

'That's very good of you.' He made a show of looking around. The blond man had long since departed, and Teresa Scott had continued to field a succession of calls. 'I am glad I spotted this place. Are there other branches?'

'No, we're very much a boutique business here.'

'And surviving the recession, I'm pleased to see.'

'Well, it's a struggle, but we have the benefit of a great reputation, as well as the fact that Brighton – and the rest of Sussex – remains very popular.'

'Certainly seems busy. Is it a large team?'

'Oh, there's . . .' She closed her eyes to count. 'Six, no, seven of us, so not many. It's a family firm.'

'Really?'

Indira gave a subtle nod in Scott's direction. 'Teresa's the owner. She started as a property developer, and the lettings agency grew out of that.'

'And her children work here, too?'

'Her son, yes. Her daughter's a lawyer. We sometimes use her firm for legal work.'

'Well, why not? Good to see small companies can still compete with those huge faceless corporations.'

'Quite,' she said. 'Who is it you work for?'

'A huge faceless corporation, I'm afraid.'

Cue appropriate laughter. It was tailing off when Teresa Scott slammed her phone down and muttered: 'Fuckwit.' She immediately glanced in their direction, frowning in apology, but Stemper pretended not to have heard.

He emerged to find a number of missed calls from Jerry. Stemper decided to take his briefcase back to the car, then stay in the vicinity of Compton's for another couple of hours.

He now knew that the proprietor had a son. Added to the presence of the BMW, this seemed extremely promising. But why was Indira driving the BMW?

Jerry greeted him with his customary agitation. 'Busy down here today, and it ain't good news.'

'What's wrong?'

'This joiner's van drove in and she's got them changing locks. All of 'em. Windows, too.'

'That's no surprise, after the break-in.'

'And this other bloke's turned up, looks a bit flash. Young guy, suit and briefcase.'

'What car?'

'A Citroën Picasso. Nothing special.'

'Have you managed to get a look at him?'

'Only from behind.'

'See if you can get closer. And take some photographs.'

'I have. I've got the reg plate, clear as a bell.'

'Not just the car. The man.'

'Yeah, easy for you to say . . .' Jerry trailed off, muttering to himself.

'Pardon?'

'It's just . . . it's like I'm expected to work bloody miracles.'

Stemper faked a sympathetic sigh. 'You and me both, Jerry. You and me both.'

Fifty-seven

Robbie was five minutes late reaching the farmhouse. Not bad by his usual standards, but with Hank's sister he wanted to make a good impression from the start. He had a feeling she'd be a stickler for timekeeping.

The delay was partly because, after driving a safe distance from Maureen Heath's, he'd sent Bree a text: Just met her, cant say Im impressd. Goin bck this pm. Can u hve a discrt wrd, tell her to improve personl hygiene asap! x

She replied immediately: Sorry, hun. Thought she had sorted that!

Great. And this was Bree's idea of an easy introduction to the role of gigolo.

Hank O'Brien's home was located at the end of a short private lane. The double gates stood open and there were two vehicles on the drive: a silver Lexus and a van bearing the livery of a carpenter and joiner.

Robbie parked, checked his appearance in the mirror and suppressed an image of Maureen Heath, naked and ravenous for pleasure. That was the last thing he wanted in his head right now.

He picked up his briefcase and strode towards the front door. He couldn't deny a twinge of trepidation. There was a chance that

DS Thomsett had already told Cheryl Wilson why her brother had been in the pub on Tuesday night – and if he had, it would be in terms that were less than complimentary to Robbie.

Could Hank's sister be luring him into a trap? The possibility had occurred to him on the drive over. Any hint of it and he would simply walk away.

The woman who came to the door was perhaps slightly younger than Maureen Heath, and not that dissimilar in shape. But she was taller, and broader in the shoulders, and she carried herself in a way that projected confidence and self-esteem. There was no attempt to look glamorous or alluring. She was smart rather than stylish, handsome rather than pretty, neat rather than feminine.

'Robbie Scott,' he said.

'Mr Scott. Thank you for coming.' Her smile, although stingy, seemed genuine enough, and Robbie decided that, for the time being at least, he was safe in her company.

Willie Denham kept a modest, cluttered office on the ground floor. Away from work he had a passion for motorbikes, especially Nortons. The walls were adorned with framed action shots from the TT races on the Isle of Man, which he'd attended religiously for almost forty years.

Dan was waved to a seat in front of the desk. He moved aside a stack of glossy brochures for Dyson washing machines and sat down. The idea that he might lose his job had engendered a bizarre sense of calm: in his mind, the worst had already happened.

Denham cleared his throat, as if preparing to embark on a speech. But all he said was, 'Now then,' and gazed thoughtfully at a spot on the wall just above Dan's shoulder.

'I'm very sorry. It was completely unprofessional.'

'Indeed.' The old man's tone was grave. 'You've not been yourself of late, that's my impression. Without wanting to pry into your affairs,

I do have to say that I'm concerned. You and Hayley have been an item for . . . how long is it now?'

'Seven years, on and off.'

'My word, is it really? I'll admit, when you started courting I had my reservations. Never easy, working with the other half, especially when she's a direct report.'

Lips pursed, he nodded at the truth of his statement. *This is where he suggests that one of us has to resign,* Dan thought. *And it will have to be me.*

'Of course,' Denham continued, 'I was delighted that you found a way to make it succeed. I have a high regard for you both – well, you know that. I wouldn't have wanted to lose either of you.'

Then a dismayed silence that seemed to say: *The ball's in your court.*

'So what happens now?' Dan asked.

'That's the question. I suppose it depends ultimately on where you feel your future lies.'

Dan shrugged. It wasn't like the old man to be so oblique. 'I don't understand.'

'No. It's awkward.' Denham gave a nervous laugh. 'I hesitate to say this, because I'm aware that marriage is . . . well, if not on the cards, then certainly a possibility. Or am I wrong?'

Startled by the question, Dan said, 'We have talked about it, but nothing's set in stone.'

'I see.' Denham was blushing, his white hair a stark contrast to his cherry-red cheeks. 'Please consider this as the benefit of an outside perspective – not that I regard myself as any sort of expert. But . . . have you considered that perhaps the two of you aren't actually suited for each other?'

This was about the last thing Dan had expected. He stared at his boss and didn't know if he should be outraged, or amused – or even impressed.

Denham added, 'I mean no offence, Daniel. But, as I say, sometimes it takes an outsider's view to illuminate the, ah, place in which we find ourselves. Especially, as I sense with you, it's by no means a happy place at present.'

Enemy territory. The thought gave Robbie a thrill as he stepped into the house. For all of Hank's threats as he'd stormed out of the pub, it was Robbie who had triumphed in the end.

He could hear the whirr of an electric screwdriver from one of the living rooms, but decided to let Cheryl explain it in her own time.

He said, 'I've brought along the relevant paperwork in case you want to go ahead, but there's no pressure to decide today. I'll answer any questions you have, then leave you to mull it over.'

'Very reasonable. Now, I assume you'd like the grand tour?'

'Please. Do you know if he'd had any work done?'

'No, I don't. I wasn't a frequent visitor.' She gave Robbie a penetrating stare. 'Hank and I were not close, if that's what you're wondering.'

He nodded, without quite conceding that he'd been fishing for information. He could see a resemblance to Hank in her features: the small round nose and in particular the rosebud mouth. They looked a lot better on her than they had on Hank. Her eyes were lively and astute, and as he smiled he was thinking: *Now if Bree had found me a woman like this . . .*

'I was sorry to hear about Mr O'Brien's death,' he said as she led him upstairs.

'It was quick, at least. He was walking on the wrong side of the road, so he didn't even see it coming.' In her chuckle, Robbie detected a hint of malice. 'Not that it would have made much difference. Try as I might, I can't picture my brother diving nimbly out of the way.'

*   *   *

They reached the landing. Robbie took a quick look round the master bedroom, which he thought might have been redecorated. He was aware that he shouldn't push his luck, but there was a delicious pleasure to be had, discussing Hank's death in this way.

'I suppose it's a comfort to know he didn't suffer?'

'Mm. It certainly isn't the end I'd have predicted for him.'

'Oh, why's that?'

'He had the most appalling diet. He drank heavily, smoked foul cigars. He was always travelling, stuffing himself with rich food. Propping up hotel bars and no doubt boring people rigid. It's a miracle he didn't keel over years ago.'

'What was it that he did—?'

Cheryl flapped a hand: she wasn't finished. 'In fact, if clogged arteries hadn't seen him off, I always thought it would be something violent, like being knifed to death on a dance floor for pawing someone else's wife. He was a rascal, you know.'

'Really?'

'Oh, he had his own weird and wonderful talents, but getting on with people was not one of them. Ignoring the convention that you don't speak ill of the dead, he was an obnoxious bastard, wasn't he?'

Robbie shrugged. 'Well, I, er, I didn't . . .'

'Of course, you feel you must be diplomatic. But I'd much rather hear the unvarnished truth.'

She smiled. There was a definite glint in her eye. An invitation of sorts, and not just to speak his mind.

'We only spoke on the phone a couple of times. I never actually met him.' He reacted to the sudden bang of a hammer and said, 'You're having some building work done?'

'Just repairs. There was a break-in. Well, more like an act of vandalism. I can't see that anything's been taken.'

Robbie swallowed. 'And it happened since your brother's death?'

'As far as I know. The odd thing is that the alarm wasn't activated.' Cheryl looked troubled for a second or two. 'Since I have no idea how many sets of keys might be out there, I thought it prudent to change all the locks.'

'Absolutely. Very wise.' Robbie hoped his voice sounded normal, but his mind was going into overdrive. He could easily guess how Dan would react if he heard about this.

There was something else going on here. Another game in play.

Fifty-eight

Cate slept late after a restless night, beset by dreams of violence. When she woke, it was a relief to run through the events of the previous evening and see that they hadn't been as terrifying as the nightmares they'd inspired.

For all his rage, Martin hadn't actually laid a finger on her. She had to focus on that, and on the fact that she'd been more than willing to fight back if he had tried anything.

But it was the *What ifs* that disturbed her. The simple fact of his physical size and strength, compared to hers, made it all too easy to imagine the damage he could have inflicted.

She was adamant about one thing. Martin would never again set foot inside her house.

Was that sufficient? She brooded on it while she showered. Didn't she owe it to Janine to warn her about Martin's behaviour? The woman was carrying his baby. Cate knew from her friends how weeks of sleepless nights could turn even the most devoted parent into a near-psychopath. Maybe Martin should look into some anger-management treatment.

She got dressed, poured a glass of cranberry juice and decided she was too churned up to want breakfast. Fortunately she hadn't planned on a busy day, although her mum had phoned yesterday and suggested some retail therapy. It was a fairly regular occurrence, so the alarm bells hadn't rung until Teresa said: 'You seeing much of Robbie?'

Cate had answered vaguely, wondering what he'd done to arouse Mum's suspicion. In her current mood Cate was tempted to come clean about the whole business with Hank O'Brien.

She gathered up her dirty laundry and put a wash on, then made for the lounge. In the hall, her attention was drawn to the spot where Martin had virtually pinned her to the wall. There was a shallow indentation where he had thumped it, a few tiny cracks in the top layer of plaster.

Once she'd put the TV on and sat down, she felt ready to take a look at her phone. She'd turned it off after Martin left, fearing the evening could succumb to a not unfamiliar pattern where her ex-husband was concerned: after the temper tantrum, the inevitable remorse and whiny self-justification.

Sure enough, there were a string of missed calls, as well as a couple of voicemail messages, but all from an unfamiliar landline number.

Maybe not Martin, then. But who . . .?

Hank O'Brien, from beyond the grave.

Cate laughed. 'Fool,' she said, and called up her voicemail.

It was Martin, after all, phoning from his brother's home in Burgess Hill. He was staying the night there, having told Janine they were going fishing early on Saturday.

'So I've got the whole day free,' he said. 'If you pick this up in the morning, please ring me. We'll meet somewhere neutral and talk about this like adults. I can change, Cate. I can be whoever you want me to be.'

Oh, please. It didn't help that he was pissed, his voice slurred, stumbling over the words.

The next message was even worse. Half a minute of sobbing into the phone, then a string of desperate pleas: 'I'm so sorry. I love you, Cate. Please give me another chance.' A long silence. She was about to ring off when his voice returned, small and distant, as if surfacing from the depths: 'You know what? If I thought I could never be with you again, I'd kill myself.'

Dan emerged from his meeting to find the showroom in one of its manic phases, quite typical for a Saturday, when a couple of dozen customers would simultaneously demand service. An hour from now the shop might be deserted.

But it meant there was no opportunity to dwell on the conversation with Denham – and, more importantly, no time to enlighten Hayley. After giving advice on one of the complicated cash-back arrangements that manufacturers loved to foist on retailers, he encountered that rarest of creatures: the dream customer. This was a man in his thirties who enquired about, chose and then purchased a two-grand television and surround-sound system. He paid on a debit card and was in and out within ten minutes.

By the time the rush eased off, there was no sign of Hayley. Dan hadn't a clue what he was going to tell her. Somehow try to reassure her that her job was safe, without revealing anything of Denham's rather astute take on their relationship.

He waylaid a colleague, Grace, and asked if she'd seen Hayley. She looked confused.

'Yeah, she needed to swap lunch with me. She said you'd okayed it.'

Dan gave an idiotic grin. 'Yes, I did. Silly me.'

Curiosity led him to check the car park. Hayley's Corsa was gone. He returned to the shop floor, plagued by a deep unease. He passed Grace as she was paging through the channels on a 50-inch TV. For a second the e-fits were on display, rendered in enormous detail. Dan's heart gave a stutter. Grace was staring straight at them.

She's going to recognise me. There's no way she can fail to see the resemblance . . .

But Grace didn't frown. She didn't turn and accuse him of being a hunted criminal. She went on paging through the channels, and there was no let-up in her sales patter.

For the first time Dan experienced a twinge of hope. A couple more days and the media would lose interest. The e-fits would be forgotten. The world would move on.

Cate busied herself with domestic chores, paid some bills online and transferred money into her current account. She decided it might be prudent to leave her credit cards at home this afternoon. Although her mother was extremely careful with the business finances, she often encouraged Cate to splash out, in a way that implied her daughter's life was lacking somehow.

She still wasn't hungry, but consumed a bowl of Cheerios to tide her over. She'd kept her phone on, despite her misgivings, and it buzzed as she was putting the bowl into the dishwasher. The number was familiar: DS Thomsett.

Cate took a deep breath. 'Hello?'

'Ah. Is it a bad time?'

'What? Oh no. Sorry.'

'No, don't apologise. This is, uh, Guy Thomsett. The, er, police officer . . .'

'Yes, I know.' Her mouth was dry. *What had he found out?*

'This isn't an official call. I wondered if you happened to be free tonight, and if you are, whether I could take you to dinner somewhere?'

'Oh.'

'Sorry. I appreciate that it's short notice. You're probably busy . . .'

No comment. 'Can you guarantee that DC Avery won't be coming along?'

He chuckled. 'You haven't warmed to him, then?'

'As it happens, no.'

'Hmm. Not many people do. He's good at his job, though. Tenacious.'

Cate went cold. Was this another warning?

Thomsett went on, 'Definitely just the two of us. I had in mind the Indonesian place in Pool Valley. Warung Tujuh.'

'Oh, I know that one. It's fantastic.'

Silence. It seemed like a startled silence.

'So . . . is that a "yes", then?' he asked.

There was no mistaking the surprise in her own voice when Cate said: 'I think it is.'

Fifty-nine

Robbie chatted easily with Cheryl as they toured the house. She'd already demonstrated that she had a finely tuned bullshit-detector, which encouraged him to shrug off his professional persona and let his natural charm do its work.

Aside from some minor redecoration, the place was just as he remembered it. Cheryl explained that her brother's employers had been in to retrieve paperwork and computers, and she'd be back at various times over the next couple of weeks to sort through his personal possessions. The property would be rented furnished, as before.

'I assume you can show it to prospective tenants in the meantime?' she said.

'No problem. The top end of the market is still pretty healthy. I'm sure we'll have it occupied very quickly.'

'Good. I'd better get my skates on with the clear-out, then. The bulk of it is destined for charity shops.' She sighed. 'Ironic, as I don't believe my brother ever donated a penny to charity.'

'Not everyone does.'

'No. But most people don't tell the Salvation Army to fuck off. He did that one Christmas, at an outdoor concert to raise money for the homeless.' Cheryl tutted at the recollection. 'In fact, the more I think about him, the more I start to wonder if it wasn't an accident at all.'

Robbie's confusion was note perfect. 'You mean . . . someone knocked him down on purpose?'

'The police haven't ruled it out. And I dare say they'll be checking to see whether I arranged to have him bumped off. Apart from a few bequests to cousins and so on, I'm the sole heir. Fortunately I have plenty of money of my own, so they won't find any grubby motives there.'

There was a flirtatious edge to her voice now. Robbie grinned, knowing he'd reached the stage where he could safely tease her.

'Sounds almost like you *did* have something to do with it.'

She giggled. 'Yes. You must think me terribly wicked, joking like this when I should be grieving for him.'

'People react in different ways.'

'Oh, you're good, Mr Scott. That must be a textbook answer.'

'Top of page seven,' he joked. 'Okay, my impression is that if you ever killed somebody you'd want to look into their eyes when you did it.'

As he spoke, Robbie looked deep into her eyes. Cheryl held his gaze, understanding precisely what he was doing. He added, 'I see you with a rifle or something.'

'God, yes! Make it an Uzi. No pussyfooting around, I'd want to mow them down in a hail of bullets.' More laughter, and then, in a decidedly admiring tone, she said, 'That little mix-up when I phoned. What exactly were you in the process of arranging?'

Robbie just grinned, allowing her to work it out.

'An assignation? No doubt with some lucky nubile young lady?'

'Not a *young* lady, necessarily.' He winked. 'I enjoy the company of women of all ages.'

She smiled, then grew wistful. 'If only Hank had possessed a quarter of your charm, he would have been a much nicer person.'

Robbie made noises of agreement, but he was thinking: *Don't bet on that, Cheryl.*

* * *

Back in the hall, they were greeted by the sweet, tangy smell of sawdust. One of the carpenters emerged from the kitchen, carrying a tool bag.

'About twenty minutes and we're done,' he said.

Cheryl turned to Robbie. 'I have a huge favour to ask. I really have to be getting back to Warwick. I own a printing firm that has a habit of imploding if I'm absent for longer than a day or two. Could I leave you to see the builders out?'

Robbie hesitated. Checked his watch. She wouldn't expect him to agree too readily.

'I have a couple of appointments this afternoon, but yes, that should be fine.'

'Thank you so much. They'll give you the new keys. I have a set myself. Oh, and the alarm. I've changed the code.'

She led him to the control panel and ran through its operation, then jotted down the code. 'I'll be back again, probably Tuesday. Though next time I'll stay in a hotel.' She didn't elaborate, but he thought he saw her shiver. 'I've no idea yet when the funeral will be held. The body hasn't been released. Worse still, I can't think who will attend.'

'His work colleagues, presumably? What was it you said he did . . .?'

'I didn't.' She gave him a wry glance. 'And I can't tell you much. I'm afraid I switched off whenever he talked about it. He never showed the slightest interest in my business, which I started from scratch and have kept in profit for more than fifteen years.'

Robbie had an image of Cate talking about him in the same disparaging manner. 'Were the two of you competitive as children?' he asked.

'Not really. He attended a private school, even though it was well beyond our parents' means. And because of that, he was bullied mercilessly. I'm sure that's partly why he grew up to become so obnoxious.'

'It didn't happen to you, though.'

Cheryl smiled to acknowledge the compliment. 'I was sent to the local state school, which was deemed to be perfectly adequate for the education of a mere *female*.'

They went through the paperwork. Cheryl seemed overly concerned that Robbie should have all her various contact numbers, and he wondered what it would take – how little it would take to seduce her.

Brushing off the thought, he insisted on carrying her bag out to the car. She objected at first, but he could tell she was touched by the offer, bullshit-detector or no. He purposely hadn't asked if there was a man in her life. He knew there wasn't – or at least not one that meant anything to her. Separated or widowed, that was his hunch.

After opening the boot, she clicked her fingers. 'Damn. I forgot to show you the barn, the sheds and whatnot.'

'Don't worry. I'll have a look round.'

'There's a fair bit of junk in the sheds, but the barn is empty. I believe Hank wanted to demolish it and build another house on the land.'

'Really?' Robbie gave the proposal his professional consideration. 'Something for you to look at in future, perhaps?'

'Mm. But the thought of finding a decent architect, and builders you can rely on . . .'

'I'm sure I could help you there. Just give me a shout.'

'I will.' They shook hands, and she said, 'A pleasure to meet you, Mr Scott.'

'The pleasure's all mine,' Robbie said, and Cheryl didn't baulk at such a smarmy phrase because she could tell that he meant it.

He remained on the drive while she got into the car. The sudden growling of a dog startled him. He looked to his right and could just make out movement through the bushes that marked the western boundary of the property. There must be a footpath running alongside it. He heard a woman shouting at the dog.

By the time he turned back, Cheryl Wilson had gone and Robbie had missed an opportunity to wave goodbye, sealing in her mind the image of him as a friendly, conscientious and thoroughly gorgeous young man.

Oh well. What mattered was that she'd willingly entrusted the house, its outbuildings and all its contents to Robbie. It was the sort of development that would have left Dan gobsmacked at what a jammy bastard he was, the way so often everything just fell into his lap.

Robbie smiled. Shut his eyes and savoured the moment.

Mine, all mine . . .

Sixty

Stemper spent the morning in the vicinity of Compton's, loitering at one or other end of the street, where he could monitor the comings and goings in relative safety.

The blond man in the Golf returned at just after eleven. Shortly after that, a Smart car with the Compton name on it parked out front. A heavyset man in his sixties carried an armload of stationery supplies into the office.

Stemper made another half-circuit of the block. Earlier he'd called Patricia to pass on Jerry's news about the locks being changed. Now he rang her again to check on the preparations for tonight.

'Gordon's gone into London to fetch the tickets and the other, um, "material".'

'Excellent. I'd like our friend kept busy till mid-afternoon. By then he should be thoroughly dejected, and a step closer to mutiny.'

'What's Plan B, if he decides to accompany her?'

'It isn't something I can spell out now, particularly not on the phone.'

Patricia gasped as though she'd been reprimanded. 'Goodness, no. You're absolutely right.'

Jerry rang less than five minutes later. He was panting like an old dog, and sounded even more hoarse than usual.

'I managed to get closer. Didn't really get a good look at him, but

I heard his voice. It's him, I'd stake money on it. One of the geezers in the BMW.'

'And he's at the farmhouse? In a Citroën Picasso.'

'Yeah. Anyway, this fucking mutt appeared, nearly tore my arse off. I had to get out of there.'

'What?' Stemper was distracted by movement along the road. The proprietor, Teresa Scott, had come out and was lighting a cigarette.

Jerry said, 'Cool down. I'm parked within sight of the access road. No way he can go anywhere without me seeing.'

Stemper wasn't so sure about that. But his reaction had to be consistent with the role he would play later.

'Good work, Jerry. Follow him out, but don't let him see you. And keep me updated.'

He ended the call, gratified that another of his theories had been proven correct. Meanwhile Teresa Scott took an appreciative drag on her cigarette, then set off in his direction. Stemper casually turned and strolled down the hill, pausing at the next corner, where he pretended to read a message on his phone.

Scott turned left, up the hill towards Queens Road. She had her handbag, but no briefcase, so he guessed this was just a quick excursion, perhaps for lunch.

He set off after her.

Midday, and Cate had had no further contact from Martin. That ought to have been cause for relief, but in fact it produced a nagging anxiety. She couldn't call to see how he was, for fear that her concern would be misinterpreted: then they'd be back to square one. But it seemed like too much to hope that he really *had* gone fishing with his brother.

She thought it might be wise to mention the situation to Guy Thomsett tonight, if only for the benefit of his professional advice. Even there, Martin's taunt continued to sting her: *Are you gonna go sobbing to your little detective friend . . .?*

She was waiting to hear from her mother when there was a distinctive rapping on the front door. *Shit.* She had no choice but to answer.

'Why didn't you ring? We could have met in town.'

'I like the exercise.' Teresa Scott leaned inside, looked upstairs and cocked her head, listening.

'There's no strange man in my bed, if that's what you were thinking.'

'I live in hope.' Her mother sniffed, still peering into the house. 'Looks suspiciously tidy.'

Cate stepped back, swooping her hand in an elaborate gesture of welcome. 'Check for yourself. I can't guarantee I'm dust-free, but the washing's up to date, though the ironing isn't. And the fridge is fully stocked, I went to Sainsbury's last—' She stopped, immediately aware of her mistake.

Her mother was withering, and only partly in jest. 'You did the supermarket on a Friday night? Oh, my dear girl. What's to become of you?'

Teresa Scott didn't follow the route that Stemper expected her to take, towards the shops and cafes of Western Road. After crossing Queens Road, she continued up the hill, into a residential district. Perhaps seeing a client?

There were fewer pedestrians up here, so he had to hang back, but she was hard to miss: a tall woman in an immaculate suit, route-marching up the hill at an athlete's pace. Stemper was able to match her, but not easily. Clearly the cigarettes didn't hamper her lung capacity.

After crossing Dyke Road next to a vast construction site, she turned along Clifton Terrace, passing a row of gleaming white stucco town houses, most of them four storeys high, offering what must have been an enviable view out to sea. Today that view was obscured by low-hanging clouds; there was a growing threat of rain in the air.

Scott finally stopped at a house in Victoria Street. Stemper, on the opposite pavement, quickened his pace, hoping to draw parallel when the front door opened. He was staring straight ahead, but saw the movement in his peripheral vision and heard an exclamation from inside the house. A female voice, to which Scott responded in a dry tone.

Risking a sideways glance, he saw Scott talking to a younger woman. She was about five six, slim, with shoulder-length dark brown hair and good skin. She was laughing, and the body language between the two women was relaxed, familiar, in a way that suggested a close connection.

He remembered what Indira had told him this morning: *Her daughter's a lawyer.* He couldn't be certain, yet, but this woman looked like a good candidate.

She also fitted the barmaid's description of the woman who'd been with Hank O'Brien on Tuesday night.

Sixty-one

It was another half an hour before the builders were done. Robbie occupied himself by wandering around outside, trying not to dwell too deeply on the break-in. There could be any number of explanations that had nothing to do with the man who'd jumped out and photographed his car on Wednesday night.

The original farm had been sold off twenty years ago, with the bulk of the land acquired by a neighbouring estate. O'Brien's property encompassed nearly two acres of well-secluded grounds, which made it ideal for Robbie's purposes.

He took a quick look at the barn, which was on the north-west corner of O'Brien's land. It was maybe sixty feet long, twenty feet wide and about the same height. Constructed on a steel frame, with block walls and corrugated-iron cladding. The traces of an old track could be seen beneath the weeds and grass, leading to a massive steel roller door at the front.

There was also an access door at the side, secured by a padlock. Robbie found a key to it on the set that Cheryl had supplied. He unlocked the door and entered a vast empty space, the air warm and stale and smelling faintly of oil. The concrete floor bore various stains from the dregs of leaking farm machinery, and Robbie stared at them for a long time, mulling over a brand new idea. The interior was relatively sterile. So long as you left the doors open for ventilation, you could burn something in here quite nicely . . .

That was fine. The real difficulty lay in convincing Dan to go along with it.

And he needed to check the roller door, in case the mechanism had seized up during Hank's years of ownership. He pressed the button on the control unit, and the door began to move with a satisfying clunking noise.

Robbie took it up ten feet – more than enough – then dropped it down again.

Perfect.

Back at the house, the carpenters insisted on showing him their handiwork before they departed. Robbie tried not to let his impatience show. Finally they were gone, and he was alone.

Time to get to work.

The idea had been brewing since Wednesday night. Once again he had Dan to thank for sowing the seed, with his suggestion that Hank's life might have been more complicated than they realised. If this was the case, so Robbie's train of thought went, there should be some indication of that to be found in the house.

He searched methodically for nearly an hour: moving furniture, lifting beds, rooting in cupboards; even checking that the carpets were securely fastened down. He climbed into the loft and nearly put his foot through the ceiling; descended a few minutes later, grimy with dust and sweat, his only reward a bruised knee.

He didn't find a thing. Dejected, he made himself a black coffee and took it into the room that had served as Hank's office. The desk drawers and filing cabinets had been emptied, and there were spaces in the dust where a computer had been removed. Nothing left but office crap: pens, staples, paperclips, Post-it pads.

He felt resentful that his time had been wasted, and decided to blame Cheryl. Why had the silly cow let her brother's employees take everything? She might have inadvertently given them something valuable.

Or perhaps whoever had broken in had already seized anything worth having?

Robbie drank the coffee slowly, and worked on his mood. Okay, so he'd been wrong about a consolation prize. But the main attraction here was the location: somewhere to destroy Dan's car.

The more he considered it, the more he liked the idea. No doubt the good old male fire-making gene was a factor, but it was undeniably a great way to destroy forensic evidence. The smoke should go unnoticed at night, but the flames might be visible to neighbouring properties. That was why he now favoured using the barn. It shouldn't cause any damage to the building, except maybe a scorch mark on the floor. And who could read anything into that?

He wandered back outside to check the other buildings. First the double garage: it was home to an old washing machine and a 2010 Range Rover Sport. Robbie whistled with admiration, all his disappointment forgotten as he wondered whether he could risk borrowing it for the weekend. Certainly a big improvement on Indira's Citroën.

Then he imagined Dan's voice screaming in his ear: *Are you trying to get arrested?*

Okay, but maybe he'd speak to Cheryl next week, offer to keep the vehicle in good running order until she was ready to sell it.

Emerging from the garage, he felt light rain falling, the sky to the south-west ominously dark. He almost didn't bother with the sheds, except that he was in no hurry to talk to Dan. So he strolled over, searching through the keyring to find the right keys.

The first shed he reached was the larger of the two. It was also newer, with heavy double doors and a proper Yale lock. Inside there was a John Deere ride-on mower and all sorts of gardening implements, as well as spare bags of compost and chipped bark: everything clean and neatly stored. Robbie sensed that this was the work of a gardener rather than O'Brien himself.

The smaller shed looked tatty by comparison. Its door was split in places, and it was secured by a cheap rusty padlock. The interior was thick with cobwebs and spotted with mould. It stank of rotting wood, and there were wet patches on the timber floor, and old stains and scuff marks similar to the ones in the barn.

This was the dumping ground for the house. Halfway between fascinated and repulsed, Robbie explored this museum of junk: old televisions and video equipment, and a reel-to-reel tape recorder. A food mixer and a kettle like something from the Ark, and crazed crockery piled up on a heavy dresser at the back, which was blotchy with gloss paint where a tin had spilled.

There was a deep, wide bookcase standing against the wall opposite the door, nothing on its shelves except a stack of yellowing newspapers and dozens of dead insects. Robbie peered as closely as he dared and saw headlines about Thatcher and Scargill and Kinnock, names that only vaguely rang a bell.

With fire on his mind, he was seized by the notion of dousing the shed in petrol and razing it to the ground. A nice way to vent his frustration. Unfortunately, it was another idea that the 'Dan' voice in his head wouldn't hesitate to veto.

The rain was coming down harder, drumming on the shed roof. Inside, a dripping noise had started up in the corner. Dejected again, Robbie made a dash back to the house, realising halfway across the lawn that he should have locked the shed behind him.

Fuck it. He ran into the house, dried his face, and called Dan. As usual, he got voicemail, and said: 'Call me, soon as. We can sort out your problem tonight.'

He was double-checking that he'd left no trace of his search when Dan rang back. 'I got your message. I take it you mean my car?'

'What else would I mean?'

'Well, offering to solve my problem, I thought that meant you were going to confess.'

Robbie laughed weakly. 'No need to be like that. We're in this together, yeah?'

'Hmm. Where have I heard that before?'

'Look, I've found a solution. But you've got to bring the car over to the farmhouse. Hank's place.'

Dan's reaction was exactly what he'd expected: 'Are you *crazy*?'

'It's on Compton's books now. I've got the whole property to myself. It's the safest place on Earth.'

Now for the tricky part. Robbie needed to keep the truth from Dan until he was here and they had the car in the barn, before revealing that he wanted to smash it up and then set it alight.

Scorch marks.

Dan said, 'Supposing I do bring it over, what then? Do you have a repairer in mind?'

'Sort of.' Robbie couldn't concentrate. There was an image in his head. It was important, but he didn't know why. Something he'd seen just now, in one of the outbuildings.

'Rob, are you listening to me?'

Something odd. A scorch mark, or something like it. But not in the barn.

'Yeah, yeah. Sorry, I'm working.'

A scuff mark. In a kind of semicircle. A shape that looked like —

'Robbie . . .'

'I've gotta go. I'll text you directions – meet you here at eight?'

'Make it nine.'

'Okay.' He nearly added: *And bring a sledgehammer.* But this past week Dan had suffered a complete sense-of-humour bypass, and Robbie's plan for tonight certainly wasn't going to reverse it.

Sixty-two

Dan regarded it as an act of insanity to take his car anywhere near Hank O'Brien's house. But try as he might, he couldn't come up with a better alternative. He had to move the Fiesta before Joan or his brother discovered the damage.

He'd made the call from the office. As he emerged, Hayley was heading into the rest room. He caught up with her as she reached the fridge and took out a bottle of Diet Coke. Her face was flushed, her cheeks red and creased as if they'd been saturated with tears and wiped dry a bit too aggressively.

'Are you all right?' he asked. The service manager, Tim Masters, was sitting at a table, reading the *Express* and no doubt listening keenly to every word.

'Fine.' Hayley found a glass, poured out some Coke and put the bottle back in the fridge.

'Where did you go?'

She shrugged. Looking up from his paper, Tim gave Dan a lazy smile. Hayley smiled, too, but at Tim. Then she walked out as though Dan wasn't there.

He followed her into the corridor. 'What's happened now?'

She turned, glaring. 'Not here, remember? What did the boss have to say?'

'I got a dressing-down. I assured him it wouldn't happen again.'

Hayley gave a caustic laugh. 'And that's all?'

'Pretty much.' His frustration growing, Dan said, 'You can tell me where you've been, can't you? Or is this just to give me a taste of my own medicine?'

It was the wrong thing to say. She blinked away fresh tears, shaking her head as if appalled by the suggestion.

'I would never treat you the way . . .'

Her voice choked up. Dan knew he should be consoling her, but even reaching out to touch her seemed beyond him.

'Tonight,' she said. 'Can we meet tonight?'

He started to nod, then remembered. 'Oh, no. I can't.'

Her mouth twitched; it was almost a smile. 'Let me guess. You're seeing Robbie?'

'I'm sorry. I've got to.' He felt like he was staggering under the weight of deception. 'There's all kinds of stuff going on. Believe me, I wouldn't if it wasn't so important—'

'More important than us, obviously.'

'No, but . . .' Dan stopped her from turning away, his hands on her arms for a second. 'Let's go somewhere tomorrow.'

Hayley arched an eyebrow. 'The wedding fair?'

'Oh, shit. I'd totally forgotten.'

'I'm joking. What would be the point?'

Nothing he could say to that. 'How about Saltdean? A walk on the beach?'

She considered for a moment. 'I suppose.'

Robbie shoved his phone in his pocket and ran from the house. He tore across the lawn, nearly losing his footing on the wet grass. The rain was pouring down now. Once in the shed, he pulled the door shut but that made it too dark to see, so he let it swing open in the wind, not caring if water blew inside.

The mark on the floor occupied his full attention. It was exactly the shape he remembered, and it made perfect sense.

Robbie hadn't much liked school, at least not the academic aspects of it, and he'd reserved a particular loathing for maths. But this was easy enough. Basic geometry.

He moved across to the bookcase, brushing off cobwebs and spitting as a long strand drifted from the roof and clung to his face. Good job he wasn't squeamish.

The bookcase was made of walnut, good solid wood, and it took some shifting. Using all his strength, he was able to manoeuvre it away from the wall. To lift it properly you'd need two people at least. One person alone could only hope to drag it, one end at a time, and as it moved the feet would scrape over the wooden floor.

As he brought the bookcase out from the wall, he could see that its course exactly matched the scuff marks on the timber. Wishing again for better light, he leaned over and peered behind the bookcase. The floor here was subtly different. He had to kneel down before he could see why.

Some of the boards had been cut and glued to form a hatch, complete with two small screw eyes acting as handles.

Robbie pushed and dragged the bookcase another foot or so until it was clear of the hatch. It left him out of breath. His suit was filthy with grime, and there was rain blowing in on him. But he didn't care about any of that.

He knelt down again and lifted the hatch to reveal a narrow void beneath the shed. It was two feet deep, lined with a damp-proof membrane, and it contained two document boxes, resistant to fire and water, each one large enough to accommodate a ream of A4 paper.

For Robbie, the excitement was immense. It felt like a hit of cocaine, like the first big one of the night, the one that chased a couple of drinks – a beer and a vodka, say – when he was set up nicely in some plush lively venue where a fit young woman or two had already caught his eye and given him that special sultry look that the boyfriend never saw: *I'm here for the taking, baby . . .*

He had no idea what lay inside those boxes, but they'd been extremely well hidden. For now that was all he needed to know.

What it meant for Robbie, if he had to sum it up in one word, was *Jackpot.*

Sixty-three

Cate had expected to spend the afternoon dodging conversational grenades, and in that sense she wasn't disappointed. Her mother wasted little time in revealing what was on her mind.

'When did you last see Robbie?' she said, mumbling around an unlit cigarette.

'A couple of days ago. Oh, Mum. Do you have to smoke?'

'Just this one. Did he say what he's up to?'

'Not really. You won't be able to go into the shops.'

'It'll be finished by then. Only he's being even more slippery than usual. I was hoping you could shed some light on his behaviour.'

'Sorry, no.'

Thankfully they were almost on Western Road, where the crowds would hamper any kind of serious conversation – or so Cate hoped.

'I know one thing. If he wasn't my son, I'd have made him redundant by now.'

'If he wasn't your son he wouldn't have been able to take so many liberties in the first place.'

Teresa's rueful humming noise signalled that her daughter had a point.

'Things haven't picked up, then?' Cate asked.

'Treading water, no better than that.' She brightened. 'There's a nice place near Steyning that's coming back on the books. One of Robbie's, actually.'

'Oh?' Cate felt a cold tingling along her spine.

'A farmhouse, should rent for at least twenty-five hundred a month. The original client died in a road accident and the executor decided to hand it back to us.'

'Did Robbie tell you that?'

Stupid, Cate, stupid.

Her mother gave her a pointed look. 'No, Indira. But Robbie's handling it. Why?'

Cate shrugged, said nothing. They turned on to Western Road, into a swarm of shoppers. She felt a nudge on her arm: hoped it was a passer-by, and not her mother.

'Come on, lady. Do you know something I don't?'

'No. Of course not.' Nearly crumbling under the force of her mother's gaze, Cate found salvation: 'Ooh, Topshop! Let's start there.'

Stemper had to move closer once they reached the shops. Even from a few yards away it was a struggle to keep them in sight. And it was pointless following them inside – he could hardly remain unobtrusive in ladies' fashion – so he had to be content with loitering on the pavement.

Not that he was complaining. The morning had yielded some impressive results. Jerry had identified one of the men who'd returned to the accident scene. From what Stemper had learned, he was confident that the man worked for Compton Property Services – and might well be the owner's son.

And now, having just spotted that the young woman was wearing a distinctive green enamel bracelet, Stemper knew that he'd found another piece of the puzzle: the woman who'd been with Hank on the night he died. Easy to understand why she'd lied about knowing the two men, if one of them was her brother.

But why had they murdered Hank? That continued to perplex him, although the money that had been discovered on Thursday morning had to figure somewhere, he thought.

Still, the woman would know. Stemper looked forward to making her tell him.

Cate couldn't begin to fathom Robbie's motives for taking on O'Brien's property. To divert her mother's attention from it, she raised the only subject that could hope to compete with Robbie's shenanigans: her love life.

'I'm on the hunt for a new outfit,' she said as they crossed the road towards Churchill Square. 'Something for the evening that I can also wear to work. Not too glamorous or sexy.'

'Not vampish.'

'No. But still a *bit* sexy.'

That earned an incredulous sidelong glance. 'You've got a date?'

Cate responded with a mysterious smile. Her mother whooped.

'About bloody time, that's all I can say. So who is he?'

'Just somebody I met through work.' After what Cate had been through this week, lying had never come so easy to her. She said nothing more as she eased past an elderly couple, entering the indoor mall a pace or two ahead of her mother.

'Not so fast, madam.' Teresa manoeuvred alongside. 'When are you seeing him?'

'Tonight.'

'Tonight! Why the chuff didn't you say? You haven't even had your hair done. Or your nails. Now you've only got a few hours—'

'Mum, calm down. It's just dinner. It might not come to anything.'

'It probably won't, if you're not going to make an effort.' Teresa huffed, as only a mother could.

Playing the role that was expected of her, Cate said, 'I wish I'd never mentioned it now.'

Teresa wasn't listening. 'Do you need shoes? Huh. Silly question.' She steered her towards ALDO. 'Let's start here.'

*　　*　　*

Stemper followed them for over an hour. Once or twice he came perilously close to attracting the attention of the centre's security guards. It was only the density of the crowd that kept him safe. The needless risk to which he was exposing himself nearly convinced him to abandon the mission – never mind the brain-rotting tedium of watching women shop. All that time and they hadn't made a single purchase.

But he couldn't give up yet. There was one more thing that he wanted.

He got it, at last, once they left the indoor centre and made their way over to North Laine, a district of narrow streets, some of them pedestrian-only, crammed with small boutiques selling esoteric art and sculpture, idiosyncratic fashion, rare books and classic vinyl. This was the bohemian heart of Brighton, and here among the shoppers there were tourists in their droves. No one would think it untoward if Stemper took a few photographs with his phone.

He timed it perfectly, just as the two women moved slowly past the gable end of a building which hosted a stunning mural in comic-book style. He managed to get three shots, and reviewed them as he walked. One of them wasn't bad, but none had caught the younger woman's face as clearly as he would have liked.

He followed them into Kensington Gardens, a densely packed thoroughfare where many of the traders had outside displays, leaving only a narrow channel for hundreds of people to negotiate. Stemper decided to stay with them for another five or ten minutes, in the hope that a better shot would present itself.

The women had fought their way into a vintage-clothing store when Stemper became conscious of a presence behind him. In the hubbub of passing shoppers he didn't register the voice until a hand grabbed his shoulder.

'I said, what the *fuck* are you doing?'

He turned to find a man looming over him: thirtyish, tall and heavy. Bloodshot eyes and a pudgy face, flushed with a degree of anger that seemed quite out of proportion to the offence.

'I beg your pardon?'

'You've been following my w— Caitlin. I saw you taking her photo.'

'I'm afraid you're mistaken.'

'It's no mistake. I want to know what the hell you're playing at. Who are you?'

He was virtually shouting, but there was enough noise around them to make it unremarkable. Even so, it wouldn't be long before he drew a crowd. Stemper couldn't let that happen.

The man was still gripping his shoulder. He had a considerable advantage in height, weight and age. In a straight fight Stemper was likely to end up pinned to the ground while a helpful spectator summoned the police.

'Listen to me,' he said, and instead of trying to break free he moved in towards his assailant, easing him against a rack of second-hand leather jackets. He angled his body in a way that concealed his right hand as it slipped into his pocket.

As a rule, Stemper avoided the use of knives. Although they had all sorts of advantages – they were quick, silent, effective – these were outweighed by one colossal disadvantage: they made a lot of mess.

Stemper carried one, an illegal switchblade, to be used only in emergencies. And this certainly qualified. He couldn't let the woman see him; nor could he face questioning from the police as to why he had taken photographs of her.

He stumbled against the larger man, blurting an apology to mask the tiny click as the blade emerged. Bending slightly, he drove the knife into the man's inner thigh, burying it deep before withdrawing it in a slashing motion. A jet of blood spurted out and hit the display of jackets. Stemper dropped the knife into his coat and was turning as the man started to collapse, making no sound other than a gasp of shock.

'I'm terribly sorry,' Stemper said, and he might have been addressing the tall man nearby who seemed to have tripped on the rack of clothing, or perhaps it was the young couple into whose path he stepped as he danced sideways across the red-brick pavement, away from the puddle of blood that was already beginning to spread into the street.

Immersed in the crowd, he turned his head at the sound of a scream: it would look odd not to. But where others stopped or responded, Stemper pushed on, ignoring the subsequent cries of horror, upping his pace as he turned left, into Gloucester Road, then right. This was Tidy Street, a name that prompted a grim smile. Stemper dipped his head and with one hand kept adjusting his glasses or gently touching his moustache. If he was unfortunate enough to be noticed, these were the details he wanted people to remember.

A couple of minutes later he'd gone far enough to seek a temporary refuge. In the empty doorway of an office block he stopped, his back to the road, appearing to study a list of the businesses within the building. He removed the glasses and the false moustache, then slipped off his raincoat and casually reversed it. Folding the coat over his arm, he put a handkerchief to his face and kept it there as he walked away.

Turning the next corner, he put the coat back on – now blue – and added a flat cap. Even nature was coming to his assistance: it had started to rain. Everyone in his vicinity began to fiddle with umbrellas or quicken their pace.

Invisible, Stemper walked briskly to his car. He couldn't pretend that this development was anything other than deeply unfortunate, and there were many searching questions arising from it: chiefly, was it a sign of age, of failing powers, that he'd been caught unawares?

But that was for later. Right now he consoled himself with the knowledge that he'd dealt with a serious threat to his liberty. He was safe, and so was the mission with which the Blakes had entrusted him.

In fact, he reasoned, Gordon and Patricia didn't have to know about this at all.

*　　*　　*

They heard shouts and screams while Cate was deliberating over a rather splendid 1960s shift dress. Her mother thought it was perfect; Cate felt it would be indecently tight.

'Maybe if I could get rid of my lumpy bits.'

'Lumpy bits? Please! In twenty years you'll look back and be amazed at how slim you were.'

Cate shrugged. 'Still. It's not for me.' She replaced the dress on the rack and frowned. 'What do you think that is?'

They moved towards the doorway, where other customers were peering into the street. As Cate and her mother fought their way through, they could see a gathering outside a clothing store across the way. Beyond the outer cordon of spectators there seemed to be an inner group who were bending or kneeling. A few people were talking in urgent, indistinct voices, but the main crowd seemed strangely silent.

'Heart attack?' said a man in the shop.

A woman on the pavement turned to him. 'There's a man bleeding. They say he's been stabbed.'

Others overheard, and there were gasps and frightened murmurs. Cate shivered but Teresa, always a little prurient, took a step towards the crowd. 'Shall we have a look?'

'Not unless you've got medical training you never told me about.' Cate took her mother's arm and jerked her forward.

'What's the hurry?'

'It's ghoulish. We can't help, so we shouldn't just stand and gawp.'

'Spoilsport.' She tutted. 'Probably kids. They all carry knives nowadays, apparently.'

'I hope he's all right, whoever he is.' There were sirens now, as harsh and insistent as a crying child. Cate imagined what a nightmare it must be for the paramedics, having to fight their way through the city-centre traffic.

Teresa grunted, then said, 'I'm getting peckish – uh.' She twitched, and Cate did, too, as a drop of rain caught her in the face.

'That seals it,' her mother declared. 'Time for coffee and cake.'

Sixty-four

Robbie knew that the afternoon was destined to stay imprinted on his memory for ever. The feel of the cold, rough wooden floor, the smell of mildew, the sound of the rain beating on the roof and drip-drip-dripping in the corner: these things would always be associated with the magical thrill of his discovery.

Each box was stuffed full of paperwork in different shapes and sizes, as well as half a dozen notebooks and a couple of plastic document wallets. A quick perusal revealed that one letterhead was predominant: Templeton Wynne. The name was vaguely familiar to Robbie, but his lack of knowledge wasn't critical. Easily remedied by Google.

There were reports, memos, printouts of long back-and-forth conversations by email, even some handwritten notes that looked to have been photocopied in a hurry, the paper curling away from the light. Robbie didn't stop to read anything in detail. Better to sift through it quickly and try to understand what he had.

Then he took a peek inside one of the document wallets and roared with laughter. No problem understanding this.

He upended it, and a cascade of banknotes fluttered out. Pounds, dollars, euros, yen, some in thick bundles secured with rubber bands, others loose. All used notes, and mostly large denominations.

So Hank O'Brien in some respects was a man after his own heart, Robbie thought. He too had a fighting fund.

He made some quick calculations and was stunned by the result. There had to be at least twenty grand here. It certainly put the money he'd lost during the week into perspective.

He stared at it for so long that he went into a kind of trance, lulled by the rain and nearly hypnotised by the possibilities that were opening up to him. Hank was a man with secrets, all right. Every instinct told Robbie that the contents of all this paperwork would make the cash almost irrelevant by comparison.

A gust of wind slammed the door, then sucked it open again. It was enough to break the spell. He thought about the man who'd photographed them on Wednesday night, and Cheryl's description of a break-in where nothing appeared to have been taken. He shivered.

Someone else is looking for this.

But they hadn't found it. And Cheryl can't have known about the hiding place, or she'd have emptied it herself. It was here for the taking—

Robbie's phone buzzed softly. He would have ignored it, but for the feeling that it had buzzed maybe once or twice before, while he was sorting through the papers.

It was Bree. A missed call, following up on a text: Where r u? Call me x

No chance, he thought, although he was astonished to find it was half past two. How had that happened?

Maureen Heath was waiting for him, but the gold mine here in the shed changed everything. He didn't have to whore himself out.

He was ready to call Maureen and cancel the meeting when the 'Dan' voice spoke up again. *Don't be so impulsive. You need Bree's alibi, remember.*

Buy some time, that was the best option. So he made the call, Maureen Heath answering the moment it rang.

'You ain't baling out on me, are you?'

Robbie was taken aback by the aggression in her voice. 'Sorry, Maureen. I've been called into a meeting. But I'll make it up to you, I promise.'

'Tomorrow.'

'What?'

'My other half's away tomorrow. From Monday he's in and out all week, so it's gotta be tomorrow.'

It sounded like an order, rather than a suggestion. Robbie bristled, but made an effort not to let it show.

'Okay.'

'Ten o'clock's good. I hope you've got lots of energy.'

'Plenty,' he said, thinking about the fresh excuse he would have to find in the morning.

'How about uniforms?'

'I'm sorry?'

'For dressing up. A fireman's sexy. Or a Navy one, like Richard Gere in that film.'

'Sorry, no. I can wear a suit.'

'Yeah. But you should get some uniforms. Women like 'em.'

Robbie put the phone away, determined that Maureen Heath wasn't going to sour his mood. With the money back in the folder, he decided it was safe to return the document boxes to their hiding place. Best to leave everything as it was till he'd done his research and understood what he was dealing with here.

As for the cash, it came down to a test of willpower. If he could bear to let the money out of his sight it meant he was strong enough to refrain from spending it. Proof of his maturity.

After he'd shoved the bookcase back into its original position, he rooted round until he found an old tin of creosote. There was an inch or so of the liquid left, enough to pour on the shed floor, obscuring the scuff mark created by the bookcase, so that nobody else could make the connection that he'd made.

Not that anyone was likely to, he thought.

'Who else can match your genius, Robert?' he said aloud.

It took him ten minutes to finish up, locking doors, setting the alarm. He had another moment of wistful longing for the Range Rover, then he climbed back into the Citroën and drove away. One of the windscreen wipers was playing up, squeaking with every motion, like there was a fucking mouse trapped behind the dashboard.

Robbie was grinning at the image when he turned out of the lane. The visibility was poor enough to need headlights, and as he got up into fifth gear he glanced in the mirror and saw a set of lights on the road behind him. He was sure they hadn't been there when he'd pulled out.

He didn't give it much thought at first. There wasn't a lot of traffic around, so he vaguely noticed when the car made the same left turn on to the A283. He paid a little more attention when it stayed with him across the Henfield roundabout, and he was sitting rigidly in his seat by the time it mimicked his last-second decision to swerve off the slip road for the Shoreham flyover and instead cross the roundabout to take the local road into Shoreham itself.

He was being followed.

Sixty-five

After they'd stopped for a snack, Cate found that she wasn't in the mood for shopping. Everywhere was too busy, too noisy. She felt shaken by her proximity to a violent crime, and realised that she was still emotionally fragile after the bust-up with Martin last night.

All she wanted was to go home and rest for a few hours before the date with DS Thomsett. That too seemed like a bad idea, the more she thought about it. But she knew that her mother would berate her for any hint of a faint heart, so dutifully she traipsed back to Churchill Square and faked enthusiasm for a little black dress that her mother promptly insisted on buying.

'Mum, it's lovely but it's too expensive.'

'Believe me, I've waited so long to hear you've got a fella, it's more than worth it. You're gonna knock him dead in this.'

Under relentless questioning, Cate had given her mother an accurate description of Guy Thomsett, including the fact that he was divorced, with children. The only thing she changed was his occupation, from policeman to solicitor.

'Shame he's in the same line of work as you,' Teresa said. 'Still, apart from that he sounds perfect. Have you met his kids yet?'

'No. This is a casual dinner, that's all.'

'Casual!' her mother scoffed. 'Well, make sure you get to know them soon. Their impression of you will be vital to what he thinks.'

She sighed to herself, and Cate knew that her mother was about to put her foot in it. 'A ready-made family, bloody perfect.'

'What do you mean?'

'None of the pain of childbirth, or all that stress when they're little. Sleepless nights and cleaning up shitty nappies. I tell you, if I could've had you and Robbie delivered when you were ready to start school I'd have leapt at the chance. Completely overrated, babies—'

'Janine's pregnant.' The words slipped out; painful to say, but not as painful as the message it conveyed: *You can be flippant about babies because you were lucky enough to have them.*

Undaunted, Teresa gave a snort. 'Oh my God, that won't last, then. He'll do another runner soon enough. Line up some other floozy.'

Me, Cate thought, and had to blink away the threat of tears. 'Do you think so?'

'Yep. Commitment-phobic, that's Martin.' And then, perhaps to remind Cate that she didn't have a monopoly on heartbreak, she added, 'Just like your father.'

Robbie drove towards Shoreham and let himself get snarled up in the traffic on the coast road. Queuing for the roundabout by the Giant bike store, he had a feeling that his tail was some four or five cars back. He couldn't see the driver, but the car kept nudging out into the road, its impatience clear to see.

Or was that just his imagination? The discovery of the cache of documents was bound to have gone to his head. And impatient drivers were hardly rare in Brighton. He was often one himself.

Twenty grand. Merely picturing the money blotted out his worries. He glanced at a window display of gleaming bikes and thought about treating himself. Get a new mountain bike, top of the range: courtesy of the late Mr O'Brien.

The traffic began to move. Robbie turned left, inched his way along Shoreham High Street and just managed to jump through the pedestrian lights before they turned red. His pursuer – if he existed – wouldn't catch him now.

He took a convoluted route up into Southwick and through Portslade, dreaming of new bikes and other treats, and by the time he brought the Citroën to a halt in the car park at Wickes in Hove he had pretty much convinced himself that there was nothing to worry about.

Working in a shop on a wet Saturday afternoon, it could feel as though time itself had stopped. The heavy rain chased most of Denham's customers away, and the last hour or two was a slow-burning agony for Dan, as he contemplated having to deliver his damaged car to Robbie's promised refuge. At the home of the man who had been knocked down and killed by that very car.

It was madness. He couldn't do it.

Even if he could do it, he *shouldn't* do it.

But if he didn't do it, what *was* he going to do?

In terms of deliberation, that was about as far as he got. Going round in pointless circles.

Then Cate rang. Dan was in the office, ostensibly checking through the staff's timesheets but in reality hiding from Hayley, who was prowling the shop floor like an injured wolf, liable to savage anyone who offered her comfort.

'Did you know Hank O'Brien's farm is back on the rental market? And Robbie has agreed to handle it.'

A difficult moment, until he decided that he wasn't lying to Cate any more. Not about this, at least.

'Uh, he did mention it.'

'What the hell is he doing?'

'Apparently the sister approached him. His argument is that it would have looked strange if he'd turned her down.'

'And what will he do when she finds out about his squalid little deal?'

315

'The usual, I suppose. Charm her pants off.'

'I've just had Mum pumping me for information. I deflected her, but at some stage she's going to hear about it. And when she does . . .'

Cate tailed off, sighing. Dan knew it was the least of their worries, but he tried to reassure her.

'I'll see if I can persuade him to come clean.'

'Get Robbie to own up to something?' She laughed. 'I admire your optimism.'

They chatted for another minute or so, just small talk, then ended the call. Dan stared at his phone, reviewing what he'd said and what he hadn't said. He heard movement in the doorway. Hayley.

'Who was that?' Her eyes narrowed when he hesitated. 'Was it Cate?'

'Yes. We were talking about Robbie.'

'And you're seeing him tonight?'

'Yes. I told you.'

He started to ask what was wrong, but she spun away. He heard her mutter: 'You must think I'm stupid.'

Dan could have followed her and tried to explain, but it wouldn't be enough unless he could tell her the truth. And he couldn't tell her the truth.

Pointless circles.

Cate was enjoying a soak in the bath when her phone rang. As soon as she saw Guy Thomsett's number she knew he was going to cancel, and instead of the relief that she had expected to feel, there was only disappointment, exacerbated by the knowledge that tomorrow her mother would be demanding a full report.

'Cate? I'm really sorry, but I have to postpone tonight.'

'Oh, that's okay.' The brittle jollity in her voice made her cringe.

'It's work, I'm afraid. A fatal stabbing in town this afternoon, so it's all hands on deck. Especially as it's Saturday night, so there'll be the usual mayhem in West Street. They need everyone they can get.'

'That's fine. I understand what it's like.' She was analysing his voice, trying to decide whether this was simply an elaborate excuse. Perhaps he'd come to his senses.

'Thank you. It was a nasty incident. Happened in broad daylight in North Laine.'

'North . . .?' The shock made Cate sit up, and the sound of the sloshing water must have been audible to him. Another reason to cringe, if she hadn't been too preoccupied. 'We were there. Mum and I came out of a shop and we saw people crowding round, but I didn't want to be a nosy onlooker.'

'You're in a minority,' he said. 'Still, a couple of people tried very hard to stem the bleeding. To no avail, unfortunately.'

'How dreadful. Have you caught the person who did it?'

'No. Hence the urgency. I'm off to a full briefing in a minute, but the word is that nobody saw a thing.'

She heard voices in the background: he was being called away. Another quick but heartfelt apology, and he was gone. Cate lay back, stretching out her foot to grip the hot tap and top up the water level. There was no hurry to get out now.

She tried to tell herself it was for the best. She'd viewed the date as an opportunity to get Thomsett off guard and find out why it was that DC Avery seemed so suspicious of her. She'd hoped to glean a clearer picture of where the investigation was heading, but that had always threatened to be a dangerous strategy.

On a personal front, at least he'd said *postpone* rather than *cancel.* That had to mean he was genuinely disappointed, didn't it? And he probably couldn't suggest an alternative date until he knew how his workload was going to be affected by this murder.

Selfish of her to be thinking like this, but it was bloody bad timing. And what was she going to tell her mum?

Sixty-six

Stemper drove out of Brighton, never once exceeding the speed limit, while assessing which of his plans would have to change as a result of the killing. The Horse and Hounds was his next destination. A calculated risk, which he decided to accept. The barmaid had criminal tendencies, and he'd given her enough of a scare to ensure her compliance.

He removed the coat and checked his suit for bloodstains. There were a few dark patches on the legs, but he didn't think they'd be noticeable.

The pub was busy, filled with hikers or ramblers or whatever they called themselves. Ruddy cheeks and muddy boots. Men drinking warm ale in beer mugs with handles. No one showed any interest in him.

Except for the barmaid, of course. Ignoring the fear on her face, he greeted her with a smile. 'Hello, Traci.'

The best of the images was ready on his phone, which he placed on the bar at a spot that wouldn't require her to come too close.

'Is this her?'

She eyed the phone warily, then dipped forward to look and said, 'Yeah.'

'You're absolutely sure? This is Hank's friend?'

A shrug. 'That's the one who was with him. Dunno if she was his friend.'

Stemper smiled again. 'Semantics. Very good.'

He snatched up the phone and was gone.

The next update from Stemper came shortly after Gordon returned from London, both pleased and mildly shaken by the success of his shopping expedition.

Patricia didn't bother with the speakerphone, so Gordon had to interpret the conversation as best he could. It seemed to be almost unequivocally good news, and yet he sensed a fretful quality in Patricia as she listened.

'The daughter? Ah, yes, I see how that could fit.' A laugh. 'Well, quite. Let's hope we see him soon.' She met Gordon's eye and frowned, but that could have meant anything.

He was feeling quietly satisfied. Everything he had been asked to do, he had done. Collected the tickets from a scalper, paying an exorbitant amount in cash, and then for the other items he'd ventured into the wilds of Soho – still thrilling, but so much tamer than the Soho of his youth, never mind the Soho of his imagination.

To think that once in a hotel suite he had lain beneath a glass coffee table, coked up to the nines and giggling like a fiend while two women and a man copulated frantically across the room, and a third woman squatted above him—

'What?' Patricia said, and for a terrifying moment he thought she'd finally found a route into his head. If she ever caught the merest hint of his secret life she would divorce him without hesitation, a fact which undeniably made his exploits seem all the more daring.

He said, 'Nothing, my sweet.'

'Why the silly grin?'

'Just pleased with the day's work.' He gestured at the phone. 'What's the news?'

'On the face of it, very positive. He thinks the woman with Hank is a solicitor, first name Caitlin, surname possibly Scott. Daughter of the proprietor of Compton Property Services.'

'Ah.'

'He has her home address, and he managed to get her picture, which the barmaid verified. He suspects that one of the men is her brother, thus explaining why she'd conceal his identity from the police.'

Gordon clapped his hands. 'It's coming together, isn't it?'

'I'm not sure. Stemper wasn't nearly as . . . ebullient as you'd expect, given these developments.'

'Really, darling. Is there anything to be gained in trying to understand a man like Stemper?'

'Good question. He's due here later. In the meantime he wants us to research the woman. We're looking at law firms in Brighton.'

'Caitlin,' Gordon said to himself. 'Why the uncertainty about her surname? Is she married?'

'Stemper believes she might be separated or divorced.'

Gordon choked on a laugh. 'How on Earth would he know that?'

Stemper had called the Blakes from a car park in Horsham. He needed a large anonymous town, and this fitted the bill. In a chain menswear store he bought a new set of clothing: suit, shirt, tie, underwear, shoes and a raincoat. He also bought a small tub of hair-styling wax.

Using a disabled toilet, he stripped off his old clothes and bagged them up, then dressed in the new outfit, making sure to crumple the suit and scuff the shoes a little. The gel was used to slick his hair back in a style that transformed his appearance.

He returned to the car and drove until he found a retail park with a hardware store. His purchases included a can of Jeyes Fluid, some heavy-duty refuse sacks and nylon rope. He drove out of the town and stopped at a large expanse of open ground: a park with playing fields, a picnic area and a lake. The lake had an ornamental bridge that gave him access to slightly deeper water.

It was still raining hard, and the car park was deserted. Stemper soaked his old clothes in Jeyes Fluid, then stuffed them into a refuse sack and added stones from the car park for extra weight. He tied it up with rope and carried it out towards the lake, on to the bridge, checked that no one was watching and then tossed it into the water.

The knife, regrettably, followed the bag to the bottom of the lake. It wasn't perfect, but Stemper didn't have time to search for anywhere better. The main thing was that, even if someone hooked the bag and pulled it out, there would be nothing to link its contents to him.

Back at the car, he realised that he ought to have heard from Jerry by now. The first call wasn't picked up. Stemper waited a couple of minutes and tried again.

'Yeah?'

'Where are you? Still at the farmhouse?'

'Nah. He left. I followed him down into . . . Shoreham-by-Sea. He was going east, towards Brighton, but I lost him. Traffic was shit. I did my best, honest.'

'Hmm.' Stemper couldn't afford to go too easy on him: Jerry wouldn't buy it. 'Was he aware of you?'

'Nah, course he wasn't. I'm not a complete amateur.'

'You know how the Blakes will react to this?'

'Oh, yeah.' Jerry sounded reconciled to his fate. 'Suppose I have to drive round and round till I see him, then?'

Stemper paused, as though the idea had its appeal. 'Actually, you've spent an awful lot of time on this. I think you can call it a day.'

'You what?'

'Get off home and put your feet up. I'll square it with the Blakes.'

'Are you sure?'

'I appreciate how hard you're working, even if they don't. And it's Saturday. You'll want to take it easy. Unwind. Recharge your batteries.'

'But how are we gonna find this bloke?'

'I'll think of something. Don't worry. Just enjoy a nice quiet evening at home.'

Satisfied that he'd placed some useful suggestions in Jerry's mind, Stemper terminated the call and drove away.

The incident this afternoon continued to perturb him. The man had seen Stemper taking the photographs, so he must have been following him for a while. Or rather, he must have noticed Stemper during his own pursuit of the woman, Caitlin. It was an unforgivable lapse, not to have spotted him first.

Back on the A24, he found a pleasant-looking pub that was still serving food. He restored his original hairstyle, added glasses, and took his briefcase with him. Over a delicious fillet of sea bass he fired up his laptop and went online, attending to various matters. There was a mildly flirtatious email from Debbie Winwood, expressing the hope that his business trip was progressing well. She asked if he knew when he'd be coming back. He sent a brief reply: within the next week, he hoped.

His gut feeling was that this would be concluded by then, even though at the moment he wasn't sure exactly how it would end. A lot to play for.

Gordon understood what Patricia had been getting at when he saw Stemper's face. It was as though the man's mask had slipped a little, and what they could see behind it was an unmistakable hint of vulnerability.

Declining refreshments, Stemper took a seat at the kitchen table. He told them about his visit to the letting agency.

'I registered as a prospective client, because I suspect that the farmhouse might soon be available to rent again. That hunch was confirmed when Hank's sister had a visitor this morning. Jerry heard his voice and believes it was one of the men from Wednesday night.'

'The brother?' Patricia said.

'It's highly likely. I've taken another look at the Compton website. There's reference to a Robert Scott. He's on Facebook, as *Robbie* Scott, with a couple of hundred friends, one of them a Cate Scott.'

'Caitlin,' Gordon said.

Stemper nodded. 'Did you identify the law firm?'

'Mitre Jeffreys Arnold,' Patricia said. 'They have offices nationwide and affiliate companies around the world. The bad news . . . they've done a lot of work for Templeton Wynne.'

'The London office, principally,' Gordon added. 'We can't find any direct links between Templeton and the Brighton branch, or Caitlin specifically. But that's not to say they don't exist.'

'It seems to get ever more complicated. Whenever we take a step in one direction, there's something else pulling us in another.'

Stemper weighed it up. 'As you say, MJA are huge. Therefore it's more likely than not to be a coincidence.'

'I hope so. Otherwise . . .' It was an almost melancholy cry from Patricia.

'Let's focus on the positives,' Gordon said. 'You've identified two of the three people from Tuesday night. That's a very significant advance.'

'Any candidates for the other man?' Patricia asked.

'Plenty on Robert's Facebook page,' Stemper said. 'Too many to hunt down one by one.'

'The better route, surely, is to question this woman Cate?' Gordon said. Patricia nodded, and both looked to Stemper for a response.

'I agree. But I want to watch her for a day or two first, see who she consorts with.'

Patricia was tight-lipped, clearly reluctant to offend Stemper, so Gordon chipped in. 'It's wise to be cautious, but we mustn't lose sight of the timescale.'

'I understand. Shall we say, until Monday? Sooner if I spot an opportunity for a fruitful conversation.'

They all smiled. Then Stemper said, 'And tonight. I take it nothing's changed?'

Another glance between them. Patricia shook her head.

'That goes ahead as planned.'

Sixty-seven

Louis's recent behaviour had one fortunate consequence: it meant he was in his brother's debt. And when Dan pointed out that it was their aunt to whom he should make amends, Louis could do little but agree.

'Will you take her out to dinner?' Dan asked. 'Casa Don Carlos. She loves it there.'

'Aren't you coming?'

'I'd like to, but there's stuff I've got to sort out with Hayley.' At least that wasn't really a lie, Dan thought.

'So this is serious, then. Are you gonna split up?'

'I don't know.' Dan handed over sixty pounds. 'Will that be enough to cover it?'

'Should be.' Louis gave him a cheeky grin. 'Do you want change?'

'No. You can keep it.'

Joan was delighted by the offer, though she too tried to persuade Dan to join them, curtailing her pleas only when Louis gave her a none too subtle look.

They were ready to leave by seven, which was earlier than Dan would have wished. Knowing his aunt, she'd eat her dinner quickly and want to be back home by eight-thirty. Just in case, Dan texted Robbie, warning him that he might be there sooner than they'd agreed.

For Joan, this was almost a dress rehearsal for her date next week. Despite the short notice she made a considerable effort, and it showed. 'You scrub up well for an old bird,' was Louis's less than respectful compliment, though he then declared that he was proud to be escorting such an attractive woman.

'You mean you won't hide if we see one of your friends?'

'Nah. They'll be well jealous. And you wait till Ron sees you on Wednesday. He'll think he's won the lottery.'

'All right, don't overdo it.' Joan kissed Dan goodbye, gripping his hand tightly for a moment. 'You're a lovely man,' she whispered in his ear. 'I hope everything works out the way you want it to.'

It was an enigmatic comment, which played on his mind during the next hour while he waited impatiently for nightfall: one eye on the window, another on the TV.

The local news was dominated by a fatal stabbing in the centre of Brighton. Dan felt a twinge of guilt that someone else's misfortune had helped dislodge the hit-and-run from the headlines.

By eight o'clock the rain had eased off, but there was enough low cloud to hasten the darkness. He realised he had no good reason to delay any longer.

As he opened the garage door he noticed that his hands were shaking. He hadn't felt this nervous about getting behind the wheel since his driving test.

The Fiesta started first time, which was a small relief. Reversing it out of the garage was a different matter. He hadn't done it for a year or two, and he'd forgotten how narrow the opening was. But it was probably the nerves that caused him to scrape the edge of a wing mirror on the wall.

'You bloody idiot!' he shrieked. He had to stop for a few seconds to compose himself. Then he got the car straight and managed to back out in one smooth motion.

The urge to panic was ever-present. Now the Fiesta was out, he wanted it away from the house as fast as possible. First he had to shut the garage and lock it. He couldn't have Joan and Louis coming back and finding it open.

He was walking back down the drive when he heard a door slam. For a second he thought his aunt was home, but then he heard the beep of a car lock and realised it was a neighbour going out.

Dan climbed into the Fiesta and watched the rear-view mirror until he saw the neighbour pass by. Then he reversed gently over the pavement and on to the road.

So far, so good.

The journey was uneventful, but still a major ordeal. His rational mind understood that the dented bodywork was virtually invisible to other motorists, but to Dan it screamed for attention as blatantly as if he had Hank O'Brien strapped to the roof.

A couple of times on the A27 he had to overtake slow-moving lorries. As he accelerated it came back to him: the way he'd set a course to pass O'Brien, then the sudden wrench as Robbie pulled on the wheel, followed by the impact, the heavy thud of a body, the weightless terror as the car lost traction on the verge.

It was all there, in perfect vivid detail, and Dan felt vomit rising in his throat. His vision swam and the road shimmered and vanished for a moment. A flick of the wheel now and the same blackness that had swallowed O'Brien for ever could swallow Dan too, if he chose.

But he couldn't do that. He knew it wasn't the answer.

For the rest of the journey he was assailed by thoughts of the man who had killed his parents. Was this how he had suffered in the days and weeks afterwards? Had he been haunted by what he'd done?

Somehow, Dan doubted it.

The directions Robbie had supplied proved easy to follow. Dan turned into the lane and his headlights picked out the open gates.

As he reached them Robbie came towards him at a fast trot, waving him in.

By the time Dan got out of the car, Robbie was already closing the gates, his attention fixed on the road beyond.

'What is it?'

'Nothing. Just . . .' Robbie went on looking that way for a moment, then turned, shook his head. 'Nothing.'

Dan surveyed the house. Apart from a single light in the hallway, the place was in darkness. The grounds were bordered by tall trees, barely visible against the charcoal sky; he could hear them swaying in the wind.

'It's safe here, though?'

'Yep. Nearest house is about three, four hundred yards away. We're good.'

Dan gestured at a Citroën Picasso parked by the garage. 'Whose is that?'

'Indira's. She needed a better car for the weekend.'

'You lent her your BMW?'

'Yeah.' Robbie made it sound as if it was commonplace to put his pride and joy into the hands of others.

Dan let him come closer, until he could see his face clearly. 'So what's the plan, exactly?'

'First things first, we've got to move your car.' Robbie pointed towards a patch of grass to the side of the garage. 'Probably best if you drive. I'll guide you.'

'Where's it going?'

'There's a barn—' Robbie broke off, staring at the bushes along the side of the driveway. Dan spun round, his heart juddering.

'What is it?'

Robbie chuckled. 'Don't worry. Makes me jumpy, all this country-side. I'm not used to it.' He shoved his hands into the pockets of his jacket. 'Follow me.'

*   *   *

327

Still full of misgivings, Dan drove on to the grass and rolled along behind Robbie until a building loomed into view. It turned out to be a large barn, its entrance gaping wide.

Once inside, Robbie pressed a button on the wall and the huge roller door descended. Then he switched on the lights and a bank of fluorescents fired up overhead. Dan got out of the car and immediately noticed a sledgehammer leaning against the wall. There was a fuel can next to it.

He turned to Robbie, who was beginning to smile. A smile that said *I can explain everything . . .*

'Did you bring those?'

'Yeah.' No bluster, for once.

'What for?'

'I looked into getting it repaired, but I couldn't find anywhere. With all the stuff over the news, and the cops testing for paint, I don't think we can risk it, to be honest.'

Dan put on a sceptical expression, but the same thing had occurred to him. 'So what, then?'

'Jed's got a mate, works in a scrapyard. He can make it disappear. But he says it's better if it's properly smashed up first.'

'Does he?' Dan sighed. In many ways the Fiesta was an old heap: nothing to be sentimental about. But it was relatively cheap to run, and it got him from A to B.

And he couldn't afford to replace it.

Then Robbie chose to rub salt into the wound. 'The guy wants three hundred. I've paid a hundred up front. I thought I'd deduct that from the cash you lent me the other night.'

Dan laughed, which was arguably wiser than punching Robbie in the mouth.

'And what am I going to do for a car?'

'Ah. You've got Third Party Fire and Theft, yeah? So report it stolen and stick a claim in.'

'No.'

'Why not? Think of all the premiums you've paid over the years. You're owed that money.'

'I doubt if the insurance company would see it like that. Besides, I'd have to report it to the police.'

'That's just to get a reference number. They won't take any action.'

'But what if they go digging into you, and the deal with O'Brien? If anything leads them to me, and they find out I had a car go missing . . .'

Robbie shrugged. 'Have it your way. But whether you claim for it or not, this is still the best answer.'

'And how do I explain that I've suddenly got no car, and no money for a new one?'

There was a heavy silence. Robbie took himself for a wander around the barn, hands shoved in his pockets. At first Dan thought he was simply being given time for it to sink in, but Robbie's body language hinted at something else, so Dan kept quiet.

Then Robbie's head snapped up. He strode decisively towards the door, indicating that Dan should follow.

'Come on. You need to see this.'

Sixty-eight

Robbie stepped outside and waited for Dan. The cloud cover meant there was no moon or starlight. He could make out the farmhouse from the glow of a light he'd left on in the hall, but everything else was vague, sinister shadow.

It wasn't just nature creeping him out. This afternoon he'd called in at the office, just so he could truthfully tell his mother he'd been at work, then dashed home to shower and change. He was back at the farmhouse by half-six, and decided to take a look at the footpath that ran round the perimeter.

There he made an unwelcome discovery: half a dozen discarded sweet wrappers, and clear signs that somebody had crushed the weeds as they delved into the bushes. He recalled a dog growling as he'd bid farewell to Hank's sister. Somebody had been hiding here.

On the drive up Robbie had kept a close eye on the traffic behind him and he was confident that he hadn't been followed. But now, with this, he knew for certain that it wasn't just his imagination running wild.

Even so, he decided to say nothing: Dan's reaction was all too easy to predict.

First stop was the house, to collect a flashlight and a couple of beers. Robbie popped the caps and offered one to Dan, who stared at it in horror.

'Are they Hank's?'

'No. I bought 'em on the way here.'

Ruefully Dan accepted the bottle. 'You're driving me home, remember.'

'As if I'd forget.'

Robbie led the way across the lawn in darkness, saving the flashlight for when they were inside. He'd expected a bombardment of questions, but there was only a moody silence, broken by a loud sniff as he entered the shed.

'Stinks, doesn't it?'

Robbie shone the light around the interior, illuminating the piles of junk. He'd been in two minds about showing Dan what he'd found. His natural inclination was to keep it to himself, but he knew that Dan's feedback could be useful, especially as Robbie had no real clue what he was dealing with.

He put his beer down and propped the flashlight on an old TV, directing the light across the shed.

'Give me a hand with this.'

He took one end of the bookcase and shifted it an inch or two. With an air of exasperation, Dan moved to the other end and they manoeuvred it clear of the hatch.

'Shine the light down here.' Robbie lifted the hatch, imagining for a second that the hiding place would be empty. But the boxes were just as he had left them.

'How did you find this?'

'Sheer brilliance.' Robbie laughed. 'Plus a soupçon of luck.'

'What's in the boxes?'

'Papers, mostly. I only found them this afternoon. Haven't had a proper look yet.' He reached for his beer and took a long pull on the bottle.

Dan was staring at the boxes, his face partly in shadow, his expression sombre. 'Why would Hank have paperwork hidden away?'

'I dunno. Intriguing, isn't it?'

Dan grunted. 'That's not the word I'd use.'

*　　*　　*

At Robbie's suggestion they carried the boxes into the barn. He opened each one, upended it and spread the papers out on the floor. He felt deflated by Dan's reaction. Not a hint of excitement: just the usual anxiety and gloom. He wasn't even drinking his beer.

'Good, isn't it?'

'Is it?' Dan seemed puzzled. 'What made you go searching in the first place?'

'Something you said Wednesday night, after that bloke jumped out on us. Got me wondering what kind of secrets Hank might have been keeping.'

Dan crouched down and examined a couple of reports. 'Templeton Wynne.'

'I think that's who Hank worked for. Heard of them?'

'Vaguely. No idea what they do.'

'Me neither.' Robbie took a swig of beer. 'Hank's got a home office, but it's been cleared out. His sister said the company collected everything.' He gestured at the boxes. 'So this was stuff he didn't want anyone to know about – not even his own employers.'

'Do you think it's insider trading?'

'Could be. Whatever it is, it must be valuable.'

Dan was nodding, working it out for himself. 'So this is what they're after. The man on Wednesday night. The reason he's trying to find us is because of *this*.'

'I reckon you're right.'

'How can you sound cheerful about it? We don't have a clue what we're involved in.' Dan looked horrified. Staring at Robbie as though he expected the world to cave in on them.

'It's not all bad news.' Robbie reached for his trump card: the document wallet. 'Look what else he'd stashed away.'

He tipped the money out, picked up a wad of notes and showed it to Dan. 'There's a good twenty thousand here.' A nod at the Fiesta. 'And that's worth, say, three grand?'

'Nearer four. It's done less than sixty thousand miles.'

'All right. Four. Christ, make it five if you like.' *But no more than that*, Robbie thought. *The rest is mine.*

'Make it five . . .?' Dan echoed. 'You're saying we take this money?'

'Yeah, why not?'

'Because it's not ours. We have no idea where it came from.'

'Yes, we do. It came from a hole in the ground.'

'You know what I mean.'

'All right, all right.' Robbie put up his hands. 'Let's take this a step at a time. You agree we've got to dispose of the car, yeah?'

Quietly fuming, Dan nodded. 'I suppose.'

'And this buddy of Jed's will do it for us. But it'll cost three hundred quid. Then there's the fact that you're left without a car, which is gonna get people asking a lot of awkward questions. Yes?'

Dan nodded again, but said, 'Taking this money is not the answer.'

'Why not? Hank's dead. This was sitting here all week and nobody came to get it—' He only just stopped short of mentioning the break-in. 'What's the point of leaving it to rot?'

'It's a matter of principle. I'm not a thief. I don't want this money.'

'You may not want it, but you *need* it. You can buy a new car and tell everyone you traded the Fiesta in.'

'I can't believe you're even thinking like this after what happened on Tuesday night. Because of your greed we had to go back the next night, and we nearly got caught.'

'But this is different. It's not gonna be missed.'

'Why not? What if Hank stole the money? In fact, what if he stole it from the man who took a photo of your car?'

Robbie shook his head. 'This isn't a fortune, not in terms of robbery. It's more like . . . petty cash. He must have travelled a lot, and got used to salting money away for emergencies.'

Dan indicated the paperwork. 'So what about this?'

'Yeah, it's a mystery. And I agree that somebody may well be after it. But there's not a lot we can do about that.'

333

'We can put it back. And then, when they come looking, they'll find it.'

Robbie stared at him in disbelief. Not for the first time he was astounded that two people whose minds worked so differently could ever have become friends.

'You'd really do that?'

'Yes.'

'You've no curiosity at all?'

'Not after this week, no. You remember what happened to the cat?'

'Eh?' It took Robbie a few seconds; then he snorted. 'Oh, curiosity killed the cat. Very witty.'

Now Dan picked up one of the documents. 'This mentions the Ministry of Defence.'

'So?'

'What if Hank was into espionage or something? We could have the security services after us.'

'Oh, come on. Your imagination's working overtime.' He climbed to his feet. 'If we're gonna do the car, I'm getting another beer first. Just the one,' he added, when Dan glared at him. 'Wanna join me?'

'No.'

'I brought pizza for later, in case we get peckish.'

Dan squinted at him, his head cocked to one side. 'Is this your idea of a celebration?'

'Why not? Let's see off your poor old car in style.'

'Yeah. Thanks.'

'Hey, five grand on the table, in cash. Plus beer and pizza.' Robbie did a little skip towards the door, half expecting Dan to lob an empty bottle at him. 'That sounds like a celebration to me.'

Sixty-nine

Jerry Conlon owned a house in Derinton Road, Tooting, in South London, the sort of tiny two-bed terrace that estate agents were prone to describe as a 'cottage'. It was currently worth about three hundred thousand, but its value was meaningless since Jerry had been forced to remortgage a few years ago to pay off his second wife and put money into a trust fund for their grown-up son, who was severely disabled. Jerry never visited the lad – couldn't even bear to think about him, if the truth were told – but felt he'd at least done the right thing financially.

It wasn't the sort of home he'd imagined himself ending up in. He'd hoped to be somewhere larger, out in the suburbs, with an en-suite bathroom and a huge great kitchen like the Blakes had. A decent garden with a hideaway shed and maybe a hot tub on the deck.

But this was what he had, this and Jen-Ling, and on his good days Jerry knew to thank his lucky stars for that.

Right now he wouldn't class this as one of the good days, but it wasn't exactly a bad day, either. He didn't actually know *how* he felt, so he was enjoying a glass or two of mid-priced brandy while he tried to decide.

The doorbell ringing came as a surprise. The sound had echoed away before he registered what it meant – a visitor – and even then he had to sit up and consider that for a moment. Normally Jen-Ling handled answering the door, along with most of the other domestic chores, so he sat back and waited for her to take care of it. Then, with a gentle start, he remembered that Jen-Ling wasn't here tonight.

Oops. Possibly he was slightly more befuddled than he'd thought.

He got up, creaking and groaning like an old fence. All the hours he'd spent outside this week, crouching in bloody fields and bushes, had caused his joints to seize up and ache to buggery.

He didn't answer the door until he'd peered through the spyhole. Basic precaution these days. He wasn't sure who he was expecting to see, but not Stemper, looking bored.

Jerry opened the door. Stemper was wearing a raincoat over a suit, and holding his briefcase. *Not more effing work to do?*

'What's up?' Jerry asked.

'I think we should talk about the Blakes.'

'Oh yeah?' Jerry wasn't going to be tricked into speaking out of turn.

'They're taking us for a ride. I've no idea what they're paying you, but now we know there's fifty million at stake, I'm willing to bet it's peanuts in comparison.'

'You didn't sound that unhappy last night.'

'You have to choose your moments, Jerry. Wait until you have the right kind of leverage.' Stemper gave a disgusted little laugh, and shifted his weight from foot to foot, as though he was cold. 'Do you know, they sent me a cheap bottle of Scotch as a "thank you" for my efforts so far? As if I'd regard that as fair compensation for all I've done.'

'I know what you mean. They're taking the piss.' Jerry opened the door wide. 'D'you wanna come in?'

Stemper followed Jerry through a narrow, gloomy hallway into a combined living-dining room with laminate flooring and beige walls. There was a large TV, tuned in to an old episode of *Dad's Army*, and a nest of tables, the smallest of which was home to an open bottle of brandy and a snifter glass.

As Jerry sat down, he pointed at the bottle and said, 'They got me that. I mean, St Remy's nice enough. I'm not gonna turn my nose up at it. But Gordon knows I like my cognac, I was talking to him about it a few weeks back. If they seriously wanted to show their appreciation they could have got me a bottle of Hine Antique XO.'

'That's the rating system?'

'Yeah. Extra Old.' Jerry snorted. 'Might've guessed you'd be an expert on booze, along with everything else.'

'Hardly.' Stemper made a show of looking around the room. 'Is your wife here?'

'That's the other thing. They sent me this pair of theatre tickets. Some friend of theirs had spares and they thought I might like to take Jen-Ling. But it's *Billy Elliot*.'

Stemper grimaced: the reaction that Jerry clearly desired.

'I mean, as if I'd wanna sit in front of *Billy* fucking *Elliot* . . .'

'I hope she hasn't had to go on her own?'

Jerry shook his head. 'She works in a laundrette. One of the girls there has gone with her.'

'So you have a night in with St Remy.' Stemper chuckled again. 'Well, I may have another treat for you.'

As he spoke he set the briefcase down on the coffee table, popped it open and shifted it round for Jerry to see. He'd placed a few official-looking documents on top, printed for him by Gordon Blake. As Jerry leaned forward, Stemper moved alongside him, directing his attention to the briefcase, and Jerry didn't see him take the bondage rope from his pocket.

Jerry was squinting at the text, wondering if Stemper was going to propose blackmailing the Blakes for a larger cut, and then he felt Stemper coming in close, as if to perch on the edge of the chair. It seemed inappropriate, far too intimate, and then in a blur of movement there was something around his throat, pulling tight, and Stemper was on him, forcing him down and off the chair.

He ended up on his knees, Stemper's weight on his back and some kind of noose around his neck, Stemper gripping it as though bringing an unruly dog under control.

Jerry tried to speak but all he managed was a gargling noise. The confusion gave way to panic as Stemper's 'friendly guy' persona dissolved like aspirin and was replaced in Jerry's mind by the knowledge that this man solved problems, in ways that nobody ever liked to describe; and in hinting to the Blakes that he felt he was being undervalued, Jerry had gone and declared himself a problem.

The unfairness of it broke his heart. Jerry knew he wouldn't get a chance to explain, much less plead for mercy. Not that it would do any good. The Blakes had ordered this: Stemper was merely the weapon they used. You might as well beg a gun not to shoot you.

Despite everything, Jerry couldn't help marvelling at their ingenuity. The theatre tickets, specifically for a show that wouldn't appeal to him. The brandy, cheap enough to make him resentful, and thus determined to drink it out of spite. The booze had softened him up, made him slow and pliable. Even the decision to let him knock off early this afternoon must have been part of it. At the time he'd thought it a bit strange not to get a bollocking for losing the guy in the Citroën.

He'd been rolled into a trap with consummate skill and cunning, and the only saving grace, as far as he could see, was that Jen-Ling was to be spared. Jerry knew he must do whatever it took to protect her, even if *whatever it took* meant dying quietly, without a fuss.

As well as bondage ropes, the generous pockets of Stemper's raincoat contained the other tools for his night's work: they included a rubber-ball gag with leather straps and a lacy bra-and-knickers set in a size that would fit Jerry.

First in was the gag, so he couldn't scream. He was still making

338

guttural noises but Stemper grabbed the remote control, upped the TV's volume and changed channels until he found a boisterous game show.

He kept the pressure on his makeshift noose, tight enough to render Jerry compliant without causing him to pass out. Hauling him to his feet, Stemper pushed and cajoled him upstairs, ignoring the muffled cries and moans.

The main bedroom was painted black and silver and boasted a hideously revealing mirror on the ceiling. Stemper couldn't have designed a better backdrop for the scenario he had in mind. Better still, there was a TV on a chest of drawers, complete with a built-in DVD player.

He laid Jerry down and sat astride him, releasing the rope around his neck while he slipped on a pair of thin leather gloves. Then he gripped Jerry's right hand by the wrist and saw to it that Jerry's fingers touched the gag and the ropes and the underwear.

Undressing the man wasn't a task he relished, but he bought compliance with a simple threat: 'If you struggle I'll revert to Plan B, which I prepared in case you chose to accompany your wife to the theatre. It involves us waiting until she gets home, and then what happens to you will also happen to her. But it will be far, far worse. Understand?'

He hadn't put Jerry down as a brave man, and he was right. But it seemed that he did possess a measure of chivalry. Without a murmur he allowed Stemper to strip off his clothes and put the lingerie on him, and then he meekly flopped over to lie face down on the bed.

Stemper looped the other bondage rope around Jerry's ankles, bent his legs at the knee and joined that rope to the one around his neck, tightening it to the point where Jerry's head was tipped back. To ease the chokehold on his neck Jerry had to move his feet closer, until his heels were almost level with the base of his spine. Although his arms were free, they could do little more than flail at the ropes. Perhaps, in sheer desperation, he might have been able to save his life by tugging on the rope at his neck, even if it meant dislocating his hips. But Stemper wasn't about to permit that.

The last touch was the amyl nitrate. Stemper pressed the bottle into Jerry's hands, then put it to his nostrils and told him to inhale. By this point Jerry seemed as eager as Stemper to get it over with. He sniffed for all he was worth. His face, already flushed and swollen, grew redder still. He began to make rapid high-pitched noises, like the cry of some exotic bird.

There was one additional task – the most distasteful of all, and not always achievable. The last time Stemper had used this method the victim hadn't shown any hint of arousal, but Jerry's physiology was more obliging.

With mechanical efficiency, Stemper ensured that there would be traces of semen to consolidate the impression that this was a sex game gone tragically wrong. While he worked, he could see Jerry weakening, the oxygen deprivation putting an enormous strain on his heart as the muscles in his legs succumbed to the will of gravity, slowly throttling the life out of him.

It was now safe for Stemper to pop downstairs and fetch the DVD from his briefcase. He added Jerry's prints to the DVD and put it into the machine. By the time the first images of hardcore amateur porn appeared on the screen, Jerry Conlon was spared the sight of them.

He was dead.

Seventy

It was both a strange and a strangely fine evening. Although he wouldn't have admitted it to Robbie, Dan found it remarkably cathartic.

He had no desire for food, but once the pizza had been microwaved and he caught a whiff of melted cheese and hot pepperoni, he realised he was starving. He didn't intend to have a second beer, either. Or a third. Or a fourth. But it was Saturday night, and he wasn't going to be driving home, so why the hell not?

'See, we're giving the Fiesta a nice send-off,' Robbie said, after he'd packed up the boxes and put them by the door.

'Like a wake?'

'More like a Viking funeral.' Robbie thought that was hilarious, for some reason.

As it turned out, destroying the car wasn't as simple as they'd anticipated. Noise was one factor that Robbie hadn't considered. It was a dry evening, and not windy enough to muffle the clang of hammer against metal.

It was Dan who found the solution, fetching a thick cushion from one of Hank O'Brien's armchairs. Then they took it in turns, one of them holding the cushion by its edges and placing it against the car, while the other swung the sledgehammer. They tried to pick random spots, working harder on some areas, but still the end result was a bizarre pattern of damage that didn't look remotely natural.

'Anyone can see it's been vandalised on purpose,' Dan said.

'Yeah. But where's the damage from Tuesday night?'

Dan peered at the bonnet and around the edge of the shattered windscreen.

'It's gone.'

'Exactly. And that's the point. Now it's just a write-off, ready for the crusher.' Robbie reached for the fuel can. '*Almost* ready.'

'I'm still not sure about this.' Dan swallowed down a burp. Four empty bottles on the barn floor, and somehow he had a fifth one on the go.

'I'm completely sober,' Robbie assured him, though there were three empties next to his pizza box.

'And you seriously want to do it in here?'

'Yeah. Why not?'

'There's no chimney.'

'It'll be fine. Trust me.'

At that, Dan burst out laughing. He couldn't explain what he found so funny, but Robbie probably had a fair idea, judging by the sour look on his face.

They opened the big roller door as well as the access door to create a through draught. Robbie carried the document boxes out and put them in his car for safety, ignoring Dan's argument that they should be returned to their hiding place. Dan watched him pick up the fuel can and start sloshing petrol over the Fiesta's upholstery.

'Don't overdo it. You're filling the air with fumes. Light a match and the whole place'll go up.'

Robbie sniffed once or twice, then shrugged. 'Yeah. All right.'

They stood outside for ten minutes, allowing the air to clear.

'Wish I still smoked,' Robbie said. 'Maybe I'll start again.' A chuckle. 'Cigars. Those big fat Cuban ones, like movie producers have.'

Dan had no comment. He was steadily consuming his beer, having decided there was every reason to get totally pissed. Perhaps Robbie was right about him. He needed to loosen up, be more like Robbie. More like Louis.

'Party animals,' he muttered.

'Eh?'

Dan shook his head. 'The other night, when Louis and his friends were causing that trouble . . .'

'Mucking around.'

'Whatever. I don't think it was just booze. I think some of them are doing drugs.'

Robbie gave a regretful smile, as though Dan was the most naive man he'd ever met.

'What d'you want me to say? I was up to all sorts at seventeen, and you could've been too, if you'd wanted.'

'So you reckon they are? Louis as well?'

'Maybe. But they'll know not to go crazy.' He tutted. 'God, Dan, even after a few drinks you're still trying to carry all the world's problems on your back. Just give it a rest, eh?'

'Wish I could.'

'It's easy enough. Just say you're gonna do it. Then do it.'

At Dan's suggestion, Robbie used one of the pizza boxes as a taper. He lit it while still in the doorway, and took a few cautious steps into the barn.

'Should be okay now, yeah?'

Dan grunted. He stepped over the threshold, but decided he didn't want to go much closer.

'I keep thinking of those cartoons,' Robbie said as he approached the car. '*Tom and Jerry*, or whatever it was.'

He imitated the sound of a burning fuse, then extended his arm and hurled the cardboard on to the back seat. The vapour inside the car ignited in a white flash and Robbie leapt back with a cry of alarm. He turned and ran, the Fiesta engulfed in fire by the time he stumbled out of the barn, laughing as he showed Dan his face.

'Anything get singed? My eyebrows feel weird.'

'No, you look okay.'

'Smart thinking, mate, to wait out here for a bit.'

They watched the car burn, the smoke growing dark and foul within the confines of the barn until they could barely see the Fiesta at all. Gradually the smoke found an escape route and was sucked into the cool night air in thin grey strands like party streamers.

Dan looked at it and said, 'Are you sure this was a good idea?'

'Yeah.'

'How long will it burn for?'

Robbie shrugged. 'Fucked if I know.'

They were startled by a couple of small explosions, which Dan thought had come from the engine compartment. Not loud enough to attract attention, or so Robbie assured him.

The smoke was billowing out now, in dark boiling clouds. They retreated further to avoid the choking fumes, and then, since they were practically halfway to the house, it seemed like a good idea to fetch another beer. They took the drinks and stood on the lawn like guests at a boring wedding.

Dan said, 'Cate knows you've got this place back on the books. She can't understand what you're doing.'

Robbie smiled. 'That's 'cause she thinks the way you do, like everything has to form part of a well-ordered plan. Whereas I prefer to act on the spur of the moment. Just wing it and see what happens.'

'Like grabbing the steering wheel of your best friend's car?'

The atmosphere could have changed then, because of the bitterness in Dan's voice. He realised the alcohol was worming its way into his brain, changing his moods with bewildering speed: one minute carefree, the next angry and resentful, spoiling for a fight.

But Robbie kept the same equanimity that had seen him through scrape after scrape, good times and bad.

'I know I should probably be saying how much I regret everything that happened this week. But the truth is, I don't. Not really. I've never felt more alive than I have in the past few days. And I bet, if you're honest, you haven't either.'

He waited a second. Dan only shrugged.

Robbie said, 'I mean, this is why we've got a pulse, isn't it? Not for the usual boring day-after-day routines, but for the times like this, when the adrenalin's pumping and it feels like your whole life is hanging in the balance. That's what we're alive for, Dan, to feel like this.'

'What, are you saying we should celebrate killing Hank?'

'No.' Robbie raised his bottle and clinked it gently against Dan's. 'I'm saying we should celebrate that *we*'re still here.'

Seventy-one

After making sure that nothing in the house contradicted the tableau he'd created, Stemper studied the street from an unlit window until he judged it was safe to depart.

Back at the car, he decided against returning to Sussex. He felt too weary for another encounter with Quills; besides, he suspected that his absence would only bind the unfortunate man still deeper into his obsession.

He drove out of London amongst the dwindling traffic of a Saturday evening, stopped off at a supermarket for a few overnight essentials, and then booked into a Premier Inn in Woking. From there he called the Blakes, and confirmed that it was done.

'Any problems?' Gordon asked.

'None at all.'

'And it looks . . .?'

'Exactly as we planned it to look.'

Patricia took the phone. 'There's been an update from across the water. The meetings were a great success, apparently. Our friend Mark could be homeward-bound as early as Wednesday or Thursday next week.'

'I see. We need to up the pace, then. I'll try and complete the search tomorrow.'

'What about the sister?'

'I'm sure I can find . . . a "workaround", shall we say?'

'Thank you. And then the woman on Monday?'

The question seemed innocuous enough, but Stemper thought he discerned another layer of meaning. In their meeting this afternoon he must have communicated some extra tension that Patricia, an impressively perceptive woman, had noted.

He said, 'Yes. Or sooner, if I can.'

'Splendid.'

But it was not at all splendid, and when the call was over Stemper brooded for some considerable time.

The Blakes had Caitlin's identity. Their research would soon unearth the names of any current or former partners, and one of those names would correspond with that of a murder victim.

Stemper knew he should tell them about it, but to do so was tantamount to admitting he was fallible. It was a question of which he valued most: their faith or their trust.

He took a shower and thought about it and decided, finally, that they were equally vital.

So then it came down to timing. If he kept silent, how long before they were likely to discover his error? How long did he have?

No. The real question was of a slightly different order.

How long did he *need*?

All day Gordon had been prey to a low-level neurosis, which the conversation with Stemper had done nothing to assuage. The news from America far outweighed these small advances in identifying their tormentors.

'Time's running out,' he said, gesturing with the tumbler that contained his fourth whisky of the night.

Patricia had also drunk rather heavily. There had been the air of a vigil about the evening as they sat together in the living room and waited for Stemper to confirm that the night's grim task was complete.

Now she swallowed the last of her Merlot and said, 'I know. Those poor children . . .'

She was maudlin again, close to tears. Gordon couldn't recall so many emotional displays in such quick succession.

'Well, at least the other thing's done.' He felt an odd reluctance to speak Jerry's name.

'I wonder if she's home yet?' Patricia said. 'The widow.'

'I doubt it. From the West End.'

'Of course. Public transport.'

Gordon stood up and offered his hand. 'There's nothing more to do tonight. Let's turn in.'

Patricia nodded, grasped his hand and rose, teetering a little, and he laughed and used the loss of balance to engineer an embrace. He held her firmly and they stayed that way for at least half a minute, Gordon at first amazed that she hadn't pushed him away; then gratified and – in spite of the other thing on his mind, or perhaps because of it – aroused.

'Bed,' he said, and kissed her.

'Mm.' She responded, taking the kiss, her tongue against his, hungrier than he had known it for years.

Gordon led her upstairs feeling ten foot tall; the man of the house, with a raging erection and a head full of twisted images: bondage ropes and ball gags and unspeakable acts on a DVD – the props in a mercy killing, but ultimately it was mercy for them, not for Jerry.

In bed, still in his arms, Patricia said, 'You know, my absolute worst nightmare is that we retrieve the papers and go ahead as planned, but when we confront him it turns out he's already signed the deal in secret, and he just laughs in our faces. Can you imagine it, Gordon? The humiliation as we slink out with our tails between our legs . . .'

He kissed her. He wanted her to put this aside for now, but she was determined to worry it down to manageable proportions.

'Then should we try it anyway? As soon as he gets to the UK?'

'Without the documentation?'

He nodded. 'Yes. Bluff it.'

'I thought you were fiercely opposed to our direct involvement. And to do it without the evidence . . .'

'Darling, it petrifies me. But I know what this means to you. If we have no other options, I'm prepared to give it a try.'

'Stemper might still pull a rabbit or two from the hat . . .' Patricia's eyes were misty. Gordon's expectation of sex was receding fast, but he had to admit that this affection was a pleasure in itself.

'Let's hope he does,' he said.

'He hasn't failed us so far.' She yawned, gazed into his eyes until all his motives were laid bare. 'Oh, Gordon, I'm so tired. Tomorrow, perhaps?'

He smiled. 'Turn over. I'll hold you.'

She faced away from him and he snuggled in close, her body large and warm and solid. He thought she was done with conversation, but after a minute of silence she spoke again.

'We have to make it succeed now. For the sake of those who are losing their lives.'

He knew what she meant. He had spent much of the day examining his conscience. A necessary act, now that people were dying for the Blakes and their cause. Gordon had privately resolved that in tribute to Jerry Conlon he would purchase a less ostentatious yacht, and donate a million pounds or so to a worthwhile charity. Not necessarily a 'selfish' charity, either: not cancer or heart disease or diabetes.

Maybe he should include Jerry's widow in the choice? Make the donation specifically in Jerry's name. Now that was a nice touch . . .

If the deal comes off, he reminded himself.

A thought struck him. It seemed like a reasonably safe time to raise the issue, so he said, 'How do you feel about Hank's death?'

'Pardon?'

'Well, you haven't commented on it. At an emotional level, I mean.'

He felt her tense, and responded by squeezing closer.

'Gordon, it was years ago. It was sex.'

'Good sex?' he asked, aiming to pitch it as a light-hearted, almost frivolous query.

'It was a mistake, you know that. But it did later pay dividends – or seemed to, at least – when he joined Templeton.'

'Was that in your mind, right at the beginning?' *When you seduced him.*

'I suppose I recognised some potential. Good with numbers, if not with people. Just the right degree of blustering arrogance that impresses political types. But no, it wasn't that calculated. Hank was brash and strong and confident.' She made a little spurting noise, which he identified as a giggle. 'And he was really rather well-endowed.'

Nothing much to add to that, Gordon thought. He was idly stroking a rough patch of skin, just above the loose swell of her breasts.

'You do realise, don't you, that you needn't have kept it secret? You didn't have to exclude me.'

She twitched, and he sensed her confusion. 'You mean . . . physically excluded, from my affair?'

'Yes.' He chuckled softly. 'For you, it's twice the pleasure. Twice the happiness.' Ever hopeful, he moved his hand lower. 'Whatever makes you happy, my darling. That's all I want. That's all I've ever wanted.'

Seventy-two

A relentless pounding noise drew Cate from sleep at what she felt sure must be stupid o'clock for a Sunday.

It was: twenty to eight. Last night she'd granted herself permission to sleep half the morning away if she wanted. Now someone was thumping steadily on her front door. Someone selfishly, spitefully determined to destroy her chances of a lie-in.

No prizes for guessing who.

She couldn't ignore him, because soon the neighbours would be complaining. She threw back her duvet and sat up, her head reeling. Too much wine last night, drowning her sorrows after the date fell through.

She grabbed a dressing gown, tying it tightly as she descended the stairs. No visible cleavage, in case Martin was deluded enough to believe she was trying to entice him into bed. Clearly she'd been right not to treat yesterday's silence as a positive sign.

I'm going to report you to the police. Those were the words forming on her lips as she checked the security chain was in place and opened the door.

'You bitch! You couldn't bear it that I gave him what he wanted, so you tried to tempt him back, didn't you? Bitch. You stinking, stealing bitch whore.'

A torrent of words, slurred and exhausted and wrapped in long hours of tears cried. Even through a sliver of open doorway Cate could see that Janine was utterly wrecked, tottering on her feet, strands of wet hair plastered to her cheeks, yesterday's mascara smeared across her temple. She wore jogging pants and a thin T-shirt that clung to the beginnings of a swollen belly. There was a violence in her eyes that belied the hopelessness in her voice. Cate had a very real impression that, had she possessed the energy, Janine would have gone for her throat.

'What are you talking about?'

Janine thumped the door again, stretching the security chain to its limit. 'You've been seeing him, haven't you?'

'What? Do you mean Martin—?'

'No, fucking Father Christmas. Who do you think I mean? I bet he wasn't even at his brother's Friday night. He said they were going fishing in the morning, but that turned out to be a lie.'

'Janine, you've got it wrong. He wasn't with me.'

'So what was he doing in Brighton then?'

'No idea,' said Cate. 'Why don't you ask him?'

The silence that greeted this question was almost physical. It was as though expanding foam had been pumped into the space around them, freezing them into position. Cate saw Janine's brain racing through a series of calculations; a glint of cruelty in the way her eyes widened, a bitter delight that it fell to her to deliver bad news.

'You're serious, aren't you?'

'I don't have a clue what you're here for. I haven't been seeing Martin and I have no interest in getting back with him. He's yours, Janine, and frankly you're welcome to—'

'He's dead.'

'—have him.' Cate's sentence was complete before she could process the interruption. If she hadn't seen the words form on Janine's lips she might have assumed she'd misheard.

'Martin's dead?' Cate had to clutch the door frame for support. 'Did he . . . was it an overdose, or . . .?'

'He was murdered.'

'What?'

'Stabbed to death, in the middle of Brighton.' Janine's lips trembled, and fresh tears flowed. Cate instinctively removed the security chain, opening the door and beckoning to her, but Janine backed away.

'Don't you touch me.' There was a crazed look in her eyes. 'You did this.'

'Janine . . .'

'I dunno how, but you're part of this. They told me. They told me.' She had to stop, swallow, and find her voice again. 'He was still alive, in the ambulance. He died before they could get him to hospital.'

'Janine, I'm so sorry.'

'Shut up! They told me he kept trying to speak. *Tell Cate*. That's what he said. That's all. *Tell Cate*. And then he died.'

Cate said nothing. Into the stunned silence came the sound of a car approaching at speed. A blue estate screeched to a halt behind Janine's car. A man of about Cate's age got out of the driver's side, and from the passenger seat came a woman in her sixties: Janine's brother and mum. Shamefully Cate recognised them from her occasional late-night prowl around Martin's Facebook page.

Janine ignored them. The emotion was roaring back, and her words were almost a shriek.

'Were you with him? You saw him Friday night, didn't you?'

She lunged at Cate just as her brother got close enough to restrain her. Perhaps she had planned it that way, Cate thought. No good could come of a physical confrontation, and even within the depths of her grief Janine must have understood that.

While her brother wrapped her in a protective embrace, Janine's mother reached out and caressed her cheek.

'Come on, darling. This isn't going to help.'

From Janine, an incomprehensible burst of speech, while her brother stared coldly at Cate.

'We didn't know she'd got out. The doctor gave her something last night. We thought she was still with us.'

'And that's where you need to be,' her mother said. 'Tucked up in bed.'

She steered Janine free of her brother's grasp and started walking her towards the car.

'You take her, Mum,' the brother said. 'I'll drive her car back.'

He glanced at Cate again, now slightly apologetic, but still far from warm. Cate thought she had perhaps less than a minute before the shock overwhelmed her.

'I don't understand. Is Martin really . . .?'

'Yeah. Bled to death in the ambulance.' He shook his head. 'Saturday afternoon, in one of the busiest shopping areas in the city.'

'Where did it happen?'

'In the Lanes somewhere.'

'The Lanes?'

'Well, not the ones with jewellery shops. The hippie ones.'

'The North Laines?'

'Yeah. That's it.'

Cate felt a coldness deep in the core of herself; a lightness in her head that she'd experienced previously when she was about to faint. Janine's brother gave her a questioning look, but Cate would have slammed the door in his face rather than respond to it.

Were you there?

For a second that question hung suspended in the air between them. Then he forgot her and hurried to the assistance of his mother, who was hugging Janine as she stood, virtually catatonic, staring at the car as if nothing in the world made sense any more.

Cate knew how she felt.

Seventy-three

Dan woke with a pounding headache in a room that reeked of smoke. All his clothes from last night were impregnated with it. He should have left them in the garden.

Still, at least the car was now only a charred lump of metal, ready for Jed's mate to collect. By two in the morning the fire had burnt itself out to a point where they'd judged it safe to lock up and leave.

Dan had been far too drunk to question Robbie's fitness to drive, or to raise many objections when Robbie insisted on taking the document boxes with them. He claimed he just wanted to look through the papers, while the cash would be stored in his safe for the time being. It was news to Dan that Robbie even *had* a safe.

Once again Dan had refused to accept any of the money. It was a decision he might regret, especially when he had to explain the Fiesta's disappearance. But his overriding instinct was to have nothing more to do with it.

He showered for five minutes, scrubbing at his body and shampooing his hair twice. Even his breath seemed to smell of smoke. After swilling with mouthwash, he dressed and took the dirty clothes downstairs, hoping to sneak them into the washing machine before anyone else was up.

☼   ☼   ☼

No such luck. Joan was at the small table in the kitchen, drinking tea and reading a Lee Child novel.

'No lie-in today?' she asked.

'I could ask you the same thing.'

'I was wide awake, so I got up.' She sniffed. 'Did you have a barbecue?'

'Those outdoor heaters,' Dan said. 'I was sitting outside with Robbie. Didn't realise how much the smoke had got into my clothes.'

'It's awful.' She was watching him rather too closely. 'From what Louis said I thought you'd be seeing Hayley last night.'

'Change of plan. We're meeting this morning.' He busied himself at the unit, making a coffee. 'And Louis shouldn't have mentioned it.'

'He doesn't mean any harm,' Joan said gently. 'Do us another tea, will you?'

'Sure. What time did you get home?'

'Oh, not late. About nine. Louis rolled in at twelve, and I have no idea what hour of the day or night you came in.'

He turned, ignoring the wry tone. 'Louis was out till midnight?'

'A couple of his friends texted while we were eating. He went off to meet them and I got the bus back.' She shook her head, dismissing the anger on his face. 'I'm quite capable of finding my way home.'

'But he was supposed to be taking you out.'

'And he did. We had a lovely meal.'

'Was he drunk again, when he came in?'

'I couldn't say for sure.' Joan had a smile playing on her lips. 'If you don't mind me saying, you look a bit delicate yourself this morning.'

She was right enough there. Dan drank a glass of water, washing down a couple of ibuprofen. Insisting that he wasn't up to a cooked breakfast, he took his coffee and a bowl of cereal into the living room.

Once again the news was dominated by the fatal stabbing in Brighton. The victim was described as a thirty-four-year-old local man, whose identity was being withheld until all members of his family had been informed. The hit-and-run and the e-fit images didn't feature at all.

The world's moving on, he thought.

Robbie overslept. His phone buzzed and he reached for it, was instantly wide awake and saw the time and Bree's name in the display and knew what was wrong.

Maureen Heath.

'Where are you?' Bree demanded, as shrill as his mother on a bad day. 'Mo's just rung me in a right state.'

'It's only ten minutes. I'm on my way.'

'Bullshit. I've just woken you up.'

'No, you haven't.'

'I know what you sound like when you've been asleep.' She exhaled like a teenager. 'This isn't fair, Robbie. You ask me to do a big favour and then you go and let me down.'

'All right. Tell her I'll be there pronto.'

'Yeah, and make sure she really enjoys it. I can't have her getting the hump with me.'

He didn't like the uncertainty in her voice. 'Are you saying you don't trust her?'

'No, but . . . she knows all about me and you. So keep her sweet, for your sake as well as mine.'

Bree was gone before he could ask what she meant by that. Robbie slapped the phone down and considered defying her wishes. Another hour's sleep had its appeal. Then there were the document boxes, sitting patiently beside the bed like faithful pets. They could wait until he'd completed this chore, this ordeal, but he didn't want them to wait. A full day, with a clear head, and perhaps he'd be able to unlock their secrets.

The alibi, though. Bree had made her point. One simple favour, and now she had him by the balls.

That was a rule he'd foolishly broken: *Don't ever let them own you.*

Seventy-four

After shutting the front door, Cate dropped to the floor and lost all track of time and space. It didn't matter that she was squashed between the bottom of the stairs and the wooden rack where she kept her everyday shoes. It didn't matter that there was a cold draught seeping beneath the door. It didn't matter that she was alone.

Martin was dead. That was tragedy enough in itself. To know he had died with her name on his lips was truly grotesque. For Janine, it must be unbearable. Cate felt sure that Martin's fixation on her would have been short-lived, but persuading Janine of that would be nigh on impossible.

A rap on the door made her jump. She looked at her watch and discovered that more than an hour had passed.

Climbing unsteadily to her feet, she called out, 'Who is it?' Her voice was hoarse, broken.

'It's Guy. DS Thomsett.'

Cate opened the door without hesitation, and realised afterwards that she had nearly thrown herself into his arms. But his body language did nothing to invite such intimacy. He was in jeans and a blue striped shirt – off-duty clothes – and yet he stood stiffly, radiating tension. It was only as he took stock of her appearance that his manner softened, and the frown became one of tender concern.

She pushed a hand through her hair. 'I look a state, don't I?'

'I won't lie. I was coming here to tell you, but I'm guessing someone beat me to it.'

She nodded. Ushered him inside, where he promptly assumed command.

'Why don't you go and freshen up, and I'll sort out some . . . coffee, isn't it? Not tea.' A quick grin, but Cate's face burned at the reminder of yet another occasion when she'd made a fool of herself.

'Are you here because of . . .' She swallowed. 'Martin?'

'I'm afraid so. I learned his name last night, but it was only when I saw the, uh, photographs this morning, and realised that I recognised his face . . .'

It took her a second to comprehend that he meant pictures not of the living Martin, but of a dead man. Tears sprang into her eyes.

'I'm sorry. That was insensitive of me.' From somewhere he produced a tissue, and after Cate had taken it his arm remained extended, as though he wished he could offer something more: physical consolation.

Then he turned away. 'Coffee coming up,' he said, and it was only as she climbed the stairs that Cate realised it probably wasn't shyness that had restrained him, but a sense of duty.

She stared at her reflection in the bathroom mirror and shuddered. This was a situation where nothing short of full warpaint would make any difference, and she had neither the time nor the inclination for that. Instead she washed her face, brushed her hair and put on black leggings and a plum-coloured tunic.

When she came down the coffee was made and the detective was bustling around her kitchen as if he belonged there.

'Hope you don't mind if I make us toast. Any jam or marmalade?'

'Next cupboard along. I'll have Marmite, thanks.'

'Really? Ugh.' A playful tone, but this wasn't the same man who had asked her out on a date. He confirmed her fears once they had taken their breakfast through to the table in the living room. 'This is quite a mess I've landed in. Even being here now puts me on thin ice.'

'What do you mean?'

'I haven't yet told anyone about your connection to this case. I'm still trying to make sense of it myself.'

'You and me both. I can't believe that Martin was killed in Kensington Gardens.'

'And you had no idea it was him? You hadn't seen him at all prior to the attack?'

Cate shook her head. In re-examining the shopping expedition it seemed to her that she had been slightly ill at ease yesterday; several times she'd felt the need to look over her shoulder. But surely that recollection was tainted by hindsight?

'No,' she said. 'I definitely didn't see him.'

'According to his partner, he was meant to have gone fishing with his brother.'

'I know. Janine was here this morning.' In describing the encounter, she was sorely tempted to say nothing about Martin's dying words, but it was Thomsett who brought it up.

'What do you suppose he was trying to say? *Tell Cate . . . I love her*? Is that it?'

'I hope not.' Cate shivered. 'We'll never know.'

'But he still had feelings for you, if he was sitting out here the other morning. And he'd lied to Janine about his plans for Saturday. Don't you think he might have been following you when he died?'

She nodded. 'I hate to portray him in such a horrible light, but he came round on Friday night. He kept saying we should get back together, even though I made it clear I wasn't interested . . .'

Thomsett, studying her closely, said, 'Did he hurt you?'

'No. But he got very angry. It was the first time I've ever felt scared of him.' She fetched her phone. 'These are the messages he left me.'

Thomsett listened to them, then said, 'I have to ask you not to delete these.'

'But I can't see this has anything to do with Martin's death. Won't it just make things worse for Janine?'

'It's evidence of his volatile state prior to his death. We don't know yet what happened. It might be that he argued with someone who will claim they stabbed him in self-defence.'

'But no one saw his attacker?'

'The only description we have is of a grey middle-aged man in a mac, average height, average build, possibly wearing glasses, and nobody can say for sure whether he was involved or just passing by. Frankly, that doesn't fit the profile of a knife-wielding maniac, does it?'

Thomsett ate some toast, a preoccupied look on his face. 'Can you think of anyone who may have objected to Martin's continuing interest in you?'

'Like who?'

'Someone in Janine's family, for instance. Her brother's got a fairly good alibi, but we'll be taking a look at him just the same. Her father's in Wales, allegedly. I wondered about anyone else in your life?'

'You want to know if I have any other deranged ex-boyfriends?' Cate couldn't help laughing. 'Well, the answer's no. In fact, the only person who's asked me out in months is you.'

He nodded sheepishly. 'That's why this is so tricky. With you having such a close connection to the victim, I think it's inevitable that you'll have to give a statement . . .'

'And you'd rather I didn't mention our date?' Cate was unable to keep the hurt from her voice.

'I'm worried about muddying the waters. DC Avery is going to be working this as well—'

'And we know he's got it in for me,' Cate muttered. 'What is his problem, exactly?'

'It's not . . .' Thomsett began, then changed tack. 'He's got a grudge against everyone, not just you. He has a few "career issues", shall we say? The trouble is, he's hankering after the old-style police force, run by people like him, not by soft, smooth politically correct PR-savvy wankers like me.' He laughed at her incredulous expression. 'And yes, I have that verbatim, reported by a very reliable colleague.'

'If Avery's that bitter, it makes him dangerous to be around, doesn't it?'

'Very. So if you're hiding something, it's best to come clean.'

'I'm not. I meant dangerous for you.' Cate could feel herself blushing. 'Are you implying that I'm a *suspect* here?'

In the act of drinking his tea, Thomsett paused and shook his head, but it wasn't entirely convincing. She almost spat with indignation.

'Credit me with some intelligence. If I was going to have Martin bumped off, I'd hardly get somebody to do it when I was in the vicinity!'

'Okay, okay.' He made a calming gesture with his hand. 'That's not what I was implying. But you've got to concede that this is troubling. Not just your ex-husband, but Hank O'Brien.'

The words acted like a slap. 'What?'

'In the space of four days we've had two men die in mysterious circumstances, their assailants unknown, and both had close contact with you prior to their deaths.'

Cate sounded winded as she tried to protest. 'But that's . . . It's got to be a coincidence. I mean, what else . . .?'

'I agree. I can't see how they can possibly be linked. But, as coincidences go, it's a very unfortunate one.'

He went through it with her, the timeline of her meeting with Hank O'Brien and the contact she'd had with Martin over the past few weeks. They explored any potential connections between the two men and came up blank. As Thomsett had said, it was just a coincidence, but a very unfortunate one . . .

For you.

That was the unspoken coda, Cate realised. And she saw that, no matter what happened now, DS Thomsett would not ask her out again. That fledgling hope of a relationship was gone for ever.

It was an unspeakably selfish thought to have, but it also spelled out that Cate might be in real trouble. In the past week two men had made unwanted advances towards her, and both of them were now dead.

Seventy-five

Robbie was there by half-ten: pretty impressive given that he'd showered, dressed, wolfed down a banana, brushed his teeth and remembered to collect a box of condoms from the bathroom cabinet.

But Maureen Heath was anything but impressed. She looked right through him, then aggressively tweaked his groin as he sidled past.

'You've got a lot of making up to do.'

'Pardon?'

'To get back in favour. I told Bree her business is off to a bloody bad start.'

Robbie wanted to yell: *It's not her business, it's only her sick fantasy.* But he nodded politely and gestured to the stairs.

'This way?'

'Uh-huh. First on your left at the top.'

He tried not to trudge up the stairs like a condemned man heading for the scaffold. If he'd been in the mood for a fair appraisal, he'd have to concede that she had at least made an effort. She looked fresher today, wearing a dress that befitted her age; her make-up subtle and all the more effective for it. And she smelled a lot better, too.

But still a pig on stilts. And with twenty grand of O'Brien's cash sitting in his safe, he really shouldn't be demeaning himself like this.

* * *

He'd expected the bedroom to be fussy and overdone, but it was modest, quite simple and stylish. A big double bed, a dressing table, built-in wardrobes along one wall. A pair of bedside tables: the one on the far side had a puzzle book and a Kindle; the nearer one was home to a couple of vibrators.

Courageously ignoring them, Robbie slipped off his shoes and removed his jacket and tie. Maureen watched greedily.

'So what happened to you yesterday?'

'Work stuff. Unavoidable.'

'I thought it was me you were trying to avoid.'

His grin was sickly and false. 'No. You look great, by the way.'

'Glad you think so.' She turned her back on him. 'Unzip me.'

He obliged, his fingers clumsy. He realised he was nervous: a strange and not entirely unwelcome sensation. Maybe he could use that to enjoy the experience in a nostalgic way, reminding him of how it was at fifteen or sixteen. That was probably when he'd last been afflicted by nerves.

He eased the dress off Maureen's shoulders, loving its falling whisper but not so entranced by the sight it revealed. She was badly in need of a tan. Even leathery skin was preferable to this: white, doughy, no muscle tone, the flesh thick and loose, as though there was no skeleton beneath it at all.

'Bra,' she said, and he undid the clasp. She shrugged it off, and from behind he glimpsed heavy breasts cascading to near her waist. Gross, and yet . . . it caused a vague stirring in his groin. He put his arms around her, managing to gather the pillowy weight of her boobs in his hands and lift them, squeezing gently, perplexed by the absence of nipples until he realised they were further south. He located them – *tuning Radio Moscow*, as he'd once heard his dad say – and heard her groan. He shut his eyes and felt it working for him, too. *Because tits are tits, after all.*

Squirming beneath his touch, Maureen turned her head, forcing herself round until she was pressed against him, her mouth seeking his, her tongue hard and rude; no sensuality, only a desperate hunger that faintly repelled him even while his body responded with automatic lust to the heat and pressure of hers.

Kissing, his eyes still firmly shut, they lost the rest of their clothes and she pushed him over to the bed and he fell back on it. He stole a moment's relief before she climbed astride him, and he felt it was going well until it hit home that he didn't want to open his eyes: he was screwing up his face like a child refusing medicine.

He thought of Bree, and her petulant temper. *No.* What he needed to visualise was her smooth, taut, tanned body. Her lips, her tongue, her clever touch—

But when he opened his eyes it wasn't Bree; it was Maureen Heath, a large, fearsome predator with a ferocious appetite and a terrifying determination to satisfy it.

Robbie was months away from thirty. Not a milestone that had troubled him unduly. His rational mind accepted that eventually he'd grow old and feeble, but at some fundamental level he hadn't begun to consider what such a concept might entail.

Now he saw the future with grim clarity, saw how his body would bloat and sag and hang, and how, as a consequence, it might seem quite unremarkable to sleep with a woman like Maureen Heath.

One day, he thought, *this will be good enough for me.*

As if she'd read his mind, Maureen slid down until she was straddling his knees, her belly hanging over his thighs. Disdainfully she said, 'I thought it would be bigger.'

'Sorry?'

'Look at it.' She flopped his dwindling cock from side to side. 'My husband gets harder than this. The way Bree was talking, I expected a superstud.'

'That's 'cause Bree . . .' he judged it unwise to say *turns me on* '. . . exaggerates.'

'Well, I ain't shelling out two hundred quid for this. You can have fifty.'

'No way. What do you think I am?'

'On this evidence? A fucking disappointment.'

Suddenly Robbie couldn't bear that she was touching him. He half sat, still able to admire the way his stomach muscles rippled with the effort, hoping she would notice and be all the more regretful that she had ruined their liaison.

'This is a mistake,' he said, and he twisted, pushing her sideways on to the bed. He wasn't rough with her. Just firm.

Maureen gasped as she hit the mattress, rolling on to her back and slapping her arms up across her chest. Robbie didn't know if she was merely concealing her breasts – no chance there – or maybe she was ready to ward off an assault.

Ignoring her, he jumped up and grabbed his clothes. She must have realised he presented no threat, because she growled at him: 'Get out of my house, you wanker.'

'Glad to. There's no money in the world that would make this worth doing.'

Over the years he'd had plenty of practice at dressing in a hurry, usually after far more pleasurable encounters. With underwear, trousers and shoes on, he grabbed the rest of his clothes and buttoned his shirt as he descended the stairs. Maureen stayed where she was. A cat padded silently through the hall and paused to regard him with solemn contempt. Robbie was tempted to kick it, very hard.

Once outside, he checked his phone. Bloody Bree again – a text: Hope your havin fun. I helped with makeup & fashn. Looks hot dont she?

Hot? *Jesus*, he thought. Gazing into Hank O'Brien's dead eyes had been more erotic than this.

Seventy-six

The sun had broken through by the time Dan stepped off the bus at Saltdean. It was a proper taste of spring, and there were plenty of people out to enjoy it, walking or cycling along the promenade that ran beneath the tall chalk cliffs all the way from here to Brighton Marina, three or four miles to the west.

Dan let the fine weather and the general air of relaxation work on his mood. Perhaps this was a good omen.

Hayley was waiting for him by the low concrete wall that separated the promenade from the shingle beach. The moment she spotted him, the barriers went up. She crossed her arms and greeted him with a curt nod. No hugs, no kisses.

'Feeling better today?' he asked.

'Not really. You look like you were on the piss last night.'

'Yeah, I had a few beers.' He started walking, leaving it to Hayley to choose whether to accompany him. 'How about Rottingdean and back?'

She caught up, but was walking sluggishly. 'I don't want to go that far.'

'Halfway, then?'

'This was supposed to be a chance to talk, not go on one of your route marches.'

'We can do both at the same time, can't we?'

'No. Because I want to look in your eyes when I ask you this.'

The serious tone brought him to a stop. 'Ask me what?'

'You're having an affair with Cate, aren't you?'

Dan laughed, from a kind of relief. The accusation was predictable enough, after all. But if he had anticipated her suspicion, he should also have anticipated the way his reaction would be received.

'You think it's funny, cheating on me with her?'

'No. I laughed because the idea of Cate and me . . . it's just absurd.'

'Sometimes absurd things happen.'

A neat touch, he thought. She wasn't denying the improbability of it.

'Well, not this time.'

He turned and walked on. Probably a tactical error, but standing in the middle of the promenade, so obviously involved in a confrontation, was earning them a lot of inquisitive glances.

Hayley hurried in pursuit, and even the busy clicking of her footsteps sounded indignant. 'So was it my imagination that I saw you kissing her in the William IV on Thursday night?'

Instead of coming to a halt, Dan veered off towards the sea wall. Here at least they could sit down and enjoy a little more privacy.

'Thursd— hold on – you *followed* me into town?'

She nodded, unrepentant. 'Only because I knew you were lying.'

'But I'm not. Cate was there first, and Robbie joined us almost straight away. It was a peck on the cheek, for God's sake.' He let out a long sigh. 'I can't believe you've been following me.'

'After the way you've behaved this week, do you really blame me?'

There was a stand-off, a long sullen silence. Dan experienced a creeping horror at the thought of what else Hayley might have done to corroborate her suspicions.

'Where did you go yesterday lunchtime?'

She blinked rapidly, and he knew that his fear was about to be confirmed.

'I popped up to your house,' she said, 'to see what was wrong with your car.'

Dan put his hands down on the cold concrete wall, aware that he needed to cling to something.

'What did Joan say?'

'She wasn't in. Neither was Louis.'

'So you came back?' A hollow laugh. 'Or did you break in?'

'No.' Hayley stared at the ground, one foot toying with a fragment of chalk. 'I borrowed your keys. You'd left them in the office.'

'I left them in my *jacket*.'

'You've no idea what it's been like. What *you*'ve been like.' There wasn't a trace of shame in her voice. 'Nothing made any sense.'

'So you followed me and stole my keys?'

'Don't get all moral on me, Daniel. I saw the damage to the bodywork. You had an accident.'

He cupped his face in his hands, overcome by weariness.

'All right. I had a couple of beers with Robbie on Tuesday night. I drove home when I shouldn't have done, and I pranged the car.'

She gasped. 'Those photofit things . . .'

'What?'

'On TV. I thought one of them looked a bit like Robbie . . .' She faltered, her bottom lip trembling.

'Don't be ridiculous.' Dan had no idea where the bluster came from. 'I misjudged the turn in a car park. Scraped the barrier in a couple of places.'

She gazed into his eyes, wanting to be convinced. 'So why did you lie?'

He shrugged. He didn't know if he could sustain the facade for much longer, but Hayley saved him with another accusation.

'Because you were with Cate. And I bet Robbie agreed to give you a cover story. He'd lie to me as easy as breathing.'

'Hayley, it's nothing like that—'

'No?' She stood over him like a prison guard. 'Then tell me how it really is.'

He opened his mouth to speak, but all that came out was a groan.

'You can't, can you?' she said. 'Not even to save our relationship.'

'After knowing you've been snooping around, I'm not sure we even have a relationship any more.'

Dan expected this to incite another barrage of criticism, but instead Hayley took a deep breath, as if steadying herself, and said, 'I thought you'd say that. And I agree with you.'

'Do you?'

She nodded. 'I think it's over.'

And with that, a peculiar calm descended. By now the cool breeze had turned cold, and when Hayley suggested they go to the cafe which overlooked the beach, Dan agreed.

The cliffs were a dazzling white in the sun, forcing them to shield their eyes as they approached the steps. They climbed in silence, Dan sensing that they needed this opportunity to recharge their emotional batteries.

The cafe was busy, with a vibrant hum of conversation. After ordering coffees at the counter, they found a table and sat down. Hayley picked up a menu for tapas and idly began turning it over in her hands. Dan didn't think she was about to suggest staying for lunch.

'Do you want us to split up?' he asked.

'It's what you want,' she countered, although – perhaps unconsciously – she was nodding as she spoke. 'I think you've been too scared to admit it, because you thought it meant so much to me.'

He was taken aback. 'Didn't it, then?'

She tapped the menu against her chin, shielding her face.

'I think I was kidding myself, too. I'm starting to believe that relationships are more about habit than love. And habits are comforting.

Safe. Breaking the habit of a relationship is like pricking your skin with a needle to remove a splinter. You know it's for the best, but you'll still put off doing it to avoid the pain.'

The waitress brought their coffees over, while Dan struggled to absorb what Hayley had said. He was deeply ashamed that he'd had no inkling she felt this way.

'You know, I hope you *are* with Cate,' she said.

'I'm not.'

'But you've always fancied her.' She had gone very red, and Dan guessed what was coming next a fraction of a second before she said it. 'I went out with Tim last night.'

'You broke off surveillance, then?'

'Don't be like that. Anyway, it was only a meal. He'd noticed how upset I was.'

'Did you pour out all your troubles to him?'

'Not really.' She took a sip of coffee, wiped her lip with her thumb. 'He'll be discreet, if that's what you're worried about.'

Dan shrugged. He didn't want to talk about Tim Masters.

'He tried to kiss me, but I wouldn't let him. Not until . . . I've told you.'

Still Dan didn't respond. He wasn't trying to antagonise her: he just had no reaction to give.

'He's asked me out again.'

'Okay.' Dan wondered if this was his cue to beg her not to go.

She regarded him coolly. 'You know, what always worried me was your reluctance to buy somewhere together. The cafe just seemed like the perfect excuse to avoid making a commitment.'

'It wasn't an excuse. Having our own business would give us a far better chance of earning a good living.'

'Maybe. But the fact is, it was always *your* big ambition. Not mine.' She held his gaze. 'Yeah, I could do with more money. Who couldn't? And I know Denham's will probably go under in a year or two – that's what Tim says. But when it does I'll get a job at Currys, or Argos, or Asda.'

Dan shook his head. 'You can do a lot better than—'

'Maybe I don't want to,' Hayley cut in, her tone sad rather than sharp. '*My* big ambition isn't very big at all, really. I want to be with someone I love, and to live in a nice house, and have a couple of kids. To be like my mum and dad, basically.' She laughed, and its warmth seemed to surprise her as much as it did him: an echo of the bubbly enthusiasm that had captured his heart in the first place. 'You want more than that, which is fine.'

Dan sat back, aware of a tension within him that wouldn't quite dissipate; a lurking fear that surely the end couldn't come so easily.

'I ought to leave Denham's,' he said.

'No. Not until you're ready to buy your cafe.' She grasped his hand. 'The past week has been a nightmare, but now I'm sort of glad it's happened this way. I feel like it's given us both a fresh chance. A chance to have the future we want.'

She smiled, and it took quite an effort for Dan to smile back. He couldn't possibly tell Hayley how wrong she was: that his future continued to depend on factors that were completely beyond his control.

Seventy-seven

Stemper slept late and checked out of the hotel in Woking just before midday, by which time he'd received three urgent messages from the Blakes. There was a change of plan.

Their anxiety had been ratcheted up by a rumour that Templeton was due back in the UK within a few days. After fretting overnight, they decided that the search for the paperwork must take priority over identifying Hank's killers.

'What about the sister?' Stemper asked.

'We'll handle her,' Patricia said. The call was on speakerphone, so Gordon was able to chip in: 'By employing tact and charm, of course.'

They arranged to rendezvous in the village and drive to the farmhouse in one car. Gordon had concocted a ruse that entailed posing as partners in a secret financial venture, anxious to ensure that Hank's proportion of the profits found their way to his rightful heir: Cheryl Wilson.

'In other words, we'll buy her off,' Patricia said.

But that wasn't necessary. They met an hour later, in a quiet lane that ran along the side of the village churchyard. A bright sun shone high in an almost cloudless sky, and only a cool wind marred what should have been a perfect spring day.

Gordon was at the wheel of their Mercedes, dressed in slacks, a pale pink shirt and a navy-blue blazer. Patricia was wrapped in a brown winter coat, her hair pulled back and piled up in some elaborate arrangement. The interior of the car was a heady mix of their competing perfumes.

So far this morning, Jerry's death hadn't featured in Stemper's thoughts, except in terms of the additional workload which now fell upon him. But this was an interesting sign – a mark of their desperation, perhaps – that the Blakes were prepared to roll up their sleeves.

'We've heard from Jen-Ling,' Patricia said as they set off for the farmhouse.

'She was barely intelligible,' Gordon said. 'A friend of hers had to take the phone.'

'We put her in touch with an excellent funeral director and said we'll meet the cost.'

'A severance payment,' Gordon quipped.

'Did she mention how he died?' Stemper asked.

'"A bad accident", that's all she would say,' Patricia told him.

'A bad accident,' Stemper repeated. 'Exactly.'

They drew up some way short of the gates. Stemper approached on foot to check the lie of the land and returned with good news. 'No cars out front.'

They walked back, putting on the gloves that Stemper had told them to wear. A little incongruous on such a fine day, but better than leaving prints everywhere. Stemper became aware of Gordon, nervously casting about as if fearing an ambush.

'We belong here, remember.'

They rang the doorbell, then knocked loudly. Gordon was sent to check the rear of the building, and when he confirmed there was no sign of activity inside Stemper tried the key he had taken from Jerry on Thursday night. It wouldn't fit.

'Do you think *all* the locks have been changed?' Gordon asked.

'I'm sure they were.' Stemper had brought his lock-picking set and a selection of bump keys. 'Let's leave the house for now, and take a look at the outbuildings.'

They set off across a large expanse of grass, somewhere between a lawn and a field, Patricia expressing bitterness that a man of only moderate talents had acquired such a vast property.

It was Gordon who first picked up on the smell, when they were some twenty or thirty feet from the barn. He gave Patricia a querying glance. She in turn looked at Stemper, who frowned but said nothing.

The side door was padlocked. Stemper found a suitable key to use with his Brockhage bump hammer, and had the padlock open within seconds. Patricia emitted a sigh of admiration as the shackle popped up.

He opened the door and the acrid stench rolled over them, causing Gordon to recoil, gagging and spitting. Inside, the air was stifling, the block walls cracked in places where the tremendous heat had buckled the roof trusses and shifted the entire building on its foundations.

The source of that heat still smouldered in the centre of the barn: the burnt-out remains of a small car.

Taking care to avoid the oily residue that blackened the floor, Stemper and Patricia studied the wreck up close, their hands covering their mouths, while Gordon hung back, bobbing on his toes like the lookout man at a robbery.

'There's been quite an effort made to destroy it,' Stemper observed. 'They've pummelled the bodywork with a sledgehammer.'

The registration plates had melted, and although he was able to find one of the VIN plates, only part of the number was legible. There would be little chance of identifying the owner.

'What's it doing here?' Gordon asked.

Stemper mused on it as they retreated to the exit in search of fresh air. 'In my view, this is the car that killed Hank.'

Patricia nodded astutely, but Gordon looked sceptical. 'How do you reach that conclusion?'

'Robert Scott. We believe he was one of the men in the pub on Tuesday evening. He was at the accident scene the following night, when Jerry got the photograph. And he was here yesterday morning, with Hank's sister. As such, I think we can assume that he's behind this.'

'But why?'

'Because it's the perfect place to dispose of the evidence.'

'You're saying Scott did this last night?' Patricia said, and he knew what she was thinking: *If we hadn't been sidetracked with Jerry Conlon . . .*

'He can't leave it here, though,' Gordon pointed out. 'Not where Hank's sister can easily see it.'

'Unless she's already signed the property over,' Stemper said. 'But I tend to agree. Chances are, he'll be back to move it before long.'

Patricia cleared her throat. 'Let's return to the immediate problem, shall we?'

Stemper nodded. 'The paperwork. Yes.'

They marched across the grass to a pair of timber sheds. Stemper immediately noticed that the door of the smaller one wasn't latched properly.

He opened the door, then held it to let Patricia go in first. The shed was filled with discarded furniture and appliances, with barely enough room for the three of them to stand inside.

A heavy bookcase stood out at an angle from the wall. Patricia stepped around it, and swore softly. Stemper and Gordon each took a turn to ease past and see what she had found: a large space beneath the floor, lined with thick plastic waterproofing. The perfect hiding place for a stash of incriminating documents.

But it was empty.

'This is where he kept it,' Patricia gasped, one hand on her chest, as if winded by the discovery. 'It was here. And somebody beat us to it.'

'But who?' Gordon said. 'Robert Scott again?'

'It must be,' Patricia said.

'How did he find it? More to the point, how did he even know to *look*?'

Stemper sighed, loudly enough to capture their attention.

'I fear I was wrong,' he said, and made no attempt to disguise how much the admission cost him. 'Perhaps it isn't two separate conspiracies, after all. Perhaps it's just the one.'

Seventy-eight

Robbie arrived home in a stinking mood. Pity Jed was out; otherwise Robbie might have found the nerve to evict him there and then . . .

Except he couldn't, because Jed's buddy hadn't yet collected the Fiesta. It made him want to scream, all these obligations: Jed, Bree, Cate, Dan. Dragging him down.

He checked that Hank's money was still in his safe, and celebrated this minuscule victory by helping himself to fifty quid. The document boxes were on top of his wardrobe. He took them down and transferred the contents to a big old sports bag. Then he walked round the corner to a pub, the Palmeira. Ordered a cheeseburger and a pint of lager.

The first few papers bored him rigid, and had him wavering in his determination to read every word. But he knew he might not find the diamond in the rough unless he was prepared to be slow and methodical.

An hour and two pints later, his eyes were glazing over. The pub had a lively lunchtime crowd and Robbie felt like Billy No Mates, languishing in a corner with only memos and contracts for company.

And his phone stayed quiet, which struck him as odd. Maureen Heath was bound to have complained to Bree by now. Unless Bree was with Jim and couldn't get away to make a call . . .

He thought about another pint, then decided not to bother. Five minutes and he'd call it a day. Perhaps go to the gym to clear his head.

Pushing aside a pile of loose photocopies, he reached for a tatty A5 notebook and flicked through it, seeing a mass of handwritten entries in the form of a diary or journal. He opened a page at random and read it.

```
Mon 15 - Wednes 17 June 2009 - Dunstable,
Bedfordshire
Auditing at TWinEx, Templeton subsidiary.
Stayed till 1am on second night and managed
to copy six invoices, memos and contract
for Dept for Work and Pensions for data
analysis and ID verification project running
2003 to present day. (Ref documents DWP081-
97: shows true costs of projects inflated
from approx. £336,000 to £681,000.)
```

Robbie read a couple more in a similar vein, then turned to the beginning. There he found an introduction of sorts, or a disclaimer. The first paragraph made him laugh out loud, drawing glances from several neighbouring tables.

```
This journal serves as the record of a
project to gather evidence of long-term
systematic fraud committed by the group of
companies owned by my employer, Mark
Templeton. What follows is strictly confi-
dential. If you are reading it without my
consent, I am probably dead. If my death
occurred in violent or unexplained circum-
stances, the perpetrators are almost
certainly acting for Templeton himself, or
I was killed by my co-conspirators: Patricia
and Gordon Blake of 8 Gadbrook Lane,
Brockham, Surrey. The project was initiated
```

at their suggestion, with the aim of
extorting money from Mark Templeton. That
sum is likely to run into tens of millions.

Robbie had to stop and read that part again, to make sure he hadn't
imagined it.

Yep. That was what it said: *Tens of millions.*

'Oh, my sweet Lord.'

Robbie had always believed he was lucky; had kept faith that at
some stage his life would take a spectacular turn for the better. It was
this belief in his destiny that had prompted him to tell Dan that he
didn't really regret what had happened on Tuesday.

As if he'd already known, deep down, that he had something truly
priceless here.

With the position between herself and Dan agreed, Hayley seemed
eager to leave the cafe. Dan was in no particular hurry, so he stood
up and offered her a quick, hesitant kiss on the cheek – not unlike
the one he'd given Cate on Thursday night – by way of farewell.

'Going home?' he asked.

She shook her head. 'Into town.' A pause. 'I might see Tim, for a
quick drink.'

'Right. He'll be waiting to hear how it went.' Dan didn't care for
the sarcasm in his voice: a remnant of a wounded male pride that
was frankly perverse in this context.

With Hayley gone, he sat and looked around the cafe, reflecting
on how much he'd love to own a place like this: a great size, nice
decor, plenty of passing trade, incredible views out to sea.

It reminded Dan that a whole world of possibilities was opening
up. He was a free agent. A single man. Not only that, but the damaged
car had gone; the threat of exposure no longer existed. A painful
chapter in his life was ending; a new chapter was about to begin.

So why did he feel so miserable, even slightly cheated? It was completely irrational. The last thing he needed was to make an enemy of Hayley, especially now she'd come so close to guessing the truth.

The problem, he realised, was a bruised ego. It bothered him that she was already cosying up to Tim Masters, while her allegations of an affair between him and Cate were completely without foundation.

He finished his coffee and decided to walk part of the way back to Brighton along the undercliff promenade. As he emerged into the blinding glare of the midday sun, the parallels with a newly released prisoner couldn't have been clearer. But still the unease persisted, a nagging feeling that this was all too straightforward, too painless.

He couldn't be that lucky, could he?

Stemper had never seen Patricia so disorientated by a setback. Gazing, bereft, at the void in the floor, she kept repeating, 'It was here for us to find. It was here for us.'

'We did say that, all along,' Gordon added, almost as if to goad her into an explosion. 'We knew Hank would keep it close at hand.'

'Thursday night.' Patricia made a fist and thumped the top of the bookcase. 'It should have been ours on Thursday night.'

'But the search was curtailed by an intruder,' Stemper reminded them. 'Killing him would have attracted a lot of attention to this place. Remember that the barmaid knew the burglar was coming here.'

Patricia, steely-eyed, said nothing. It was Gordon who protested.

'But after you'd sent him packing, why didn't you—?'

'He made threats about an accomplice. I didn't believe him, but that's not to say he wouldn't have been capable of rounding up a few like-minded pals to return and settle the score. At that stage my brief was to go unnoticed. I didn't think you'd welcome a bloodbath.'

'Nobody's suggesting a bloodbath.'

'My point is that we're discussing this with the benefit of hindsight. At the time it was prudent to abandon the search. Unfortunately, Hank's sister arrived the following day.'

Patricia gasped. 'Do you think she found this?'

'I doubt it. There's another consideration, too.' With Gordon's help, Stemper moved the bookcase back against the wall. They all shuffled round into gaps between the junk and surveyed the shed as it must have looked prior to the discovery.

Patricia saw what he was getting at. 'It was very skilfully hidden.'

'Exactly. I can't say for certain that I'd have found it on Thursday night.'

'And yet this man Scott had no such difficulty.'

'The only explanation,' Gordon ventured, 'is that he knew where to look.'

Stemper nodded. 'We can't rule that out.'

'So he's our number one priority?' Gordon turned to Patricia for confirmation. 'And he should be back here for the car—'

'The woman's our best route,' Patricia cut in. 'We already know where she lives. We can make her talk, can't we?'

A savage glance at Stemper, who said, 'She'll be unwilling to betray her brother, once she appreciates the danger he's in.'

Impatiently, Gordon said, 'What are you getting at?'

'After I've questioned her, she'll probably have to die. She's a young, attractive female lawyer. And the police already know of her link to Hank O'Brien. Her death is guaranteed to generate a huge amount of police activity, not to mention media interest.' He looked at each of them in turn, his face solemn. 'You have to be convinced it's the right step.'

Patricia made a growling noise. 'I'd dearly like to see all three of them hung, drawn and quartered, and to hell with the consequences. But what other options do we have?'

The question seemed rhetorical: certainly Gordon made no move to answer it. Instead they regarded one another for a moment, and Stemper had a sense of marital telepathy at work.

'No. I'm not sure that we have any,' Gordon said at last.

Patricia nodded vehemently. 'Not with time running out.' She addressed Stemper: 'The way I see it, we've come this far — now we have nothing to lose. We do whatever's necessary.'

Seventy-nine

Robbie hurried back to the flat, the sports bag slung over his shoulder. He had the twitchy, watchful paranoia of a man in possession of a winning lottery ticket, with a big neon sign above his head proclaiming that fact to the world.

But he made it home unscathed. Jed was still out, so Robbie bolted the front door to make sure he wouldn't be disturbed, then emptied the papers on to the kitchen counter. He made coffee and fired up his laptop. Googled 'Mark Templeton' and came up with thousands of relevant hits, most of them relating to the group of companies that went under the name Templeton Wynne. A big business – and about to get a lot bigger if the rumours of an American takeover were to be believed.

While he surfed, Robbie was simultaneously browsing through the journal. A strange scribbled phrase seemed to be repeated throughout the document, often placed close to an entry that pointed to massive overcharging or downright fraud. It said: *More in the box*.

An odd comment, given that the journal entries were carefully cross-referenced with the rest of the paperwork, each document marked in hand with a date and a reference number. *More in the box* seemed far too vague.

It plucked at his concentration until, after swiftly draining a mug of coffee, he hurried into the bedroom and retrieved the empty

384

document boxes. First he held them, one in each hand, comparing the weight. Maybe there was a secret compartment.

He turned them over, examining the undersides, then reached into each one and felt around the base and sides, his fingertips carefully tracing the smooth metal surfaces. With the second box, something interrupted the glide of his fingers: a small bump just beneath the rim. Looking closely, he saw a tiny square of plastic: a micro SD card.

It had been attached with a dab of Blu-Tack. Robbie prised it off and stared at it for a moment. His heart was pounding in a way that made it feel entirely separate from his body: a discomforting and vaguely nauseous sensation. But he could withstand a little nausea in return for a discovery on this scale.

He'd had a similar card to this in one of his mobile phones. Somewhere there was a plastic sleeve that would convert the micro SD into a standard SD card, and thus fit into the card reader on his laptop. But where was it?

He swore the place blue as he searched, riffling through the drawer full of office stuff and junk: rubber bands wrapped in dust and half-bent paper clips, pens and coins and batteries, instruction books and chargers for electronic devices that had been thrown out years ago. Finally he yanked out the entire drawer, breaking one of the runners in the process, and upended it on his bedroom floor. A hell of a mess, but ten seconds later he had the adapter.

The memory card, no larger than a fingernail, had a capacity of 32 gigabytes. Less than half of this was used, which had Robbie wondering how much more data Hank had been hoping to collect.

The files were arranged in a couple of dozen folders, and each one had dozens of documents. The first few he checked appeared to be high-resolution scans of the physical paperwork already in his posses-sion. Feeling slightly disappointed, he broke off for another coffee.

Back at the laptop, he studied the folders and selected one with the intriguing name *Primafacie*. It contained a number of sound files, a sequence called *Templeton1, 2, 3* and so on, and a similar sequence: *Blakes 1–4*. There was also an AVI file, called *Blakes July10*.

Robbie double-clicked, then remembered that he probably should have run a virus check on the contents first. Too late now.

The media player opened and brought up a grainy image of a place Robbie knew quite well: Hank O'Brien's living room. For a moment he thought he was going to be seeing a clip of the movie that had been filmed there.

Instead, Hank O'Brien was in the shot, wearing a garish summer shirt and indecently tight shorts. A well-groomed, snotty-looking couple were with him, sipping from tall glasses that might have contained Pimm's. Robbie had the impression that they were unaware of the camera's presence, whereas certain subtle movements on Hank's part suggested that he knew it was there.

A covert recording, then. With the benefit of sound. The clip lasted just short of six minutes, but Robbie heard what he needed within the first thirty seconds.

The woman – it had to be Patricia Blake – was holding forth in a fashion that reminded him of Hank's sister, Cheryl.

'We knew exactly what you'd find because it's in the nature of the man to steal from others. Mark Templeton is a thief, a liar and a cheat. He deserves nothing, so what we're going to take from him is remarkably fair.'

Hank was nodding. He was red in the face, his piggy eyes gleaming, and Robbie thought of how he'd looked in the ditch on Tuesday night. *I had the last laugh, Hank.*

On screen, O'Brien said, 'I'm concerned about how he'll react, when the time comes to approach him. I mean, it's blackmail, pure and simple.'

The woman was dismissive. 'I don't care how he reacts. As long as he pays up, that's all that matters.'

'And he'll have to pay up,' her partner cut in, his voice smooth to the point of annoyance. 'We've got him by the short and curlies, as they say.'

'Don't worry,' Patricia assured Hank. 'We'll be there to look after you, every step of the way. We've put a great deal of effort into this. Just keep on playing your part, and we're all going to be very rich.'

Laughing, Robbie hit pause and said to the screen, 'Correction, my dear lady. I'm going to be very rich.'

It wasn't the happiest of journeys back to Surrey. Before leaving, the Blakes had discussed with Stemper what they required, and what actions they would sanction to achieve their aims. It was a heavy, sombre conversation, stretched tight with a palpable sense of desperation. Now they were on the move again, just the two of them, and Gordon did his best to lift the mood. But he knew he was pushing a boulder uphill.

'We don't know for sure that it's a conspiracy. It could be just a run of ghastly luck.'

'Oh, Gordon. Please . . .'

'All right, bear with me. If they don't have prior knowledge of our plan, the chances are that this paperwork will be completely meaningless to them.'

'Whether it makes sense or not, the very fact of its concealment tells them something.'

'True. But it's bound to take them a while to figure out what they've got . . .'

Encouraged, Patricia said, 'By which time Stemper will have them. We hope.'

'Hmm.' Choosing his words carefully, Gordon said, 'Did you, ah, detect anything awry?'

'With Stemper? Yes, I did.'

'My impression was that he seemed almost unwilling to act.'

'I never thought I'd say this, but I hope he's not going the way of Jerry.'

Dead? Gordon thought. He choked back a laugh. 'Oh. Losing his touch, you mean?'

'Well, he's been comprehensively outwitted, hasn't he?'

'And he can't like that one bit,' Gordon said with unconcealed relish. 'A man with such ridiculous levels of pride. Hubris, even.'

Patricia said nothing. They ate up another mile, crossed a roundabout, overtook a lorry, the silence easy but building to something, a slow ratcheting of the tension in the air around them.

'You know,' Patricia said at last. 'Once we're concluded, I'm not sure if it's wise that Stemper should be permitted to waltz off into the sunset . . .'

'I won't argue with that. But how would we prevent it?'

'It depends on the final outcome, I suppose.' A short laugh. 'Fifty million pounds ought to buy one rather a lot of options.'

After Robbie walked out on her, Maureen Heath stewed for a couple of hours. She knew she wanted satisfaction – revenge might be a better word – but was unsure of the best way to achieve it. She was also aware that Bree was a conniving little bitch, and could in future use her knowledge of this morning's disaster to humiliate Maureen within their little circle.

Having worked herself into an indignant rage, Maureen called Donna. Donna was a proper mate, but unlike the rest of them her marriage remained blissfully happy after thirty-two years. Donna and Mike still whispered and canoodled like a pair of horny teenagers.

Donna answered the call like the trouper she was, coming round with chocolate cake and a decent bottle of red wine. Maureen had already knocked back a couple of vodkas, so even one glass of vino was enough to convince her that she ought to tell Donna *everything*.

That marked something of a departure. Up till now the rest of them had agreed it was best not to burden Donna with the details of their sometimes 'complicated' love lives. *It's for her own sake*, they all stressed. *It's not fair to weigh her down, not when she can't keep a secret. Every word you tell her gets passed straight to Mike.*

But today it seemed like an insult that they'd kept such things to themselves. Donna was part of the gang. She had a right to know.

Of course, it helped that Donna's husband wasn't particularly close to Maureen's other half. Whereas Mike and Bree's hubby, that was a whole different story. Mike and Jim were the very best of buddies and had been for years.

In fact, Maureen couldn't imagine those two ever keeping secrets from each other.

Stemper knew the Blakes were dissatisfied with his performance. Not sufficiently dissatisfied to dispense with his services – on that score he was safe, not least because they had nowhere else to go – but it was a warning shot. In failing to recover the paperwork, he had let them down. But he'd also made the situation more complicated by killing Caitlin's former partner.

Once again he was reminded of Jerry's gloomy assessment of a curse on Hank O'Brien.

And everyone who came into contact with him, perhaps.

Stemper had tried to put such nonsense aside when he set out what the next stage might entail. The Blakes hadn't baulked at the prospect of extreme measures, so now Stemper had to make it happen. Increase the pace, increase the pressure, even though it meant ignoring the voice of caution.

He had no choice. He had painted himself into this corner, and only he could extricate himself.

Eighty

Dan walked as far as Roedean, then climbed the steps to the clifftop and caught a bus into Brighton. He'd reached the stage where he'd been alone with his thoughts for long enough, but equally couldn't face returning home. He wasn't ready yet to break the news of the separation to his aunt.

He got off the bus at Churchill Square, crossed the road and climbed the hill. He tried not to think about where he was heading, because this really wasn't a wise thing to do. But then she'd probably be out, in which case wisdom didn't come into it.

He rang the doorbell. Caught himself clenching and unclenching his hands.

'Who is it?'

Cate's voice – although he wasn't immediately certain of that.

'It's me. Dan.' Now his own voice sounded strange, and the very bad feeling was suddenly crystallised in his mind: *Don't go inside there are too many things you mustn't discuss and you know you'll crack if she pressures you—*

'Dan. Sorry. Come in.'

The door opened. Cate was clinging to it with one hand, the other gripping the security chain that hung from the frame. He took a step forward, but had to wait for her to realise she was blocking his path. Her face was ashen, and she looked years older, somehow.

She stood back, tried a smile. 'What can I do for you?'

'Cate, are you all right?' It was clear that something terrible had happened. He wondered if somehow she had discovered the truth about Tuesday night.

Then she said, 'Not really. I've just found out that Martin's dead.'

Cate saw the way it hit him: as if he'd tensed in anticipation of a blow to the stomach, only to be punched in the face. It was the same kind of reaction that had crippled Cate when Janine sprang the news on her.

To think that on Friday evening she had been threatened, harangued, almost assaulted by her ex-husband: in the aftermath of their fight she would gladly have wished him gone from her life, but never in this way.

How hollow and cruel now was her jealousy of Janine, of the baby that Martin's girlfriend was carrying: a child who would never know his or her father. It put Cate's own pitiful woes into perspective.

Once Dan was inside, she shut the front door and summoned the effort to walk into the living room. No: the kitchen. She had to offer him refreshments, as though this was a normal visit, a normal day.

But there was something wrong with Dan, too. It wasn't just her revelation that was making him appear so uneasy.

She said, 'I take it you didn't already know?'

'God, no. How did he . . .?'

'I don't have many details. He was stabbed, yesterday afternoon. In the North Laines.'

He drew in a breath. 'I saw that on the news. I never dreamt . . .'

'You don't.' Cate shrugged, wrapping her arms around herself. 'It's always somebody else's tragedy, isn't it?'

At that, Dan seemed to shudder. She took this as her cue to ask: 'What's been happening with you?'

Embarrassed, he said, 'Hayley and I have split up.'

'Oh, I'm sorry to hear that. I thought you had plans for marriage, buying a coffee shop together?'

'Turns out she was never really interested in the cafe idea. I don't know.' He grinned, trying to make light of it. 'Probably for the best to end it now, while we're still young. No mortgage, no kids—'

It was such a clumsy thing to say, Dan wanted to headbutt the wall. He knew from Robbie that Cate's split from Martin had been largely to do with having children. Cate had been in favour, Martin hadn't.

Now her whole face seemed to crumple. Big bright tears formed in her eyes and rolled down her cheeks. She shook her head as he went to apologise.

'H-his girlfriend, Janine . . . she's pregnant.'

There wasn't any more to be said, or any consolation that Dan could offer, other than to put his arms around her. She moved into the embrace as if they had been designed to fit together, and the awkwardness he so often felt in her company dissolved in an instant. He clung to her as much as she to him, their bodies pressed so tightly together it was almost painful, as though they were forcing the comfort from one another.

It seemed to go on for a long time, but Dan tried not to count the seconds. He didn't want to miss the experience in recording its passing, or ruin it by becoming self-conscious.

Before that could happen, he kissed her. His hand stroked her hair, gently cupping the back of her head while he placed a kiss on her forehead. She answered it with a playful squeeze, so he kissed her again, on the forehead, the temple, the cheek, each kiss lasting a fraction longer, his movements slow, deliberate: it seemed important that he didn't startle her.

The same instinct had him relaxing his hold, making it clear she could break away if it was unwelcome, if he had misjudged. But Cate's response was to pull him closer, her face turning, guiding him towards her mouth, to the kiss that mattered more than all the rest.

Dan believed it was the most desperate and the most generous, the hungriest and most nourishing kiss he'd ever had. He kept his eyes open, and so did Cate, their gazes locked in silent communication: *Here and now, this is the right thing, the best thing that can happen.*

They broke apart, just to snatch a breath, and then they were back together, the kisses long and deep and thrilling. Once or twice a voice in Cate's head tried to assert itself: This is a mistake. You might love Dan, but you'll never be *in love* with him. You'll break his heart.

But those were long-term considerations – and besides, weren't all hearts broken in the end? More immediate was the pleasure of feeling his body against hers, the way his hands moved, his touch firm and strong; the expert kisses, the way they ignited her lust for sex with him, with *somebody*.

That was the brutal truth – the basic imperative for human contact – but for now Cate was able to brush it aside, even when they paused again and she saw how different it was for him: that hint of a cheeky grin, putting her in mind of a jubilant schoolboy who can barely credit that his wildest dream is coming true.

'Robbie used to tease me about how much you fancied me,' she said.

'He teased me, too. Said I must need my eyes testing.'

'Well, he's got a point these days. I'm practically an old woman.'

'Don't be silly.'

'I look dreadful.'

'No. You look upset. But you're beautiful. You always will be.'

She had to kiss him again, before he made her cry. Another of her brother's criticisms came to mind: that she was too cautious, always having to stop and analyse everything. Sometimes it was better to take a leap into the unknown. As Robbie liked to say: *If something feels right, just do it.*

Cate pulled away from the kiss. Dan looked disappointed until he registered the wicked gleam in her eyes.

'Bedroom. Now.'

Eighty-one

Stemper caught only a brief glimpse of Caitlin's visitor as the man entered the house. If he'd arrived a few seconds earlier he might have had a clearer look. As it was, he tormented himself with the thought that this could be a contender for the second man in the pub on Tuesday night. If only Traci's description had been more detailed.

Equally, Stemper couldn't rule out that the man was a police officer, visiting Caitlin in connection with yesterday's murder. Loitering near the home of the victim's former partner was asking for trouble, but of course the Blakes knew nothing about that. No doubt they'd want him to burst into the house and threaten the couple with their lives, which was well within his capabilities, of course. But was it the right thing to do?

Ultimately, he decided, it wasn't. He explored the area on foot and found there was no access to the back of the building. Keeping a watch on the front was made difficult by the lack of hiding places and a shortage of on-street parking. He had to keep circling the block, sometimes in the car, sometimes on foot. This method held the risk that he'd miss something crucial, but it also meant he was less likely to be noticed.

Right now – to Stemper if not to the Blakes – that was more important.

* * *

Jed returned while Robbie was still trawling through paperwork. He ignored the key scratching in the lock, ignored a couple of thumps on the door, but finally had to respond to an angry shout.

'Oy, Robbie. Let us in, ya wanker!'

Robbie didn't want grief from the neighbours, so he opened up, claiming the lock was faulty. Jed almost spat with disdain. His pupils were dilated, and he was swaying on his feet like a lamp post in a hurricane.

'Are you off your head?'

'Day of rest, innit?' Jed slurred. 'I'm following the orders of the Lord Almighty.'

He stumbled to the bathroom, left the door wide open while he urinated for about half an hour at full volume, then disappeared into his bedroom.

'Good riddance,' Robbie muttered, and got back to work.

According to O'Brien's journal, the sound files had been recorded at board meetings and small social gatherings when only Templeton's most trusted colleagues were present. There was a lot of distortion from background noise – chairs shifting and creaking, the clink of crockery, coughs and sniffs and mumbled asides – but through all that emerged stunningly clear evidence that the Templeton group was rigorously fleecing a variety of government departments in the UK and half a dozen other major economies.

'Fucking civil servants,' Templeton was heard to say. 'Doesn't matter where you go, the top brass are just the same. Fat, privileged, self-important, pompous fools. Isn't that right, Hank – I mean, you were one yourself once, weren't you?'

Guffaws from around the table: even Hank, the butt of the joke, was chuckling politely.

'Well, I have repented of *that* sin, I'm glad to report.'

'Not before time,' Templeton said. 'Still, it's those inflated egos that make it so easy to get one over on them. They equate job security with professional superiority. And at the end of the day it doesn't matter if they piss away billions of public money. Nobody's going to take a penny from their gold-plated pensions.'

Another occasion – a long and boozy lunch. There were a couple of women present, described by Hank as 'overpriced tarts', and Templeton couldn't resist the temptation to boast. 'Sometimes it feels too bloody easy. There's no sport in it. They put a contract out to tender, and usually, if you've made the right connections beforehand, it's a done deal. You think of a number, double it, then double it again, and that's the going rate for the job. And it doesn't matter if there's a competitor, because they're doing the same. In most places there's only ever two or three companies in contention for the plum jobs – and let's face it, we all know the score.'

After listening to several more comments along these lines, Robbie was drawn to ponder the significance of the video file. If Hank had secured such rock-solid leverage on Templeton, why would he take the trouble to film the Blakes?

The answer made him laugh out loud. *Hank, you crafty sod . . .*

His phone buzzed again: Bree. But Robbie had no intention of talking to her yet. He had much bigger fish to fry.

Bree had to endure lunch at Singing Hills, a golf club near Henfield, with Jim and a couple of his friends who hated her guts. Using her phone in such company was strictly forbidden. When she tried to sneak a look at it in the car park Jimmy had slapped her arm and said, 'Leave that alone. You're not a fucking teenager.'

They were back home around two and Jimmy went for a nap, making it plain that she wasn't welcome to join him. Bree curled up in front of the TV and checked for messages. Nothing from Robbie. Nothing from Maureen.

Was that good or bad? Bree couldn't decide.

With a glance at the door, she tried Robbie's mobile. It tripped over to voicemail, so she texted – How did it go? – and waited a whole ten minutes before calling again. Same result.

She felt nervous now, wary of trying Maureen's number. But the need to know overcame her fears.

The phone rang and rang. She was about to give up when Maureen answered.

'All right, Bree.'

'I've been dying to hear. How d'you get on?'

A pause. 'Yeah, it was an eye-opener.'

'Are you okay? Can you talk?'

'Nah. Sorry, have to catch you later.'

Bree was staring in dismay at the phone when she heard thumping on the stairs. She just had time to grab a magazine before Jimmy came in, pulling on a jacket.

'I thought you wanted a lie-down?'

'Not tired no more.' He picked up his keys.

'Where you off to?'

'Drink with Mike.'

Bree twisted round and sat up, praying that Robbie wouldn't choose this moment to call back.

'How long's that been arranged?'

'He just rang, said he needed a word. Soon as.'

He left the house without kissing her goodbye, which propelled Bree into a sulk. If Jimmy was going to treat her like this, it served him right that she had Robbie to make her feel warm and wanted. In fact, she was almost tempted to pop over to his flat right now . . .

Then she remembered that Robbie had spent the morning screwing Maureen Heath, and her enthusiasm waned a little. And with Maureen sounding so ungrateful . . .

Honestly, Bree didn't know why she tried so hard to help people. She never got the thanks she deserved.

It's time you put yourself first for a change, she thought.

* * *

Dan and Cate raced upstairs, tearing off their clothes with the urgency of desire and perhaps a sneaking awareness that doubts might set in, should they pause to consider what they were doing.

I've known her since I was four, Dan thought. *And I've wanted to sleep with her since I was about twelve . . .*

Only when they were in bed could they afford to slow down, because by then nothing existed except the sensation of each touch. They made love with passion and humour, sometimes solemn and assured, sometimes clumsy and giggling, finding a tempo that suited them equally, their communication enhanced by the deep knowledge of an almost lifelong friendship.

Then the finish, fast and noisy and uninhibited, as though for that moment they were determined to be strangers to one another: perfect strangers.

'Well,' said Cate, when they had lain in silence for a few minutes, recovering. 'That was a bit weird.'

'I thought it was amazing.'

'Oh, me too.' She moved up on to one elbow, placing her other hand on his stomach. 'It's just, I've always regarded you as . . . well, the brother I wish I had, instead of the one I've got.'

Dan wasn't sure what to say, and perhaps Cate sensed his reluctance to bring Robbie into the conversation, for she quickly changed the subject.

'So when did you and Hayley split up?'

'This morning.' He gave her a brief summary of their conversation. 'She followed me Thursday night, and on the strength of the kiss I gave you in the pub, she concluded that we were having an affair.'

'But that was a little peck on the cheek!'

'She chose to interpret it as something more.'

With a rueful sigh, Cate said, 'And now it's happened anyway.'

Dan felt his face burn. 'I didn't come here with this in mind—'

'It wasn't just a sympathy shag, then?' Laughing, she lay back, staring at the ceiling. 'Hey, it wouldn't be so bad, really, if that's what it was.'

Again, Dan had the uncomfortable sensation that they weren't quite on the same page. 'This is the best thing that's happened to me for God knows how long,' he said, and he ached when she passed up the opportunity to agree. Instead she looked pensive.

'But isn't it horrible how soon all the trouble comes roaring back? I can't stop thinking about Martin, and Janine, and whether I'm to blame in some way.'

'Why? It's not your fault.'

'Not directly, maybe.' She told him that Martin had visited, most recently on Friday night, convinced they still had a future together. 'When he was in the ambulance, he said my name. *Tell Cate* . . . That's all he said. You can imagine what it's done to Janine.'

'And to you,' Dan pointed out.

'That's not all. On Saturday afternoon I was shopping with Mum, in the North Laines. Right where it happened.'

'What?' Dan had to think about that for a few seconds. 'Are you saying he was following you?'

'That's what DS Thomsett suspects.' She acknowledged Dan's surprise. 'He's involved in this inquiry as well. He was the one who linked the two cases.'

'What do you mean?'

'He popped in this morning, unofficially. He's worried because —' She stopped abruptly, shaking her head. 'Well, as he pointed out, it does seem a bit sinister. Two men dying in unusual circumstances, and both of them had a direct connection to me just before they were killed.'

Dan, listening in astonishment, said, 'That's crazy. There isn't any link between them. Why on Earth would he think that?'

He was looking at her as the words spilled out, and he saw the way something changed in her eyes and the room went very quiet, and in that silence his blood turned to ice.

'Why *wouldn't* he think that, Dan? Nobody knows who killed either of them.'

'No, that's true. But it just seems . . . unlikely, I suppose.'

Even Dan could hear how feeble he sounded. He shut his eyes. Thirty seconds ago he wouldn't have wished himself anywhere but here, in bed with Cate. Now he wished he was anywhere else.

'You do know something, though? About Hank O'Brien.'

He said nothing. Didn't admit it. Didn't deny it, either.

'Tell me. Please.'

Dan sighed. Even if he'd wanted to, lying to her now was utterly beyond him.

He nodded slowly. 'We killed him.'

Eighty-two

All the doubts that Cate had been trying to suppress, and now in one terrible moment they were released and made real. Her brother had lied to her. *Dan* had lied to her.

'But you were driving. That's what you told me.'

'I was.'

'Then how did it happen? Was it deliberate?'

'Not really. At least, I don't think so.' Dan rubbed his head: a touch of the Stan Laurel, but not remotely endearing in this situation. 'We spotted him up ahead, walking in the road. As I went to pass him, Robbie grabbed the steering wheel.'

'He what?'

'He claims it was meant to be a joke, to give the guy a fright. But Hank had his back to us, so he wouldn't have realised.'

She cupped her hands over her mouth, horrified by the image. 'And you knocked him down?'

'Yes. A glancing blow, but it . . . he was dead.' Dan looked stricken as he relived it. 'We couldn't help him, and there was no signal on my phone. Robbie said to go home, call the police from his flat.'

'Why not return to the pub?'

'We should have done. Only I let myself get talked into driving away, and then he started saying it was pointless to report it. We'd only be destroying our lives, causing heartbreak for our families . . .'

He pressed his hands together, as if in prayer. 'I hate myself for agreeing to it.'

'Robbie's very skilful when it comes to emotional blackmail.'

'He also made it clear that if I went to the police, I'd be on my own. He'd deny grabbing the wheel, and I wouldn't be able to prove otherwise.'

Dan knew it might be yet another mistake to tell her this, but he couldn't bring himself to regret it. Cate, however, looked shell-shocked. Little wonder, coming on top of Martin's brutal murder. And with DS Thomsett searching for links between the two deaths, Dan realised that their problems were going to be compounded by more police resources, more media interest, more scrutiny . . .

His phone was ringing. After a look from Cate, he scooped his jeans up from the floor and dug out his mobile. It was Robbie.

'Talk of the devil,' he muttered.

'You'd better see what he wants.'

Cate sounded distant, and Dan felt a wrench of anxiety that he would lose her because of this. He was so stupid not to have seen that; so incredibly clumsy and stupid about everything . . .

Robbie said, 'Dan, you've gotta take a look at something. Can you come over?'

'Not really. I don't have a car, remember.'

'This is mega-important. Turns out the late Mr O'Brien was a total frigging genius.'

'Robbie, I'm not in the mood—'

'Where are you? You with somebody?'

Dan sighed. Robbie in his excitable terrier mode was not easily dissuaded.

'I'll pop round later, but you're giving me a lift home.'

'Deal.'

As Dan ended the call Cate was sitting up. He noticed how she pulled the sheet with her, careful to cover her breasts.

'What have you done with your car?'

'It's being crushed. Someone Robbie knows . . .'

She nodded. 'Probably wise. And what does my brother want?'

'He didn't say. I thought I'd better see him, to break the news that you know the truth.'

Cate shook her head. 'No. Don't tell him yet.'

It made Cate uncomfortable, having to confront such momentous issues while she was in bed, naked. But she wasn't quite persuaded to throw Dan out, in part because there was still so much she needed to know.

She drew herself up, resting her elbows on her knees and her chin in her hands. A thinking pose.

'I have to get this clear in my mind. I'm now party to a conspiracy to cover up an unlawful killing. If we're caught, any of us, we'll be sent to prison for a long time. There's no question about that.'

Looking contrite, Dan reached out to touch her arm, but withdrew at once when she flinched.

She went on: 'DS Thomsett said they'll probably have to interview me about Martin. And they're still searching for the men from the pub, relying on e-fits that I helped to amend – inaccurately.' She paused, recalling DC Avery's threat: *Lie to us, or hold something back, and we'll destroy you.* 'From now on, every contact I have with the police will be like walking a tightrope . . .'

'That's why we kept you in the dark. Robbie thought it was better not to compromise you.'

'Mm. And I'm sure he had only my best interests at heart.'

'Of course not. But it's a valid argument.' Dan began to add something, then dropped his head. 'Look, if you decide that your best option is to report this, I won't argue. Go ahead and tell DS Thomsett the whole story.'

'You want me to shop you to the police? You can't make the decision to hand yourself in, so you're transferring that burden on to me?'

'I don't *want* you to. But you're right in saying that I've ducked responsibility. I'm a coward, I know that.'

'Not really. I don't see why you should take the rap for what Robbie did.' Despairing, Cate let out a long sigh. 'It's impossible. There's no right answer here.'

Dan saw the misery he'd inflicted on her, and was debating how he could possibly explain the rest of it when she let out an exclamation.

'Robbie took O'Brien's place back on the books. He's cheerfully doing business with Hank's sister, even though he was responsible for the man's death . . .'

Nodding, Dan said, 'It's sheer insanity.'

'God knows, he's played with fire in the past, but this is just . . .' She gave a disgusted sigh. 'I should have ratted on him to Mum years ago. Or even to the police.'

'For doing what?'

'Where do I start?' Cate rubbed her eyes, looking almost too weary to continue. 'Sleeping with clients. Taking backhanders. Renting properties off the books.'

'That all sounds unethical, but would the police want to get involved?'

She waved a hand, as though he'd got mixed up. 'Not for that stuff, but the drugs.'

'Well, I know he smokes some weed occasionally. Does a bit of coke. But that's no different to thousands of other—'

'He deals in it, as well.'

'What?'

'On a small scale, I think. Hard to tell, because with me he's always either bragging or trying to wind me up.'

Dan was staggered; could barely absorb yet another shock. 'Where does he get it? And who does he sell it to?'

'No idea on the first one. As for selling it . . . to friends of his, to clients. You know what a massive social network he's got. He said something a few months back about developing a route into the student market.' Cate looked forlorn. 'I always knew his behaviour would blow up in his face one day. I suppose I took the view that it would serve him right when it did.' She blinked away tears. 'I just never dreamt he'd take so many people with him.'

Eighty-three

Bree must have been dozing, because the sound of the front door opening made her jump. A dribble of saliva had cooled on her cheek. On TV, Reece Witherspoon was smiling prettily, but Bree couldn't place the film.

Then Jimmy was in the room, shrugging off his jacket, tossing it aside like it disgusted him.

Flustered, she wiped her face. 'You're back early.'

'Didn't take long to put me in the picture.'

Before she could ask what he meant, he came steaming towards her. She raised her arms to ward him off but he was too quick. He grabbed her wrist and yanked her off balance, then clubbed her with his other hand, hard enough to rattle her brain.

'You cheating little slut.'

'Jimmy, no—' She screamed. She couldn't help it, even though she knew there was nothing Jimmy hated more than women screaming. It set his teeth on edge, and that was plenty of justification for giving her another slap, never mind what he thought she'd done.

'Please, Jimmy, what's happened?'

'Don't come the innocent. I had a feeling you were up to something. Now that fat slag Maureen's dropped you right in it.'

'What?'

'She told Donna, who told Mike. And Mike told me.'

And then he spat on her: literally spat in her face, as though she was a worthless piece of . . .

She'd never seen him this angry before. As if he could kill her with his bare hands. When the doorbell rang it felt like a lifesaver, but Jimmy only sniggered. 'Ding ding. Round two.'

He drew back a fist. The doorbell rang again, long and loud. Cursing, he pointed a meaty finger at her. 'You stay there.'

Bree obeyed him – almost. She crept to the door so she could see who the visitor was. Robbie wouldn't have been crazy enough to come round, would he?

She heard a man's voice, a northern accent, and the relief was incredible. But short-lived.

'What the hell do *you* want?' Jimmy snarled, adding, with fake politeness: '*Dee Cee* Avery . . .'

'No need to take that tone, sir,' the man said. 'It's actually your wife I'm here to see.'

Robbie was like a kid waiting for Christmas morning, almost bursting with the need to share the secret. It was nearly four in the afternoon when Dan turned up, and then he was in a sour mood, barely responding to Robbie's greeting.

'Come on, look at this.' Robbie led him through to the bedroom. He'd spread the documents out on the bed, and had the laptop there so he could play the video.

'I want to talk to you about something.'

'Yeah, in a minute. First, you've gotta hear about Gordon and Patricia Blake. Remember those names.'

'Why?'

'The Blakes are long-term acquaintances of Hank O'Brien. They dreamt up a plot to extort fifty million quid from the owner of Templeton Wynne.'

'That's Hank's employers?'

'Yeah.' Robbie waited. 'Didn't you hear what I said? *Fifty million pounds.*'

Dan shrugged. Robbie pressed on, for fear of losing his momentum.

'Hank's journal explains it all. He had this auditing role at Templeton's, so for years he went round collecting up proof of fraud. He'd stay late at night, steal pass codes, even break into filing cabinets to get his hands on this lot.' He indicated the paperwork. 'They've got government contracts all over the place, and they are ripping them off on a mind-blowing scale.'

'So is it the Blakes who are trying to find us?'

Robbie scowled. 'Probably. Anyway, they employed this old guy called Jerry to act as a messenger, but also to keep an eye on Hank. Only Hank saw through it straight away . . .'

Robbie tailed off, watching Dan grow fidgety, as though none of it meant anything to him.

'You see, if the dirt on Templeton wasn't enough, Hank gathered stuff on the Blakes as well. At any point he could have switched it round and sold *them* out to Templeton.'

'Except that we came along. So what do you think the Blakes are going to do now?'

'Ah. I've got a plan there.'

Still nothing. Dan looked calm enough on the surface, but he seemed to be trembling slightly, like a boiler with a faulty pressure gauge. Robbie threw up his hands.

'All right, mate. I can see you're not impressed. So what's up?'

'Lots of things. I assume you don't know about Martin?'

'Cate's ex? What's he done?'

'He's dead. Someone stabbed him in Brighton, yesterday afternoon.'

'No? Bloody hell!' Robbie laughed, which probably wasn't the right reaction. But when he thought about it, he realised that this news meant very little to him. 'Do they know who did it?'

'Nope.'

'He was a chippy old bastard, though. Always used to piss me off.'

'Yeah, well, Cate's pretty cut up, so be careful what you say to her.'

'Aren't I always? Besides, I thought she was glad to see the back of him.'

Dan grunted: not relevant. 'What's this about you dealing drugs?'

'Eh?' The abrupt change of subject threw Robbie off balance. 'Dunno what you mean.'

'Bollocks, you don't.'

'Who've you been talking to?'

'Doesn't matter. Is it true?'

Robbie spotted a weak point, a chink of hope. 'Not my sister?'

Dan's face coloured. He went to speak but Robbie snickered. 'Oh, Jesus! Don't tell me you've gone to bed with my bloody sister?'

Dan knew his feelings were transparent, but he wasn't going to be deterred: not by that, nor by the manner in which Robbie swept a hand towards the papers littering the bed.

'You'd better not have mentioned any of this.'

Dan shook his head. He had few qualms about lying to Robbie.

'Let's get back to you and your death wish. Are you really dealing in drugs?'

'You're making it sound like I'm Pablo fucking Escobar. It was just something I dabbled in from time to time, helping people out.'

'So you've stopped?'

'Pretty much.'

'What does that mean? You haven't stopped?'

'Hey, less of the interrogation. Just because you're Mr Perfect. Like I said the other day, some of us prefer to have a bit of fun, you know?'

Like I said the other day.

It was an innocuous phrase, but a shadow crossed Robbie's eyes as he said it; as though he wished he could reel the words back in. He was referring to Thursday night, the conversation they'd had after Dan broke up the tussle in North Street . . .

And what was it Cate had said? Something about *developing a route into the student market*.

'My brother.'

Robbie feigned confusion. 'What about him?'

They were standing a couple of feet apart. It took less than half a second for Dan to grab Robbie by his shirt, pinning him to the spot.

'Have you supplied drugs to Louis?'

'Let me go. Will you calm the fuck down?'

Dan tightened his grip. 'I'll get the truth from him, so you may as well tell me.'

'It was weed. Practically harmless. The booze is far worse for him.'

'He's *seventeen*.' Dan shoved Robbie backwards, and he stumbled and dropped on to the bed, scattering paper everywhere and knocking the laptop on to the floor.

'How could you look me in the eye when you've been pushing drugs to my kid brother?'

'You think he won't get hold of it if I don't help him? At least with me he's not gonna get conned, or turned over by the cops.'

'How much do you give him? And how often?' Dan stood over Robbie, primed for violence: one move, one wrong reaction and he would pile in.

Robbie shook his head. 'Just a taste, every now and then.' A beat of silence; deliberating. 'And he wanted some for his mates.'

'You turned Louis into your subcontractor?'

'No. Dan, will you calm down?'

Robbie tried to climb to his feet but he never got further than Dan's fist. It connected neatly with his chin and Robbie fell back again, this time rolling and then falling from the bed with a loud thud.

'Stay away from him, do you hear me? You give him anything ever again and I'll kill you.'

'Don't get so—'

'And stay away from me. We're finished.'

Robbie let out a laugh: half scorn, half regret. 'You've gotta be joking. You can't walk out on this.'

'Watch me.'

'But what about the money?'

'There won't be any money. Don't you get it? You think everything's going to slip smoothly into place, but it won't. There's always something you haven't allowed for, Robbie. There's always a catch.'

'Not every time. You're just looking at it from a loser's perspective. And I'm not a loser like you.'

It was Robbie who had the last word. Dan stormed out, slamming the door so hard that the whole building seemed to shudder. Robbie groaned. This wasn't how he'd imagined their meeting would end; not even close.

Still, he felt curiously light-headed, aware of an inexplicable desire to giggle and then throw things, like a demented toddler. So what if there was a catch? He wasn't stupid. He'd find a way round it.

A sharp rap on the bedroom door. Jed was standing there, bemused, taking in the mess of papers, the fallen laptop, the sight of Robbie gingerly patting his face.

'You're not bleeding.'

Robbie grunted. 'Second time in a week he's done that.'

'Yeah? If that's how your friends show their respect, I don't wanna be around when your enemies come calling.'

'Who says I've got enemies?'

Jed's mocking laugh was dry as sawdust. 'That pal of mine? He can collect the car first thing tomorrow.'

'Perfect.'

'Got the rest of what's owed?'

Robbie nodded, ignoring Jed's knowing look. Once he was alone again, he began to gather up the papers, trying to restore some order both physically and in his head. But his attention kept wandering, distracted by Dan's fit of temper. And this news about Martin.

Robbie was one of the few people who'd predicted from the start that Cate was making a mistake. He'd even wondered on occasion if she had persevered with the relationship to spite him – or to prove him wrong, at least.

But he hadn't been wrong. Martin was a tosser.

It occurred to Robbie that he should call his sister to offer his condolences. Then he decided to wait a day or two. He had too much on his plate at the moment.

Martin's death was unfortunate, but it had nothing to do with him.

Eighty-four

Cate's first action after Dan left was to run a bath. It was a tried and tested method to counteract emotional stress.

She didn't regret what had happened this afternoon: the sex, in truth, had been a wonderful respite. But Dan's betrayal had cut her deeply, even allowing for Robbie's justification that she was better off not knowing. He shouldn't have lied to her.

That conviction wavered shortly after she climbed from the bath to find a couple of missed calls from her mother, along with a crude text: R u too busy shagging him to give me the gossip?!!

A reference to the date that never was. Cate swore softly. She'd have to respond, but she couldn't tell her mother about Martin. Not today. Not on top of everything else.

And that made her a hypocrite, didn't it? For she too was lying and deceiving at every turn.

She drifted over to the bedroom window, and was briefly tempted to pack a suitcase and drive far away. Then she took a deep breath and made the call.

'How was it? Did he pay for the grub? Did you end up in bed togeth—?'

'Mum, stop there. I didn't see him.'

'Don't say you chickened out?'

'No. He had to postpone. Some sort of problem with one of his kids.'

'Hmm.' Either she didn't believe Cate, or she didn't believe the story Cate had been given.

'It's no big deal. Maybe in a week or two.'

'Haven't you fixed another date?'

'No. I told you all along it was only casual. You shouldn't have got so worked up about it.'

'Are you all right? You sound upset.'

'I'm fine. Look, I've got to go. I think there's somebody at the door.'

'Who?'

'Just a neighbour.' Another lie. 'I'll talk to you tomorrow.'

Cate ended the call, her heart thudding. She had seen a familiar car draw up outside. She retreated from the window, hurriedly pulling on jeans and a sweatshirt, Dan's revelations all too fresh in her mind.

From now on, every contact I have with the police will be like walking a tightrope . . .

From the way he thumped on the door, refusing to answer wasn't an option. Cate walked slowly downstairs, willing herself to appear calm.

She opened the door, nodded curtly at his warrant card. She knew perfectly well who he was. This was simply to remind her of the power he wielded.

'What can I do for you, DC Avery?'

'A bit more friendly advice heading your way. DS Thomsett tells me you already know about your ex?'

Cate saw she was supposed to be intimidated by his manner, but she had been through too much already today; the result was a sudden fearlessness.

'Yes. I heard about it this morning.'

'Well, the lovely Guy, he who makes the ladies go weak at the knees, thinks it's just coincidence. Poor old Martin, poor old Hank, boo hoo. Two unlucky fellers in the wrong place at the wrong time.' Avery jerked his thumb towards his chest. 'Whereas me, I take a different line. To my mind, you're up to your neck in something. I reckon you know far more than you're letting on, and I can't for the life of me see why my sergeant has bought into your act.'

'Because it's not an act,' Cate said, still surfing a bizarre wave of confidence. 'And DS Thomsett is an immeasurably better police officer than you'll ever be.'

'Aw, sounds like true love,' Avery drawled. 'But it won't get you off the hook. As a lawyer . . .' he sneered, his lips pressing together as if longing to spit '. . . you'll know the consequences of lying to the police. So think carefully about the hole you're digging, and decide whether it's gonna be your grave.'

'Are you threatening me?'

'Course not, love. This is a prudent warning. Soon as I can sort it, I'm having you in for questioning. If need be I'll go over Thomsett's head. And if it turns out the DS was protecting you . . .' He whistled, feigning regret. 'Well, that's him for the chop 'n all.'

'And you'll step into his job?' Cate suggested.

Avery shrugged. 'We'll see, won't we? I'm going to enjoy wiping that smirk off your face, madam. Because you might not have killed Hank O'Brien yourself. But you damn well know who did, don't you?'

Cate said nothing. They stared at each other for an interminable length of time. Cate noted the detective's growing frustration, and added to it with a demure smile.

'This is a fishing expedition. If you suspect me of something, go and find the evidence, then come back and arrest me. Until then, please stay out of my life.'

She shut the door in his face, then made fists with her hands and clamped them against her cheeks to hold in the scream of anger and relief and sheer amazement that she had performed so well.

* * *

The arrival of a second visitor brought Stemper's surveillance to an end. This time there was no doubting that the man was a police officer, and Caitlin looked decidedly unhappy to see him.

Stemper watched them converse for a minute and decided he had seen enough. He was achieving little and risking a lot.

He returned to the guest house. Quills was checking in a party of tourists: German or Danish, perhaps. Stemper saw the proprietor's face transform as he walked past; a hope rekindled. His gaze took in Stemper's new raincoat, which he'd folded over his arm, and then the suit. These weren't the clothes he'd gone out in yesterday morning.

'I thought you'd abandoned me,' Quills said, with a mirthless chuckle.

'An all-night meeting,' Stemper said. 'I'm exhausted now. Perhaps we can talk later?'

From Quills, barely concealed delight. He was desperate to say more, but the tourists were demanding his attention. Stemper thanked them silently and slipped away.

Eighty-five

The Blakes passed a slow, dull evening. While Patricia read a Max Hastings book on Churchill, Gordon spent a couple of hours online, hunting for connections between Templeton and the law firm that employed Caitlin Scott. Finally he concluded it was nothing more than happenstance, though it emphasised the problem they had: with so many unknowns it became impossible to evaluate the threats and decide which must be faced and which could be dismissed.

Two bright notes. First, as they sat down to a light supper, Jen-Ling phoned, now sufficiently recovered to speak to them herself. It was Gordon who took the call: Patricia could fake the sympathy, but not the patience.

He was pleasantly surprised at how fluently she spoke English – rather more coherent than Jerry himself, in some respects. She was humble and polite, thanking the Blakes for their help. Gordon quickly established a rapport and was able to enquire about the progress of the police investigation.

The response was encouraging. Everyone seemed satisfied that Jerry had died at his own hand. Jen-Ling had confirmed that he'd been a difficult man to live with, a man who could all too feasibly have concealed his exotic sexual proclivities from his family and friends.

Then their daughter called, apologetic that it was so long since the last visit. She suggested joining them for dinner during the week, but Gordon had to put her off.

'Can we make it the week after? Things are rather hectic with us at the moment.'

Lisa scoffed. 'Goodness, Dad. When are you going to slow down a bit?'

'When your mother lets me,' Gordon said, quietly. Neither of them had laughed. He came off the phone to find Patricia working herself into another frenzy.

'I've reviewed it all once again, and I'm convinced it's a deliberate plot to usurp us. But Hank, to his credit, must have refused to go along with it—'

'Or demanded too high a price.'

'Well, yes. Either way, they killed him and stole the documentation. What if they're already beyond our reach? They could be on their way to Templeton as we speak.'

'They won't leave the country. Far too dangerous.' Gordon sat beside her, placing a hand on her knee. 'What did we say earlier? Let's not go shooting off on these flights of morbid fantasy.'

'Normally I'd agree with you. But we've never faced something like this.' Patricia's hand grasped his, and she turned towards him, tears glinting in her eyes. 'I can't bear it. The uncertainty, the pain of losing what we've held so dear to our hearts for so long.'

Gordon did his utmost to console her, but she was right. The work of a lifetime hung in the balance.

One of the young MPs befriended by Patricia in the early 1980s had later held a number of portfolios, including that of Minister for Overseas Development. By that stage the Blakes were providing PR and consultancy services across a range of departments, and they had accepted an invitation to accompany the minister on a fact-finding mission to some godforsaken country in the Horn of Africa.

Gordon would be the first to admit that they'd arrived with the standard preconceptions about the continent, not to mention a healthy contempt for the practice of pouring foreign aid into badly run Third World administrations. Just a few years earlier Patricia had been openly derisive of the high-profile mission launched by a group of pop stars to relieve the suffering in Ethiopia. A lot of leftie heart-on-sleeve posturing.

But the experience of Africa in the raw did something to them: to Patricia, certainly. It changed her in some fundamental way, those long convoys by Land Rover to dusty, drought-ravaged villages, touring absurdly inadequate schools where children clustered rapturously around these strange, sombre visitors; attending makeshift classes that fizzed with joyful laughter. They had frequently been moved to tears by the laughter.

Then the desperation of the refugee camps, and the almost unfathomable sight of men and women and children who literally possessed *nothing*, and yet still went on living, still smiled, still loved and cared and hoped enough to survive. It had awakened in Patricia a desire to nurture that had barely surfaced when her own child had needed it most.

Since then they had been active where they could, revisiting several times, donating money particularly in the areas of primary health and in education. Patricia was passionate in her support of projects that focused on educating and empowering girls, and when Templeton's undeserved success first inspired the Blakes to gain recompense, it was these projects that had motivated them to act.

Fifty million pounds. That had been their target. Hank O'Brien had fought bitterly for half, but since the whole scheme was conceived by the Blakes, they had negotiated him down to fifteen. From their share, once Jerry had been paid and various other expenses settled, the Blakes had estimated there would be around thirty-three million remaining, of which two-thirds – twenty-two million – were to be allocated to their favoured projects.

Now, if the scheme could somehow be resuscitated, virtually the entire fifty million would be theirs. Gordon had suggested going halves but Patricia was insisting on thirty-five for their philanthropic efforts, leaving fifteen to add to their personal wealth, which currently stood at just under three million, including the Surrey home and their villa in Tuscany.

Plenty of money by most people's standards. At times this past week, Gordon had wondered why they didn't just turn away, forget the African dream and make do with what they had.

But then he thought of his restless mid-life craving for a yacht, and the tumbling value of some of their key investments, and the idea of spending maybe twenty or thirty years in retirement with an inexorably falling income. Bye-bye villa, bye-bye exotic holidays and sumptuous meals and earth-shattering sex with his pneumatic playmates in Kingston-upon-Thames . . .

Patricia was right. There was too much to lose. And if they had to gamble everything now on a last desperate throw of the dice, then so be it.

Stemper slept for nearly six hours. He bathed, dressed and slipped out while Quills was holding forth in the dining room. Perhaps one of the tourists had caught his eye.

He found a restaurant near the Theatre Royal that was still open to new customers at eleven p.m. He fuelled up, allowed himself a couple of glasses of wine, and was back at the guest house at just before one.

The building was quiet, save for a faint peal of laughter from a bedroom on the second floor. The door to the private apartment had been left unlocked, as per Stemper's instructions.

Quills was still awake, eyes bright, face flushed. Heavily inebriated, by the look of him. Excellent.

'Are you sleepy?' Stemper crouched by the bed. 'It works better if you're sleepy.'

'Too excited to sleep.'

'I take it you made some new friends tonight. Were you drinking with them?'

'One or two.' Quills giggled. 'I wish you'd been there.' Beneath the old-fashioned eiderdown his body was gently writhing, his arm stretched across his belly, lying there, awaiting the signal to move.

'Do it,' Stemper said. 'It'll help you relax.'

'I am relaxed.' The movement began, rhythmic, fast.

'Slow down.'

'It feels wonderful. But I wish you'd—'

'Not tonight. Tonight you have to do as I say. Close your eyes. Remember how it was last time. How you listened to my voice and felt yourself sinking. A gloriously heavy weight, Bernard, sinking into the dark. And as you go, I want you to picture the treat I'll give you on my last night here.'

'When . . .?' Quills's voice was thick, drowsy.

'Soon. Tomorrow, or Tuesday. We'll have a drink together. What is it you like best? What's your tipple?'

'Cham . . . champagne.'

'Champagne it is. In fact, you choose the bottle. Have it ready on ice, and think about what you're going to do that night, the pleasure you'll feel as you lie back and sink into the warmth, the heavy warmth and the peace, the stillness. The pleasure. Think about it all, think about me, and then I want you to sleep deeply.'

A long, soft groan accompanied a series of spasms beneath the covers, and then Quills lay still, wearing a dreamy smile. For several minutes nothing was said; neither man moved at all.

One of Stemper's knees popped as he straightened up, but the proprietor did not stir. It had not escaped Stemper's notice that he could so easily have picked up a pillow and pressed it down on the poor man's face.

But where was the challenge in that?

Eighty-six

Dan had found the perfect business. It was an almost exact replica of the cafe in Saltdean, but located on a hillside in the Cuckmere valley, with fine views of Friston Forest and even a glimpse of sparkling blue sea. Dan was racing to get it ready for opening time, but no one else had turned up to help.

And Cate was outside, on the terrace. Dan kept beckoning to her but she ignored his pleas, staring at him with a sad regretful smile, and somehow he understood that she dare not come in because she was afraid of breaking his heart.

He woke with a desperate sense of longing, and a realisation that his subconscious was a good deal more perceptive than his conscious mind.

For once Robbie was all set to go at six in the morning – and a *Monday* morning at that. He'd got his head down early and slept like a baby. He showered, dressed in tatty clothes, then trotted into the kitchen and found Jed already at the table, drinking a concoction so dark and thick that it might have been tar.

'Did you go to bed?' Robbie asked.

'Not exactly. We having brekkie here or stopping by Maccy D's on the way?'

'Maccy D's sounds good to me.'

*　　*　　*

Dan lay and drifted until his alarm went off, by which time the effect of the dream had begun to fade. Another half an hour and he'd restored enough hope to send Cate a text, suggesting they meet for dinner one night this week.

It had been the same yesterday, his emotions on a see-saw after he'd left Robbie's flat and walked home across the city. He had said nothing to his aunt about splitting up with Hayley – that news could wait until he'd come to terms with it himself. But Joan had asked what he was planning to do about his car, and he'd told her it was in hand.

'A friend of Robbie's came and got it last night. He's taking a look at it for me.'

'Let's hope it's nothing serious,' Joan said. 'But either way I'll pick up the bill.'

Dan had begun to argue, then remembered that it was never actually going to happen.

Louis hadn't come home until eight, by which time Dan's anger had cooled. In any case, this wasn't the right moment to discuss Robbie or the drugs. Sunday nights were traditionally about family time: the three of them together in the living room, Joan busy with a sudoku and sipping a glass of sherry, Dan watching TV, Louis glancing at the screen while messaging his friends on his BlackBerry.

Now, as he walked to work, Dan reflected on a tumultuous weekend. He'd lost his car, his fiancée and his best friend, and although it might be the case that he had gained a new lover, deep down he couldn't bring himself to believe there was any prospect of a lasting relationship with Cate.

He checked his phone yet again, but she still hadn't replied. Perhaps, having thought it over, she had decided to go to the police. Dan waited for the idea to provoke a stab of panic, but nothing came. He truly felt that he didn't care what happened to him now.

✵   ✵   ✵

The text from Dan made Cate's heart sink. She wouldn't answer it until she had given some thought to a tactful response. Despite Dan's role in Hank O'Brien's death and the subsequent cover-up, Cate was still disposed to let him down gently.

In the light of a new day, she'd concluded that going to bed with him hadn't been a mistake, exactly, but neither had it represented the beginning of something. She was in two minds as to whether she should meet Dan to warn him about DC Avery. Or would it be safer if she and Robbie stayed well away from Dan for the time being?

She was thinking about reporting Avery's behaviour to DS Thomsett when her phone rang. It was her mother, sounding uncharacteristically solemn.

'Darling, are you still at home?'

'Yes. Why?'

'I wish I could be there, but I'm in East Grinstead and I've only just seen the paper. It's Martin . . .'

Cate released the breath she'd been holding. 'I know. DS Thomsett came to—' She faltered: *Mum doesn't know about Thomsett, or Hank O'Brien.*

'DS who?'

'He's one of the detectives on the case.'

'Oh.' A sniff. 'Why didn't you call me?'

'I've . . . I was in shock, I suppose.'

'You realise it happened in Kensington Gardens? It must have been that disturbance we saw. What was it, a fight with someone?'

'They don't seem to know at this stage. Look, Mum, I'm late for work. If you're in the office at lunchtime I'll pop round and we can discuss it then.'

A little put out, her mother agreed, then clicked her tongue. 'Martin was a bit of a pillock, but still. What a dreadful thing to happen.'

'It's terrible,' Cate agreed, and managed not to hurl the phone across the room.

She was surprised her mother hadn't raised the thorny issue of coincidence. Then again, Mum had twice bumped into friends in Churchill Square. Half the city went out shopping on a Saturday afternoon, so maybe Martin hadn't been following her at all . . .

An encouraging thought, until she remembered his final words in the ambulance: *Tell Cate.*

And now she had gone and mentioned DS Thomsett, which would stir up many more questions. Cate would have to come clean about Martin's visit on Friday night, and Janine's tirade, and God knew what else. As Dan had proved, it was incredibly hard to maintain a deception for any length of time.

It's spiralling out of control, she thought. And sooner or later there'll be a reckoning.

It was a weight off Robbie's mind to see the burned-out Fiesta carted away, and while other niggling worries remained, they were as nothing compared with the optimism that coursed through his veins.

The only bugbear was that Jed's buddy turned up late. It meant waiting around for nearly an hour, trying to make conversation with a man he didn't understand, didn't much like, and wanted out of his life as soon as possible. But Jed seemed sublimely unaware of Robbie's irritation. He was far more talkative than Robbie had ever known him, his comments and questions always gently probing, overlaid with an amusement that suggested he knew all of Robbie's secrets.

And that, when Robbie stopped to consider it, was no small matter. He realised that this shabby, chaotic waster could, from what he'd seen and heard over the past few days, assemble enough information to make a real nuisance of himself.

At last a recovery truck rumbled in through the gates. Robbie directed it across the lawn to the barn, wincing at the furrows it was carving in the grass. He'd have to devise an explanation for Hank's sister.

After reversing partway into the barn, the driver used a winch to drag the wreck up on to the flatbed. Another ten minutes and it was covered with a tarpaulin and strapped up tight.

Robbie produced the rest of the payment but Jed took it from him and retreated to the far side of the truck, conferring quietly with the driver. *Bastard's taking a cut for himself,* Robbie thought. If not for the small fortune resting in his safe – and the much larger one promised by Hank's stash of paperwork – he might have made a fuss about it.

Instead he was glad just to have this over with. They saw the truck off the premises, then returned to Robbie's BMW. Jed took one last admiring glance at the farmhouse.

'Hell of a place, this. Could take to living here myself.'

'In your dreams,' Robbie muttered.

'Why's that?' Jed asked, as if genuinely surprised. ''S not as though the owner's got any use for it.'

Robbie gave him a sharp look. He hadn't breathed a word about Hank O'Brien's fate.

'What makes you say that?'

'Well, you said this is one of your rental places. Nobody living here, by the look of it.' A chuckle. 'Why, what did you think I meant?'

Robbie scowled. 'Nothing.'

Cate checked the street from her bedroom window before leaving the house. A furtive, guilty action, but she wanted to make sure DC Avery wasn't lying in wait.

There was no sign of him, thank God. She hurried downstairs, set the burglar alarm and stepped outside. It was a fresh morning, a warmish breeze coursing uphill from the sea. No pedestrians in sight, no passing cars; just a delivery truck double parked at the top of the road and a car with its engine running in the side street almost adjacent to her home.

She set off down the hill, towards the magnificent red-brick church of St Mary Magdalen; beyond it, the whitecaps scudding over a greeny-blue sea. She loved the changing colours, the moods of the sea; a different landscape every day—

'Miss Scott?'

She hadn't heard footsteps, but when she turned there was a man only yards away. In his fifties, medium height, slim, wearing a suit and a raincoat. Grey-brown hair in a side parting, silver-framed glasses, a nondescript face.

At that moment, only one thing explained who he was and what he was doing here: Avery had made good on his threat. This must be DS Thomsett's boss.

'Caitlin Scott?' he said again. He had a smooth monotone voice; no discernible accent.

'Yes. Do I know you?'

Ignoring the question, he grasped her arm firmly at a point just above the elbow and steered her towards the side street, Victoria Place. 'Come with me, please.'

'What? Let me go. Who are you?'

He moved with the agility of a much younger man, urging her forward while positioning himself slightly behind her. Cate was so startled that her body obeyed, her mind whirring uselessly like a slipped gear.

His destination was the car with its engine running, a silver Ford Focus. Would a detective inspector or higher drive a Focus . . .?

You silly cow, she thought. He hasn't arrested you, hasn't cautioned you.

He's not a cop.

The panic spiked through her like a bolt of lightning, but he anticipated the impulse to break away, tightening his grip on her arm. At the same time something dug into her side. She looked down, saw the muzzle of a gun. Her legs almost gave way.

'You're not going to be hurt, but I need you to cooperate. Can you do that?' His tone was friendly, relaxed, and it induced a strong desire to believe him.

There were duelling voices in her head: one trying to maintain order, anxious not to make a scene; the other furious and afraid, berating her for being so meek.

Tell Cate . . .

Too late, it came to her: *A grey middle-aged man,* the witnesses had told the police.

Martin had been trying to warn her.

It was a paralysing thought. And now they were at the car. One of the rear doors had been left ajar – easy for her captor to flick it open without relinquishing hold of her arm or the gun.

He had her blocked in. The street was still deserted. Cate could try to break away, or cry for help, but it wouldn't save her.

There'll be a better chance than this, the calm voice told her. So she made the decision, possibly the most momentous decision of her life, and climbed into the back seat; and the other voice screamed and bawled, told her she was spineless, a coward and a fool, and that she'd just made a terrible, terrible mistake.

Eighty-seven

Dan's worst fears about his future at Denham's seemed to be realised within the first ten minutes. He arrived to find Hayley sitting in the restroom, Tim Masters perched on the table above her as though waiting for an opportunity to tumble into her lap.

Hayley took a sip from a carton of Ribena. A lock of hair fell across her forehead and Tim caressed it back into place, only to see her flinch. Confused, he glanced round, clocked Dan and gave a triumphant smile.

'Morning . . .' The tone cheery but clipped, as if the full greeting would have been: *Morning, loser.*

Dan nodded to them both, then set about making coffee. A few of their colleagues ambled in, and each time there were little starts and abrupt silences as they took in the intimate body language displayed by the couple at the table, then turned to examine what Dan was making of it. The more unconcerned he tried to appear, the more ridiculous he must have looked: any more nonchalant and he could have slithered under the door.

Checking his phone was a reliable displacement activity, but even that brought disappointment. Silence from Cate.

Then the old man walked in, dwarfed by his classic Crombie overcoat, complete with beloved TT Race lapel pin. He reacted in broadly the same way as everyone else: first a confused look at Hayley and Tim, then a questioning glance at Dan. But with Denham there was also an unmistakable hint of satisfaction.

Diffident as ever, he said, 'Uh, Dan, could we have a quick word, do you think?'

'Sure. Here?'

'Oh no.' Denham's eyes gleamed. 'This is strictly between us.'

Robbie was home before nine. A flying visit, so he left his car on the street. Jed sloped off to his room: back to bed, Robbie would have guessed, although the occasional thump and clatter suggested otherwise.

Robbie was due in the office by now, but he'd checked his mother's schedule and fortunately she was out for most of the day. He called Indira, who was less than impressed to hear he was throwing a sickie.

'I have to be in Saltdean at four, and there's no one else to cover.'

'Just close early,' he said. 'I'll square it with the old bat.'

He put the phone down on her protest, then took a shower to wash off the smell of smoke that seemed to have adhered to him again. He put on a good suit – a dark grey Hugo Boss – and transferred Hank's paperwork into a small suitcase. His Antler cabin bag was the perfect size and its combination lock, while insufficient to deter a serious thief, would at least keep prying eyes at bay. That was all he needed for now.

He left the flat, his only farewell a spectacularly loud burp: the sausage-and-egg McMuffin repeating on him. He trotted down the stairs in a buoyant mood, partly because he'd kept a watchful eye out for anyone following him this morning and he hadn't seen a thing.

For that reason he relaxed his guard, striding towards his car with barely a glance to his left or right. He didn't notice his attackers until one of them spoke, a gruff voice that wasn't addressing Robbie at all: 'That's him.'

Three heavyset men in their late forties or early fifties, dressed in designer sports gear. Tough characters gone flabby from years of fine living, but still strong, still vicious. They were on him in an instant, tearing the suitcase from his grasp. One of them held him from behind, making sure he stayed upright under the barrage of blows. Robbie dimly registered that this was a good sign: fall to the ground and you're dead.

So he *had* been followed, he thought, barely hearing the abuse they were raining on him. He wondered if they'd have the brains to search him, or if taking the papers would be enough. The memory card was in his—

'And keep your filthy hands off Jim's missus,' one of them growled, and at last the message penetrated Robbie's skull.

This isn't about Hank O'Brien.

The relief was sweeter than morphine. Ignoring the blood streaming from his nose and mouth, he lurched sideways, abandoning the effort to protect his vital organs, and made sure the suitcase was still there. It had been kicked across the pavement and now sat in the gutter next to his BMW. All it would take was for some opportunistic little scrote to wander past and nick it while everyone else was focusing on the assault . . .

Then he lost his footing and went down, his elbow striking the ground with such a loud crack that even one his assailants sucked in a breath. The other two laughed. Robbie felt like he was going to throw up. Or pass out. Or both.

He heard a scream, thought for a second that it was coming from him. As it rose in pitch it transformed into a kind of war cry. The thugs were turning away when Robbie, through his tear-distorted vision, saw Jed hurtling towards them, brandishing a carving knife in one hand and a can of something in the other. Mace?

'Who's this fucking nut?' one of the men said.

'Dunno, but we're finished here. Let's go.'

They backed off, crossing the road to a Jeep Cherokee. Jed slowed as soon as he saw the attack was over; at close range it was apparent that he had no real appetite for a fight. But he stood guard until the Cherokee roared away, then pocketed the Mace and went to help Robbie up. He froze when he saw the grin on Robbie's face.

'What's up with you?'

Robbie laughed, choked, spat a gob of blood on to the pavement, then laughed again.

'Celebrating.' He ran his tongue over his teeth, testing to see if any had come loose. 'I'm the luckiest man alive.'

Jed shook his head slowly. 'You're a fucking lunatic, Rob.'

'Yeah, I won't argue.' Robbie pointed at the suitcase. 'Gimme a hand with that, will you?'

Denham waved Dan to a seat, then hung his coat on the back of the office door and eased behind his desk.

'Am I to assume that things have moved on?'

'If you mean Hayley and me, yes. We've split up.'

'I see. Well, I hope it wasn't precipitated by our conversation on Saturday.' Denham frowned. 'Or should I hope that it *was*?'

'It had been on the cards for a while. If it affects how we work together, I'll look for another job.'

'I hope you'll do nothing of the sort.' Denham sounded unusually stern, but there was still a twinkle in his eyes. 'In any case, I don't believe such drastic action will be necessary.'

'Oh?'

Denham idly inspected a pile of mail on his desk; lifting the first envelope, he read the return address and threw it aside in disgust.

'They say that nothing is certain but death and taxes. To that, I'd currently add the obliteration of the High Street retailer. Now, I've denied it in staff presentations, and I'll go on denying it for the sake of morale, but I can see the truth as well as anyone.' He leaned back, lacing his hands behind his head, a relaxed posture that seemed at odds with his message. 'The one saving grace is that we own this site. It's the land we're sitting on that's the only true asset – and I say "we", but actually it's just me. At present.'

Another pause. Dan had the impression that he should have cottoned on to something by now, but he remained mystified.

'Here's what I'm proposing,' Denham said. 'A management restructure, appointing you as general manager with responsibility for both sales and service.'

A promotion, when Dan's dream was to strike out on his own. He opened his mouth to explain but Denham raised a hand. 'Hear me out. I won't be able to employ a new sales manager, unfortunately, so there'll be some increase in your workload, but I'll be around as much as ever. Between us, I'm sure we'll cope.'

'This is going to put Tim's nose out of joint.'

'Oh? Why do you say that?'

'Well, he's always been ambitious. And if it came down to the two of us, I bet he'd fancy himself as the winning candidate.'

Denham nodded happily. 'Let's hope so, because then he's liable to bugger off in a fit of pique.'

'You don't want to keep him?'

'Give it a year, eighteen months at most, and we won't need a service manager.'

'Is that how long we've got?'

'The end may come sooner still, if I'm made the right sort of offer.'

'You're selling—' Dan began; and at last he understood. 'But not as a going concern?'

'Residential development, with some sheltered housing, that's the likeliest option. I hope you won't think too badly of me,' Denham added gravely. 'The staff will be looked after, I promise you that. Well, you'll have a say, of course.'

'Will I?'

'Along with the post of general manager, I'm proposing to give you a share in the business. How does ten per cent sound?'

Dan was stunned. Perhaps misreading the look, Denham gave a dismissive wave. 'Oh, it means nothing now. We've made fresh air for profits, the past few years. But come the sale, after fees and expenses, I expect we'll realise about two million for the site.'

It was one of those silly cartoon moments, as though pound signs had appeared on Dan's eyeballs. Ten per cent of two million was *two hundred thousand pounds.*

'That should be enough to finance this business proposition of yours.' He smiled at Dan's incredulous expression. 'As it happens, I thoroughly approve of a coffee shop. Low overheads, high margins, and best of all the online vultures and supermarkets can't muscle in, because location is the key. Even in hard times folk like to treat themselves to a drink and a cake made for them by someone else.' He winked at Dan. 'In my retirement, I look forward to becoming a regular customer.'

Robbie stood up, shrugging off Jed's help. A few people loitered nearby, one of his neighbours among them. Robbie had no idea how long they'd been there. The neighbour asked if he should call the police, but Robbie shook his head.

'No real harm done,' he said.

He trudged back to the flat, clutching the suitcase to his chest as if slow-dancing a lover. His suit was a write-off, covered in blood and torn at the elbow and knee. He stripped off, got back in the shower and carefully washed the blood from his face.

His elbow hurt like crazy, but there were no bones broken, and once he'd cleaned up none of his injuries was visible. That curious sense of elation persisted, perhaps because the beating hadn't disrupted his plans in the slightest.

He put on another good suit, then came out into the hall and stopped dead. A battered old army-surplus kitbag stood by the front door. Jed emerged from his bedroom, wearing his green parka and carrying a rucksack. He saw Robbie's expression and nodded.

'I'm out of here.'

'Oh. Right.' Robbie was temporarily lost for words.

'Seems like you're getting yourself into all kinds of shit. I don't wanna be around when it hits the fan.'

Robbie didn't comment. 'Where are you going?'

'Pal in Swansea, for starters. So I'd appreciate some cash to tide us over. Let's make it a grand.'

'What?'

'Golden handshake, sort of thing.' Jed sniffed, aggressively. 'I mean, to thank us for saving you from a kicking just now.'

Robbie wanted to say, *They'd practically gone by the time you got there*. But Jed had a mean look in his eyes.

'I would, but I don't have that kind of money.'

'You're a shit liar, Robbie. It's sitting in your safe, that and a lot more besides.'

'What? No, it's n—'

'6-8-4-3-1,' Jed recited in a sing-song voice. 'I could've cleaned you out whenever I wanted. Could've strolled away with the whole lot and left you in a bleeding heap on the pavement.'

Robbie was taken aback, but tried to recover. 'All right. I appreciate that. The thing is, it's not my money.'

Jed roared with laughter. 'Since when did that ever stop you, ye cheeky bastard?'

Eighty-eight

'He's binding us in.' This was Patricia's reaction to the call from Stemper.

On Sunday they had agreed with him that drastic action might be necessary. But it was one thing to discuss in theory; quite another to know the woman was coming here, right now. Their prisoner.

While Gordon could hardly move for the excitement, his wife was rather more measured. Shaking her head as Gordon tried to argue that there was nowhere else as suitable.

'It's about ensuring that we sink with him, if anything goes wrong.' Then a harrumph. '*If* anything goes wrong. What am I saying? So far virtually *everything* has gone wrong.'

'That's not true. We've dealt with Jerry. We've identified our rivals. And now we have one of them in our possession . . .' Gordon decided it was safe to stand up. 'I'd better get the room prepared.'

'She's not a house guest.'

'Make it secure, I mean. Just in case . . .'

She mistook his breathlessness for reticence. 'I hope you're not having second thoughts?'

'I'm not. I promise.'

'It's what we agreed. A couple of lives, in exchange for all that good work . . .'

'More than a couple, potentially.'

'But none of them exactly innocent. It's still morally justified, isn't it?'

'Absolutely.' Earlier Gordon had been dreaming about his yacht, how occasionally he might enjoy a week away on his own – or, rather, minus Patricia. He wouldn't be *alone*. One or two of his lady friends would accompany him. Or half a dozen, if the mood took him.

Moral justification didn't come into it.

Stemper thought he might have trouble with the woman, but she turned out to be remarkably compliant. Once he had her in the car it was child's play. He made her lie face down on the back seat, then tied her hands with a length of the nylon rope that he'd bought on Saturday.

She was warned that he would gag her if she screamed. She agreed to keep silent, and so she was, until they had driven out of Brighton and were heading north on the A23. At first her voice was dry with fear. She cleared her throat, made smacking noises with her tongue, and tried again.

'Did you kill Martin?'

He was moderately impressed by the question. It showed a lawyer's mind at work. A truthful answer would tell her a lot about who he was and what he was doing. And it seemed an unselfish enquiry, though there was a subtext: *If you killed him, you might kill me.*

'What did the police say?' he asked.

'They have your description.' Her tone now was overly confident: a bluff. 'But no motive. They don't understand why he died, and neither do I.'

'You must have a theory, at least?'

'No.' The word emerged on a sob. 'I haven't a clue. But I promise, if you pull over somewhere and let me out, I won't report you to the police. In any case, I can't identify—'

'I'm disappointed. I expected better from you.'

'Please. I just think you've made a mistake.'

'There's no mistake. You're Caitlin Scott, aren't you? Sister of Robert?'

She gave a sigh of pure dejection. 'What's Robbie got to do with this?'

'That,' he said, 'is what you need to tell us.'

Robbie. Somehow, directly or indirectly, it was her brother who had put Cate in this position.

DS Thomsett must have got it right, after a fashion. The two deaths were linked, and the link couldn't just be her, or Robbie. It had to be Hank O'Brien.

But why had she and Martin been targeted, if it was Robbie they wanted?

Presumably she would find out, if she was being taken somewhere to be questioned. That sparked a new kind of terror, not so much numbing as galvanising, because she realised she had nothing to lose. She couldn't believe she'd been so weak, so passive before.

She lay still, listening to the rumble of passing traffic, the burr of tyres on tarmac, eating up the miles between here and her destiny. She fell into a strange dreamlike state, alert and yet sleepy, and tried not to think about the next step. Her attempt to escape, when it happened, should be spontaneous, not constrained or telegraphed by too much planning.

From her position on the back seat it was impossible to see the route they were taking, but the noise and the speed at which they were travelling suggested a motorway. She had driven on the M23 and M25 often enough to track the long westward curve of the slip road, then the steep climb into the Surrey hills.

Before long they left the motorway and followed a sharply meandering route on roads with far less traffic. She guessed they were in countryside just south of the M25: maybe the Guildford, Dorking area.

Then a sharp turn, the car bumping over a rougher surface, slowing, then jerking to a halt. The driver's door opened and Cate's heart began to race, her throat closing up, every nerve primed and every hope she had pinned on the next few seconds.

Make it count. Don't shame yourself now.

Eighty-nine

The rear door opened, but it was the one by her feet, not the other side as she'd expected. Her abductor grasped her ankles and dragged her over the seat.

'Get out. Slowly.'

Cate did as she was told, wriggling and shuffling, having to use her chin to help propel herself along. With her hands behind her back, her only real weapon was her head, but he'd neutralised the threat by making her climb out backwards.

She was barely upright before he wrenched her towards him, forcing her head down. He had something in his hands, a hood, and even as she caught a glimpse of a large house – a red and white Victorian villa – he swept it over her head and she was blind.

'This guarantees your safety,' he said. 'If it's removed, you will die.'

Cate heard footsteps approaching on the driveway and knew that this was it: her last chance. Turning towards her abductor, she went up on tiptoe and launched a headbutt which seemed to catch him somewhere – his cheek, perhaps – and she drove her body forward, bumping past him and staggering blindly away from the car, her hands useless; no way to save herself other than to scream at the top of her lungs.

'Help me! Please, help me! Call 999! I've been—'

A hand clamped over her mouth, through the hood, and she was dragged backwards and felt other people moving in, one of them possibly a woman. Definitely a woman's fragrance, sickly and old-fashioned; everyone breathing hard from exertion and stress; grunts and whispered instructions as Cate kicked and fought against the hands that restrained her, knowing it was useless but determined to go down fighting.

'Got a feisty one here,' a man said, and his voice was smooth and cultured, a little in love with itself.

Then someone punched her, the blow so fast and strong that she had no time to tense in anticipation. It drove the breath from her lungs and made her light-headed, but she battled to stay conscious, hating herself with a ferocity that should properly have been reserved for her attackers.

She had wasted her opportunity, and knew there might not be another.

Gordon had chosen the smaller of the spare bedrooms to use as a cell. The door was reasonably sturdy, and could be locked with a key. The room had one window, but with some effort he was able to shift a heavy wardrobe across it. The only other furniture was a single bed and a chest of drawers. He removed the latter, but left the bed.

Then Stemper arrived, and the woman made a spirited effort to escape. It was only after they'd manhandled her inside and up the stairs that Gordon could take a good look at her. Not her face, of course. That remained hooded. But her body . . .

Patricia caught him staring greedily at Caitlin's breasts. She exhaled sharply but said nothing. She and Gordon were supposed to keep conversation to a minimum in the woman's presence, though to Gordon it seemed a superfluous effort. Now they had her, he couldn't envisage being able to let her go.

She was placed on the bed, face up, hands still bound behind her back. She wore a functional suit – M&S or Next, probably – in dark blue, the skirt riding well above her knees. Tights, not stockings, and simple black court shoes. The hood was an unwelcome addition, not even erotic in a fetishistic kind of way. It put Gordon in mind of that film, *The Elephant Man*.

Stemper fetched his briefcase and set it down on the bed. Caitlin flinched when the catches sprang open. He removed a set of pliers, looked at Patricia and gave a sombre nod.

'Now, Caitlin, I have some questions to ask you.' His voice, as ever, was so soft and mild, the delivery so steady in its pace, it was impossible not to hang on every word.

Caitlin said, 'Please. I don't know anything.'

'Well, now, I had a feeling you would say that.'

Stemper slipped off the woman's shoes. Caitlin jumped at the contract, drawing her knees up. He nodded an instruction: *Hold her still*.

This was Gordon's first chance to lay his hands on her, and the prospect of it gave him palpitations. Standing at the side of the bed, he gripped the calf of her right leg, the flesh warm and soft, with strong muscles beneath. Stemper held her foot and carefully placed the pliers around the woman's little toe. She began to breathe in short, urgent gasps. A whining noise issued from her throat, a long single note that grew in pitch until Stemper brought the pliers together.

Then a ferocious, spine-chilling scream. Gordon swallowed, and looked away from the business end of the bed. This was like Lisa's birth all over again. Even Patricia, watching sternly at close range, seemed to blanch.

Only Stemper was unaffected. He eased the pliers off, the metal sticky with the blood that was seeping through her tights.

'You see, Caitlin, the pain of a crush injury is out of all proportion to the damage done. You'll know that if you've ever trapped your hand in a door. I doubt if I've even broken a bone here, and yet you're going to suffer pure agony now, as it swells, as it burns. Think about that, and then imagine how it might feel if I repeat this procedure on every single toe, and then on every finger . . .'

Caitlin whimpered, breathing in great hitching gasps that for Gordon prompted another recollection of his daughter: this time her legendary temper tantrums at the age of two or three. Patricia used to curtail them with a hard slap, and she was itching to do the same thing here, Gordon could tell.

But Stemper was in command of this process, and he merely waited.

'Now, Caitlin, my first question. If you lie to me, I'll do two more toes before I'll even consider giving you an opportunity to speak. Was your brother, Robert Scott, involved in Hank O'Brien's death?'

Silence. Maybe ten seconds of deliberation, and then she nodded. 'It . . . it was an accident. He didn't mean to knock him down, I swear.'

'Where does Robert live? I want his address.'

Gordon expected this question to meet resistance, but she gave it up almost immediately. An apartment in Hove.

'And does he have what we want?'

'I don't understand . . .'

'You're trying to say that you're not part of the conspiracy?'

'There's no conspiracy. It was an accident.'

'And who else was present? Who was with your brother on that night?'

A long pause. Stemper opened the pliers, a small but significant noise.

'Just . . . one of his friends.'

'But they were in the pub with you. They helped you out when Hank overstepped the mark, remember?'

She gasped, as if taken aback by how much they knew. Gordon was desperate to speak himself, to crow a little, but that urge – along with all his other urges – had to be repressed.

She said, 'I think his name was Tom. I really don't know.'

'Then Robert will tell me,' Stemper said. 'And I'll move on to the next toe.'

'No, please!' She sobbed a couple of times. She sounded weak, defeated. 'The dispute was over money. Robbie agreed three thousand with Hank, but he'd made five thousand. From . . . using the farmhouse. For a film.'

'*Entwined*,' Stemper said. 'Yes, we're aware of that.'

'But no one killed Hank on purpose. It was late at night. A dark road. It just happened.'

'So how did Robbie know about the documents?'

A baffled silence. Then she said: 'The what?'

Stemper gave Patricia a peevish look. Gordon thought he understood why: Caitlin genuinely didn't know about the paperwork.

At Stemper's signal they filed out and gathered on the landing. He said, 'I suspect she won't be able to tell us what's happened to the paperwork. In which case, finding her brother is far more important.'

The Blakes were in agreement. Gordon said, 'And what about this other man, "Tom"?'

'She's lying. She knows who he is.'

'My feeling exactly,' Patricia said. 'Why don't you go after Robert? I'm sure we can get the rest out of her. Can't we, Gordon?'

'Oh, yes,' Gordon agreed.

Ninety

Probably less than wise, Robbie thought, turning up here after what had happened. And only a small comfort that Jimmy's car was nowhere in sight.

Robbie had parked his BMW down the road, the precious suitcase locked in the boot. After ringing the doorbell he dabbed at his nostrils to make sure the bleeding hadn't started again.

The front door opened an inch. 'Yeah?'

Robbie couldn't see anyone through the gap, but it was Bree's voice, at least.

'I wanna know what the hell happened. I got jumped on this morning.'

Silence, then the door opened wider to reveal Bree, in trackie bottoms and a sweatshirt; no make-up, no bling. One eye swollen almost closed, the whole corner of her face a reddish-purple lump of flesh. A bandage around her left wrist; deep scratches on her hands and neck.

He took a step back. 'Jesus.' Then he got it. 'Maureen?'

'You pissed her off. This is her revenge.'

'The bitch. Jimmy swallowed every word, I suppose?'

'He did when DC Avery turned up, asking me where I was Tuesday night.'

Robbie shut his eyes for a second. 'Oh, shit.'

'Means you got your alibi, though.'

'So this cop . . . he did believe you, then?'

'Yeah, especially once he saw the mood Jimmy was in. And soon as Avery left, Jimmy had his fun.' A brittle smile. 'Still, it's worked out all right for you, eh?'

Robbie nodded sadly. He couldn't begrudge her this bitterness; nor could he let on how relieved he felt.

'I'm sorry, Bree. That's really out of order, what he's done to you.'

'Yeah, well. Shit happens.' She gave an anxious look over his shoulder. 'He'll be back soon. If he finds you here . . .'

Robbie nodded. He had no desire to be caught. 'Is this it, then?' he asked.

'Think it had better be, don't you?' There was a hint of a smile, but the door shut before he could offer a farewell, much less kiss her.

He returned to his car, feeling self-righteously aggrieved about Jimmy's behaviour. No matter what the provocation, you didn't beat up a woman.

A wealthy man wouldn't stand for it, Robbie thought. A wealthy man would hire some serious muscle and give Jimmy a taste of his own medicine.

And soon Robbie was going to be a very wealthy man indeed . . .

Dan emerged from his meeting in a pleasant daze, then realised that Cate might be with DS Thomsett right now, spilling out the whole miserable story. If he'd known yesterday what Denham had in mind, perhaps he wouldn't have been so eager to let justice take its course.

He rang her mobile but there was no answer, so he sent a bland text: Hope you're ok? He was on his way to the shop floor when Tim Masters pounced.

'Uh-oh, here's a man in trouble!'

'Pardon?'

'I s'pose Denham's trying to decide if you can cut it under the new regime.'

Dan managed to look puzzled. 'What new regime is that?'

'Ah, he'll be playing it close to his chest.' Tim winked. 'Some of us can read between the lines.'

'Glad to hear it.'

'No hard feelings, though, what with Hales as well?'

'None at all.'

He walked away, but he'd only gone a few feet when Tim said, 'So, when the big day comes . . .'

Dan turned. 'Yes?'

'You reckon you can get used to calling me "sir"?'

Dan's laughter echoed down the corridor, and might have been audible in the shop.

Robbie took an indirect route to Hollingbury, not discounting the possibility of somebody on his tail, but he saw nothing suspicious. Various parts of him still ached to buggery, but the news that Bree's alibi had put him in the clear over Hank's death acted as a very effective analgesic.

He knew Dan wouldn't be home. It was a bonus when he discovered that Joan was out, too. She was a tough old bird, and nobody's fool. Robbie's charm worked on her up to a point, but never if there was any hint of tension between him and Dan.

Fortunately it was only Louis there, the lazy sod in Calvin Kleins and a *Stewie* T-shirt, bloodshot eyes and hair like a haystack.

'No college?'

'Going in for twelve.'

'Jesus. The pressures of higher education.'

'And you work hard for a living, do you?'

Robbie cackled. That was what he liked about Louis: only seventeen, but not afraid to dish out the backchat.

'Need a small favour.' Robbie held up the suitcase. 'Just gotta stash this here for a day or two.'

Louis stared at it for a moment, then he let Robbie inside. 'Better not be anything illegal.'

'It's not, I promise.' Robbie gave him a close look. 'Has Dan spoken to you?'

Louis twitched. 'What about?'

'Somebody ratted me out on my little sideline, and from that your big brother came to the conclusion that I was plying you with narcotics.'

'Oh, fuck.' Louis frowned. 'He hasn't mentioned it, though. And he can't have told Joan, either. She'd go mental.'

'Maybe he's decided to say nothing. Anyway, for your info, I'm out of that game now.'

Louis was despondent. 'So what am I supposed to do?'

'Give up. Dan's probably right. It's bad for your health in the long run.'

Turning away, Louis muttered: 'Who gives a toss about the long run?'

Robbie followed him upstairs, wrinkling his nose at the smell of Louis's room. He wondered if his own pit had stunk like this at the same age.

'They used to reckon it made you go blind, too much wanking.'

'You'd know, I suppose,' Louis said, and ducked away from Robbie's playful swipe.

They stashed the case at the bottom of an old wicker laundry basket that held spare bedding. Then, from his wallet, Robbie brought out the micro-SD card.

'You see what this is?'

Louis pulled a sarcastic face. 'Duh. I do have an acquaintance with modern technology.'

'Not what I meant,' Robbie snapped. 'Treat this like the most precious thing you'll ever possess. And don't let anyone know about it. Definitely not your big bruv.'

At this, Louis looked troubled, but he took the card, studying it in a manner that conveyed just how his greedy little mind was working.

'Yeah, yeah, there's a nice bonus heading your way. *If* you keep it safe. And you keep your mouth shut. Deal?'

'Deal.' A beat of silence. 'So what are you up to?'

Robbie shook his head. 'You don't wanna know.'

* * *

Dan kept on trying Cate's mobile, with no success. He became prey to a creeping paranoia, wondering if the police were about to march in and arrest him. He pictured Hayley, tearfully vindicated as he was led away in handcuffs, Tim consoling her; old man Denham thanking providence that he hadn't yet signed over a share of the business to this low-life criminal . . .

At eleven o'clock he phoned the law firm where she worked. He was put through to an administrative assistant, who crisply informed him that Ms Scott was unavailable.

'I'm Dan, a friend of hers. A friend of Robbie's, as well. And I urgently need to speak to her.'

'You can't. She hasn't come in.'

'Is she off sick?'

'I don't know.' The woman's attitude softened. 'She's already missed an important meeting, and I can't get hold of her on the phone.'

'Me neither,' Dan said. 'And you're sure she hasn't been in touch?'

'No. It's really not like her . . .' The assistant's voice trailed off, and Dan had the sense of someone passing her desk. When she spoke again it was in a confidential tone: 'She had a visitor earlier, a detective sergeant. He seemed surprised that she wasn't here.'

Dan thanked her, a tremor in his hand as he put his phone away. *Where was she?*

He remembered what Cate had said about the possibility of a link between Hank O'Brien's death and the murder of her ex-husband. Dan had clumsily poured scorn on the suggestion, because he knew there wasn't a link – at least not in the way that DS Thomsett had meant it.

But now Dan wondered if he'd been wrong to dismiss the idea.

What if there *was* a connection?

What if the connection was Cate?

Ninety-one

The Blakes saw Stemper off, then retired to the kitchen. Gordon had picked up Caitlin's handbag and riffled through it with a prurient curiosity. Other than her phone, which Stemper had switched off, there was nothing of interest in the bag – not so much as a pocket vibrator. He tutted. *Young woman of today* . . .

'We should set some ground rules,' Patricia said, 'since you so blatantly want to screw her.'

Gordon, still smirking at the absence of sex toys, felt that an outright denial would be unconvincing. 'Not desperately.'

'No? I imagine she's a step up from your usual "outlets".'

Gordon was flabbergasted. He'd always been *so* careful. 'Patricia, I—'

'Save it. The reason you mustn't is that you might leave DNA on her body. Now, promise me you can control yourself in there. Because it *will* be a temptation, a nubile young woman tied up and at your mercy . . .' Patricia licked her lips, as if deliberately trying to push him over the edge.

'I'm certain.' He coughed to hide his embarrassment. 'I thought, with Stemper having hurt her, that I'd take the role of "good cop", as it were.'

Patricia nodded. 'It plays to your strengths.' And when Gordon looked puzzled, she added: 'Well, you're hardly the threatening type, are you?'

*   *   *

It was a relief to be left alone, even though the solitude offered no distractions from the pain. Cate's torturer had been right: as the damaged toe swelled up it only hurt more and more, a throbbing so huge that it seemed to inhabit the whole room.

She felt wretched about giving them Robbie's address, but it was something they'd find easily enough by other means. And Robbie, she had to pray, could look after himself. Better than she had done, at least.

She had no idea how her colleagues would react to her absence. The assumption, surely, would be that she was ill, or grieving for Martin. Her mother was expecting to see her at lunchtime, but even if Mum went to the house there were no clues to her whereabouts. Cate found herself wishing that DC Avery had turned up this morning and taken her in for questioning . . .

She heard the door open, a thump as it swung back and hit somebody's foot. Little sighs and the clink of crockery: something was being manoeuvred through the doorway.

'Caitlin, I'm so very sorry about all this.'

It was the man who had labelled her as 'feisty'. The smoothie. He set down what he was carrying and came over to her. He smelled of shower gel and moisturiser; a subtle cologne, as he leaned in very close, and when he spoke she felt the soft pressure of his breath against the hood.

'Eyes shut tightly for a moment, my dear.'

She felt his weight settle on the bed alongside her. As the hood was removed she opened her eyes a fraction, glimpsed a bare room lit by a single bulb, a heavy wardrobe blocking the window.

'No peeking.' His arm brushed her neck and she was sure he gasped at the contact. Some soft, smooth material slid over her head and covered her eyes. A silk scarf?

The man was breathing rapidly, radiating tension, and Cate had a sudden clear sense of why he was alone with her. She bit down hard on her lip.

'Don't be alarmed,' he said, because of course now he could see her face; her emotions were there to be read. 'I thought you'd welcome refreshments. Paracetamol, too, after that gruesome business earlier . . .'

He sounded so pleasant, so gentle, Cate longed to believe he was being sincere, but deep down she felt sure he was playing a part. Not that she objected to his offer of painkillers: anything to alleviate the throbbing in her foot.

He fed her the pills, then held a glass of water at her mouth and let her drink. Coffee to follow, he said, and he asked how she liked it, as though she was a friend who'd popped in for cake and a gossip.

'I'll have to hold the cup, of course,' he said.

'You could untie my hands.'

His lips smacked together, as if cutting off the answer he would like to give. 'Sorry, no.'

You're not allowed, she thought.

'The man who brought me here, what does he want?'

He sighed. 'My dear, why don't we run through my questions first, and then we'll see about yours?'

The aroma as he lifted the coffee to her lips was like manna from heaven. His hand was trembling, so it was difficult to drink without scalding her mouth, but the first taste produced an almost ridiculous surge of pleasure.

'Nice?' he asked. 'Now, let's begin with this movie connection, just so we understand it correctly.'

Her voice shaky, Cate explained the deal that Robbie had made. She described her part in the negotiations, and the dispute with Hank in the pub, and she went on insisting that his death had been a tragic accident.

'I don't know how many times I have to say it.' To her disgust, she sounded whiny and afraid. 'Why won't you believe me?'

'Ssh, don't get upset.' She felt him briefly stroking her head, his fingers gliding through her hair.

He moved on to the fact that O'Brien's property was back on Compton's books.

'You know your brother has taken the car there? The one that hit O'Brien.'

Her reaction was quite genuine: No, she didn't know anything about that

'But you can see how it all appears so convenient? Not to mention that he seemed to know just where to look.'

'Where to look for what?'

'Oh, Caitlin, please.' He chuckled, and she felt his breath on her face. She sensed his hands floating just millimetres above her skin and fought to conceal her revulsion.

'I have no idea what you want. Please. You must be able to see I'm telling the truth.'

'You were lying to us earlier, about the other man in the pub. What's his real name?'

'I don't know,' Cate said, and understood that for Dan's sake she had to change the subject. 'I wish I could help you, because I think you're just trying to soften me up, before that psychopath comes back.'

'Caitlin, my dear, that's nonsense—'

'It's not. He's going to torture me again, and you'll stand by and let him do it.'

She turned on the waterworks, bawling like a child, with an intensity that was about eighty per cent genuine. Her interrogator hushed her, whispering soft assurances, his hands finally settling on her skin, crawling over her shoulders and back before slipping round to the front. This was appalling, but better than selling Dan out to them.

'I-I know he . . . he killed Martin, and you w-won't stop him from—'

She broke off as she registered the jolt of shock that passed through him.

'Martin?'

*　*　*

453

A big mistake, to phrase it as a question. A big, big mistake.

And it had been going so well. Had the environment been more conducive, Gordon wouldn't have ruled out a mutual attraction; and in the startling new landscape of a life where Patricia was privy to his darkest secrets, who could say what adventures lay in store?

He'd been skilfully gaining Caitlin's trust, developing a strategy to tease out the truth about the second man in the pub, when she had lobbed this at him:

Martin?

'My ex-husband. He was stabbed to death on Saturday afternoon.'

Without a word, Gordon carried the coffee tray to the door. He was fumbling with the handle when Patricia opened it. She must have been lurking outside. Her lack of trust rankled, but there were more pressing matters to discuss.

'Did you hear that?'

'Something about a stabbing.'

'Her ex-husband, Martin-somebody. She claims that Stemper killed him.'

Patricia spread her hands. 'Why wouldn't he have told us?'

'I don't know. But it seems a bizarre thing for her to lie about.'

'I'm sure Stemper will have an explan—'

A noise downstairs cut her off: a heavy rapping on the front door. But Stemper wasn't due back for hours, and they weren't expecting anyone else.

The police, he thought. Perhaps Stemper had been seen, bundling Caitlin into the car.

A second of speechless panic. There was no disputing the gravity of their crimes: a woman held prisoner in their home, the victim of physical torture . . .

'What are we going to do?' he said.

Patricia, not entirely unperturbed, said, 'Well, see who it is, I suppose.'

*   *   *

Stemper returned to Sussex, calling first at the farmhouse. As he might have predicted, the burnt-out car had gone. A chance to intercept Robert Scott – and possibly the other member of the gang – had been squandered.

His next stop was Robert Scott's apartment. The building was a dark, Gothic pile, one of several in the street: a cluster of Transylvanian mansions transported to a seaside resort. At the communal entrance he buzzed several numbers at random and someone duly released the door.

He was in a decidedly positive mood as he climbed the stairs. After the misstep on Saturday afternoon he had brought the operation back on track. The ultimate prize, he felt sure, was very close now.

No answer at the flat. There was only a single lock, easily bumped. Once inside, a quick check to ensure he was alone, and then the proper search could begin.

Kitchen, living room, bathroom: all unremarkable. A guest bedroom, occupied until very recently by the look of it. The tenant had been a drug-user, a devotee of cheap booze and junk food. The sense of a hasty abandonment troubled him slightly.

The master bedroom offered limited reassurance – plenty of clothes in the wardrobe – but in the en-suite bathroom he found an expensive suit, torn and dirty and soiled with blood. Another cause for concern – until he saw the opportunity it presented.

There was a moderately secure floor safe, probably a 3k-cash rating. Stemper didn't have the equipment to open it, but in any case it didn't look large enough for the volume of paperwork he was expecting to find.

A moment later he spotted two document boxes on top of the wardrobe. Both empty. He took a photo of them with his phone, then called Gordon Blake.

'I'm sending you a picture of something.'

'Oh yes?' A strange wry tone to Gordon's voice.

'I'm at the apartment. No sign of the owner, or the paperwork, but

I'm certain he has it. I may have to wait here and question him when he comes back.'

Gordon gave a joyous laugh. 'There's really no need.'

'What do you mean?'

'He's already here.'

Stemper exhaled slowly. Discretion forgotten, he said, '*Robert Scott* is there, with you?'

'Correct,' Gordon said. 'Only I think he prefers "Robbie".'

Ninety-two

Cate felt sure her captor's abrupt departure spelled trouble. He'd seemed confused by what she said about Martin, which suggested that the man who had abducted her was keeping secrets from his accomplices.

She heard low voices outside the room, and then a distant knocking. She felt a leap of hope: she could cry for help.

Unless it was one of the gang?

Worth the risk. She wriggled forward, straining to make out the variations of light through the blindfold. She had a sliver of vision if she looked directly below her. She used it to guide her off the bed, and then across the room in a slow shuffle. She reached the door and was paralysed by fear and indecision. Should she shout, scream, what?

Too late. She heard urgent footsteps along the landing. The door opened and Cate twisted away from a large, powerful presence; her nostrils filling with that cloying flowery scent. So it was the woman this time. It was the woman who grabbed Cate by the throat and forced her back on to the bed. It was the woman who tied her ankles together and lashed them to the bed frame. It was the woman who stuffed a cloth into her mouth, sealed it with tape and snarled: 'Don't make a sound, you skinny little bitch, or I'll kill you myself.'

*   *   *

Dan hated having to approach his boss for a favour so soon after their meeting. But Willie Denham was happy to grant his request for an extended lunch, especially when Dan explained that a friend of his was in trouble.

He jumped on a bus to Western Road, then ran up the hill to Cate's home. After he'd knocked and called through the letter box several times, an elderly woman emerged from the house next door and told him that Cate was probably at work.

'Did you see her leave this morning?'

'Sorry, just got in myself. But where else would she be on a Monday morning?'

His next stop was Compton's. As soon as he pushed through the door he sensed an air of crisis. Teresa Scott was deep in conference with Robbie's colleague, Indira, but broke off when she spotted Dan.

'Hello! This is a surprise.'

'I'm trying to get hold of Cate.'

He saw a little bloom of hope wither in her eyes. 'So are we. We've had the police here, looking for her. DS Thomsett.'

Dan kept his expression neutral. 'What did he want?'

'Something to do with Martin. Did you hear . . .?'

'Yes. Dreadful.'

Teresa nodded, as eager as Dan was to return the focus to Cate. 'I have a spare key, and I've been round to the house. There's no sign of her. When we spoke this morning she said she was late for work, and was coming to see me at lunchtime. I don't see why she'd lie.'

'Me neither. So she's been reported missing?'

'DS Thomsett says it's still a bit soon to make it official, but he did say they'd be paying a visit to Janine's brother.'

Dan was shocked. 'Why would they do that?'

'Some bonkers theory that Cate was trying to lure Martin back. Janine's been hysterical about it, so it's just possible that one of her family . . .' Teresa tailed off. 'Sorry, love, I'm scaring you.'

But it was herself she was scaring, and they could all see it. Indira

458

put an arm around her and said, 'Could be she's just gone off to get some space.'

'She's not answering her phone,' Dan pointed out.

'Unless the battery died?' Teresa said. 'I know mine always packs up at the most inconvenient time.'

She had been toying with a box of Marlboro Lights, unconsciously teasing a cigarette from the pack; now she noticed and crossly pushed it away. To Dan, she said, 'I don't suppose you know where Robbie is?'

'What?' It was almost a yelp. 'Do you mean he's missing as well?'

'No. Just being an awkward sod, ignoring his messages. Probably up to no good, as usual . . .'

Dan raised an eyebrow; playing dumb.

'His floozies,' Teresa said, and Indira went tight-lipped and wouldn't meet Dan's eye.

He said, 'I'll try and find him.'

'Can you? Not that he'll be much help, but he may know something.'

Dan agreed, thinking: *Damn right Robbie knows something.* He knew what Hank O'Brien had been hiding. He knew what that information was worth, and he knew who wanted it.

And Dan was going to force him to reveal it all.

It was an infatuation, as far as Gordon was concerned, though he had no intention of describing it in such terms, least of all to Patricia.

While she had hovered anxiously on the stairs, he'd checked from a window in the hall, then exclaimed, 'I think it's the brother. Robert Scott.'

'Are you serious?'

'Well, we've only seen the Facebook picture, but that's who it resembles.'

'And he's alone?' When he nodded, Patricia had shook her head and muttered, 'He can't know we've got his sister. He simply can't.'

'Then why is he here?'

Her face was slowly transformed by a smile. 'Only one possible reason. Open up.'

Gordon braced himself, but it was evident at once that the man on their doorstep had no violent intent. He was wearing a navy pinstripe suit: probably Italian tailoring, and rather too narrow in the cut for Gordon's taste, but undeniably a very smart, appropriate style for a young man in such great shape.

What the Facebook portrait hadn't revealed was that Robert Scott was, to use a common phrase, *drop-dead gorgeous*. He had a killer-watt smile, too. And a good handshake: dry, firm, strong.

'Gordon Blake?' he said. 'I'm Robbie Scott.'

Just in time, Gordon remembered that he shouldn't know who Robert was. He allowed his hand to be pumped and then, looking suitably mystified, said, 'How can I help you?'

'I've come about your little problem. With Templeton Wynne. I thought maybe I could discuss it with you and . . . er, Patricia, if she's available?'

'I'm here,' Patricia said, and while Gordon went on faking confusion she stepped forward and offered her hand. 'Sounds fascinating. Please do come in. My husband will sort out refreshments, if you'll just excuse me for a moment.'

She was well ahead of them in reaching the kitchen, emerging again as Gordon led Robbie through. He couldn't see what she was holding behind her back, but from her discreet nod he guessed it had something to do with ensuring Cate's silence.

She was gone for a couple of minutes, leaving Gordon to spew out some routine babble about the local housing market. Robbie introduced himself as a property developer and letting agent from a Brighton-based company. The way he described it you'd think the company was his, rather than his mother's, which Gordon found highly amusing.

No sooner had he made the coffee than the phone rang. A look from Patricia: *You answer it.* She was keen to get to know Mr Scott herself.

Gordon took the call in the living room. It was Stemper, reporting that Robbie wasn't at home. Gordon derived great pleasure from revealing that they knew precisely where he could be found.

Sounding disgruntled, Stemper said, 'That's a bold move on his part.'

'Isn't it?' Gordon was tempted to spring a question about this Martin chap, but knew he had to discuss it with Patricia first.

'Shall I come up—?' Stemper began. 'Actually, no. Better that he's unaware of my existence.'

'That's what we thought,' Gordon said, and wanted to add: *We're not complete morons, Patricia and I.*

Robbie felt supremely confident. He liked this large, cosy house, nestled in the Surrey hills, and he liked these people, the Blakes, far more than he had expected to. He sensed kindred spirits here.

In the case of Patricia, Robbie couldn't recall when he'd last been in the presence of such a strong, incisive personality. Formidable, and yet still appreciably feminine. To Robbie it was like encountering some weird combination of ideal mother figure, naughty aunt, mentor and femme fatale.

'Fantastic coffee,' he said, smiling at Gordon, and then he got down to business. 'And it was a fantastic plan, too. With one massive flaw.'

Gordon, who was openly basking in the compliment, said, 'Oh?'

'Hank had far too much power over you. The proof is that I'm sitting here now, in possession of everything I need to know about your scheme.'

They conceded the point, nodding sagely. It impressed Robbie that they were content for him to take the floor like this; not butting in or trying to impose their views. Smart, considerate people.

He said, 'And Hank was wise to that gofer of yours, too. This guy Jerry.'

Gordon frowned, gave Patricia a wary glance, and she said, 'Jerry wasn't up to scratch, it's true. We've now dispensed with his services.'

Her husband added, 'You're remarkably well-informed, Mr Scott.'

Robbie took another mouthful of coffee. 'Hank kept a journal, along with all the paperwork he'd collected. It told me all about you two, all about Templeton Wynne, and how Hank insisted on keeping the evidence so you couldn't cut him out of the deal.'

'Well, that's a moot point,' Patricia said, 'since Hank was so cruelly taken from us.'

'Yeah, I heard about that. Knocked down by a car or something, wasn't he?'

Silence for a moment, all three of them smiling, nobody saying what they thought. Robbie felt sure they'd have at least a suspicion of his involvement, but this was all part of the game: a little test of nerves.

Finally Patricia tipped her head. 'Apparently so.'

'A tragic loss,' Gordon said.

'Certainly is. Because you didn't just need him to gather the evidence against this Templeton guy. You two have history with him, yeah?' Robbie waited, and got a somewhat grudging nod from Gordon. 'Much better if Hank made the demand on your behalf, set up the payments and all the rest of it.' He stopped, cocking his head. 'How was that gonna happen, by the way?'

'My word, there's something you don't know!' Patricia said, gently mocking.

Robbie grinned, leaned forward and contrived to brush his fingertips over the back of her hand. 'There's actually quite a lot I don't know. But I can put on a very convincing performance.'

Gordon snorted. If he'd noted Robbie's move, he didn't seem unduly concerned about it.

'Offshore accounts,' he said. 'A whole network of shell companies in different territories around the world. Within an hour of Templeton's payment hitting the first account, the money will be utterly beyond retrieval by anyone but us.'

'So there's no physical handover of cash?'

Patricia laughed gaily. 'Oh, Robert, do you have any idea how much space fifty million pounds would take up?'

'We'd need a damn truck,' Gordon said. 'And then what do we do with it? Cash is toxic these days.'

'Absolutely.' Robbie was nodding briskly. 'No, that's a good system.'

'You mean you approve?' Patricia asked, coquettishly enough that Robbie risked another touch, a slightly longer contact this time.

'I do. Because it means you don't have to worry about me running off with more than my fair share.'

At this, Gordon looked like he dearly wanted to take Robbie down a notch or two, but Patricia was still smiling warmly.

'Your suggestion being . . .?'

'Let me screw the fifty mil out of Templeton.'

Gordon spluttered: 'I beg your pardon?'

'It makes perfect sense.' Robbie beamed at them both. 'I'm your new frontman.'

Ninety-three

Dan took a bus back to work, alternately trying Robbie and Cate's numbers and getting no response from either. At the shop, he learned that Denham was out. He found Hayley at the till.

'I need to ask a big favour.'

He'd anticipated resistance, but the look she gave him wasn't hostile; it was pitying.

'I've just seen it on the news.'

'Seen what?'

'Martin. That was Cate's ex, wasn't it? Stabbed to death.'

He told her the little he knew. 'Cate's gone missing. I need to borrow your car.'

A brief hesitation, then she nodded. 'The keys are in my bag. Will you have it back by half-five?'

'If I don't, can Tim give you a lift home?'

Her eyes narrowed, but he wasn't point-scoring, and she knew it. She leaned over the counter and drew him into a friendly embrace.

'For God's sake, be careful, will you?' she said.

It was a long and serious discussion. Gordon sensed a growing excitement take hold as they began to recognise the viability of Scott's proposal.

Robbie left them in no doubt that the papers were at his disposal

– while safely beyond their reach, of course. He also displayed an impressive understanding of the sometimes complicated methods by which Templeton had perpetrated his fraud.

'I always thought paying tax was a mug's game,' he muttered at one point. 'Now I know I was right. Half the money gets siphoned off by a load of rich, clever businessmen. Well, to put it bluntly, I wanna join the club!'

Beautifully direct, but essentially Robbie was telling the Blakes what they wanted to hear. This young man was, at heart, a salesman, possessing all the easy charm and confidence of his breed. From their perspective, all that mattered was whether Templeton would take him seriously – and Gordon felt that he would.

Then a brand new angle was suggested: what if Robbie approached Templeton, claiming that Hank O'Brien had been preparing to expose him for purely malicious reasons? Robbie had ridden to the rescue by liquidating Hank, and was now offering the return of the documentation, providing his own demands were met.

'Fifty million quid, though.' Robbie gave a laugh of pure delight. 'It's one hell of a finder's fee. Are you sure he'll be willing to pay up?'

Patricia nodded. 'If this information is made public at such a sensitive time, the deal will fall through and he'll lose twice that.'

'Though it will stick in his craw,' Gordon warned. 'He's an exceptionally greedy man.'

'But he'll see sense,' Patricia said. 'Whatever else he may be, he's no fool.'

Cate strained to hear evidence of a visitor, but there was nothing. No movement outside the door, no voices. So why had she been restrained like this?

The gag made it hard to breathe. Each swallow of saliva carried with it the foul taste of the cloth, part of which kept slipping down her throat; she had to cough and retch it back out, her cheeks bulging before the air and snot was expelled from her nose.

465

In search of relief she twisted round to lie on her front, her head partly over the edge of the bed. She focused obsessively on the sliver of vision available to her: a strip of beige carpet. She resorted to counting the individual fibres as a way of blanking out the threat, the danger of choking to death.

For all her efforts, more tears came, soaking slowly through the blindfold. A pathetic whimpering that she tried and failed to stem, until the reverberating thud of footsteps reached her ears. Then voices, no more than a low-pitched vibration. But if *she* could hear *them* . . .

The only way to make a loud noise was by rolling off the bed. Even then only her upper body would reach the floor, because her feet had been tied to the bed frame.

She pushed forward, letting out a muffled screech of agony as her injured toe was squashed against the mattress. Her shoulder hit the floor with a thump that sent vibrations through the floorboards and must have been audible downstairs.

The move left her in an ungainly heap, half on and half off the bed, unable to move in either direction. The pain from her toe was excruciating, but Cate was too busy praying to care.

She had done what she could, but was it enough?

Gordon expected tensions to arise over the question of remuneration, but even there Robbie blindsided them.

'I'll leave that to you two. I'm sure you'll have a fair idea of what's appropriate.'

It was a masterstroke. With Robbie in such a dominant position, Gordon thought it likely that their offer would exceed whatever figure Robbie might have demanded, had he taken the more predictable approach.

'We'll give it some thought,' Patricia said. 'Let's reconvene tomorrow morning. If we go ahead, it may be later this week.'

'Great. I'm ready any time.'

Robbie exchanged mobile-phone numbers with Gordon. Leading

him through the hall, Patricia gently held his arm. 'The papers are safe, aren't they?'

'I guarantee it,' Robbie said. 'Nobody's gonna—'

The noise wasn't particularly obtrusive, but it put Robbie off his stride. He hesitated, turning to look at the stairs.

'We have a dog,' Patricia said. 'Border collie, very excitable.'

Gordon didn't care for the anxiety in her voice, so he added drily, 'Actually, it's the deformed child we keep imprisoned in the attic.'

Robbie just nodded: not interested. There were handshakes all round, and Robbie even had the nerve to give Patricia a kiss on the cheek. His car was on the drive: a black BMW. Undoubtedly the one that Jerry had photographed.

'Cheeky rascal,' Gordon said. 'Ten minutes alone with Stemper and he'd be begging us to take that paperwork off his hands.'

'Is that a route you favour, then?'

'I suppose not. It's breathtaking arrogance on his part, but he's got us over a barrel and we may as well be pragmatic.' He sighed. 'How do you think he'll react to his sister's disappearance?'

'We must hope it won't affect him unduly. I still see the advantage in keeping her as insurance.' Patricia rubbed her hands together, a lustre in her eyes. 'You know, I really do believe we're going to come up trumps.'

'I wonder how Stemper will feel about this.'

'Frankly, I don't much care either way. Stemper is hired help, nothing more.'

Gordon liked the sound of that. 'So from here on in, we can go it alone. The two of us, plus your hot new beau.'

'Oh, nonsense.' She slapped him lightly. 'I'm old enough to be his mother.'

'Ah, but you're *not* his mother. Believe me, he was interested.'

'Interested in the money. That was avarice you saw, Gordon, not lust.'

He grinned. 'What I saw was a bit of both.'

'Hmm. At least he was refreshingly honest about his ambitions.' It seemed to Gordon that she was blushing slightly. Then a harsh change of mood as she gestured at the ceiling. 'Except that bitch nearly spoiled everything.'

Watching Patricia advance on the stairs, he felt moved to issue a warning. 'Don't hurt her. Not too badly, I mean.'

'Will you call Stemper?' she said. 'Hired help he may be, but we should run this past him all the same.'

'I agree. And we'll still need him to deal with Caitlin.'

Patricia looked back at him, smiling fiercely. 'Oh, I don't know. Maybe we can do that ourselves.'

Ninety-four

Robbie stopped at the first pub that looked like it might serve decent food and ordered a steak and a pint to celebrate.

In his view, the meeting had been a stunning success. The only niggling worry was whether the Blakes had accepted his proposal a little too readily. On reflection, Robbie decided not. They were basically in the same boat as Templeton. If somebody had you outmanoeuvred, you had to bite the bullet and do the best deal available.

Still, he'd need to be careful with what he handed over and when. He'd certainly hold back the evidence he had on the Blakes until they'd paid him. And that point about cash being toxic . . . maybe Robbie should ask for a mix. An offshore account sounded appealing, but who to approach for information? He wouldn't want his mother's accountant knowing about this.

He wondered what their opening bid would be. He was planning to push for ten, although he'd settle for five. Made him want to giggle hysterically just thinking about it. *Five million pounds.*

He took out his phone and found a ton of missed calls and texts, mostly from his mum and Dan. He wasn't sure if he could be bothered with them.

A pity that Dan hadn't played ball. His advice might have been useful, and in return Robbie would have bunged him a hundred grand to buy a cafe. In fact, perhaps he'd do it anyway, to prove to Dan how badly he had misjudged his oldest friend.

Same with his sister. He'd pay off her mortgage. And for his mother, a piece of jewellery – something really extravagant and tacky – he'd hand it over and then tell her where to stick her job . . .

No, better still: bail out the business with a hefty injection of cash, in return for a full partnership.

And poor old Bree. If only she'd found him a woman like Patricia Blake. He wouldn't have believed it possible that he could have such a strong reaction to someone of that age, but there was no denying the chemistry. Even the sad sack of a husband had picked up on it.

An unorthodox relationship there, Robbie guessed. In the past he'd had wealthy clients invite him to swingers' parties, and he knew the type.

His phone buzzed again. Another text from Dan. In the absence of something better to do, he opened it up.

`Where the hell are you? Yr sister is missing. This is SERIOUS!`

Robbie had to read it three times, and even then it didn't make a lot of sense.

Missing?

Hayley's Vauxhall Corsa had a smaller engine than Dan's Fiesta, but it was newer and felt considerably more powerful. In other circumstances Dan might have enjoyed pushing the small car to the limit, throwing it around corners and stamping on the brakes.

He went first to Robbie's flat, but no one answered. Then he cruised up and down Woodland Drive, unsure of Bree's exact address but looking out for Robbie's BMW. Again he drew a blank.

He couldn't return to work. He was too worried. He drove to Cate's, checked with the neighbour to see if anyone had come or gone, and only then, feeling defeated, he went home. Thankfully Louis was at college, and Joan was out visiting a friend.

He made himself a cheese sandwich and slumped on the sofa. No TV: he needed a respite from bad news.

His phone rang. Hardly daring to believe it could be Cate, he snatched it up and read the display. Robbie.

Dan answered in a fury. 'Pick up your messages, will you? Your sister's life could be in danger—'

'Hey, hey, calm it. What's happened?'

'She didn't make it into work earlier. Have you heard from her?'

'Not a thing. Is that why Mum's trying to get hold of me?'

'Of course it is. DS Thomsett was at Compton's earlier. It sounds like they're investigating Janine's family, in case it's some kind of reprisal. Because of Cate and Martin . . .'

'Jesus,' Robbie said. 'I suppose you never know how people will react.'

'Can you think of anywhere to look?'

'Nope. Maybe she's just gone off for some peace and quiet?' Robbie lowered his voice. 'I can see why you want to help here, Dan, especially now you're all loved up. But make sure your path doesn't cross with DS Thomsett. The last thing we need is him seeing you and making a link to those e-fits.'

'Right now finding Cate is all that matters. Where are you?'

'Nowhere special. Why?'

'Something else I want to talk about, but not on the phone. Can you meet me?'

'Okay.' A long-suffering sigh. 'The Black Lion in Patcham? Say about four?'

'That's nearly an hour and a half.'

'Yeah. I'm up in Surrey. Earliest I can do.'

He rang off before Dan could respond. *Surrey.* What was Robbie doing in Surrey?

The answer was obvious, he realised. Robbie was doing what Robbie always did.

Looking after number one.

* * *

Cate had failed. She knew that from the silence that followed her fall.

Then the bedroom door was flung open and somebody marched in. That heavy, aggressive stride: the woman again.

'I ought to leave you like this.' She grabbed Cate's foot and pinched the damaged toe.

Cate screamed, choking on the gag, tears streaming from her eyes. The woman heaved her back on to the bed as though she were a lump of meat.

'Pull a stunt like that again and you'll really know what pain is.'

Gordon fidgeted. He felt irritated, unhappy, for reasons he couldn't put into words. When Patricia returned he said curtly, 'Stemper's ten minutes away.'

She gave him a curious look. 'Something wrong?'

He knew his protest would sound petulant, but he went ahead and said it anyway. 'I thought we didn't want her to know about you.'

'Rather academic now, isn't it?'

'Are you serious?'

She nodded, as relaxed as if they were discussing how to dispose of an old fridge. 'Don't you find, after the first one, there are far fewer qualms the next time?'

He took a moment before he replied. He didn't want to snap; nor did he wish to appear faint-hearted.

'I'm not sure. In my view it's important that we don't get too blasé. This is the taking of another human life we're talking about.'

'For the greater good. That's what we agreed.'

He nodded glumly. No sense arguing when she was feeling so unstoppable, buoyed by the knowledge that the scheme was saved, and her ego flattered by the attentions of a handsome young man.

She took herself off to freshen up. When the doorbell rang she called out that she would get it, and shortly afterwards Stemper swept into the kitchen with Patricia at his shoulder.

Gordon's first impression was of a man just beginning to crack under the strain, while valiantly striving to ignore that fact. His suit was crumpled, the jacket lopsided, as though it didn't fit him properly. Gordon wouldn't have dreamt of going out in public looking this shabby.

He realised that he and Patricia hadn't decided how to broach the issue of Caitlin's ex-husband. It seemed a low priority for Patricia, who spent several minutes gushing about Robert Scott, and how perfect he would be in the role of frontman.

Stemper greeted the proposal with muted scepticism. 'Does Scott have any idea that you're holding his sister?'

Gordon shook his head. Patricia said, 'None at all.'

Quite emphatic. And that was fine, Gordon thought. There was only the little commotion as Robbie was leaving, which they'd explained plausibly enough.

Patricia added, 'Our other great advantage is that he knows nothing about you.'

'So once he's secured the payout, my job is to remove him from the scene?'

'If you'd be so kind.' Patricia had agreed with Gordon that this was the line to take, even though she currently favoured sparing Robbie and eliminating Stemper.

'And the girl?' Stemper asked.

'The same fate, alas. Though we keep her alive for now.'

'Do you mind if I check on her?'

'Not at all,' Patricia said, stepping forward. 'I'll accompany you.'

She exchanged the briefest of glances with Gordon, which he took to mean that she preferred to discuss the 'Martin' issue discreetly, just the two of them.

'A coffee, in the meantime?' she asked brightly.

'Actually,' Stemper said, 'a pot of tea would be marvellously refreshing.'

Patricia looked to Gordon – the skivvy – who as usual felt he had little choice but to bury his resentment and grin like the imbecile he probably was.

'Coming right up.'

Ninety-five

Stemper had anticipated that Cate would tell them about Martin, which no doubt explained the rather taut atmosphere as they climbed the stairs. But he was intrigued by Patricia's fulsome admiration for Robert Scott.

'This is a transformation,' she said. 'I've told Gordon we should swallow our pride and accept that it's a godsend, of sorts.'

'Indeed.'

'He's coming back in the morning. I wonder if that's when we should make the first approach to Templeton. Have Robbie phone from here, so we can gauge how well he performs.'

'But you'd prefer that I was absent?'

'I think so.' She chuckled. 'Unless you'd care to hide in a cupboard?'

Stemper laughed politely. Patricia unlocked the bedroom door, then stood aside to let him take a look. The woman was now blind-folded with a scarf, and she had been crudely gagged. Stemper regarded her for a few seconds, her body frozen in terror.

He withdrew, and as Patricia locked up he said, 'The gag is a good idea, but you have to be careful of the suffocation risk.'

His tone was deliberately stern. He saw her frown as she moved towards the stairs. Stemper cleared his throat to regain her attention. At the same time he took the gun from his jacket. It was a Glock 26, complete with noise suppressor. The magazine contained seventeen rounds of 9mm ammunition.

Patricia looked faintly aghast but perceived no danger to herself, judging by the way she said, 'What's that thing for?'

He raised the gun. 'For killing you, I'm afraid.'

Patricia said, 'No.' Then, 'Stemper, please—'

He fired once, hitting her in the chest. The noise was little more than a click, easily misinterpreted at close range. The sound of the spent shell hitting the wall was only slightly louder.

Stemper darted forward, reaching for Patricia's arm while pressing the silencer into her belly and firing again. Her eyes, still open as she slumped against him, shone with desolation.

He lowered her to the floor to lessen the impact, and when she was down he fired once more, to the head. Messy, but it looked passionate. It looked like an act of rage and retribution, exactly as he wanted it.

Cate heard it all, a succession of strange noises that she struggled to place in context. She'd sensed two people approaching the door and had braced herself for pain. But after a brief look inside, the door closed and there was a murmur of voices. One of them was the woman from earlier, the vicious cow who'd hurt her.

Then a click, and a pinging noise, as if something metal had struck the wall. A groan, and the creak of a floorboard, then more clicks and pings, and after that a single set of footsteps that receded and left Cate with only silence and a sickening impression that a bad situation had just become very much worse.

Gordon was trying to remember if he'd seen Stemper drink tea before. Normally he had coffee, or water. Why tea all of a sudden? Then the man himself was back in the kitchen. Alone.

'Where's Patricia?'

'With our prisoner,' Stemper said. 'I think she's as keen on Caitlin as you are.'

Ignoring the impertinence, Gordon said, 'Did she mention Cate's ex-husband?'

'Martin? No. She may have intended to, but she didn't quite get the chance.'

A mystifying comment. Gordon expressed that mystification in a single word: 'Didn't . . .?'

By then Stemper had brought out a gun and was pulling the trigger. Three times, in quick succession, and with each one he took a step closer. All three shots hit Gordon with a very distinct impact, but he was aware of no pain, so there was a millisecond when he was riddled with bullets but still alive, not hurting – a survivor, he thought, against impossible odds – and then he realised that his legs were giving way beneath him and understood that he was quite, quite dead.

Not dead enough for Stemper. He fired another three shots, including one to the face. He had never liked Gordon's face. Too smooth and tanned and smug.

To a degree, Stemper enjoyed this hit more than most. Not that it was personal, really; just immensely satisfying, from a professional point of view. Like any good magician, Stemper loved to spring surprises.

There was plenty to do: clean up, remove evidence, plant other evidence, report back on the success of his mission. But first he pulled on latex gloves. Then he checked on the progress of his tea.

As much as Cate could track the passage of time, she thought it was around twenty minutes before the door opened again. The footsteps were firm, not heavy. No perfume in the air.

If it was the man who'd questioned her earlier, she knew what he would be after. She had steeled herself to encourage him, to exploit his lust in exchange for making her more comfortable – and perhaps giving her a chance to escape. Nothing robbed a man of his good sense more than a hard-on.

She tensed as he touched her leg, examining the injured toe. Her stomach cramped with horror; maybe it was his scent, or the rhythm of his breathing, but she realised it wasn't the man from earlier. This was her abductor. The man who had tortured her.

A spasm of panic made her body jerk as if electrocuted. In response he gently squeezed her arm.

'Settle down. I'm not going to hurt you.' His bedside manner as dispassionate as ever, like an efficient but jaded GP.

Holding her still with one hand, he used his other to peel off the tape that covered her mouth. Cate coughed and spat, trying to eject the gag. His fingers were on her lips; she tasted latex, but the sinister implication of the gloves was lost in the wave of relief that the gag was out and she could breathe freely again. She could swallow. She could talk.

'There's something I want you to do for me,' he told her. 'If you cooperate, I'm prepared to make things easier for you. If you don't, I'll make you suffer.'

Ninety-six

Robbie didn't dawdle over his meal, but he didn't rush it, either. He felt sure that Cate was fine. She'd always been the moody sort, and was probably just trying to get her head straight after Martin's death.

The drive back was hampered by school-run traffic, but it was still one of the most enjoyable journeys of his life. Figuring out how to blow a couple of million quid – even if only hypothetically at this point – made any tailback bearable.

He was in Brighton for ten to four. His phone rang as he was crossing the city boundary. He had it on hands-free, and leaned forward to read the display. It was the number the Blakes had given him, so he answered breezily, radiating confidence and good cheer.

'Hello there!'

A drab male voice said, 'Mr Scott, I'm acting on behalf of Gordon and Patricia for the next stage of the operation. From now on you'll deal with me.'

'Hold on.' Distracted by the roundabout he was trying to negotiate, Robbie couldn't adjust to what he was hearing. 'When did that get decided?'

'This afternoon, shortly after your meeting.'

'So who are you?'

'You can call me Jerry.' The voice was soft, dry and humourless.

'If you're driving at the moment, can I suggest you pull over? I have a message from your sister, and you need to give it your full attention.'

A car in front braked. Robbie gunned the engine and overtook, cutting back in just before a traffic island, then took a sharp left into the pub car park. He slewed into an empty space and grabbed the phone.

'Let me speak to Patricia.'

'That's not possible. Her instructions are very clear.'

'Bollocks. How do I know this isn't a bluff?'

In response, a different voice in his ear. His sister, though it didn't quite sound like Cate. It was a recording, he realised, and fear had constricted her throat.

'Robbie, it's me. Please . . . please do what he says. My life depends on you. Please don't let me down.'

A sob, cut short as the recording ended. Then Jerry was back. 'First rule: no contact with the police. I'm sure you're only too happy to comply with that.'

'What do you want?'

'The paperwork you took from Hank O'Brien.'

Robbie glanced out of the window, saw a red Corsa turning into the car park. Dan was at the wheel. What was it he'd said yesterday afternoon? *There's always a catch.*

Robbie took a deep breath and said, in his most commanding voice: 'I need to speak to the Blakes.'

'No, Mr Scott. What you need to do is think very carefully about this. Caitlin will remain safe for as long as you follow instructions.'

For a second – one long, greedy, shameful second – Robbie was tempted to call this man's bluff. Tell him to piss off, to do what he liked with Cate: the paperwork was going nowhere till Robbie had his cash.

Then Jerry said, 'If you're wavering, consider what happened to your former brother-in-law. I opened up his femoral artery in the middle of a crowded shopping street. As deaths go, it was relatively quick and painless. Your sister won't be nearly so lucky. I'll be in touch again.'

'Wait a—'

Dan had fled the house before either Joan or his brother returned. He made one more futile trip to Caitlin's home, then reached the pub for four o'clock. As he got out of the Corsa he noticed Robbie on the phone and saw the tension in his posture. Running to the BMW, he snatched the door open and heard Robbie exclaim: 'Wait a—'

'Who was that?'

Robbie was staring at the phone as though it were a black hole about to swallow him up. Dan had to repeat the question before Robbie acknowledged his presence.

'It . . . it was Jerry. Claimed to be Jerry, anyway.'

'What about Cate? Is she all right?'

'She's alive.'

'Have you spoken to her?'

Robbie gave a dazed shrug, still cut adrift from reality.

'For Christ's sake . . .' Dan snatched the phone from his grasp. 'Tell me what's going on or I'll call the police and you can tell them instead.'

He started to walk away. Robbie scrambled out of the car, frantically calling him back.

'All right, all right.' He raised his hands in surrender. 'But let's go inside. I need a drink.'

Ignoring a protest from Dan, Robbie ordered a Scotch. Dan had grapefruit juice. They found a table, and Robbie described his visit to the Blakes, their apparent enthusiasm for his proposal, and then this strange, disturbing call.

'According to Hank's journal, the Blakes employed a guy called Jerry to run errands and act as go-between. This Jerry now seems to have taken Cate hostage. He wants to exchange her for the stuff I found at the farm.'

Dan was sitting forward on a low chair, his chin in his hands. 'You have to go to the police.'

'No way. Do that and we won't see her again.'

'How can you be sure?'

'You don't wanna know.' That earned a glare from Dan. Robbie gulped down the Scotch and said, 'This guy isn't bluffing. He killed Martin.'

Dan rocked back in his seat. 'So DS Thomsett was right about a link?' He searched out Robbie's gaze. 'You realise what this means? Our actions last Tuesday led directly to Martin being stabbed . . .'

Robbie preferred not to dwell on it. The situation still hadn't assumed the full weight of reality in his mind.

'It makes no sense,' he said. 'Why change tack like this?'

'You're trying to extort a fortune out of them. Didn't you think there would be consequences?'

'Keep your voice down.' Robbie checked that no one was listening, then said, 'Honestly, Dan, if you'd been there, if you'd seen how they reacted . . . it was like I was their bloody saviour. I wasn't taking money off them. I was gonna help them get very, very rich.'

'Then what are the other possibilities? Why would Jerry be doing this?'

Robbie clicked his fingers, a sudden recollection. 'They told me they'd sacked him. So maybe he's gone rogue.' He stopped. 'But he rang me from their phone. And what he actually said was "You can call me Jerry." That's a funny phrase to use.'

Dan agreed. 'If he's holding Cate hostage he's hardly going to reveal his true identity.'

'No, but I wonder . . .' Robbie picked up his phone, found the number and called it back.

'What are you doing?'

'I want to see who answers.'

Nobody did. Robbie endured Dan's disapproving gaze for half a minute and finally gave up.

'How did he leave it with you?' Dan asked.

'Told me to wait for his call.'

'So he wants to demonstrate that he's in charge. He won't do that by answering when you phone him. Have you got the documents ready?'

Absently, Robbie shook his head. 'They're hidden.'

'You'd better get them. Where are they, at the flat?'

Robbie tried a grin; not one of his better attempts to charm.

'Ah,' he said.

Ninety-seven

'My house? You hid them at *my* fucking house?'

'I knew they'd be safe there. Nobody knows about you.'

'And what if you were wrong about that, like all the other things you've been wrong about?'

Robbie shrugged, sulky and unrepentant. 'You haven't noticed anyone following you, have you?'

'No, but that's not the point.' Dan found himself wondering if he would have picked up on it, until a more important consideration struck him. 'Have you, then?'

'Once or twice, maybe. I was never certain.'

Dan buried his face in his hands. He heard the groan of a chair as Robbie stood up.

'Come on. We ought to go and get the stuff.'

They took both cars. Dan pulled up first, intercepting Robbie as he opened his door.

'You stay here. Where will I find them?'

'In a cabin bag, stashed in an old laundry basket. In your brother's room.'

'Louis's . . .?'

'Sorry, mate. He did it as a favour. But I also told him the drugs thing was over—'

Dan slammed Robbie's door and strode away. He had to keep his temper in check, at least until he knew that Cate was safe.

Joan greeted him as he opened the front door. 'You're home early.'

'Decided to take the afternoon off to sort a few things. Is Louis here?'

'He's in his room. Why?' She stepped in front of him as he shook his head; gently she grasped his arms and made him look at her. 'What's wrong?'

Dan forced a smile. 'Nothing much, I promise.'

He kissed her cheek, feeling worse than crummy for a week of relentless lies, then hurried upstairs. The music playing in Louis's room was a beautiful, melancholy piece from Morricone's *The Mission* soundtrack, another favourite of their parents.

'Louis, can I come in?'

Dan opened the door. His brother was lying flat out on the bed, hands laced behind his head. His eyes not exactly tearful, but filmy.

'You okay?'

'Not really. What I need right now is a joint.'

'Yeah, well. I've come for Robbie's stuff.'

'The suitcase?' Louis twisted his foot towards the old laundry basket. 'It's in there.'

He didn't move while Dan opened the basket and pulled out a couple of spare pillows.

'Are you gonna tell me what's going on?'

'I can't.'

'You're in some serious trouble, then?'

Dan turned and examined his brother, who was still staring at the ceiling. 'Why do you say that?'

'How you've been acting lately. No way this is just about Hayley. Is Robbie part of it?'

Dan couldn't see any point in lying, so he nodded. 'Yeah.'

'And Cate?'

'Why'd you think she would be involved?'

Louis shrugged. 'I heard her ex-husband got murdered on Saturday. Is that true?'

'Yes. And Cate's—' Dan stopped himself in time.

'What?'

'Nothing. She's . . . well, suffering a bit, that's all. I'm trying to help her.'

'Right.' A loaded tone.

Dan removed the case and refilled the laundry basket. As he stood up to leave he had a sudden conviction that he would never see his brother again. The thought left him rooted to the spot, staring at Louis as though they were at opposite ends of a long, dark tunnel.

Louis sat up, offering a conciliatory smile. 'I wasn't taking the piss. I just mean, you've always fancied her, haven't you? I reckon you'd make a great couple.'

'Thanks.' Dan set the case down. 'Give us a hug, Louis.'

'What?'

'Please.'

Bemused and a little embarrassed, Louis stood up and they embraced. It was the first such contact they'd had in a long time, and Dan was struck by how tall Louis was, how strong. *My boy's become a man.* Isn't that what a father would say at a moment like this?

Slowly they broke away, and Louis wasn't so immature that he didn't appreciate the significance of this occasion, even though he had no idea *why* it mattered so much.

'An unhappy accident,' he murmured.

'Sorry?'

'That's the reason I'm so screwed up.' Louis scraped a tear from his eye with the edge of his hand. 'I remember what Joan used to tell me, about how Mum and Dad were so overjoyed when I came along, all those years after you. I was their "happy accident".'

Dan nodded. That phrase had always been Joan's way of conveying to Louis how important he'd been to the parents he had barely known.

'I was the happy accident. Two years later came the *un*happy accident. Because life finds a way to balance out.'

'Oh, Louis, you can't think like that.'

'I know it's not rational. But that's how it feels. Like I was a curse on them.'

'No.' Dan held his brother by the arms. 'You represent what was best about Mum and Dad. You carry them into the future. Don't ever forget that.'

Louis nodded, sheepish again. 'This is getting too heavy. You'd better piss off before I start blubbing or something.'

'Yeah, me too.' Dan slapped Louis on the shoulder. 'Love you.'

'Where you going, anyway?'

Dan shrugged, and found the fuel for one more lie. 'Nowhere, really.'

He trotted downstairs and heard laughter. Robbie was deep in conversation with Joan, who was giggling at a joke he'd made. She saw Dan and tutted.

'You didn't say Robbie was with you. Why didn't you invite him in?'

'It's just a flying visit.'

'Forgetting your manners, Dan,' Robbie said with mock severity.

'He is, you're right,' Joan said. 'I wish you could stay longer.'

'Me too. Next time, yeah?' Robbie gave Joan a hug, then turned and made his exit without catching Dan's eye.

'And you're off as well?' Joan noticed the small suitcase and frowned.

'It's a long story.' Dan kissed her and was gone, knowing he trailed all kinds of fear and anxiety in his wake. He wondered if he would ever have a chance to explain.

He carried the case to the BMW and put it in the boot. Robbie had fetched an old road atlas from his glove compartment, which he handed to Dan.

'Look up Brockham, near Box Hill. That's where the Blakes live. 8 Gadbrook Lane.'

'Okay. But why, exactly?'

'Because it's likely that Jerry is based somewhere close by, don't you think? He had to go to the Blakes to get their phone.'

Dan shrugged. It was credible enough. But he was conscious of a mutual reluctance to discuss what might have happened to the Blakes themselves.

While Dan studied the map, Robbie punched in the combination and opened the case, gazing at the contents as if unwilling to part with them.

'I'd say we should head up that way, so we're in the area when he calls me again.'

'In one car, or both?'

'Both. I want you to follow at a bit of a distance. We can keep in touch by phone. Don't suppose you've got a hands-free kit?'

Dan snorted: *as if*. Robbie sighed, then consulted the map.

'Let's head for Kingsfold on the A24. There's a pub that we can make our base till we hear from him.'

He handed Dan the road atlas – Robbie had satnav, of course – and shut the boot. He took a step towards the driver's door and then real-ised that Dan hadn't moved.

'Dan . . .'

'I'm just thinking about last week, when you talked me out of phoning the police. We both know that was the wrong thing then. Aren't we making the same mistake again?'

For once, Robbie displayed none of his usual bravado. He ran a hand through his hair and admitted that Dan had a valid point.

'Whether you believe it or not, I want to do what's best for my sister. If I thought that meant going to the cops and giving them a full confession, I'd do it. But, first, we don't have a clue where she is, or who this "Jerry" really is. Second, any conversation with the author-ities will have to include the background to all this, and as soon as we mention the hit-and-run it'll be the two of us getting thrown into a cell. And then how are we gonna help Cate?'

'Okay.' Dan had reached a similar conclusion himself, but he'd wanted to hear Robbie lay it out for him.

This time round, Robbie was right. They had to do this themselves. They had to find Cate, and bring her back safely.

'Let's go,' he said.

Ninety-eight

Befriend your captor. That had been Cate's objective. That was why she obediently supplied the message to her brother. In return, he agreed not to gag her again, which not only eased her discomfort but meant she could speak. First she asked his name.

'Jerry.' The question didn't seem to anger him; he wasn't amused, intrigued or anything else. And with no verbal or visual cues, establishing a rapport was impossible.

'I don't understand what's happening. Please can you explain it to me?'

'No.'

'I don't mean a lot of detail. Even just—'

'I can replace the gag, if you'd prefer?' He sounded distant, almost bored.

Cate gave up. He left the room and was gone for what felt like a couple of hours, though it might have been much less. At times she heard movements from within the house, and gathered that he was at work in some way.

Then he was back, and a revolting smell accompanied him into the room: the stench of human waste.

'We're leaving. I take it you need to use the toilet?'

Cate hadn't realised her desperation was so visible. Her bladder ached to the point where she had been negotiating away the shame of letting it go on the mattress. Her body was enveloped in a cold, foul sweat, and she shivered as he untied her legs.

He let her sit up and wait for her circulation to recover. She set her injured foot down on the floor, testing whether it could bear her weight. She thought it would be okay, so long as she angled it slightly, keeping her little toe off the ground.

He untied the blindfold and replaced it with the hood. Then prodded his gun in her back.

'I'm going to release your hands. If you've any thoughts of rebellion, look down as you cross the landing and you'll get a taste of the consequences.'

Cate stood up, crying out as her limbs protested after hours of enforced immobility. She hobbled across the room, and by gazing at her feet she was able to see a small section of the floor.

Once out of the bedroom the source of the smell became clear. A woman's body, slumped and twisted in death, the face a mess of dark sticky blood.

'What happened?'

'It doesn't concern you,' he said. 'In here.'

He guided her to the bathroom and insisted on staying while she sat on the toilet. By now the need was so urgent that she hardly cared what he saw. Unlike the other man – who she presumed was also dead – there was nothing lecherous in his demeanour.

When Cate was done he tied her hands, manoeuvred her down the stairs and out to the same car that had brought her here. Once again she was made to lie along the back seat, but in addition he looped the rope around the base of the driver's seat, making it impossible for her to rise more than a few inches.

Then he was gone for perhaps another half an hour. Apart from the occasional rumble of a car, there was no other human activity. Calling for help was futile, but she tried it anyway.

She managed to rub her head back and forth until a little of her face was exposed beneath the hood, allowing her to breathe more freely. Despite this, the panic returned in waves, sending her heartbeat into a frenzy and leaving her to wonder if her ordeal would be cut short by a cardiac arrest.

He returned and covered her with a rough blanket. To passing traffic she would be only a formless lump.

One more try, she decided as he got into the car. Because Cate had always believed she was tougher than this; a fighter.

'Have you spoken to Robbie?'

He shifted in his seat, which she took as a sign of irritation. 'I played him the message.'

'And has he agreed . . . to do what you want?'

He subjected her to a few seconds of agony before replying. This time there was a trace of grim humour: 'Did you doubt that he'd be prepared to save you?'

Cate mumbled a non-committal response. Her prize, at least, was confirmation that Robbie was still alive. She prayed that he'd have the good sense to talk to Dan, and that between them they could figure out a way to end this without more bloodshed.

When Jerry phoned, Robbie had just skirted Horsham on the A24, Dan trailing some four or five cars back. It was ten to six. The roads were busy, hindering their progress, but that didn't worry Robbie.

In fact, he felt intensely relaxed: just as he'd demonstrated on Tuesday night, he was at his best in a crisis. He'd hooked up his iPod and was playing a selection of classic soul: Sam and Dave, Jackie Wilson, Marvin Gaye. Music to make you feel alive and potent and formidable.

He switched it off and took the call. 'Jerry.'

'Where are you?'

'Just been for a McDonald's.' Robbie congratulated himself on his quick thinking: they'd passed one a few minutes ago. 'I was peckish.'

'I hope you enjoyed it. Now, I want you to drive to the town of Midhurst, in West Sussex.'

'I know it.'

'If you're coming from the east, you'll find a large car park just before the town proper. Park at the bottom and wait there till exactly seven-thirty.'

'Is that where we're doing the handover?'

In a slow monotone, Jerry said, 'If you fail to follow these instructions, your sister will die. At seven-thirty take the A286 north to Haslemere, and on towards Godalming. I'll call when you're under way.'

There was a roundabout coming up. Robbie moved to the right-hand lane and left the indicator on, hoping that Dan would spot the change of direction.

'I want to speak to Cate,' he said.

'Not possible. Your sister won't be harmed, on the condition that you do as I say. I warn you now: if you've gone to the police the repercussions will be severe.'

The line went dead. Robbie swore a few times, swinging the BMW around the roundabout. Dan was tracking him, probably confused as hell. For a second Robbie thought about flooring the pedal and losing him altogether. This guy Jerry was the real deal. Could Robbie really hope to get one over on him?

Then he thought: *You betcha.* If Robbie was smart, if he was careful, of course he could. A couple of hours and he'd have Cate back, and this twat would have his bundle of documents. Even then, all was not lost, providing Robbie moved fast enough.

That was what irked him the most: the delays. It wouldn't take more than forty minutes to reach Midhurst. Then he'd be sitting there like a lemon for an hour or so.

He rang Dan, half expecting him to ignore the call until he could pull over and answer safely. But Dan picked it up at once.

'Midhurst,' Robbie said, and relayed the instructions. 'You need to stop for a bit, say at Petworth. Come into the car park about fifteen minutes after me, at quarter to seven.'

'And then we have to stay till half-past?'

'Yeah. Though again, you should leave a few minutes early. I can't really see that he'll be watching us, but it pays to be careful, eh?'

'This is very thorough, Robbie. I think he knows exactly what he's doing.'

'Yeah, so imagine if we *had* gone to the cops. Cate would be in big trouble.'

Dan just grunted. 'I wonder if the delays are because he's waiting for it to get dark. Less chance of being seen when we do the exchange.'

'Good point. And looks like I was right about Surrey. I bet the final destination will be near where the Blakes live.' *Lived*, he amended silently, because his gut feeling was that they were dead. 'Maybe we should just head straight there?'

'What? Do you want to go and get your sister killed—?'

Chuckling, Robbie said, 'Chill, mate. Of course I'm not gonna put her at risk.'

'You idiot. You already have.'

Robbie's laughter made Dan feel sick. A man who refused to take even this situation seriously was a man whose judgement shouldn't be trusted.

'Why are you sounding so cheerful?' he asked.

'Because I'm the eternal optimist, me. Because there's no disaster so bad that you can't salvage something from it.'

Dan had heard enough. 'Midhurst, at six-forty-five.'

The churning in his gut wouldn't be subdued, even when he tried to accept that Robbie was right in one sense. Involving the police probably would have made things worse.

Easing up on the accelerator – there was no longer any need to match the BMW's speed – Dan took the A264 to Billingshurst, where he joined the A272 heading west. It was a murky evening, the setting sun obscured by streaks of thin cloud, a soft pink light diffused across the sky. The fields and copses of Sussex were falling into gentle shadow, while the road that ran between them was transformed into a glittering chain of red and white lights.

Dan couldn't stop tormenting himself with images of Cate held prisoner, perhaps in pain, certainly terrified, confused – and no doubt able to deduce that Robbie wouldn't call the police for fear of ending up in jail.

So they were all she had: Robbie and Dan.

Right now, it didn't seem like enough.

The congestion didn't bother Robbie: it meant less waiting around at the other end. But he nearly had a run-in with some idiot who kept tailgating him. That put him on edge, the thought that this arsehole might hit the car and throw the whole evening into chaos.

It was almost exactly half past six when he reached Midhurst and drove into the car park. There were dozens of empty spaces, but Robbie kept to the instructions and parked at the furthest point from the entrance. The car park backed on to fields, and there were trees and bushes along the perimeter.

Robbie was pleased to see that. He was dying for a piss. He hadn't noticed any signs for toilets as he'd passed the bus station on his way in, and in any case it was too far to walk. He sat for a minute, gauging how many pedestrians were likely to stray into the vicinity, and decided it would be safe. Hardly anyone around.

He locked the BMW – because of the suitcase in the boot – then nipped behind a bush and relieved himself. Probably the most pleasurable moment of his evening, he thought. And it was gonna get worse before it got better.

As if to prove it, there was an indignant cry as he got back to the car. He turned to see a man hurrying towards him, eyebrows knotted with displeasure. Robbie knew the type at once: a grey, middle-aged small-town bureaucrat with a stick up his arse.

'Urinating in public, you know that's tantamount to indecent exposure?'

Tantamount? Robbie grinned. 'Fuck off, matey, and get a life.'

'No, I won't. I've a good mind to . . .' The man tailed off, as his sort always tended to do, in Robbie's experience. They never had the balls to back up their threats with action.

Settling into his seat, Robbie leaned out to shut the car door. At the same time he glanced up to see if the bloke's nerve had failed him yet.

Not quite. Mr Bumptious had come closer, almost to the door, and he was reaching inside his suit jacket. Robbie gave a silent groan.

What's he gonna threaten me with now? His Rotary Club member-ship card?

Ninety-nine

Dan pulled in to a lay-by near the small town of Petworth. En route it had occurred to him that they should have brought weapons of some sort. In the boot of the Corsa he found a wheelbrace, which he placed beside him on the passenger seat. Better than nothing.

He sat back, shut his eyes and let his mind drift. He thought about Hayley and Tim, and decided that he wished them well. He worried about his aunt, and Louis, and the effects on them both when the truth finally emerged. For it *would* come out, he was sure of that.

Unhappy accidents.

What nagged him was a disturbing sense that they were getting this wrong. Dan didn't like it that Jerry had them driving from place to place; it felt like misdirection. They'd had no chance to discuss what was happening, no chance to think about it clearly.

So think about it now . . .

Jerry was holding Cate hostage. For reasons unknown, he had killed Martin. And it seemed likely that he'd turned on his former employers, the Blakes. Now he was after the paperwork that could be used to extort a fortune from Mark Templeton, presumably because he'd spotted a better opportunity to enrich himself.

Either he was going to blackmail Templeton – or perhaps he was working for Templeton. Perhaps he'd been a double agent all along.

All perfectly logical, but for one huge obstacle. How could he murder on this scale and hope to get away with it?

When Dan opened his eyes it was just after six-thirty. Time to go.

He joined the line of traffic and drove the last few miles to Midhurst, still brooding over the missing piece of the puzzle. As he drove into the main parking area he spotted Robbie's BMW sitting alone at the bottom of a slight incline. Too obvious to drive right up to it, so Dan settled for a space in one of the central sections, about a hundred feet away.

He didn't glance at Robbie until he'd got out of the Corsa, and then he tried to disguise it with a casual sweep of the area. But one clear look at the BMW and the pretence was forgotten.

He could see Robbie inside the car, but he wasn't sitting properly. Seemed like he was leaning sideways, reaching for something in the glove compartment.

Dan jogged towards the car, slowing as he drew level with the BMW. Then he bent at the waist, hands on his knees in the manner of an exhausted athlete, and turned his head towards the car. He saw the truth at once.

Robbie was dead, a dark, blood-filled hole in his forehead, as if someone had drilled into his skull. His expression was a kind of surprised scowl. He couldn't believe this was happening; couldn't credit that someone had actually got the better of him at last.

Shock might have frozen Dan to the spot. Robbie was dead; there was absolutely no doubt about that. But it must have happened in the past ten or fifteen minutes, so the killer could still be here . . .

That got Dan moving, his neck tingling at the thought of someone training a gun on him. But as he straightened up he noticed something else. The BMW's boot was open a fraction.

Checking to make sure he was unobserved, Dan lifted the boot lid and looked inside. Apart from a rolled-up picnic blanket and a bottle of screenwash, the compartment was empty. The flight bag had gone.

So now Jerry had Cate, he had the paperwork, and Dan had no way of tracking him.

The growl of an engine made him jump. A small van drove into a space just forty or fifty feet from the BMW. Dan shut the boot without slamming it, then tried to saunter away, his legs jerking spasmodically, as though he was learning how to walk. He drove from the car park on autopilot, holding his shock and grief at bay and trying strenuously to deny the fact that Cate might be lost to him for ever.

He considered the instructions from Jerry. Wait till seven-thirty, then head for Godalming. Back towards Surrey, Robbie had said. Because Cate was probably being held close to where the Blakes lived.

And Dan had suspected that Jerry was stringing this out until nightfall. So what had changed? Had Robbie disobeyed or confronted Jerry, and this was his punishment? Or had the instructions been a bluff from the beginning? A misdirection.

The confusion kept Dan sharp, although his hands trembled every time he lifted them from the steering wheel. He knew that at some future point he might succumb to the shock, but right now he was sustained by his determination to find Cate.

So go back over it again. Jerry: what he's done, why he's doing it and what he'll do next. Answer those questions and you can find him.

A possibility seemed to flash across his mind like a meteor, its illumination too fleeting to reveal the solution. Furious with himself, Dan turned on to the A272, back towards Brighton, towards home.

Where else could he go?

Stemper had positioned his Ford Focus on the far side of the car park, where it wouldn't be noticed by Robert Scott's accomplice. He felt sure that the man who approached the BMW was the same man he'd spotted yesterday afternoon at Caitlin's home.

A slip-up, of sorts. Ultimately, though, it hardly mattered. Yesterday afternoon he hadn't quite finalised the terms of his deal with Mark Templeton.

Now he watched the Corsa depart, waiting to see which way it went before he pulled out to follow. It was a slow single-lane road, and he knew he could afford to lag behind. There was little chance of losing it and even less chance of being noticed.

As a precaution, before he reached the car park he had pulled up in a quiet country lane and gagged Caitlin. She had thrashed and fought, to the extent that Stemper had been forced to cut off her oxygen for almost a minute before she would be subdued. Even then she remained wildly agitated, as if she'd guessed the fate he had in mind for her brother.

Killing Robbie had been child's play: a silenced weapon, two shots fired at close range – head and heart – in an encounter where the victim had felt confident of his physical superiority. Stemper couldn't have asked for more. But he'd taken a significant risk in staying at the scene. If the body was discovered by someone other than the accomplice, the police would be swarming all over the area.

But it had worked out perfectly, and he had told her so.

'I'm on the trail of your brother's friend. I believe he's your friend, too, despite the lies you told me. He doesn't look much like the e-fit, I have to say. And as for Robbie, I can promise that the two of you will be reunited very soon.'

Not Surrey: on that point, at least, Dan was clear. He felt increasingly sure that the instructions were a bluff. Jerry was here, in West Sussex, right now. It made sense that he'd minimise the risks by having a base much closer at hand.

Identifying the key to the mystery was a tougher prospect. Dan went over it again and again. Jerry had everything: all he had to do was deliver the papers, collect his payment and disappear. However hard it was for Dan to accept, it seemed likely that Cate was already dead or would die very soon.

But the bodies were stacking up. Once Robbie's was found, it would spark a massive police investigation. Add to that his sister's disappearance and the media were bound to go crazy, even before they made any connections to the Blakes. Or Martin. Or Hank O'Brien . . .

Connections. Jerry couldn't afford to leave any sort of trail that might lead the authorities to Templeton Wynne. Therefore he had to give them something else.

A different trail.

If Jerry knew about Hank O'Brien's death, he'd also know that Cate and the two men who'd helped her were engaged in a conspiracy to evade justice – and thus couldn't go anywhere near the police.

He'd be aware that one of those two men was Robbie – and Robbie had mentioned that he might have been followed. But Dan hadn't noticed anything untoward.

They don't know about me, he thought. Jerry, the Blakes: they had two of the three of us, Cate and Robbie. But they weren't able to identify me.

I'm the key to this.

That was when he had it. That simple. That dangerous.

I'm the key to this.

One Hundred

Cate felt sure that something dreadful had happened during the last stop. Jerry hadn't been gone for long, but upon his return he had whistled with quiet satisfaction, then sat in silence for about twenty minutes.

In Cate's view, this was another stage of a plan that went beyond simply eradicating the people who stood in his way. If you considered it rationally, she decided, the other element he required for success was a fall guy. He had to craft a scenario that would supply the police with an obvious suspect.

Either it was her – which might explain why she was still alive – or it was somebody else: Robbie or Dan. Certainly one of the three. But that only worked if the other two were dead—

No. It worked even better if all three of them were dead.

He seemed to confirm that when they set off again. He said he was following the other man from the pub, and that soon she'd be 'reunited' with her brother. Cate didn't believe a word of it.

She asked herself: what was the most reliable, the most elegant solution here?

And the answer filled her with terror.

The young man surprised Stemper by turning south when he reached Petworth. That wasn't the natural route towards Box Hill. Maybe Robbie hadn't told him about the Blakes. Maybe he was just going to return to Brighton and forget what he'd witnessed this evening.

That was fine with Stemper, though a showdown at the Blakes' home would have made his job much easier.

He had killed Patricia and Gordon – and now Robbie – with the same gun. That gun would also be used on Cate, and then, most crucially, on their accomplice – but the young man's death would be made to look self-inflicted. The result: a bizarre and puzzling sequence of events with no obvious motives, but with a chain of evidence so unequivocal that Stemper doubted anyone would search beyond this little group for the killer.

He'd arranged many such endings before: for peace campaigners, trade unionists, rogue government employees. So long as the deaths were grisly and plausible, it didn't matter what unanswered questions they raised. In fact, sometimes his paymasters welcomed outlandish speculation. Let the conspiracy theorists have their fun. Nobody ever listened to conspiracy theorists.

The traffic thinned out as Dan joined the A283 south of Petworth. He was able to drive at between forty and fifty miles an hour, a speed that normally was quite fast enough for him. It was a meandering single-lane road with only occasional stretches where overtaking was permitted.

At the first opportunity, Dan shifted into third gear and moved up tight on the car in front, nudging out towards the centre line to make his intentions clear. Several cars passed in the opposite direction, and then there was a gap of several hundred yards, although he could see the headlights of more oncoming traffic in the distance.

Had to risk it. He floored the accelerator and moved out, passing a couple of cars easily, then ignored a chance to slip into the gap behind a high-sided lorry that was doing about forty-five miles per hour.

Dan was squarely alongside the lorry when he saw that he wouldn't make it. The first of the oncoming cars had reached the same conclusion, the driver flashing his main beams in warning. Dan moved in closer to the lorry, his wing mirror almost touching the side of a massive wheel arch as he willed the Corsa to find a little extra speed. He could hear the long blast of a horn as the approaching traffic had to veer on to the grass verge to avoid a head-on collision.

Then he was past the lorry, with a clear road ahead. He pushed the speed up from sixty to seventy, then to eighty. He met the next group of slow vehicles on a straight section and this time he didn't hesitate, sailing around them as if the road was his alone to command.

He was driving like a maniac, breaking every rule imaginable, and he knew full well that if he resembled anyone right now it was the man whose driving had robbed him and Louis of their mother and father.

Stemper noted the burst of speed, the reckless overtaking, and he was intrigued. He didn't think this was merely an urge to flee from his friend's murder. More likely that the young man saw himself as the white knight, riding to Cate's rescue.

That explained where he was heading. Not back to Brighton, but to the most credible hiding place within close range.

Jerry was on his trail. That was Dan's assumption, although he hoped that the way he'd driven for the past few miles had been enough to open up a good distance between them. He needed to buy some time.

He'd concluded that the rendezvous in Midhurst hadn't just been about handing over the paperwork. It was also a chance to lure Robbie's partner into the open – and Dan had walked right into that trap.

The road conditions forced him to trundle slowly through the villages of Pulborough and Storrington, but he managed one or two more bursts of speed. It was around seven-thirty when he reached the Steyning bypass, and a few minutes after that he was racing north along the same road where, six days before, a moment's foolishness had set so much tragedy in motion.

Dan slowed for the tight turn into the lane that led to O'Brien's farmhouse. He was obsessively checking his mirror, but there were no other vehicles in sight.

He rolled along the lane until the farm's double gates came into view. They were standing open, which meant either Robbie had left them like this after the Fiesta had been collected, or else it was another trap.

Dan had to take the chance. He sped up, crossing the driveway and on to the grass. The sky overhead glowed with the last of the light, a subtle purple-blue sheen, while the trees and bushes around him were retreating into the gloom.

He parked behind the barn, cut the engine and got out, armed with the wheelbrace. He ran back the way he'd come, listening for an approaching car, but all he could hear was some sporadic birdsong and the distant thrum of traffic.

The farmhouse seemed like the ideal place to hide Cate away until Dan had been captured. He felt sure she would be kept alive until the last possible moment: Jerry needed her as an insurance policy, as well as a source of information.

Now, having lost his target, what could Jerry do but come here and force his hostage to reveal Dan's identity?

There was a hedge bordering the driveway. Dan managed to hide himself in a gap close to the gates. He crouched down, confident that he would be hard to spot in the growing darkness. He'd decided to wait here for fifteen minutes. If no one turned up he would search the property, and if that proved fruitless he'd have no option but to phone the police and tell them everything.

It was less than three minutes before he heard the engine, then saw the prowling lights of a car.

One Hundred & One

Stemper pulled up on the driveway and peered into the dark. The Corsa was nowhere to be seen. He'd lost sight of it fifteen minutes ago but had assumed it was heading this way. Had he got it wrong?

He picked up the gun, removed the magazine and checked how many shells remained: six. Plenty.

He looked around cautiously as he climbed out of the car. There was no sign of life, no lights on in the house. He opened the back door, untied the rope binding the woman's feet, then moved to the other side, removed the hood and tore off the tape over her mouth. Caitlin spat and coughed, blinking in surprise that he had shown her his face again.

'I was expecting to find your friend here,' he said. 'Clearly self-preservation overcame chivalry.'

Once he'd released the ropes, he hauled her out of the car. Cramp made her wince and gasp as she stood upright, stretching and flexing her muscles. Stemper kept one hand on the rope around her wrists, while the other held the gun at waist height.

'My patience is running low,' he said. 'Who is he?'

'Just one of Robbie's friends.'

'I saw him visit you yesterday afternoon. Think harder.'

A surly silence. He glanced at a line of bushes flanking the driveway. When he turned back Cate was shaking her head, a sudden defiance in her posture.

'No. I'm not telling you.'

'So you *do* know? That's progress.' He kicked the side of her knee. Her leg buckled and he forced her to the ground, driving the Glock into the back of her neck.

Cate felt the gun digging into her skin and thought: *This is my moment to die.*

She swallowed, took a breath. 'You're going to kill me anyway. Go ahead. But I won't tell you. That way he wins, you lose.'

She forced her head up, turning so she had sight of the bland face gazing down at her, the pale eyes strangely expressionless, as if nothing ever truly mattered to him.

'A fine speech, but I suspect your courage will be no match for the reality.' A pause. 'I can shoot you without killing you,' he declared. 'I can inflict half a dozen non-fatal wounds and still keep you conscious.'

She had the impression that the threat wasn't intended for her ears. Sure enough, he spun and fired a shot into the bushes. Cate flinched, even though the noise was no louder than a click.

'What are you doing?' she asked.

Ignoring her, he called out: 'I know you're here. Are you prepared to see her suffer?'

Dan's legs were starting to cramp, but he didn't dare move an inch. The man – Jerry – had the gun aimed in his direction. The bullet had missed by a couple of feet; it was only when he heard it thudding into a tree that Dan understood he'd been shot at. If not for the silencer, the noise would almost certainly have freaked him into revealing his position.

Now he assessed the threat to Cate. She hadn't been a prisoner in the house: Jerry had kept her with him all along. And if Dan was right about the gunman's priorities, he wouldn't hesitate to kill her the moment that Dan showed himself.

Jerry was standing over Cate, some twenty feet away. The only weapon Dan had was the wheelbrace. He knew he couldn't throw it with any accuracy; nor could he hope to get close enough to use it before Jerry opened fire.

The only option was to stay put and watch him carry out his threat, or take action, but accept that it was a suicide mission. At least Cate could use the distraction to make a run for it.

Cate realised that Dan must have come here after all. She had no idea why, but she wasn't about to let this bastard kill them both. If she had to die, so be it, but she was going to die fighting.

Jerry was still staring at the bushes when she sprang up. Remembering how she'd made a mess of it earlier, she drove her head into his groin. Her arms were useless behind her back, so there was little chance of wrestling the gun away from him. All she could do was go on pushing forward and hope he would lose his footing and perhaps drop the gun as he fell.

Dan saw Cate fling herself at Jerry. She rammed her head into his midriff, driving him backwards, but although he stumbled he was better placed than Cate to keep his balance. He grabbed at her hair, meaning to take her with him if he went down.

As Dan burst from his hiding place Jerry struggled to raise the gun and let off a shot. It went past Dan at chest height, no more than inches away, and he was sure he felt its lethal power in the rush of displaced air.

But he kept on moving, head forward, the wheelbrace raised in his right hand. If he could cover the distance in time, he would take Jerry's head off, even if it meant he ended up dead.

* * *

Cate turned to track the bullet's trajectory, saw Dan and understood that Jerry was trying to get a better aim. She was already losing the battle to stay on her feet, but as her knees hit the ground she managed to throw her upper body against Jerry, clamping her mouth on his arm, just above the wrist.

She bit down with all her strength and felt skin split and tendons crush and blood begin to flow. She heard him scream and his other hand pushed against her forehead, his thumb seeking her eye socket, trying to blind her.

But he hadn't dropped the gun. He let off three more shots, thankfully wasted, all of them driving into the ground a few yards away. And then Dan was on him, swinging some kind of metal bar, and Jerry twisted round, tearing his arm free of Cate's mouth, and her teeth were dripping with hot blood as she collapsed and instinctively rolled to avoid smashing her face on the tarmac.

Dan's swing was fast and strong but too well-telegraphed. Jerry dodged the worst of it, but still caught a heavy impact on his upper arm, the wheelbrace pounding against his bicep with a deep thwack. It should have knocked him off his feet but somehow he only reeled back, blood pouring down his other wrist from Cate's attack.

He had dropped the gun. Both men saw it at the same moment, but Jerry was closer.

Stemper knew he'd never retrieve the gun in time to fire it: the instant he bent down his assailant would crack his skull.

Plan A had failed, just as he'd feared it would. Time for Plan B.

He kicked the Glock away from him. It went skittering over the driveway and the young man watched it go, seemingly stunned by what he was seeing. Then he made a belated lunge for it, and that was Stemper's cue to run.

Cate was quicker, and smarter, snatching at Stemper as he fled. But she couldn't move freely, and it was easy enough to evade her as he dashed to the car.

He threw himself in and started the engine. The young man had picked up the gun and was standing about fifteen feet away, slightly behind and to the left of the Ford Focus.

Turning the car was impossible. Stemper put it into reverse and revved the engine. Heard a shout and realised the gun was coming up.

The man yelled at him: 'Stop!'

Six rounds. Stemper had fired once into the bushes, once at his assailant, then three times at the ground, deliberately leaving only one shot.

He prayed that the young man would use it.

Dan thought he was capable of shooting. But now the moment had come, he wasn't sure if that was the right thing to do. He wanted justice, which meant a trial. It meant keeping this man alive.

But not letting him escape.

The Ford Focus reversed about six feet in a single jerking movement. It brought the driver level with Dan. He was a bland-looking man in his fifties; the sort of face that would melt into a crowd.

Dan used both hands to steady his aim. He didn't want Jerry to see how much he was shaking.

'Get out of the car,' he ordered.

Jerry turned away, his gaze calm but distant, as if he required a second to reflect on the instruction he'd been given.

He'll see sense, Dan thought. He'll surrender.

Then the man reversed again, wildly, the wheels screaming for traction as the Focus wobbled and swerved and raced backwards through the gates and down the lane.

For an instant Dan was frozen with indecision. Then he turned, lined up on the figure silhouetted at the wheel, and fired.

He thought the bullet hit the windscreen, but the car didn't slow down or deviate from its path. Dan ran forward a few paces, aware that he had only a split second to get off another shot before the Focus was gone. He aimed, pulled the trigger, but there was only an empty click. He tried it again, realised he was out of ammunition.

The killer had got away.

One Hundred & Two

But we're alive. That was his next thought. *We're alive.*

He ran to Cate, who was struggling to stand. He helped her up and saw that her hands were bound with nylon rope, knotted too tightly to prise apart with his fingers.

As he groped in his pocket for his keys, Cate was spitting frantically. 'Wipe it off, wipe it off!'

Dan tore his shirt open and used it to clean the blood from her mouth and chin. Her face was bruised and scratched, but she didn't seem to be badly hurt. She leaned to see past him, while he dug a key into the knot to loosen it.

'He's gone, hasn't he?' she said.

'Yes. It's safe.'

'But he might come back.'

'I know. We have to get out of here.'

'What's happened to Robbie? I thought he'd . . .' The words petered out as she read the expression on Dan's face. Her shoulders dropped. He caught her as her legs gave way, her body almost deflating before his eyes.

'Oh no. No.'

'I'm sorry, Cate. I really am. But we need to hold it together for a bit longer.'

* * *

The warning made her unreasonably cross. 'You don't have to tell me that.'

'God, no. I'm sorry.' The rope came free and Cate let out a groan of relief as she brought her hands in front of her and rubbed some life into them. Fighting back tears, she said, 'I heard the phone call, when he was arranging to meet Robbie. It was a trap, wasn't it?'

'I'm afraid so. And now he's got away, and we don't know the first thing about him.'

'He told me his name was Jerry . . .'

Dan nodded. 'I don't think that's true. I'm pretty sure he wasn't the man I saw . . .' He faltered.

'What?'

'I'm sorry. Robbie *did* pocket the money on Tuesday night. I didn't find out until Wednesday, after we'd seen you. I made him take it back, but someone was lying in wait. He tried to photograph us.'

'So you knew there were people looking for you?'

Another nod, forlorn and apologetic. Cate realised this wasn't the time for recriminations. With his help, she tried to take a few steps, her knee throbbing from where she'd been kicked. Dan led her into the darkness beyond the house and explained that Jerry, whoever he was, had been trying to kill all three of them, probably to frame them for a number of other deaths.

Cate confirmed it. 'He killed the people he was working with. I saw one of the bodies at the house where they were holding me.'

'So how come he wasn't able to identify me?'

'Because I swore that I didn't know you.'

'And Jerry believed you? He didn't threaten to torture you or something?'

'Oh, yes.' Even she was surprised by her matter-of-fact tone. 'He hurt me. But I didn't tell him.'

*   *   *

They exchanged what other information they had while they hurried to the Corsa. Dan couldn't dispel the fear that Jerry had merely gone off to regroup. What if he'd kept a spare gun in the car and was hiding in the lane?

'You know we could be driving into an ambush,' he said as he started the car.

'I don't care. We can't stay here.' Cate gasped. 'Oh God. I have to tell Mum about Robbie . . .'

'The police might beat us to it, if the body's been discovered by now.' Dan sighed. 'I wonder if we should call them right away, from here.'

Cate shook her head. 'No. Let's go. Take our chances.'

He steered the car past the barn. The echoes of last week's dispute with Robbie didn't immediately occur to him, but the thought must have been lurking at the back of his mind.

We're doing it again. We're running away.

He leaned forward as they reached the driveway, craning to see into every shadow. Once they were through the gates he accelerated, and they raced down the lane to the main road without incident. It was only when they'd gone a mile or so towards the A283 that the reality of it struck him. He swore under his breath.

'What's the catch?'

Cate looked at him, confused. 'Dan . . .?'

The shock was so profound, he wasn't sure if he could put it into words for her. 'He's got us. This is no different than if he'd killed us back there.'

Cate made a sceptical sound. 'Well, it is. Because we're still in one piece.'

'No. In terms of his objectives. The set-up is the same. We're going to take the blame for this.'

At first Cate thought he was just being dramatic. Her grief at the loss of her brother weighed heavily enough as it was, but as the car sped towards Brighton she reviewed what she knew as though it were a brief to be mastered in double quick time. She put together the case for the prosecution, and the case for the defence, and she saw that Dan was right.

It was a brilliant stitch-up.

The brains behind the extortion – the Blakes – were dead in one location. Robbie was dead in another. The paperwork that supported the plot was gone. Cate and Dan had nothing: no evidence of Jerry's involvement, no clue as to his real identity.

'Apart from what might be at the house in Surrey,' she said. 'There'll be DNA to prove I was a prisoner.'

Dan groaned, slapping a hand against his forehead. 'I fired the gun.'

'What?'

'Forensics. For his strategy to work, it helps if I've fired the same gun that was used in all these killings. And I did. I shot at him as he drove away, but I missed. There was only one bullet left in the gun. I bet he knew that. I bet he planned it that way.'

'You think he allowed for the fact that you'd miss?'

'Why not? A moving target, and I'd never picked up a gun in my life before. Of course I was going to miss.'

'Where is the gun now?'

'Shit. I put it down to untie you and left it on the drive.'

Cate sighed. 'Maybe we should go back and get it?'

Dan saw the pensive look on her face. It was another grim reminder of last Tuesday with Robbie, running through their options without a thought for morality.

'And do what?' he asked.

'I don't know. But if we've got it with us, we can decide whether to . . . hand it in. Or get rid of it.'

'No. We're not covering this up. We can't.'

'But you've just said it yourself, if there's no evidence to trace the real killer, the police are bound to suspect us. Well, not us. You. Especially when they hear that you knocked down Hank O'Brien.'

'I'm still going to tell them.'

'Dan, please. Think about this. You don't deserve to go to prison for crimes you didn't commit.'

But what about the crimes I did commit? He wanted to say it, but for some reason he couldn't. He sneaked another glance and saw that Cate was shattered, utterly drained, and so was he. They were running out of energy, running out of options.

'Shall I take you home?'

'Please.' Then she said: 'No. He knows where I live.'

'All right. My place.'

He thought Cate might protest, but she didn't. They drove on in silence for a few minutes, enveloped in a misty darkness, the beams of approaching headlights spearing the sky. For Dan it was a relief to be out here, just one more anonymous vehicle, gliding through the night like a ship far out at sea: lonely, distant, safe.

But soon they would have to dock, back in the real world. And then it had to be faced: what he had done, who he really was.

Stemper felt relatively sanguine on the journey to Brighton. He'd had to depart from his original plan, but the essential elements were still in place.

He had recovered the paperwork before it was made public. He'd eliminated Jerry and the Blakes – the only people who could have supplied the authorities with substantial information about him – and he had left Cate and her friend in a position where they would inevitably come under suspicion for the murder of Robert Scott. To confuse the issue further, he had deposited Robbie's bloodstained suit at the home of the Blakes.

Now only one loose end remained.

One Hundred & Three

At Dan's suggestion, Cate used his phone to send her mother a text, insisting she was all right and apologising for any fuss she'd caused. Then she switched the phone off before she or anyone else could call them. They were on the edge of the city, emerging from the Southwick tunnel and cresting the hill where the glittering sweep of lights first came into view.

Dan had continued to brood, and now he said, 'Another reason for going to the police is that it's safer.'

'How'd you work that out?'

'Because his key motive for trying again is to silence us once and for all. Right now he's relying on the fact that we'll keep quiet, because of our part in Hank's death. If the police manage to connect us to any of this, we'll look all the more guilty for not coming forward. And if they don't, all Jerry needs to do is wait a decent interval, then finish the job when it suits him.'

'Okay. I can see the logic there.'

'Whereas, if we own up to it immediately, there's nothing to be gained by killing us.'

She conceded the point, but said, 'Are you really willing to go to prison? Because you will, Dan. Once you're in the interview room, facing somebody like DC Avery, somebody determined to put you away . . .'

'Cate, I know—'

She raised a hand. 'Even if I can get DS Thomsett to believe what I tell him about this man who abducted me, I still can't prove that Jerry killed my brother. And you can't prove that you *didn't* kill him.'

'No, you're right. The accident with O'Brien will give them the perfect motive. And the gun has my prints on it.'

To Cate's ears, he sounded grimly satisfied, but she was disconsolate. 'It's a slam dunk. You won't be able to fight it.'

'Maybe. Maybe not.' He said nothing else for a while. They were climbing the last steep hill that separated Hove from Brighton, the slip road to Devil's Dyke off to their left. The Corsa was struggling with the gradient, forcing Dan to ease up on his speed.

In a quiet voice, he said, 'My parents used to say, if you do something wrong you should put your hand up to it and take your punishment. Last week I failed to do that, and what I've realised is that I can't accept the way I behaved. I can't live with myself. It's as simple as that.'

They drew up outside the house. 'Have you seen what we look like?' Cate said as they got out of the car. Dan nodded.

Joan must have spotted them: she opened the front door, frowning when she recognised Cate. 'Oh, I thought it was Hayley—' Then she registered the state they were in, looking down to see Cate's stockinged feet encrusted with blood. 'Good Lord, what's happened to you two?'

'Not now, Joan.' Dan sounded brusque rather than rude, but still regretted it at once. 'Just let us get sorted out, and we'll try to explain.'

'Well, was it a fight or something? Were you in an accident?'

He shook his head sadly, took Cate's hand and led her upstairs.

'Are you really going to tell her about this?' she asked.

'I'll have to. I've got to prepare her somehow.'

As they reached the landing, Louis's door opened and he came out, jerking to a halt.

'Shit, look at you two . . . This wouldn't be connected to that suitcase Robbie gave me?'

Dan nodded. 'Yeah. But it's all done with now. And I want to apologise for how I've been over the past week.'

Louis shrugged, reluctant to discuss it in Cate's presence. 'Nah, I probably deserved it.'

Dan started to go past but Louis stopped him, digging in his pocket. 'Oh. I ought to have mentioned this.'

He handed over a micro SD card. 'Robbie asked me to keep it safe, along with the case. He swore me to secrecy, but . . .' He shrugged. 'I figured there have been too many secrets round here.'

Dan stared at it for a second, then looked at Louis. 'Is your laptop on?'

Cate stayed out on the landing while Dan fetched the computer from his brother's bedroom, along with an adaptor for the memory card. Louis was clearly eager to see what the card contained, but Dan told him that they needed some time alone.

'Okay. Cool.' Louis made brief eye contact with Cate, a silent question: *Are you two together . . .?*

Cate looked away.

They went into Dan's room and shut the door. Dan sat down on the bed, and Cate knew she would have to join him. It made perfect sense, if they were both to look at the laptop.

As she sat down the mattress compressed beneath her and for a moment their bodies touched. Cate didn't think that she recoiled, certainly not so it was visible, but Dan shuffled an inch or two away from her.

'I feel bad about this,' he said, and she misunderstood until he added, 'I should be finding you some spare clothes, so you can clean up and get changed.'

'That can wait. I want to see what's on here.'

'Me too.' He inserted the card, selected the folder-view option, and a window opened that contained about a dozen folders, with names like 'Defence 0809' and 'Social Sec 00s'. Others were marked 'Overseas' and 'Journal' and 'Templeton Vids'. And there was a folder called 'Blakes'.

'Is this what it was about?' Cate asked.

'I think so.' He opened a folder at random, changed the view to Extra Large Icons and found dozens of scanned documents. 'These are copies of all the paper evidence.' Dan shut his eyes, his face briefly contorted as if in pain. 'That's why Robbie was so blasé about the handover.'

'He had this as a backup.' The discovery made Cate want to laugh and cry at the same time. 'But if Jerry had had any idea that the memory card existed, he might have . . .'

Killed me as retribution.

Dan said, 'Don't forget, Jerry never intended to play it straight.' A thoughtful silence. 'But surely he'd have allowed for the possibility of an electronic copy?'

'Unless he doesn't much care either way. If his brief was to recover the paperwork, and he's done that, the existence of a memory card isn't his problem.'

At this, Dan brightened a little. 'But it *will* be Templeton's problem. With this, we can put a stop to the takeover.'

Cate wasn't impressed. 'Perhaps we can. But you'll still have a lot of questions to answer.'

Dan kept quiet as Cate stood up and walked to the window. She needed space, he realised. Because of her recent captivity, the bedroom must have seemed horribly confined.

Or maybe it was his presence that was making her so edgy.

'This is such a mess,' he muttered, putting the laptop aside and pushing his hands through his hair. 'You know what I'd like to do now?'

'What?' She sounded hesitant.

'I'd like us both to have a shower, and something to eat, and then crawl under this duvet, and I'd like to hold you close and sleep for about three days with you in my arms.'

He paused, his stomach like a ball of lead. He sensed the effort it took for her to turn and face him. She had fresh tears in her eyes, but she made an effort to sound enthusiastic.

'Sounds lovely.'

'*But.*' He raised a hand. 'You don't have to say it, really.'

'No, but I will. I think we were destined to be best friends. Not lovers.'

He grinned sadly, feeling skewered by that last phrase.

'I sort of hate myself for agreeing, but you're right. So that's what I'd *like* to do. But this is what I'm *going* to do.'

He took out his phone and held it up for her to see. After gazing at it for a moment, she returned to the bed and sat down.

'Okay, Dan. As your best friend, will you think about what I've been saying? The memory card might screw up this man Templeton, but it doesn't get you out of the mess you're in.'

'I know. Despite how I look, I'm in full possession of my faculties.'

'Dan, I'm serious.'

'So am I. Deadly serious. Now, DS Thomsett. Do you remember his number, or will I need to ring Sussex Police?'

He was braced for more objections, but instead she relented. 'I think I know it.' She took the phone from him, started keying in a number. 'You definitely want to do this? And you're happy to go wherever it takes you?'

'I wouldn't use the word "happy". But certainly "prepared". Because wherever I end up, I'll be able to look myself in the eye once again.'

Cate handed the phone back, and as he put it to his ear Dan heard the final burr of the ring tone and then a male voice said: 'Hello?'

'Is that DS Thomsett? My name is Daniel Wade. I need to arrange an urgent meeting with you.'

A glance at Cate. He expected her to look away but she held his gaze, nodding her approval.

At the other end of the line, Thomsett said, 'Can I ask what it's about?'

Dan said, 'Yes. I want to tell you who killed Hank O'Brien.'

One Hundred & Four

Stemper returned to Kemptown, stopping only to make a brief transatlantic phone call. He didn't speak to Mark Templeton himself, but to one of his key aides. Stemper assured him that the threat to the imminent merger had been nullified. The papers were to be deposited on Wednesday afternoon at an agreed location near Regents Park, while the balance of Stemper's fee – two million in sterling – would be transferred to a UK trust account.

The deal had guaranteed them the return of the original documentation. It had crossed Stemper's mind that O'Brien might have kept duplicates, or more likely electronic copies, but even if they existed it would be a simple matter for Templeton's lawyers to challenge their provenance in court.

In any case, by that stage Stemper would be long gone. And he had ensured that he was untraceable.

Back at the guest house, he made it to his room without being seen. He took a shower, tended to the wound on his wrist where the woman had bitten him, then lay down for a short nap. His sleep was untroubled by doubts or fear. He woke in time to catch a late-night news bulletin, which reported on the discovery of a man, believed to have been shot dead in his car in a small West Sussex town. 'Police are at the scene,' the newscaster told him, 'and we hope to have more information for you very soon . . .'

You can hope all you like, Stemper thought. He pictured Cate and her accomplice hiding out somewhere, haunted by guilt, waiting for the knock at the door.

At one in the morning, with his bag packed and the room sanitised, Stemper put on a fresh pair of latex gloves and crept down to the proprietor's private quarters. He tapped gently on the bedroom door, opened it and saw Quills lying beneath the covers, his eyes glittering with excitement.

Stemper said, 'Stay where you are. I have a treat for you.'

He set a bath running. From a wide selection of bath lotions he chose one with green tea, rice milk and jasmine.

In the kitchen there was a bottle of Veuve Clicquot in the fridge. He poured two glasses and carried them into the bathroom, then he searched the cabinet above the sink and found a box of paracetamol. Two blister packs of twelve tablets each, with four missing.

Twenty tablets. That should be sufficient.

If it wasn't, Stemper would suggest that he used a knife.

Quills was in a state of hyper-arousal when Stemper finally returned and told him it was time. Regrettably, a certain amount of physical contact was necessary, but Stemper closed his mind to it, as he was accustomed to doing, and before long he had Quills luxuriating in a steaming hot bath, playfully blowing bubbles across the bathroom floor.

Stemper, sitting just beyond reach on the toilet seat, feigned coquettish amusement while encouraging Quills to finish his champagne. He was pouring a refill when Quills noticed the gloves and snorted. 'Kinky.'

Stemper nodded. 'There are many such surprises in store for you.'

'Mmm.' Quills shut his eyes, resting his head back on the edge of the bath. The water lapped at his neck, the foam on his chin like a child's approximation of a Santa Claus beard.

'That's good,' Stemper murmured. 'Now, just as we did before, I'm going to talk and I want you to listen. I want you to trust me, and let me guide you to the ultimate pleasure.'

From Quills, a long sigh of contentment.

'Listen carefully, follow my instructions and after tonight, my dear man, you won't ever be bored or lonely again. All your troubles will be soothed away and disappear to nothing. Because just as you've known all along, I have the answer, Bernard. I'm the solution to all your problems.'

Stemper leaned over and picked up the first pack of tablets.

'Listen to me, and I'll show you the way to pure bliss. To pure, pure oblivion.'

He departed an hour later. There were five other guests in residence that night, but no one saw him go. Later, during a cursory police investigation which swiftly ruled out foul play, none of them could recall if anyone else had been staying there. It turned out that the proprietor's record-keeping was somewhat erratic, and a crucial bookings diary had been dropped into the same bath that had claimed the poor man's life.

Stemper drove slowly through the night. He wanted to coordinate his arrival in Suffolk with the breakfast hour. Ideally he would let himself into the house in time to have a pot of tea ready when Debbie Winwood came downstairs.

Debbie, he knew, would be *overjoyed* to see him.

Acknowledgements

I'd like to thank my editor, Rosie de Courcy, as well as Trevor Dolby, Nicola Taplin, Katherine Murphy, Nick Austin, David Mitchell, Najma Finlay, Rob Waddington and the whole team at Random House. Thanks also to my agent, Will Francis, and everyone at Janklow & Nesbit: Claire, Rebecca, Kirsty, Tim and Jessie.

For help with research I'm indebted to Traffic Officer PC Simon Dove and to Dan Rosling, Crew Manager, London Fire Brigade – though I must stress that responsibility for any mistakes or inaccuracies rests firmly with the author. Thanks also to my family, friends and first readers, in particular Stuart and Karen Marsom, Claire Burrell and Sarah Hitt. As always, I owe a huge amount to Niki, James and Emily for their love and support.

This was a novel written in cafes, and I'm grateful to the proprietors and staff who put up with the long hours I spent tapping away (and longer still gazing out of the windows): in Brighton & Hove the Rotunda and St Ann's Well Garden Cafe; in Shoreham the Thunkshop cafe and Toast by the Coast; also Whitecliffs Beach Cafe in Saltdean and Kiki & Cole in Hurstpierpoint.

Finally, a very special thank you to everyone who has bought, borrowed, read, reviewed or recommended one of my books.

ALSO BY TOM BALE

SKIN AND BONES

On a cold January morning, a nightmare awaits in a small Sussex village. A deranged young man goes on the rampage, shooting everyone in his path before taking his own life. It is a senseless, tragic event, but sadly not an unfamiliar one. At least, that's what everyone thinks.

Only Julia Trent – believed to be the sole survivor – knows that there was a second man involved. But after being shot and badly injured, her account of the massacre is ignored. Together with Craig Walker, the journalist son of one of the victims, Julia determines to find out the truth. As they peel back the layers of a dark and dangerous conspiracy, they discover the slaughter did not begin on that bitter day in January. And worst of all, it won't end there . . .

'Bale keeps us guessing as our heroes edge towards a shocking climax' *Guardian*

'This first-time thriller cuts the mustard' *Daily Mail*

'A spellbinding thriller . . . Quite simply the best book I've read this year' *Latest*

arrow books

TERROR'S REACH

A burning summer's day explodes into violence. A murderous gang targets the exclusive south-coast island of Terror's Reach, playground for the super-rich. But who has hired them and what do they want?

There are plenty of people with secrets on Terror's Reach. Among them is Joe Clayton, a CID officer hiding from his past under a new identity, working now as a bodyguard to the family of Russian oligarch Valentin Nasenko. As the terrible night of murder and betrayal gathers momentum, Joe Clayton emerges as the only man who can save the innocent. But can he save himself and everything he has worked so hard to protect?

'A gripping thriller' *Closer*

'Tom Bale has produced a great second book with a pace that matched his previous . . . The plot has many twists and turns and the book holds your interest right up to the last page'
Eurocrime

arrow books

ALSO BY TOM BALE

BLOOD FALLS

Joe Clayton thought the dangers of his undercover career were behind him. He was wrong. One grey October morning, while working in a quiet Bristol street, he hears the voice of the man who has sworn to destroy him. Minutes later Joe is running for his life again.

Desperate for sanctuary, he heads for the small Cornish town of Trelennan, and the home of Diana Bamber, widow of a former police colleague. But Diana reacts strangely to his arrival, and gradually Joe discovers that Trelennan is far from the idyllic, law-abiding resort it claims to be.

The town is in the grip of one man. Leon Race doesn't welcome strangers, especially ex-cops who start asking questions about missing women. Soon Joe is caught up in another undercover role, but as he penetrates the web of secrets that ensnares the town's elite, his own secret is at risk of discovery. And all the time his old enemy is circling . . .

'A neat British gangster thriller written with élan and substance.' *Daily Mail*

arrow books

THE POWER OF READING

Visit the Random House website and get connected with information on all our books and authors

EXTRACTS from our recently published books and selected backlist titles

COMPETITIONS AND PRIZE DRAWS Win signed books, audiobooks and more

AUTHOR EVENTS Find out which of our authors are on tour and where you can meet them

LATEST NEWS on bestsellers, awards and new publications

MINISITES with exclusive special features dedicated to our authors and their titles

READING GROUPS Reading guides, special features and all the information you need for your reading group

LISTEN to extracts from the latest audiobook publications

WATCH video clips of interviews and readings with our authors

RANDOM HOUSE INFORMATION including advice for writers, job vacancies and all your general queries answered

Come home to Random House

www.randomhouse.co.uk